IRONBARK

S.L. Venables

Published in 2012 by FeedARead.com Publishing – Arts Council funded

First Edition

A CIP catalogue record for this title is available from the British Library.

For: Vienna and Tomos.

Look out World!

IRONBARK,

(Noun).
{Botanical}.

Native Australian tree.
Member of the Eucalyptus family.
Eucalyptus Sideroxylon.
Identified by deep lines or tracks in its stems and trunk.
Hardwood.
Preferred use: as a general construction product, and for the building of ships.
Also known as "ironwood" and "rockwood".

<u>1972</u>

The good sister had read his book, then had written it. She had passed it on with promises and secrets, and awkward knowings that made difficulties in her vows.

The bones of his tale had scorched the ashes of her own ancestors, and she had screamed at God.

Told him off.

Rebuked him.

The notebook would travel the world, and she would save some of it.

Almost at the same sad time, (possibly a little later my Father recalled, though not reliably); a flimsy airmail envelope as blue as the sky flopped through Mrs. Amethysts letter box. It was addressed to Dilwyn and Ellis.

It was from my uncles, Murray and Wilf.

It said that they were all wrong, and that there was nothing to it, that Spinksy had been right, and that they wanted nothing more to do with it.

Nothing at all.

Ever!

<u>Darwin.</u>
<u>Northern Territories,</u>
<u>Australia.</u>
<u>August 3rd 1933</u>

The Aborigine had parked the stock truck outside the gaping stone and marble entrance doorway to Darwin Railway Terminus. He had just paid for a one week rental on a storage locker in the 'Left Luggage Hall', and had placed inside it the brown paper package.

All as he had been instructed.

As he walked across the road to the hotel opposite he slipped the locker key into the envelope he had been given, and had brought with him, and licked it, and sealed it shut.

He would give the hotel reception clerk five dollars, again as instructed, and which had been given to him, to hold the envelope until someone came to collect it.

That persons name was written on the front of the envelope.

Desert Hills,

Kalgoorlie-Boulder:

Prison Service of Western Australia:

Penal Work Camp Number 18.

Western Australia,

January 3rd , 1943.

It was a sweltering, humid January day.

The height of the antipodean summer.

Though still early morning, the Spotted Crakes and Blue Winged Kookaburras, were already hunting out the shading refuge of foliage in the Shining Gum Trees and the Grey Ironbarks.

Prisoner number 89855812 squinted up at the vulture Sun which pecked at his irises.

He wondered, (for that brief moment he allowed himself each morning for such wonderings); if he would ever be free again?

Wondered if he would ever shovel anything for himself again, anything he could call a morsel of his bones?

Play the metal banjo for a penny a push again?

Wondered if the burial place was still there, still undisturbed, still with its old finger pressed tight against its hushing lips?

6

Wondered if she was still alive, still fucking strangers when it took her fancy, still making them scream for her in the middle of the night long after she had gone, moved on?

And if she was alive, where was she alive?

Was she alive in some marble mansion, some polished corner of her skull, or only in his, or someone else's?

He had been wondering the same wonderings for too long. Wanking in the speckled night of his prison bed, spurting the energy he could not afford to spurt on the callused hands he would need for every tomorrow's labour.

He wondered if any of it had been worth the while?

Wondered as he always wondered?

Of course it had!

He decided, as he always decided.

Then he collected up his lump hammer and wrecking bar, and set about the Governments rocks.

It begins.
The Brisbane Bandolero's
Brisbane St. John's Bank, (Ekibin Branch),
The corner of Rochdale St. and Barr St.
The Ekibin district of Brisbane,
Queensland, Australia.
February 24th 1932,

The first one was easy.

Easier than any of them had thought.

Like the first time you kill someone.

Like the first time you fuck someone.

It's all adrenaline, all quick, then it's done, almost like a mistake. It's when you have to plan it that things get harder. Things go wrong.

Killing they had done before.

Stealing they had done before.

Lying they had done before.

Running and hiding they had done before as well.

It was the planning that was new.

It was the planning that would fuck them up.

Dylan drove the job car, Eloise waited with the switch car, and Boyden was the outside watcher. Banjo and Itzak stood in the public foyer for a short while with their backs to the tellers, pretending to write something at the waist high polished counters that lined the walls. They waited until the bank was as empty as they thought they could safely handle. The public was an unpredictable animal, one or two 'have a go Joe's' was all it took to turn the whole thing into blood bath.

They had no grouse with 'Mr. and Mrs. Get Born, Live, Then Die'; but if they were the price of this, then they were the price.

The two brothers wore Donkey Jacket coats, too thick for this time of year. They looked like 'Bank Robbers for Christ's sake', Eloise had told them, and she had laughed.

Around their necks they wore red scarf's, tied in a way which allowed them to be pulled up easily, and in one movement, over mouths and noses in concealment.

The short stub nosed revolver that Banjo had removed from Gonda's body, a life and death ago back in Pietermaritzburg, was pulled from inside his Donkey Jacket and pointed at the customers in the foyer of the small banking hall. With his other hand he had yanked the bandana up and over his features, only his wide blue eyes and his thick dark hair could be seen.

"No body move!"

Banjo heard his brother say, as he strode over to the metal full height gate which led to the teller counter. As he looked across the foyer he saw Itzak, his face covered with the scarf, pointing the extra long barrelled Colt 45, (Dykka's old gun), at a young girl on the other side of the gate. Banjo heard him say:

"Open this bloody gate! Now!"

He pointed the gun through the bars and waggled its barrel noisily against the metal.

The young girl was crying, and Itzak was shouting at her over and over again to open the gate. She didn't move, she was stuck there as if some invisible Roman cunt had crept up and nailed her feet to the floor.

"Banker Rex, (or more accurately, 'Regina) Iudeorum". They would have scrawled across her forehead.

She stood where she had always stood, next to her cash drawer and stool, and she pissed herself.

The hammer on the Colt drew back, almost gracefully as Itzak applied not very much pressure to the trigger.

"I'll let you in!"

Said a middle aged woman who stood one cash window away from the terrified girl. She walked around behind the youngster and opened the gate. Itzak burst through it, sending the woman crashing to the ground, striking her head on the corner of the tellers counter as she fell.

A gash opened there and blood streamed from her forehead into her eyes. A crown of paperclips fell upon her from the counter top and glued themselves to the sticky thick blood.

Itzak stepped over her, and yelled that the tellers should empty their tills and cash drawers into the two hessian sacks he had just thrown on the counter top from inside his jacket.

Behind the teller windows and the metal gate were four women; these included the crying girl and the injured and bleeding woman on the floor. There were also two men, both of whom now stood behind their large redwood desks and in front of their maroon leather chairs. Their matching thin grey flannel suits fluttered gently. There was either a delicate breeze dancing through the bank, or they were shaking.

Both men had their hands in the air.

Against the panelled wall behind them stood a huge dark green McFarlane and Dunn Safe, it was about four feet tall with gold edging painted around its door, and a keyhole in its centre, (below the name plate), that was big enough for a small boy to get his finger stuck in. It was parked there for all the customers to see. Parked beyond the bars of the teller's windows, a symbol of how solid the bank was, and

9

how well they would look after your money, if you were lucky enough to still have any.

Itzak told the tellers to fill the sacks, and not say a word. He shouted to Banjo to watch them and shoot anyone who tried 'anything stupid'.

Banjo had already told the five customers to lay face down on the foyer floor, with their hands behind their heads. They had been most obliging.

"Who's got the keys to the safe?"

Itzak asked, waving the Colt at the two men in grey flannel suits. One was balding with gold rimmed spectacles and in his fifties; the other was younger, more dapper, tall with brylcream'd hair parted on the left side, probably thirty two or thirty three.

"We don't have a key to the safe".

The younger man said,

"Only the head office in……",

Before he could finish his sentence 'The Bloody Elephant' once more rose inside Itzak, and his left fist ploughed into the right ear of the young man, sending him careening across his desk. Itzak grabbed the man's oily hair and banged his head hard on the leather inlay of the desk top. The man's eyes rolled, upwards and backwards, and he felt two or three cold inches of the barrel of the Colt 45 cut his tongue and scrape skin from the corrugated roof of his mouth as Itzak forced the gun into his throat. He gagged and began to turn purple.

"The key's in the bottom drawer of the filing cabinet", said the older man pointing to a pair of large wooden and brass handled cabinets against the far wall. They stood between two frosted glass windows, each with the name of the bank painted on the outside.

"The one on the left".

He concluded, a quiver in his voice, and nodded towards it.

Itzak threw the younger man to the floor as one discards a failed betting slip, and retrieved the key from the cabinet. Hurling it on the desk in front of the older man, (who was still standing with his hands aloft), he screamed, as if racked by some immense secret, yelling:

"Open it!"

The older man did as he was told.

Inside there were bundles of ten and twenty dollar bills, some new, some old, some in between.

"Fill these!"

Itzak said, speaking generally to both men. The younger of the two was now kneeling on the floor, he had blood coming from his ear, and a thick single trickle also coursed over his lips and down his chin, staining his white collar and his pale blue tie.

Itzak threw two more hessian sacks on the floor, he had eight or ten of them slung around his waist on a piece of chord.

The two men duly complied.

Banjo told the women tellers to bring their sacks around through the gate and into the foyer, then put them on the floor and lay down next to them with their hands on their heads, just like the customers were doing.

He told the crying girl to help the woman on the floor, the one with the cut head, around to the front and then to lie down next to her.

Banjo then collected up the four sacks and placed them by the door. He poked his head outside, around the door, only a little, and said to Teddy Boyden, who was leaning against the door pillar, smoking, and pretending to smoke, but really watching, watching everything.

"Call Dylan over we'll be out in a shake".

Inside, the two sacks by the safe were now full and bulging, and crammed as tight as a cow's udder before milking; and the safe's shelves were empty, lonely, and impoverished as a man without love.

"Which one of you two is C'nute Hyfeffer?"

The two men in flannel suits looked at each other with mirror images of acute bemusement.

"I am!"

Replied the man with the brylcream'd hair.

"How did you know my na......"

The two shots from the Colt 45 were deafening in the reverberating closeness of the banking hall.

11

Mr. Hyfeffer's head exploded like a bladder filled with a mixture of thin oil and baked beans, spitting over the walls, the ceiling, the inside emptiness of the McFarlane and Dunn, and floating through the air in light droplets, which rained down on the tellers and customers laying on the floor beyond the bars of the cash windows. What was left of the Branch Manager, Mr. Hyfeffer, spilled out onto the dark patina'd floorboards, making a stain there of about five feet by three feet.

Itzak turned back to face the older man, who now, like the young girl earlier, had pissed himself, leaving a growing damp stain in the crotch of his grey flannel trousers. Itzak looked down and smirked beneath his bandana.

"That's what writing nasty letters gets you!"

He said, pointing his revolver at the bubbling lump on the floor.

"Tell your friends Banker! Tell them all, if you have any, tell them we're coming".

Malakye Wylachi O.B.E.
Sugardock Apartments, Penthouse 8,
Sydney Harbour,
New South Wales,
Australia.
31st August 2012.

As he lay in his bed, the crisp whiteness of the ghosts of his linen fell gently about him.

He was aware of, but not conscious of, the spectres of his nurses clipping and unclipping drips and pipes, and twisting things in his arm, and occasionally flicking open his eyelid, or gently tugging his catheter. Emptying this, or re-filling that.

He could feel the plastic edge of the oxygen mask burrowing the wizened haggard indents of his cheeks. It sucked against the tender, paper thin skin of his nose, and left red marks there if anyone lifted it.

He was dying.

Though motionless, his memory tumbled backwards inside his parching skull, and spun, as flipped coins spin, then pattered to a tinkling halt some seventy odd years earlier.

Her turquoise dress let the sun in, and she moved like a new found colt. He could not recall the day, nor the incidental periphery of the moment. But he could see her as if it were yesterday, today and tomorrow; forever. He could smell her gentle perfume; taste the painful perfection of her skin, her tongue, her lips, the curving inside sweep of her thigh.

He recalled the slippery wetness of her, the gasps of warm breath she funnelled on his neck, his ear, his lips.

He re-lived, (as he had re-lived a thousand times), the rasping movement of her stocking'd legs about the small of his back, his arm beneath her pinched waste, pulling her towards him, forcing into her as much as the begging bed would allow. These sensations reminded him of the life he would shortly lose.

He hated them for it, but cajoled them to stay.

It was the first and only time he had seen her, met her, touched her, fucked her, emptied his soul into her.

It was some cheap room, some stay-over, squeeze-over, some escape hole in a dusty 'bed and breakfast'. He thought it was either Coolinar Hill or Payne's Find. He couldn't remember.

He didn't care.

He had saved her life that day, saved it as sure as if he was Jesus Christ, and she had taken him into her world, and swallowed the sacrament and the opaque wine.

Wherever it was, this moth house hotel, this den of absolute pleasure, this Eden on the edge of the Great Victoria Desert, it had been the place of her salvation.

For it was here, in the aftermath of their each-othering, that he had warned her of his sins, sought her forgiveness that she would never again see the giver of her Ironbark wedding ring. Confessed the greed of his crimes, and shared their guilt's in the moaning, clenching thefts of their joint innocence.

Their ignorance.

Their guilt.

He told her never to return to the Stockman's Hut, nor the place of the burial.

13

He left her an address he knew of in Darwin. Some place he had stayed once with his Uncle Mordichae, some hotel opposite a large Railway Station. In there, beneath the domed colonialism of transport architecture, in the ornate lobby, was a left luggage hall. It had polished steel lockers with Ironbark doors, each with a key and innards that would keep a secret forever, for enough dollars.

Before he left, he made her promise once more.

"Promise!"

He had heard himself scream at her, and left thumb and fingerprints on the smooth soft whiteness of her upper arms. The whiteness marked with red pressings of bruised memories.

"Promise!"

He whispered now.

He was begging.

He took refuge in his youth, as she hid in her experience.

She promised.

Amidst the tears and the pleadings.

She promised.

Kneeling on the crumplings of bedclothes, amongst the uncomfortable stains, half dressed, more undressed.

She promised.

The word cut her with every uttering, skewered her, as his penis had skewered her.

This was an end and a beginning, and all the in-betweens gone before and yet to come.

The young man left without so much as a tender kiss.

As he cracked the bedroom door, he said, with no regard.

"Remember Darwin, It'll be there by the weeks end, the key will be at the reception of the hotel opposite. I'll have paid for a full weeks rental on the locker. After that.....".

He paused, smiled at her, an almost callous smile, but it wasn't meant that way. He finished his sentence, repeating the first two words for emphasis:

"After that": he said, pausing once again; "who cares?"

Then, he was gone, back to the life before her.

Pietermaritzburg;
Kwa Zula Natal, South Africa.
'The Bonded Warehouse',
behind the Railway Sidings.
Sometime in August 1921.

The two huge fists moved like well greased connecting rods on the wheels of a monstrous steam locomotive. The young man was massive, muscular, over six feet tall, and only just in his early twenties, if not younger.

He was stripped to the waist; his trousers were oil stained, and his boots, thick, heavy and worn, with dirty frayed strings for laces.

His knuckles were cut, and stained red from the broken teeth and blood of his opponent. He glistened with slippery, sticky, smelly, sweat.

The other man was older, in his thirties, shaven head, with swollen eyes that could no longer see past the bulging bruises. His nose was broken, and he sucked in air through his mouth, spitting out gobs of spittle and blood that exploded on the floor like Howitzer shells, splashing the boots of the onlookers.

The welts on his midriff bore testament to the punishment his ribcage had taken this day.

He went down for the fifth time.

As he fell, the young man fired two devastating straight right handers into his protagonists' kidneys. The older man squeezed out a pitiful mix of grunt and squeal, reminiscent of a slaughterhouse hall as he hit the concrete floor.

The watching circle of observers, cheered and clapped, or jeered and hurled abuse, some spat on the older fighter as he lay on the floor, face down in his own blood and phlegm. The blows to his kidney, as he fell, had caused him to shit himself, and his dungaree trousers were beginning to emit the foul odour of wet diarrhoea.

A small Negro in overalls, threw a bucket of water over the man's back and head, and unceremoniously dumped an ice pack on the back of his neck as he lay prone.

The man eased a quiet, throaty, gurgling groan, then, after a few seconds, another. After a few more seconds his hands and feet began to twitch, painfully, back to consciousness.

Satisfied; the Negro dropped the bucket, and walked silently away.

A Wet Friday in late March 1943.
Port Keats,
Northern Territories,
Australia.

She had caught two trains and five buses to get to Port Keats.

Her last bus ride had started outside Darwin Central Railway Station, at the Bus Terminus opposite the 'Duchess Mags Hotel'.

It had been raining as she had checked the timetable on the wall posters of the terminus ticket hall. She had visited the small window, with the small man in the small uniform behind it, and had slid a scrunched up five dollar bill through its slot.

"Return to Port Keats, route eighteen", she had said, and smiled.

Then walked outside.

It had been a warm rain.

A sensuous rain.

A drizzling fumbling foreplay kind of rain.

A rain that made her wet.

A rain that pricked her memory.

It would become a drenching rain.

She had gathered up the return bus ticket, comforted it, folded it in the warm dampness of her palm as she had walked across the road.

She looked around the square, across towards the 'Duchess Mags'. The place had changed, but not much, some new paint, some better pavements.

It had only changed a spit.

It had taken a decade, and a cruel practical joke of fate to drag her back here. A chance encounter with a tortured sliver of a shard of time long gone; it had become a splinter under her milk white skin, a splinter she could not squeeze.

At first, she had fought the urge to leave her safeness.

Fought it as she always did.

Then lost, as she always had.

It had been nothing but misfortune which had brought her back this way. If only she had not chanced upon that newspaper in the coffee shop, if she had not had a quarter of an hour to kill before her appointment at the hair salon. Or even if the journalist had not phrased his article in the way he had, or if the Ships Captain had not emphasised the particular skills of his un-named 'Stoker'.

An insignificant two or three inch column, reproduced in hundreds of local rags. Rags which ninety nine percent of the Countries population failed to read, and which wound up on shit house hooks, or wrapping vinegar soaked chips.

Jammed in the cracks between the gazillions of gargantuan stories that filled this bloody war, sat this story, struggling to be left alone like some weed creeping through a kerb.

She could have missed it.

But she didn't.

She had to poke her painted nail into this one.

"Why, for fuck's sake?"

She asked herself over and over.

As the world had flicked past on her outward journey, she continued to question her motives for this unwelcome return.

"Why?"

The diagonal rain striped windows of the bus distorted her view. Outside, as if in a damaged film, she saw the inarticulate images of ordinary people's ordinary lives, just ticking away in the same old way, the same old tick; she asked herself again.

"Why?"

After all perhaps it wasn't even him, just an unfortunate expression, three or four words that could have easily been edited out. She had nursed the bag across her lap, and the tin box had jostled inside it as the road lost its occasional smoothness.

"Why?"

She knew why!

It was him.

She felt it in those parts of her that missed him most, that part that made the wetness between her thighs, that other part that hid like a child needing comfort in her dark wonderful soul.

Betrayal is a "funny" concept, she had said one night between whiskies and soldiers. Everyone, (she had decided), betrays up to a point. We betray others as they betray us; she had convinced herself of this.

She was, after all, the victim.

No doubt of that.

She was, most definitely, most assuredly, that victim.

Arthur Du Pont, had given Captain Tynsdale of the H.M.A.S. Waterhen the tin box, as he had been asked to do.

He had dried her shoes, warmed her with coffee from his flask, and sheltered her from the now striking, piercing, penetrating rain. He had seen her safely across the road from his security hut, and onto her bus, the first one heading back towards Darwin; and had agreed to her wishes.

"Promise?"

She had demanded as she left; and he had given his word.

In less than an hour, he had fallen in love with her; exactly as she knew he would.

The box was delivered by Officer Du-Pont, and Captain Tynsdale was asked not to pass it to his Stoker until they had been at sea for three days and three nights.

Then.

The honourable Captain should allow his Saviour one whole hour of solitude.

Then.

He should never mention the matter again.

Arthur Du Pont had refused to hand over the box, until the Captain had sworn, (again, as had been requested of by Arthur), that, as an 'Officer and a Gentleman', Iestyn Tynsdale would abide by these requests.

He had done so, but only reluctantly, as he had not himself met the woman.

He was unaccustomed to betrayal.

When the H.M.A.S. Waterhen sailed with the tide the following morning, Captain Tynsdale struggled, over his coffee, his sausages and his scrambled eggs, with his own concept of this particular demon which had boarded his ship.

This creature of betrayal.

This tacit stowaway whose silence he must beg for three days and three nights.

It was the weight of his oath, his word, and her desire, pitted against friendship, gratitude and an ultimately un-payable debt.

She won.

This was a Saturday; it would be Tuesday before 'Stoko' would suffer his hour of solitude.

When the hour came, like the thief it was:

Iestyn Tynsdale loaned his friend and Saviour the privacy of his Captains quarters for one hour.

All as requested.

The good Captains self imposed punishment for his own betrayal; was to stand outside his cabin in the corridor, resting on his Ironbark walking stick, smoking his Meerschaum pipe, and listening for sixty long minutes as his Saviour wept alone.

Malakye Wylachi O.B.E.
1916 – 2012, still going, but only just.
Sydney,
New South Wales,
Australia.
September 2nd 2012

St. Vincent's Hospital, in Darlinghurst, Sydney, New South Wales, was a premier centre, for the treatment of Ischaemic Heart Disease.

Malakye Wylachi had moved to Sydney, in August 2008, six months after he was first diagnosed.

He had taken a penthouse apartment in Sugardock, overlooking Sydney Harbour Bridge, and the iconic Opera House, on Bennalong Point. It was one of the best views in the city, and the apartment sagged with luxurious fixtures and fittings, paintings and sculptures.

Most of the interior furnishings had been chosen by his two surviving daughters in law, Glynnis and Toraya, with some unsolicited help from his five grandchildren. Particularly Stanforth, (who couldn't keep his nose out of anything), and spent his time, when he visited the apartment, checking that Glynnis and Toraya had receipts for all the purchases. Much the same as he did every day in the family business.

The great grandchildren, all twelve of them, whose ages ranged from seventeen to thirty, and whose names varied from Arbuthnot to Luscinda, and everywhere in between. With no two having a Christian name starting with the same letter, (and, incidentally, none of them being called Malakye either), used the apartment as a weekend crash-pad, for the bright lights and fast life of the big city.

Malakye, (when he had still been a functioning human being), had been fairly certain, that somewhere on their collective e-mails, out there in the ether, was an excel spread sheet with some sort of 'usage rota' on it, for HIS apartment.

He had now cheated the Grim Reaper, for nearly four years, and had dodged and weaved his sweeping scythe with amazing dexterity for a man of ninety six. However, he knew who would ultimately win this fight, and it wasn't going to be Malakye Wylachi O.B.E. He also knew that the bell had already rung for the last round, and he may not even make the count.

He had been in bed for the last three days, unable to rise, and Glynnis and Toraya, his self appointed carers, and arranged for six, private agency nurses, to be at the apartment around the clock. With a minimum of two always on shift at any time.

He had worsened overnight, and his breathing had become laboured. His clear plastic oxygen mask was now a permanent fixture, as he drifted in and out of consciousness.

A private ambulance had been organised to collect him at two p.m., and take him to St. Vincent's, where an equally private room awaited him.

Stanforth Wylachi, and Hugo Wylachi, the Chairman and Vice Chairman respectively, of the, Wylachi Herds, Stockman Corporation Ltd., and the W.H.S. Group of Companies; were already at St. Vincent's. They had flown in from Perth, earlier that day, for a meeting with two of the Senior Cardiologists, and, Thoracic and Cardiac Surgeons.

Hugo's twin sister, Ronda; and Stanforth's sisters Ethel May and Gwyneth, had not been to the apartment for a few weeks. Since Malakye's deterioration they had preferred to stay in Sandstone.

They had never been interested in the family empire, and, other than to collect their monthly bank transfers they had shown little desire to acquire any financial or business acumen. Though, it has to be said, Ronda and Gwyneth could argue into the small hours as to the competing qualities of 'Manolo Blahnik's' versus 'Jimmy Choo's'. The pair were tanned, manicured, coiffured, plasticized and lean.

As far as Ethel May went, well she lived for golf. She played every day, sometimes twice on a Saturday, and never missed an 'Open'. She was currently in Atlanta cheering on Tiger Woods, who neither knew nor cared that she even existed.

She had once paid thirty thousand dollars for a putter which he had, (allegedly), used in a 'Davis Cup' match, and had then donated it to the 'Payne's Find Golf and Country Club', where she was now in her third tenure as Club Captain. The putter stands in a glass case in the clubs entrance foyer, next to a black and white chequered pullover mounted in a pale green picture frame, with a gold label proclaiming it to have been worn by Arnold Palmer in the 'British Open' of 1968. This artefact again purchased by Ethel May Wylachi, for the "absolute snip", as she said at every available opportunity, of eighteen thousand dollars.

Despite their journey, and the circumstances, both men, Hugo and Stanforth Wylachi, looked sharp, in dark business suits, crisp white shirts, and plain coloured ties. One tie in pale blue, the other bright yellow. The yellow tie had a gold and onyx tie pin, the blue one was allowed to hang loose. Both wore dark leather lace up shoes, and carried handmade pig-skin briefcases. The men were tall, each over six feet, tanned, with thick well kempt hair, greying at the temples; and one would say handsome.

The yellow tie man wore gold rimmed, pilot type glasses, with photo-tint lenses, which had slightly darkened in the glare, creeping in through the meeting room window. He was Stanforth. His clothes were slightly looser fitting, a conscious effort to hide his spreading midriff. He was in his early fifties.

Hugo was leaner, his skin more taught, and his eyes more keen. He was five years younger than his cousin, and although they exercised a vibrant rivalry, (both in the business, and on the squash court, which they shared three times a week), they actually quite liked each other, and made a formidable force.

Their respective wives however loathed each other, and despite them being mutually young, attractive, rich, blond and inherently lazy; seemed to have no common ground upon which for them to construct a relationship. Shardaka was thirty six and liked horses; Chelsea was thirty eight and liked her Ferrari. Both liked money and knew how to spend it, a skill which they were religiously and diligently trying to pass on to their children.

Indeed there seemed to be a degree of healthy competition emerging in this department between Hugo and Stanforth's children, and the offspring of Gwyneth and Ronda.

Ethel May, and her husband, Eric, had seen fit never to re-produce.

It was around 11.45 a.m., and the medical team had concluded their briefing of the two men.

They all sat around the elliptical granite topped meeting table, with their respective coffees or teas, in front of each, in plain, utilitarian, (but elegant), white china cups, complete with saucers.

A too large sugar bowl, a carafe of water, and a too small stack of glasses, along with a lonely plate of bourbon biscuits, sat incongruously, and untouched between them all.

22

"So that's it then Gentlemen", said Hugo, in his deep velvet voice, and he rested his chin on his pyramid clasped hands, with elbows on the table top, either side of his cup and saucer.

"So your certain that our Grandfather would not survive any further surgery?", asked Stanforth, for probably the third time, leaning back in his chair, hands clasped on top of his head, like some naughty schoolboy.

The medical team confirmed their prognosis yet again.

Malakye's heart condition had deteriorated dramatically over the last three months. And his recent bout of pneumonia, although cured, had caused a severe weakening, and reduction in his general health and strength.

The medical teams had been fantastic, and, by their skill, had given 'The King of the Stockmen', (as he had been known for the last half century), at least two years more than he should have reasonably expected, given the severity of his condition.

It was a brutal truth, but Malakye Wylachi O.B.E.; was dyeing. From this point on, there was no recovery; there was pain relief, and making comfortable. And that, basically, was that.

For the family, there was clock watching, and re-organising, forms to get drafted, transfers to be finalised, agreements ratified, and re-structures to be completed. And Malakye Wylachi's frail, scrawled signature would still be needed on probably hundreds of documents in the time remaining.

There would be a time for grieving, a time to mourn. But like everything else, that time would have to stand in line behind company business.

He always was, and still remained, up until the last month or so, a 'hands on' patriarch of the 'W.H.S. Group'. He still retained his title as 'Company Secretary and Managing Director', to all of the businesses.

Whatever lucid moments he would have over the next hours, days or weeks, (probably not weeks): it looked as though they would be spent with a fountain pen in one hand, and a Bible in the other.

His death-bed would have a Priest on its left, and a lawyer on its right.

"Probably how the old buzzard would have wanted it!"

Mused Hugo and Stanforth as they left the hospital later that evening.

Their late night flight back to Perth, (after a good meal in one of Sydney's swisher restaurants), would pass in reminiscences, and too many little plastic bottles of Scotch.

Not only would they wax lyrical in semi-sobriety about their grandfather; a trait delivered by indulgent alcohol; but about their own respective late fathers as well.

"Useless cunts!" Hugo had whispered, slurring slightly. Stanforth, (who tried to avoid, "profanity", as he called foul language), nodded in agreement.

They would talk of their wives, their children, their homes, the business, squash, cars, rugby, air travel, and many other things. It was a long flight, and eventually they would have to talk about their grandfather's funeral.

Stanforth pressed the overhead buzzer, and ordered more Scotch from the stewardess that arrived in response. As she walked away, Hugo asked:

"What do you reckon to those new automatic barriers at the security lodge, at Mount Magnet abattoir then; too long or what?"

The 'right time' had clearly still to arrive.

The 'Send Off'.
Eglwys Ilan,
Senghenydd,
South Wales.
A Thursday in February or March 1972

The morning of the funeral was one of those days that fell like a stumbling drunk, between foggy, wet, and miserable; and misty and becalmed.

The month; as my father had recalled, (but only when pressed), staggered somewhere between February and April. A tri-mester often only discernable in these parts, by the progressive dog-eardness of a calendar behind a snug-room bar, with no hint whatsoever provided by climactic conditions.

So even today, the exact date remains, like a youthful catholic, as unconfirmed.

Glam rock still topped the charts, Marc Bolan was 'Getting It On', and page 3 of 'The Sun' newspaper was getting it off. Beer was dark, warm, and served in chipped pint glasses with handles, (not piddle sized bottles), by barmaids named Gloria or Beryl, with low cut chests and cherry red lipstick; all slightly passed their fuck by date.

The closest thing to the internet was Ena Sharples hair net, and crash helmets were not obligatory. British motorcycles with kick starts were still on the roads, smokers were normal people, and Alan Sugar was flogging 'stereos', not sacking would be 'has-beens' on the telly.

It was a day that couldn't make up its mind.

Much like the age.

Much like the congregation.

Some wore overcoats, gloves and scarves, and togged themselves up like Arctic explorers. Others just wore suits: but every man was wedged in a pressed white shirt and black tie, and every foot crumpled in a polished shoe that only came out to play for funerals and weddings.

No last wishes for carnations to be worn, or brightly coloured ties, or meaningful tunes by 'Mott the Hoople'. This was a time when proper send off's demanded proper dignity. Black was a mark of respect, and respect deserved recognition and due deference to those that had gone before.

Music came from hymns, sung by the congregation, with backing from a proper organ with a proper organist, and tubes that didn't work properly. 'Guide Me Oh Thou Great Jehovah' and 'How Great Thou Art', were two ubiquitous stalwarts that made an appearance that day, with 'The Old Rugged Cross' providing a less conventional edge; almost groundbreaking in its non-conformity.

This was the time.

This: was 'The Seventies', the decade that fashion forgot. The decade where rebellion rose like an unexpected erection, only to be tossed off, sharply and expertly by successive Governments.

The difficult birth of the technical revolution had hacked to death the preceding decade of Peace, Love, and The Vietnam War. All of which, by 1972, had by-passed Senghenydd, as had all the other revolutions, innovations, social upheavals and cultural assimilations of the last three hundred years.

Paradise to one such as Yuris Pavel…..um, something or another: 'Stalin' to his gathered 'already missing him's', and the 'already forgetting him's'.

Every sniffling woman to a solitary dark soul was cast in bible black frocks, stilettos and stockings.

The uniform of death.

Mourning with the morning crows and starlings; and each as sad as the sky was full of ink and dirty linen.

The only splashes of colour were those from the flickering white and floral hankies, dabbing frosty penny marked cheeks and peeping out of sleeve cuffs, like snowy ferrets from mucky rabbit holes.

Eglwys Ilan chapel was a stone built cosy little refuge of Christ, nestling in the fist of the Aber Valley.

It overlooked Abertridwr to the south and Pontypridd to the north, with the village of Senghenydd snuggling behind the nearby crouching hill; which, (at this time of year), was constantly infested with fluffy sheep with blue and red dots on them.

Next to the chapel was the Rose and Crown pub; known to everyone as 'The Eglwys'.

It begged the question had it ever been known as the Rose and Crown? In the same way that Senghenydd had become 'Sneggy', the Rose and Crown had become 'The Eglwys', not so much by evolution, but more of a big bang. No one could remember when either was not thus.

Mind you, most of them couldn't remember what they had for breakfast, let alone tackle abstract ideas of a conceptual nature. Still; things are what they are!

The funeral had gone well.

There had been no scenes; people who weren't talking had politely avoided each other, the weather had held its breath, and the reasonably early kick off had meant that the Reverend Iolo Pugsley had been a study in sobriety; instead of a slobbering piss-head.

Only twice had he fumbled: once when 'Jo's' surname had become a jumbled mixture of 'K's' and 'W's'; when, for that one brief moment the Right Reverend had turned into a cross bred mongrel of Alf Ippytittymus and the stuttering Norman Collier.

So, henceforth, the unpronounceable unknown word was subsequently avoided, side-stepped, coughed around or just became 'Jo'. Then, secondly, when he referred to 'Jo's' 'wife', or 'um friend', or just 'um'; and his eye fell, (albeit inadvertently), on Bethany Harrington, spinster of this parish, and 'Jo's' landlady for thirty odd years.

It was, (in fairness), such an inadvertent glance as would normally cause no offence; but then again it was a glance that only Right Reverends can conjure up.

Invoke it they can, from the purulent bowels of heretical souls past. They can spew and spit it with contemptuous ease from a squinting casual blink, or a sideward dart that would make even Eric Bristow proud.

This practiced glance of condemnation had been known to turn new boiled jam bitter.

And, (it is said), on comparison between 'The Glance' and Dante's forecast of torment, one Arch-Bishop had commented, (of the Italian Renaissance poet), that:

'His inferno was not quite up to the task".

But on this occasion, in fairness, the glance was just an inadvertent accident.

Jo, like 'The Eglwys', and 'Sneggy', to everyone apart from Bethany Harrington, was always known as 'Stalin', primarily because, (like the Reverend Pugsley), no one could pronounce his second name, so the nickname 'Stalin' was coined, and became common currency.

Stalin was well known, and well liked throughout the Aber Valley; he had arrived as a stranger in the tortured villages of South Wales around the end of the Second World War, or at least before people had started numbering them, (Wars that is), and when strangers were a welcome distraction; like the 'Darkies' down Tiger Bay, and 'Swansea Jacks' anywhere except Swansea.

'Stalin' had fitted in, he was a grafter, and had dirt under his fingernails, and coke smuts in his ears.

He worked underground at 'Lady Windsor Colliery', and had the miners blue snaking tattoos over his eyebrows, and across his knuckles.

He was a man.

A giant green oak of a man, with spreading shoulders, the size of screaming drams and hands like coal shovels; and apparently he could shag wild women as quick as two strong men could throw them under him.

The Reverend Pugsley, (by sad contrast); was a twisted, dead oak stump of a man; knarled by the newly numbered war, and life in general.

He was a widower who lodged above the Piccadilly Pub; on the square in Caerphilly, less than three miles down the valley. What an unfortunate homestead for someone with a propensity for 'Trophy Bitter', no car, and equal detestations, of both walking and public transport.

His parish missed him as he had missed it; by a good long way on a dark cold night.

He had been posted to Eglwys Ilan from goodness knows where by goodness knows who. He had never met 'Jo', nor most of the congregation. He was resigned to delivering poor sermons to poor congregations, and collecting his poor wages every Friday, and spending most of it on poor beer by the following Wednesday. Today was a Thursday, so he would rely on the benevolence and consciences of the congregation in 'The Eglwys' later; to provide his sustenance.

But deep down, and buried where only a collier could have winkled it out, there was a walnut sized space in him, screaming, not pleading, but screaming, for the blessed agony, to take upon himself, the sins of the world, or at least Senghenydd.

The Reverend Pugsley concluded with the expected "Ashes To Ashes" etc., and 'Jo' was duly planted.

A steady procession, a scar of stooped, black mourners hopped, and slipped passed the hole, this new wound in the graveyard. They seemed to shrink as they did so.

As they went they threw, (some with a thud, and some with a tinkle), handfuls of sand onto the top of 'Jo's' Co-Op box; covering the brass plate which had the word 'STALIN' in copper plate engraving, with inverted commas at either end; final as the 'Lights Out' in 'Cardiff Nick'; and the single date; 1972 carved under his name.

The procession continued on, and marched in dignified order, respectfully silent, and duly deferential, through the lich gate, and across the ten or twelve paces of rough car park, to the entrance door of 'The Eglwys'. Like columns of first day schoolboys and schoolgirls they paced; looking neither left nor right, exchanging neither pleasantries nor specifics, each actively maintaining the demeanour of this solemn transit.

Secret fags held at their sides as they went.

Each soul demure and tutored from countless other funerals they had shared.

They danced in formation, a measured trudge, no one breaking into a rush despite the light drizzle which was now spitting on these stooped starling participants. They hunched in the way only funeral-goers can hunch. Each stooped in recognition of their own, individual, personal, transience and self appraisal.

For that short trek betwixt graveyard and public bar, like the short trek betwixt whining, puking infancy and certain death; each mourner incanted a silent personal vow. A fish-bowl hollow promise to themselves to make more of the time left to them. Each mourner knowing in their shallow hearts that these crumbling vows would shatter at the first whiff of overtime, or an 'obble' to knock down 'so and so's wall' for a tenner cash.

As each of these trudging incantations of a life entered 'The Eglwys', they were transformed.

The magical portal, the open fire, the exposed beams, the littered horse brasses, and the round dark wood tables, (abused through the stale tobacco and alcohol which hung like a traitor in the air), recovered their ambivalence.

"Enough!" It said.

And clenching a fist of misery, it whispered, (waving it at God):

"The mourning is done; the now is for the living!"

And so it was that the 'making more of the time left' bits of the promises were fresh; as green as life can be shit sometimes, and as honest as a tax return!

These new found vows of hedonism were taking on a religious zeal, as the mourners attacked the bar.

Like Zulu's they clamoured against the brass foot rail, ordering round after round of pints of bitter, halves of Mackesson, port and lemon's and Babychams, with the tops left on.

Filled with bubbles!

Filled with dreams!

The bar staff defending the 'ridout', like men with 'bayonets Sir; and some guts behind it', they should have been awarded a dozen Victoria Sponges for their actions that day. Or at least a plate of prawn *vol'au'vents*

The reception had begun.

The last they saw of Greniko, November 18th, 1918.

Men on grey horses, brandishing sabres and revolvers, and holding their reins in their teeth, galloped through the small, rural village of Greniko.

Slashing glinting steel, and firing dull lead as they went.

The horses' hooves thumping into the early winter mud, leaving brown spatters up their legs and under their bellies. Occasionally one would stumble, hurling its rider over its head, and into cold stone walls, or onto piles of sharp farming implements and clawing machinery.

Some horses staggered back to their feet, others did not; as did, or did not, their riders.

The screams of injured animals and people filled the crisp morning air. The piercing yelps of pigs and goats; shot, or gashed by sword swipes, the crippled horses, terrified fleeing sheep, chickens and ducks. Then the people: men, women and children:

"No Prisoners!"

The shout from the horsemen.

"No Prisoners!"

The human animals fell like the farmyard animals, crying in their own blood and their own muck.

Spilling their own entrails onto their own ground. Their own village burning all around them.

The few men remaining in the village were shot, or cut down as they ran, becoming bogged down in the stewed mud.

This abattoir.

The women, raped first, then shot or hacked to death, their remains littering the single street and central square of the village, scattered around the frozen communal water pump, still wrapped in its winter sacking.

Even on the steps of the clinker built Synagogue they lay.

After two or three hours, the village was a mish-mash of smouldering piles of isolated debris, like lonely spent volcanoes, in a small and insignificant mountain range of nightmare and disaster.

Human and animal remains spotted and dotted the mud roads, trampled into the muck by the horses of the White Guards. Small puddles of red bubbled in the hollows, then, the blood, like the people, like the village, soaked away without trace into the gobbling, sucking mud.

From the small copse on the hill, the woman and the two boys watched.

She knew well enough this inevitable outcome the instant she had first seen the horsemen riding down the valley sides towards their small village.

No clairvoyance was required.

She had called the boys to her side, away from their wood gathering, and crouched them down next to her in the bracken. Crouched like piglets at a slaughterhouse, penned by the undergrowth which hid them.

Waiting.

They had watched silently as the carnage unfolded. Grew before them.

Just two withering fields away, their world was changing.

31

All knew that silence was their saviour, there was no movement, breaths were shallow, eyes were wide, and hands held each other tightly, until their knuckles gleamed as white as the frightened eyes of new caught slaves.

And with such slaves they shared a common reality.

A common understanding.

They would never return to their village.

Once darkness had begun to cloak them, they would begin the twenty eight mile walk to Gwalikin Palatinsk, the next village, further down the valley toward the Black Sea port of Odessa.

The next village where three Jews could trust to God for shelter amidst some of their own kind.

Amidst Bolsheviks, Russians, and Jews; but most importantly; most of all, amidst Jews.

As in all revolutions, the minorities seek solace with other minorities. At least until the larger 'other minorities' slowly evolve into majorities, and then begin to fear those minorities they invariably leave behind. Already the Jews were being left behind by the Bolsheviks.

From here, (the woman knew); it was only a matter of time until the Bolsheviks, like the 'White*s*', turned on the Jews.

But for now, the pressing necessity was the cover of night. Then a cold, wet, arduous, (but hopefully safe and uneventful), journey to Gwalikin Palatinsk.

The Office of Ambrose Suda-Iwo,
'Mimex Fuller, Mimex Law',
Sydney,
New South Wales,
Australia.
October 10th 2012.

Ambrose Suda-Iwo spoke bluntly with Stanforth and Hugo.

The voices from the conference call desk pods were as clear as a mountain stream, despite the two halves of the conference call being the length of the country apart. 'The Wylachi Group of Companies' end of the conversation being in Perth, and the 'Mimex Fuller, Mimex Law' end, being in Sydney.

Mr Suda-Iwo's tone made it plain that there was to be no debate, no misunderstanding. He said, in a voice that could crack marble, at several paces with nothing more than a well placed syllable.

"Your Grandfather wanted it this way. It all comes out of his money, not the companies, not the trust funds, not the endowments. You can contest it if you wish; but as your company's solicitors, and more importantly, as your Grandfathers personal solicitor for over fifty years, and the person who drafted this document. I would advise very strongly against it. There are matters being resolved here which you know nothing about".

"What matters?" demanded Hugo.

Mr. Suda-Iwo cut him short from two thousand miles away.

"Matters which do not concern either of you!"

Stanforth now interjected:

"Ambrose, we pay your firm very fat fees every short month, there is nothing which doesn't concern us, and if we ask for......."

Mr Suda-Iwo fielded Stanforth's demands with the same dispatch he had handed out to Hugo's.

"I am not acting for you in this matter, or the companies. I am acting for your late Grandfather, as executor of his will. There is over twenty million dollars set aside for this in that document, and I also have certain specific instructions as to how this whole task is to be administered."

Hugo spoke again;

"Let me guess Ambrose, those instructions are not our concern; am I right?"

Mr. Suda-Iwo's sigh was audible over the conference line speakers, then he spoke;

"Now you're getting it boys".

He used the word 'Boys' because he knew how much it annoyed them.

Knew how condescending it was.

Knew how much he enjoyed using it.

With Malakye dead, Ambrose also knew that the long relationship 'Mimex Fuller, Mimex Law' had enjoyed with 'The W.H.S. Group of Companies' under Malakye Wylachi Jnr. O.B.E., would very soon be terminated.

Hugo and Stanforth disliked Ambrose Suda-Iwo, they considered him too 'Old School', and too close to their late Grandfather. They also thought that he knew too much about the company business, which was not necessarily business, if you see what I mean.

They had been quietly moving their legal affairs and contract work, to practices in Perth, Canberra and Melbourne for over three months now. Ambrose had been aware of this turning tide; his octogenarian ears were close to the ground, and he had not been in legal practice in Australia for over six decades without making certain connections.

He had realised some time ago that once Malakye was gone, there would be no delay in this particular axe being wielded by his grandson's.

Ambrose Suda-Iwo, Senior Partner in the Sydney office of 'Mimex Fuller, Mimex Law', would make the most of this last task given to him by his old associate, (friend is the wrong word), Malakye Wylachi. As he sat back in his leather Chesterfield chair in the well of his business-like office on the twentieth floor of the Chifley Tower, alone, except for the conference pod in the centre of the coffee table; he began to realise how much he would miss Malakye.

The two men had shared triumphs and disasters over the last half century, shared times when they had needed each other, and times when they had hated the sight of each other, times when they had lied to each other, times when they had shared their inner-most secrets, and cried with each other.

It was the depth of this mutual comprehension that 'The Boys' now objected to.

"So?"

Asked the conference pod speaker on the coffee table.

"So Nothing!"

Snapped Ambrose, and then continued without waiting for any further response.

"There's over three hundred million in cash to be distributed between the family members. You two get fifty five million each. Plus there are the properties, the boat, the cars, the stock portfolio and the art collection, and something a little over three million dollars worth of wine in the cellar at Sandstone".

Hugo's voice spat from the speakers once more;

"Are there any other bequests we should know about Ambrose?"

There was a slightly uncomfortable pause, a pause wherein Ambrose, (briefly), could not decide properly and finally on his delivery of the answer. He was of course not obliged to divulge anything; but he chose to. In the end he did it matter-of-factly.

"There are a few, yes, in fact there are three, each of five hundred thousand dollars. There is one to Mr. and Mrs. Amos Duval, your Grandfathers housekeepers at Sandstone Farmstead, one to an anonymous person in Queensland, and one to myself."

There was a thunderous silence, a crashing, crushing pause of apocalyptic proportions. Ambrose seized the moment and continued.

"Oh, and I almost forgot; Malakye has made provision for a small gathering with a meal and the like, for all the employees at each of your abattoirs, ranches, packing plants, and distribution depots etcetera. He has allowed a sum of two hundred and fifty thousand dollars, with a further ten thousand dollars to be paid to the 'Shillington Arms' at Sandstone for the, as he puts it here", Ambrose, pausing deliberately, thumbed the pages of the will document which he rested across his knee. "Ah yes, here it is, it say's;

'To be put over the bar at the 'Shillington Arms,
Sandstone, W.A., for the future enjoyment of
beverages and food, provided that the purchasers
make a toast to me with their first sip'.

I think that's quite nice, don't you boys?"

Stanforth exploded verbally down the conference line.

"Drinks and food in the 'Shillington' for all our employees!"

Ambrose Suda-Iwo interrupted him.

"And former employees as well, in the case of the Sandstone bequest"

Stanforth continued, getting more agitated with each sentence.

"And who's this anonymous person with a half a million bucks of our bloody money?"

Ambrose was beginning to enjoy himself, he replied, saying:

"I am not at liberty to divulge that information Stanforth, I'm dreadfully sorry". He, of course, wasn't, sorry I mean.

Stanforth carried on, Ambrose could feel the venom rising, 'Come on Stanforth' he thought to himself, 'Gob it out, you know it's the one that's really eating you up, come on, spit it out'.

The speakers burst into life.

Here it comes, Ambrose thought.

"And you, half a million bucks on top of all the fees you've had out of us over the years, are you really going to accept it? I can't believe you're even considering it?"

Ambrose replied without delay.

"Of course I'm not considering it. There's nothing to consider."

Ambrose felt the Wylachi cousins breathe a collective sigh of relief and satisfaction. He allowed them, their brief few seconds of anticipated victory.

Then he continued.

"Malakye has left it to me, and I'm definitely taking it. As for the fees; well, we've provided a service, and we've charged for it".

Hugo was now losing his temper, fuming, stuttering, spluttering; he interrupted Ambrose.

"Charged for it! Charged for it!" He screamed.

"You can charge like a fucking Rhino Ambrose, and now you're telling me you'll take this half million on top".

Ambrose replied, a measured response, a cool response, designed to inform and inflame, he said.

"Not only will I take the five hundred thousand dollars bequeathed to me personally; but, and having considered the time involved in finalising matters, for myself, and my staff, I would assess that a reasonable estimate for my practices fees in the execution of your Grandfathers will, should be something in the region of seventy thousand dollars".

He waited for a reply, none came.

As the conference line died with no further exchange, Ambrose imagined Hugo and Stanforth smashing the conference pod against the wall, and throwing cups and pens and anything else that was to hand around the room. Swearing and cursing as they did so. Throttling secretaries at random as they rampaged through their offices, crazed with angst and vinegar. Beating unfortunate employees to death with desk legs to save the cost of a free four 'X' in the 'Shillington Arms'.

Ambrose smiled to himself, leaned forward, and pressed the 'end call' button on his own conference pod.

"Brats" he said, with no emotion whatsoever, as he leaned back in his chair.

"Third bloody generation brats".

The Reception at 'The Eglwys',
And the introduction of, 'THE BOX'.
February or March 1972.

My Father, and his friend from the Railway Sheds, Jimmy Calabria, were sipping on 'Manns-Tops', and edging, wriggling and squirming closer to the fireplace. Its bubbling warmth, inviting, with beckoning tongues of flames.

'Come and warm your bum', it said, in the common language of the hearth.

The chairs and stools were for the ladies, and the old folk.

Men stood in pubs.

"Who the fuck was this 'Jo' feller; I thought I was at the wrong funeral!"

Some wag had mused during their skirmish towards the fireplace; the entire pub had laughed. It was a laugh at the Reverend Pugsleys expense, though he was, and would ever be, blissfully ignorant of it.

Jo Stalin was that Rusky bloke with the big moustache, who changed his name from, Ioseb Besarionis dze Jughashvili, and had five year plans. Sneggy's Stalin was just 'Stalin'.

He too had changed his name, or, more accurately, his world had changed it for him, invented him, suckled him, absorbed him, protected and hid him.

He was just 'Stalin'.

Or 'Sneggy Stalin', if you came from Abertridwr, Ponty, or Caerphilly.

A shout squealed through the crescendoing, spiralling, thermal conversation like an unexpected gale.

"Jimmy! Jimmy bach!"

It sliced the buzzing breeze of release, (which wafted like a gliding, hunting, stalking condor in the air); sliced it like a bread knife in the wrong hands.

Eeeeh! Eeeeh! Eeeeh!

It would have said if it was a shower scene in a Hitchcock film.

The screech was buoyed up on gusts of last night's stale tobacco, mingling delicately with little typhoons of freshly puffed Players Navy Cut and Embassy Regal.

It would stink like a mongrels fart to twenty first century cosseters, but it was just how proper pubs smelt then.

"Jimmy! Jimmy!"

Squalled Bethany Harrington once more, from across the snug.

She was holding aloft, (like an assegai), an old Jacobs biscuit tin, with aging sepia selotape around it, and a bit of paper stuck on the side; browned with Capstan Full Strength, Rough Shag and hard years.

Jimmy Calabria took a long pull on his pint of 'Manns-Top', and waved,

"Over here Beth!"

He yelled, in a voice as deep as a shopkeeper's pocket.

Bethany Harrington's ample frame squeezed between the other participants of the funeral reception. ('Wake', is a far too Irish expression, and somehow, not quite suitable for such a sombre occasion in a Welsh mining valley. The Irish are a much more irreverent race, and their abuse of sobriety reflects their abuse of society, morality, and religion; Catholicism, after all is no competition for 'Chapel').

Bethany dodged and weaved between the condolences like 'Tasker Watkins' ducking machine gun bullets on 'D-Day'. For a woman in her mid-sixties, and a tad on the rotund side, she was as agile as an eel. Within seconds she was standing by the fire with Jimmy and my father, her impressive bosom heaving with the exertion of her dribble across the snug.

She was an attractive woman, (given her age); and always wore a dab too much make up, as a last ditch effort against the onslaught of that age. She had lied for years that she was 'fifty nine', and had vowed to remain so for another four years when she would become 'sixty one.

She put her glass of Babycham on the stone mantelpiece, (she never spilt a solitary drop on her traverse across the snug).

She stood in front of my Father and held out, in both hands now, like some ancient offering, the Jacobs biscuit tin.

Her black funeral dress, which was at least one size too small, and with a hemm at least two inches too short, was on the cusp of exploding; and it was likely that only the applied pressure of the surrounding throng was all that was holding Bethany Harringtons clothes in place.

"What's that you're clutching there then Beth?"

Enquired Jimmy.

"It's for you!"

She replied, and held it forward towards Jim, he handed his pint to my father to guard, and took the tin.

"What is it?"

Jimmy asked, holding it to the side of his head, and rattling it in mock inquisition. When he studied it closer, the paper on the side of the tin said.

'For my friend Jimmy C, when I'm gone'.

Jimmy looked at the tin for a moment, and then at Beth, an awkward tear bloomed in his eye: blinking it away, he asked.

"What's in it?"

Bethany shrugged her shoulders the inch or so her dress would allow, trying desperately not to spill her Babycham, (which she had retrieved in a single deft movement from the mantelpiece at the same time as handing over the box to Jimmy

39

'C'). Despite the bumping jostling mob, the meniscus of Bethany's Babycham never wavered by more than one or two degrees from true.

As indeed was the case with Bethany's answer.

"Don't know!"

She shouted above the hullabaloo.

"He wanted you to have it; Yuris kept it under the bed".

She paused; an embarrassed pause, an unnecessary pause, she continued, but amended.

"Under HIS bed".

She emphasised, the word, HIS; (an altogether different form of 'Rough Shag' springs to mind).

Bethany was the only person who called 'Stalin', 'Yuris'; and the only person not to admit that their relationship was something more than landlady and lodger, but nearer to landlady and Roger(er).

She took an immense swig of Babycham, which drained her glass and nearly choked her.

Bethany Harrington could drink like a fish with hollow legs, when the circumstances demanded, and today was demanding. She was beginning to slur, and flirt, a dangerous combination, and one very difficult to fight against in one such as Bethany Harrington. She continued.

"Anyway, I'll leave that with you Jim; I've got to go and mingle now".

She glanced across the snug. Then frowned, paused, winked at a young barman, and said.

"Reverend Pugsley's getting a bit pissed over there, and cadging drinks that should be coming my way. Well man of the cloth or not, he can just fuck off!"

They all exchanged some condolences, (of the obligatory fashion), and Bethany made another attempt at escape. With a sweeping swerve and a drop of her left shoulder, she was gone, smuggling into the beating crowd like a weavel into bread.

Jimmy placed the biscuit tin on the stone mantelshelf above the fire and he and my Father gazed at it for several long minutes, musing as to its contents.

Could it be cash?

Or letters?

Old medals perhaps?

Some photos?

Or maybe just a full tin of Jacobs crackers and a chunk of Caerphilly Cheese?

That would be the kind of joke old 'Stalin' would play, knowing Jimmy was partial to a bit of cheese, (the 'Ben Gunn' of Senghenydd he was). That would be 'Stalin', get Jimmy's hopes up, and then spring the trap. My father and Jimmy 'C' laughed between themselves, convinced of the box's eventual utter pointlessness.

Shortly, they were joined at the fireside by other black tied, and black dressed send-offers, like ravens pecking at the warmth, they talked the embers by.

Jimmy told a few of them about the box, and it, (like most things on mantle shelves), had become something of a conversation piece. Johnny Spinks, a Highways Inspector with the Council, and an old friend of both my Father and Jimmy 'C', mused that the box may be a bomb, designed to blow up at the reception, and convey the entire congregation to the hereafter, so that 'Stalin' would not be lonely.

"Is it ticking?"

Dilys Pugh had asked.

"No, I think it's turkey".

Spinksy had replied. The little fireside gathering chuckled, as only half cut mourners can chuckle. Slightly embarrassed at the intrusion of humour, and wholly grateful for the late arrival of such a welcome interloper.

The remainder of the day degenerated into disjointed conversations about disjointed memories about disjointed anecdotes about 'Stalin', the Aber Valley, football, the Labour party, bricklaying, coal-mining, the price of fish and chips, and, how beer wasn't what it used to be, so no wonder 'poufs' were drinking wine, and there were more 'poufs' every day. All present agreed that the growing availability of wine in society was a direct cause of homosexuality.

Every tale slurred and buffeted around the fag end banter of snug bars, and spilt 'Barley Wine', as thick and sticky on the carpet as the stories were dark and funny, and funny and lies.

Occasionally someone would strike up a tune on the presumption that such behaviour was an expectation of a South Wales Valley funeral, having watched 'How Green Was My Valley', dozens too many times.

A 'Calon Lan' was attempted quite early on, and in fairness, was not a discreditable version, for a bunch of drunks with no Welsh speakers amongst them, (save for Bethany who knew two proper words and nine swear words). Also, everybody seemed to know most of the words, which always helps. Thank goodness for the efforts of the 'Twyn Infants School', and 'The Gwyndy Secondary Modern' to instil a modicum of cultural awareness into pupils who, (in reality), didn't give a fuck.

The Reverend Pugsley had even joined in the 'Calon Lan'. It had come at the right time for his eminence; somewhere between three and six pints, somewhere between amiable and affable, and just before belligerent, rude, foul-mouthed, pissed, and ignorant: or his seven pints limit, as Selwyn, the Landlord of the Piccadilly Inn, called it.

By the time 'Ar Hyd Yr Nos' came along, the first verse was barely completed before the entire pub ran out of words, and the haunting melody decayed into a mumbled, bumbling, unrecognisable pile of shit.

Later, when the inevitable 'Myfanwy' sprang up, there was some debate as to whether it was in fact T.Rex's, 'Ride A White Swan', or 'Mama We're All Crazee Now' by Slade.

It was eventually, (almost unanimously), agreed to be a soulful version of 'Long Haired Lover From Liverpool', by little Jimmy Osmond. The scamp!

Thankfully, by this time the Reverend Pugsley, was propped on a stool at the end of the bar, having well exceeded his *tourettes* inducing seven pint limit.

"Cunts!"

He had cursed as his drinks donations slowly dried up, in reciprocal proportion to his manners.

"Tight fisted Welsh cunts!"

Slumping into the stone wall behind him, and partially assuaged by an alcoholic sleep, the Right Reverend looked like a bonfire night 'Guy' recently rescued from a skip; a skip full of sick.

He had a slug trail of spittle that ran down his chin, over his dog collar, down the lapel of his jacket, down his trousers, over his shoe, across the carpet, out of the door, and down the hillside to Pontypridd.

Well, at least some dribble was on his face, and he was fast asleep, snoring, and driving them home like a good 'un.

Not what one expects from ones local Minister on these occasions.

Another day in the sun,
Western Australian Prison Service,
Penal Work Camp number 18.
Kalgoorlie Boulder.
Western Australia.
January 5th, 1943.

It was another sweltering, humid January day.

The same as every other

sweltering, humid day of every other

sweltering, humid sickening week, of ever other

sweltering, humid, sickening, numbing, month, of every other

sweltering, humid, sickening, numbing, thieving antipodean year;

that Prisoner number 89855812 could remember.

Though still early morning, the whining Spotted Crakes and flea infested Blue Winged Kookaburras, were already hunting out the shading refuge of mouldy foliage, so that they could look down on, and occasionally shit on Prisoner number 89855812 from the Shining Gum Trees and those fucking Grey Ironbarks that stood like extra 'Screws', (as if any more were needed), around the perimeter fence.

The huge red sun had swollen again like a blister over 'Bluff Knoll', a craggy granite mountain in the 'Stirling Range' of Western Australia, about two hundred and fifty miles south-east of Perth, and fifty miles or so north, of the Pacific ports of Albany, Denmark and Wallpole.

43

"Wakey wakey, you lazy good for nothing buckets of shit, there's a bloody war on, and you fucking 'Galahs' are helping us beat those little yellow bastards that want to shag the fuck out of your mothers and sisters, and fill up their fanny's with rice guzzling Nips. Now get, fucking, up!"

It was the unmistakable voice of Sergeant Fuzzy Dolenz, 'Top Sarge', of the, 'Western Australian Prison Service Penal Work Camp Number 18'. He stood like a brick khazi in the doorway of the hut, flanked by two prison guards with unclipped side arms, and each, swaying gently, a two foot long hardwood club, made from the seasoned Ironbark of the surrounding trees.

Each club comfortably capable of cracking disobedient skulls with the gentlest of clouts.

The prime function of 'Penal Camp 18', was to smash big rocks into small rocks, so the factories, further in land, could extract zinc from them, so the factories on the coast could use it to make ships, so the Japs could get the hammering they deserved, and not get to shag your mothers or your sisters.

Under Sergeant Dolenz' command, there were exactly thirty two armed guards, who constantly patrolled a fenced compound of at least twenty acres. The camp was located on the southerly slopes of 'Bluff Knoll'.

Above Sergeant Dolenz, in the pecking hierarchy of the 'Western Australian Prison Service Penal Work Camp Number 18', were Deputy Warden Frank Summersby, and a small band of seven or eight administrators and accountants, who kept the books for the Government. Presumably there was a 'Proper Warden' above Deputy Warden Summersby, but no one had ever seen him.

Camp 18 was the arse end of the Australian Penal System. Far enough out not to be noticed, and sorry enough that if it ever did get noticed, it wouldn't be cared about.

From shit packed dawn till shit packed dusk lorries full of rocks rolled through the gates. Rocks, ranging from the size of your head to the size of a pair of doors poured through the 'pig-mesh' gates in an endless procession.

They got tipped in an ever growing pile in the east corner of the compound. The rocks then got smashed into smaller rocks the size of your fist, using sledge hammers, lump hammers, chisels and wrecking bars. All powered by raw muscle, bread with weevils, meat with maggots, and Australia's just desire for punishment and retribution on the social miscreants she had spawned.

The convicts here, had all been sentenced to prison terms suffixed by the codicil, "Hard Labour". They all deserved it. They were all cunts!

The satisfactorily re-sized rocks, were then carted in wheelbarrows, across the uneven dust and gravel ground of the compound, and re-piled in another ever-growing hillock, (this time), of fist sized rocks, on the west side of the compound.

The emptied lorries were then driven around the compound perimeter from east to west, like the sweeping hands of a clock ticking down sentences. Then they were re-filled with the re-sized rocks, and then driven back out of the gates.

The only mechanical assistance in this entire process was the small, tracked, maroon and yellow crane and bucket, thick with dust and rust, which loaded the west side rock hillock, back onto the recently tipped lorries. This machine was manned and operated by a civilian named 'Scud', who was constantly accompanied by three armed guards, in buff coloured uniforms, with salt rings under the armpits, and down their shirt backs, and around the arses of their trousers.

'Scud' would spit on the prisoners if they came close enough to the cab of his little crane. He chewed tobacco and was constantly pissed, but all-in-all he wasn't a bad stick.

If he got pissed enough, he would sometimes clamber onto the metal roof of his cab and recite foul limericks about girls with big arses, or about guards sucking each others cocks.

The screws would always try and shut him up before Fuzzy heard him, but the con's would laugh and clap.

He was the only bloke who could drive the crane, so he took the piss a bit.

Each guard carried two canteens of water slung at their webbing belts. They had clubs, pistols and rifles. Some of them were o.k., but most of them, (Prisoner number 89855812 thought), "were cunts!"

They wore wide brimmed hats, and sweat stained neckerchiefs, and walked persistently around the rock pile. It was their sentence too, they got paid, but it was still their sentence too. Occasionally one of them would shoot the odd buzzard that flew overhead, or a rare rabbit that strayed too near the fence. The guards, (as the

45

prisoners), would urinate against the wooden posts of the thick galvanised 'pig-wire' compound fencing; urine which dried in seconds under the beating, punishing sun.

The fence itself was a good twelve foot high, with randomly attached, rusting barbed wire, draped, in sagging curtains of tetanus across the top; designed to deter and infect.

The compound as a whole was an irregular pentagon, neither level nor true in any plain.

At three of its five corners stood flimsy, tall, cast iron sentry towers, with a hoop ladder for access, extending from the 'Free Side' of the fence, (as the guards called it), to a rectangular hole in the underside of the wood planked viewing platform.

Each tower held two guards, one with a double barrel shot gun, the other with an Enfield 303 rifle. And the one opposite the compounds pair of entry gates, also snuggled an aging 'Maxim Machine Gun', above its platform, that nosed, cheekily, and menacingly, out over its timber guardrail.

Every Saturday morning before 'Grub Break One', the guards in that tower had to test fire the Maxim Gun, just to make sure it was working properly. Once, a round had hit the iron leg of the tower next to it, the bullet had bounced off with a deafening ping and hit an old feller from a place called Jumbla, who was doing a five stretch for persistent sodomy. It had taken the top of his head clean off.

He had no next of kin, so he got buried outside the perimeter fence.

One morning about a week later bits of him were scattered all around the bottom of one of the guard towers. Some Dingo's had dug him up over night and ate most of him. The guards hadn't buried him deep enough so Fuzzy Dolenz had them pile the bits that were left up, douse them in diesel and put a match to them. The bits smouldered for hours and put the cons off their grub.

The viewing platforms were enclosed by scruffy, and uneven, timber palisade rails, painted in a peeling olive green; and covered from the sun by a flat corrugated tin roof, rusty as an old nail. Each platform contained a five gallon jerry can of water, a piss-pot bucket, and two tall wooden stools, the sort you find in school laboratories.

The sentry towers overlooked the two hundred and eight, 'Hard Labour Convicts'. They all wore thick blue denim trousers, and thin blue denim shirts. Hats were not permitted. Both the shirts and the trousers had a white stencilled eight digit number on their backs. The shirts also had a name badge sewn onto the left breast, some names were filled in, others weren't, it was the numbers that mattered, not the names. The labels were all white cotton, with thick black embroidery.

All the convicts' uniforms were showing signs of wear, knees were open, and tears and scags remained unstitched. Neither shirts nor trousers had any pockets. Pockets weren't needed. The boots were cut down rubber Wellingtons, distinctly unsuitable for these conditions, and very, (deliberately), un-conducive to thoughts of escape.

The prisoners slept in five large Nissan huts, almost central in the compound, with a latrine hut which could accommodate five inmates at a time, and a shower hut, with a capacity of twelve inmates at a time.

Meals were served in the open, and from the back of an old, surplus army truck, painted in rusting desert camouflage; which drove up to the camp three times a day,

The meals were always the same, boiled potatoes with crawling things, something that looked like pork with crawling things, a chunk of bread with crawling things, and at 'Grub Break Three', an apple with crawling things.

Near the large entrance gates, flanked by guard boxes on both sides, and on the 'Free Side' of the fence, there stood a pair of grey, two thousand gallon water bowsers. On the side of the left one, in bright red, uneven letters was painted the words.

'Don't ask cos the answers NO'.

On the right hand one, in the same demented lettering it said.

'It's still fucking NO'.

At least they had put the 'G' in 'fucking'. If there was one thing Fuzzy Dolenz could not abide, it was poor grammar.

The guards' conditions were not much better, except that their huts were outside the compound, and had better latrines and shower facilities. They also had a small lounge hut with a radio, a film show every other evening, and telephones that occasionally worked.

47

It was January 12th, 1943. The 'Yanks' were in the War proper, (at last), and the convicts, under the able management of 'Top Sarge' Fuzzy Dolenz, were all paying for their crimes, with interest. At the same time they were satisfying the wartime lust for metals of all descriptions, by aiding the production of zinc, which was, (Fuzzy had been told, by Deputy Warden Summersby), a national priority.

'Penal Work Camp Number 18', was doing its job.

The mid-day klaxon for end of grub break two had just sounded. The life of the camp was governed by rigid regime. Ten minutes for breakfast, 'grub break one', at 8.30 a.m. Twenty minutes for dinner, 'grub break two', at 1.30 p.m. Then Twenty minutes for supper, 'grub break three', at 6.30 p.m. Five minute water breaks, at two hour intervals further split up the back breaking monotony of the day.

Prisoner number 89855812 was on barrow duty after 'grub break two'.

It was worse than smashing rocks.

The wheelbarrows were all busted and bent, and the tyres were mostly flat. The guards made sure the barrowers jogged across the compound to the west pile, to keep up with the rock breakers, who outnumbered barrowers by five or six to one. Every convict had a shift on the barrows at least every other day; they called it 'Pain On Wheels'; and it was.

By 5.30 p.m., the aching back, calf and forearm muscles of Prisoner number 89855812, were beginning to scream for release.

He had ceased to sweat over an hour ago, and his lips had begun to crack, and his tongue to swell. Although he was used to the daily muscular and dermatological trauma that the camp inflicted by its imposed labour; barrow duty seemed to make it all ten times worse.

There was still an hour to go until 'grub break three'. Then probably, another two and a half hours after that, until sundown, and 'Hog Hour'.

'Hog Hour', was the one hour period after sundown, when the crane drove out of the compound, and pushed one of the water bowsers, inside, through the gates. Five guards would then circle the bowser, and an orange tinged searchlight would shine down on it, from one of the sentry towers. Then; for a whole hour, the convicts could drink as much water as they liked, using the half a dozen steel ladles which hung on secure chains, (each chain, no more that three foot long), from the pull rail above the bowsers nozzle.

The first twenty minutes or so was always a free for all, with a few punch ups between the cons., and a few clips dolled out by the Ironbark clubs of the guards. But after this initial frenzy, their thirst slaked, the cons would generally plonk themselves down on the nearest available rock, slump into abstract positions of repose, and let the falling temperature of the night air, cool their agonising bones, sinews and muscles.

But 'Hog Hour' was still an eternity away for Prisoner number 89855812, still three or more hours of barrowing. Still at least fifty more barrow fulls, eight thousand more jogged paces, one hundred more stops, releases, tips, pulls, shakes and turns on the callous causing rust covered handles of the wheelbarrow.

He thought about anything except the wheelbarrow.

He thought about home.

He thought about his brother.

He thought about his mother.

He thought about Eloise.

He thought about lamb chops.

He thought about Eloise again.

He thought about playing in the snow as a child.

He thought about Eloise again.

Then Eloise some more.

Then again, and again.

It had been over twenty five years since he had seen snow, let alone played in it.

He tried not to remember how many years it had been, since he had last seen Eloise; or touched her, or fucked her, cursed her, missed her, laughed at her, got drunk with her, walked with her, went to sleep with her, woke up with her; wanted to kill her, wanted to fall in love with her all over again.

He would always remember.

It was eight years, one hundred, and sixty six days.

A day more than yesterday.

Pietermaritzburg;
Kwa Zula Natal, South Africa.
The Bonded Warehouse,
behind the Railway Sidings.
Sometime in August 1921.
After his first fight.

Dykka Van Hoost, was a smuggler, a pimp, a fraudster, and a thief. Nothing for him was too hot or too heavy.

It was said, that for every ten tons of coal that went into Pietermaritzburg railway yards, one and a half tons went back out to 'Dykka's Sidings', as they were known locally. He would then ship this 'black hard stuff', as he termed it, (never being too open about his business), to every dockyard around the Cape. From Saldanha in the west, to Durban in the east, with East London, Port Elizabeth and Cape Town in between; few ships left South Africa without some of Dykka Van Hoosts fuel coal aboard.

In return, and for a discounted rate, or for fifty free tons of 'the hard black stuff', in the right place; or the odd barrel of rum, to a ships captain who was 'in the know'; Dykka would purchase inside information about "Sweet Cargos", (as he called them).

Rolls of fabric, or tyres, or tobacco; anything he could turn a coin on.

He would simply grease the right palms to look the wrong way, or to fiddle some paperwork. Then other palms, (equally greased), would load up his trucks, and drive them out of the dock gates; while the gatekeepers, (again with greasy palms), would be conveniently out on their rounds, or having a sneaky fag, or in the toilet.

He would often say to his closest associates that his business could be summed up, as:

"Black stuff in; Luckies out!"

He also supplied coal to the dozens of small, privately owned railway companies, which proliferated throughout central and West Africa after the First

World War. In turn, (and as something of a reciprocal arrangement), he made use of the services provided by these less than scrupulous small lines, to transport, collect, and deliver his contraband throughout the region. From French wines to Irish Whisky, Dykka always knew where to get it, who wanted it, and how much they would pay.

His business was basically, anything anyone wanted, anything anyone would pay for.

But his passion was diamonds.

He liked gold too, but he loved diamonds.

Not to buy.

Just to own.

Just to steal.

He had first come across Itzhak and Yuris Androskewowicz, when they were working as labourers, shovelling coal into steam locomotive tenders for The Natal Railway Company, at two shillings a tender-full.

He had 'fixed them up' with one of the Pietermaritzburg Railway Yard Supervisors, (a man called Gonda Vischen); from the Cape Government Railways Company, to shovel coal from some of their freight wagons, into Dykka's Lorries.

Stealing it.

He paid them one shilling and sixpence per lorry full. The lorries were about half the size of a locomotive tender; and Dykka paid cash on the night, with no waiting until Friday for your pay, and no questions asked.

He paid the Railways Supervisor five bob a lorry-load.

Dykka Van Hoost, was a thick set, tall, dapper, very smart man. Always in a light, tweed, three piece suit, with a gleaming white wing collar shirt, and a silk tie, with a gold tie pin. The tie pin held in its ornate clasp, a single diamond, the size of a woman's little finger nail.

His features were square, with dark slicked back hair, and a neat pencil moustache. He had no hint of grey to give away his age. Although he was in his late forties, he could pass for a decade younger. He chain smoked long thin cheroots, which he lit from a gold Vesta case with his initials engraved on it in luxurious copper plate. His shoes were hand made brogues, and, as he loved to say;

"So shiny that a fat nigger could see his own arse in them".

He hated 'Blacks', and had a way with words.

As he strode across the rough concrete floor of the warehouse, he collected money, (his winnings), from various members of the audience, men and women who had watched the fight, and had clearly bet on the loser.

There were very few members of this audience who were not well dressed and well heeled.

Dykka said to one man, who was wearing a brown astrakhan coat with a thick silken mink fur collar, and who was carrying a silver topped cane.

"I told you yesterday Banger was past his best, he's nudging forty for fuck sake: he should be at home bangin' that little black tart of his. Still; made good dosh off him over the years, can't grizzle too much".

At the same time, the man with the cane was counting out, into Dykka's outstretched hand, twenty five South African Pounds, all in large crisp fivers.

Dykka Van Hoost smiled at the man with the cane, a huge white smile, full of teeth, full of greed.

He walked on without further discussion, continuing to mingle with the crowd, collecting his winnings from various members as he went.

As he walked passed Banger, the aging pugilist had just managed to get to his knees, and was trying, (somewhat unsuccessfully), to cover one nostril with a thumb, and blow the blood and snot out of the other. He coughed, a horrible guttural sound, hawked loudly and gobbed on the floor between his thighs. He was, (at the same time), trying to pull a loosened front tooth out by the roots with his other hand, and yelped at his self inflicted pain.

Dykka stood behind him, clutching the better part of three hundred South African Pounds in his fingers. His gold and diamond rings glinting in the half light from the overhead cone lamps, high in the warehouse's cast iron roof trusses. He peeled three one pound notes from his winnings, and, crouching down, placed them carefully on the floor in front of Banger, avoiding the little patches of blood, snot and phlegm. He waved a hand, exaggeratedly in front of his face; wafting away the stench of the fighter's diarrhoea soiled dungarees. Dykka leaned forward, so that his mouth was close to Banger's ear, and whispered:

"We'll see if we can you a couple of easy bouts, over in Kokstad or Ulundi in a couple of weeks time, try and line up some 'Blacks' for you, bit of ready snatch cash if you know what I mean old son".

Dykka paused for a moment, (he called people 'old son' when he was being condescending, but thought it made things sound as though he wasn't), he stared across the cold concrete floor at the young man opposite. He turned back towards Banger, and as he rose he continued in his thick Afrikaans accent.

"There's not much here for you now my old son, I'll see if I can't get you a loaders spot in Durban; down on the docks, as well as some easy bouts. And maybe something for that black bitch of yours as well. I'll see what I can do".

He walked away without glancing back, walked towards the young fighter opposite.

"Hey; Jew boy, here's your pay, and a bit more for the winnings".

Dykka peeled of a single five pound note from his wad, a half smoked cheroot smouldering between his large teeth. Teeth that looked strangely too big for his mouth. A mouth that looked strangely too big for his head.

As the young man took hold of the fiver, Dykka, snatched, (mockingly), at the end he still held, before eventually letting it go. He laughed, and then said, pointing at the note.

"That's nearly a hundred lorry loads of hard black stuff you'd have to shovel there boy. You want another fiver next week, Saturday night, here?"

The young man looked at another young man, who stood next to him, the other young man was holding a bucket of blood stained water, and had some strips of rag draped over his shoulder. Dykka, laughed out loud, and carried on speaking:

"Is this your fucking manager then?"

He looked at the young man with the rags and bucket. The young fighter spoke, pulling back Dykka's attention.

"Saturday night then".

Dykka took this as the response he required.

"Good; I'll catch up with you pair, in the railway yard in the week".

As he turned to walk away, he stopped briefly, and, turning back towards the young men, he said:

"See Gonda, the railway Supervisor tomorrow, he'll sort out some extra lorries for you to fill in the evenings. Tell him I said so".

He paused again, this time he took a few steps back towards the pair.

"Do you know what the 'Blacks' call this town?"

The two brothers both moved their heads, indicating that they didn't know; Dykka continued.

"They call it 'Um Gungundlovo'; it means, 'The Place Where The Elephant Wins'".

He nodded towards the young fighter, who was still sweating, still stripped to the waist, wiping his knuckles with some of the rags. Dykka looked him in the eyes, and said.

"From now on that's you; 'The Elephant'; that's what your going to be called, 'The Elephant'; 'The Bloody Elephant'".

He laughed loudly, dabbed out his cheroot on the floor, with his gleaming brogue, and strode off, thrusting his money into the inside pocket of his jacket.

Whistling brightly as he went.

The day of the funeral.
The Church of the Resurrection,
Sandstone,
Western Australia.
October 18th 2012.

It was a solemn occasion.

The invited congregation numbered less than three hundred, and was to be presided over by none less than the Archbishop of Perth himself.

At the Nave, a silver grey coffin of well grained Ironbark stood forlornly; draped softly in silken strands of multi-coloured sunlight spilling through the stained glass window above it, creating an almost ethereal hue.

The florist had scattered random pink and white blossom delicately across its lid, and on the floor beneath it.

The casket was the work of craftsmen whose clenched knuckles must have stiffened and ached with the sanding and repeated polishing. The moulded silver Cherubim's that held up its six silver handles caught the light from the elliptical stained glass, and sent dainty reflected angels of golden glow dancing around the plain white walls of the Church.

All was tranquil.

All was peace.

The inlaid lead-work of the stained glass depicted the moment when Christ had rescued Mary Magdalene from the angry partisan crowd; willing to stone her for her adultery, willing to steal her days.

They were consumed with self righteous indignation.

Christ did not appear in the glasswork, merely his hand. Mary Magdalene was set centre stage, crouching on crumpled cloth, clutching her dishevelled garments about her fragile but detailed body.

Her face gazing upwards towards her unseen saviour.

The window, which, (like most of the Church's upgrades and repairs), had been paid for by the Wylachi family, had been a particular and personal passion of Malakye's.

He had taken a close interest in its creation.

He had chosen the subject matter himself.

He had over-ruled the Church's Management Committee.

He had crossed swords with the then Vicar, Turner Quentin Jones.

He had pulled 'strings' to have The Reverend Quintin Jones replaced in 1992.

He had 'arranged' the appointment of the Church's present incumbent Arturo Moia who was now in his twentieth year of service.

He had got his own way.

He always did.

In the twenty years since his appointment, (and the installation of the stained glass window), The Reverend Arturo Moia had seen Malakye Wylachi O.B.E., only on occasional Christmases, and at even less occasional funding meetings. Even then,

Malakye had only attended when work had been required on the Church building, and he had provided the signature on a cheque confirming an additional donation.

All of which came from his personal accounts.

Arturo had however seen him, (early morning), on each and every twenty eighth day of July, in each and every year since he had taken up his ministry.

On these clockwork annual occasions Malakye, alone, would visit the church at six a.m., and stay until eight.

He did not pray.

It was not his nature.

He would sit alone in the front pew, and study the window. Not as a student would study a book, but as a poor quality artist would study an El Greco or a Da Vinci.

As someone seeking something beyond their grasp.

Beyond their abilities.

Beyond their comprehension.

The figure of The Magdalene, (like Malakye's Ironbark coffin), was beautifully crafted; depicted with a delicacy and love not readily discernable in her patron.

Malakye himself had paid particular attention to her creation though, being very specific in his instructions, and having caused several revisions until he was wholly satisfied with the result.

It was a work of extreme love.

Extreme devotion.

A work of piety.

But not necessarily religion.

A work of redemption.

Arturo Moia was casting a last critical eye over the floral arrangements, and picking odd bits of fluff from the choristers' surpluses. He had added more white blossom to the top of the coffin as a pointless aesthetic gesture.

It was ten fifteen a.m.

56

The congregation were beginning to arrive, and in the front rows of pews, sat the immediate blood relatives, along with Malakye Wylachi's closest friends. The family filled three complete rows, on both sides of the isle.

The close friends could have been counted on the fingers of Karem Tortruk's thumb-less hand, and even then, (maybe), with digits to spare.

"I've got three invoices on my desk relating to that coffin, Ambrose".

Whispered Hugo Wylachi, as he leaned forward into the eternally cocked ear of Ambrose Suda-Iwo.

"One from a tree surgeon in Bindi-Bindi for twelve hundred dollars, for removing two big boughs of Ironbark from the old tree on the Cutters Lane roundabout; another for one thousand eight hundred dollars from a lumber mill in Mount Magnet for planking it and special kiln drying; and a third for eight thousand eight hundred dollars from a joinery shop in Payne's Find for making that monstrosity!".

Hugo's voice rose slightly, and without control as he spat out the last item, and nodded towards the coffin. He reined himself in, biting his bottom lip.

"Really?"

Replied Ambrose, in his best quizzical and tempered voice.

He was smiling inside.

He turned his head back slightly, and whispered.

"There should be four invoices; you'll be getting another one Hugo, from an upholsterer in New Norcia. She made the lining out of the Hessian Sacking".

He was chuckling inside.

He paused, strictly for effect, then said,

"I think that was about eighteen hundred dollars too".

He didn't look back towards Hugo, but merely revelled in his discomfort.

"Are those handles real silver Ambrose?" interjected Stanforth who was next to his cousin Hugo; and now in Ambrose's other ear.

Suda-Iwo was now laughing loudly inside.

Belly laughs.

Side splitting laughs.

Vengeful, cruel laughs.

"They certainly are Stanforth, and very smart they are too and all fully in accordance with your late grandfathers wishes".

The penny pincher surfaced in Stanforth Wylachi and he said with an exasperation that was impossible to hide. He whispered his anger, an almost impossible skill, and one which he failed at.

"Twelve grand or more for a coffin, plus all the other stuff, where the fuck does all this end Ambrose, it's just fucking ridiculous?"

Ambrose Suda-Iwo smiled wryly, more of a smirk really, more of a grin; he could keep it in no longer, and felt the satisfaction escape his curving lips. Again he did not look back, preferring to keep his satisfaction private. Stanforth of all people, he thought to himself, swearing, and in a Church. Tut, Tut, Tut.

Now it was Hugo's turn again.

"Hessian Sacking?" He whispered, a little too loudly. "Why for heavens sake? Why?"

Had he turned around at that moment, Ambrose Suda-Iwo would have seen Hugo Wylachi pulling his handsome features into puzzled grimaces, reminiscent of those of schoolboys whose sherbet has been stolen from beneath their desk lids.

Ambrose turned his gaze to the coffin, and replied softly.

"Perhaps he was seeking redemption, or taking something with him, something he valued. Or perhaps it's for penance".

He allowed himself another grin.

"Poenitentiam Agite!"

He said with a single exhale, hiding under his breath.

The expression escaped so silently that a flapping butterfly passing by would have muffled his words.

"We need to talk about this thing Ambrose!"

Demanded Hugo Wylachi, carrying on where Stanforth's frustrations had left off.

Ambrose cut the cousins short, in terse whispers and without turning to face them, he said simply.

"Not today! Not here! As beneficiaries of the 'Will', you can ask any questions you wish. As Executor, I will carry out your grandfather's......."

He paused again, as if searching for conciseness, then added, as if his search had failed.

"My friend's", (part of him still resented uttering the word), "wishes to the letter!"

He raised a hand, almost imperceptibly.

Then all was silence.

The service commenced.

Western Australian Prison Service,
Penal Work Camp number 18.
Kalgoorlie Boulder,
Western Australia.
Late in the afternoon;
January 5th, 1943.

He tried every day, not to think of her.

Yet every day she still burrowed into his skull.

He was finding it increasingly difficult to picture her face as the years had crept by.

He longed for the day when her memory would no longer come to him.

He longed for the day she would leave him forever.

He longed for the day she would disappear.

He dreaded that day!

Every day he thought the same thoughts; there were no new thoughts anymore. He thought about water, what socks felt like, what a brand new cigarette would taste of, what women's perfume smelt like. He found himself running faster and faster.

"Slow down you silly fucker!"

He heard a fellow barrower running in the opposite direction say to him as they passed one another. The sweaty scruffy inmate then added as he faded behind him.

"Stupid cunt! If Fuzzy sees you, he'll have us all up the pace. You'll get us all fucking killed!"

Prisoner number 89855812 slowed to his regular jog, and roughly calculated that twelve thousand seconds should see the shift out.

He began counting, out loud sometimes, but mostly under his breath.

"One, two, three......."

As he had counted down his barrow shifts thousands of times before.

Soon he would get to a thousand, then two, then three, then four, then five, then pain, then more pain.

Time.

The principal enemy of all prisoners; was paying Prisoner number 89855812 his daily visit.

He would call again tomorrow.

And the next day.

And the next day.

And the next day.

Scottsville Racecourse,

Pietermaritzburg,

South Africa,

The last Sunday in May, 1924.

Eloise Van Hoost, was the twenty one year old step daughter of Dykka Van Hoost, and the biological daughter of his recently acquired wife of two years; Vienna Van Hoost, (nee Schmeizer, nee Cutter, nee Kleist).

Eloise was elegant, tall, with huge green eyes, and auburn hair, her lips were cherry red, and her skin the colour and texture of the finest alabaster. She had a figure that bordered between voluptuous and girl-like, and a gaze that could destroy a man.

Today she sat alongside her mother in the rear of Dykka Van Hoosts brand new, bright yellow 'Austin Twenty Convertible'.

She held in her lace gloved hand, a pale mimosa parasol, edged in blue taffeta and white embroidery. She wore a full length silk gown, also in mimosa, also edged in delicate embroidery and blue taffeta.

She spun the parasol gently, as the world spun around her.

Despite the hustle and bustle of the racecourse, for those whose eyes were lucky enough to fall on Eloise Van Hoost, their senses would be magnified, multiplied, glorified.

They would hear the sky creaking in the early afternoon warmth.

They would feel the miniscule temperature changes on the surface of the sun.

They would taste from a distance every sweet breath that she exhaled.

They would envy the air inside her.

Such a jealous onlooker was Yuris Pavel Androskewowicz.

He heard the grandstand clock tower chime the quarter hour. It was in a different world, the real world. For this brief time he was in her world, a better world, a more beautiful world.

As he walked behind his brother, across the track from the betting circle towards the centre ring, he shoved his ten shilling betting slip deep into his pocket. He could not drag his gaze from the girl in the back of Dykka Van Hoosts car.

Though he tried.

Though he didn't.

It was the day of the 'Railwayman's Cup'; sponsored by the 'Cape Government Railway Company' and the 'Gonda Vischer Land Freight Transport Company Limited'. It was the races third annual running, and was always held on the last Sunday in May, at this, 'The Scottsville Park Racecourse and Jockey Club', in Pietermaritzburg.

All the cities finest, (for it had recently become a city, elevated to that status in 1923, by Royal Decree); were present. They strutted in their best, and drank imported champagne from cut lead crystal glasses, that stole wandering sunbeams as they tilted and made them dance, like ballerinas, in the windshields of the parked cars.

It was a site to behold.

Darkie chauffeurs stood at the side of each car in the central ring, each sweating in the melting air.

Their thick woollen uniforms and peaked caps, all pristine in light grey or charcoal.

Their beaming black or brown leather boots grinned in the brightness of other peoples worlds.

Their toes strained at 'ten to two' like the hands on the grandstand clock, and black thumbs fiddled down the seams of their trousers.

The more brass buttons on the chauffeurs jacket, the 'bigger noise' his boss was in Pietermaritzburg. The Darkie chauffeurs were polished to out do each other, polished to make their bosses shine.

The rows of cars were ten deep in the middle of the racetrack grounds. Black waiters in white jackets, and green trousers, buzzed between them like wasps, carrying trays of champagne for the ladies and gentlemen, and lemonade for the fat white kids.

The kids made fun of them dripping in the sun. They poked their tongues out and called them 'Darkie' or 'Sambo' as they shouted for more lemonade, or a sandwich, or an ice cream. The waiters smiled and brought what they asked. They spat in the lemonade and buried snot in the Rum and Raisin.

Dykka Van Hoost was standing at the front of his 'Austin Twenty', with Gonda Vischer. Both men were dressed in fine morning suits with with grey silk edging, and a shiny top hat. Dykka wore a yellow orchid in his lapel, and a mimosa and blue silk handkerchief peeped cheekily from his jacket breast pocket.

He was showing Gonda the cars horse head bonnet mount, and exclaiming loudly as he stroked the ornament.

"Solid gold Gonda! Forty eight pure ounces, twenty two carets, best South African yellow!"

He took a large gulp from the cut glass champagne flute he was holding, before continuing, too loudly, and too brash for this audience.

"Shining like a silver shilling on a niggers arse that is! Look at it, bloody gorgeous!"

He turned to his chauffeur, standing at attention by the drivers side running boards, and asked, (albeit rhetorically, for the day when Dykka Van Hoost would give a flying fuck what a black man thought was a lifetime away).

"What do you reckon then Mambo, gorgeous or what?"

Mambo smiled broadly and nodded his agreement, then resumed the actions of a statue.

Gonda Vischer was patently relieved when he was rescued from Dykkas' dialogue by a racecourse official, wanting him in the parade ring for the pre-race photographs. He made his grateful excuses to Dykka, his 'Lady Wife', (as he called all women over thirty), and to Eloise. He then walked briskly, (and gratefully), away with the official; whispering to him as they went, saying.

"Perfect timing Otto, perfect bloody timing; remind me to buy you a case of Scotch next week".

He paused; then added, almost apologetically.

"And not that fucking 'gutt rot' that Dykka brings in either!"

For all his brashness, Dykka was well connected in Pietermaritzburg society; and for all Gonda Vischers bravado to Otto; he would never have walked away from Dykka Van Hoost without an excuse; and it would need to be a bloody good one too.

There were not many people in this neck of the woods, who didn't owe something to Dykka Van Hoost, however much they may resent it, and however much they may want to hide it.

That went for Gonda as well.

Dykka did after all own thirty five percent of the 'Gonda Vischer Land Freight Transport Company Limited', and he made sure Gonda never forgot it.

As his business partner walked away, Dykka again turned to Mambo, and, taking a bundle of notes from his inside pocket, he licked his thumb, and, swaying very slightly, almost imperceptibly, he sliced off ten five pound notes, and handed them to his chauffeur. He said.

"Take this over to the bookies at the bottom of the grandstand, and shove it all on 'Kerasons'; shop around until you get six to four on, or better".

He waved his hand and Mambo took off at a trot. Kerasons was Dykka's thoroughbred stallion; he owned him in thirds with two business associates from Bloemfontein. They had paid over two thousand guineas for him three years earlier, and he had won the 'Railwayman's Cup' for Dykka the year before.

Today's purse was two hundred and fifty guineas, and the trophy already had Kerasons name on it. At least according to the bookies, (and to Dykka).

"Good afternoon Mr Van Hoost; Mrs Van Hoost, Miss Eloise".

The voice came from behind Dykka, and somewhere to his left; it was deep, and rich flavoured, like syrup dropped on the back of a warm spoon. It had an accent, but not Afrikaans, more eastern European. Dykka turned. A large smile of recognition trundled across his jaw.

"The Elephant!"

He gestured to his wife and Eloise, who had not budged from the back seat of the car for at least two hours, and five glasses of best Perrier Jouet. They had turned elegantly and occasionally to chat with passers by over the door rails, or to collect champagne from the Darkie waiters.

"Look girls, it's 'The Bloody Elephant', you've met before haven't you; come on boy, have a drink with us before the race!"

Dykka turned, and shouted to one of the waiters to bring a tray of champagne over.

Vienna Van Hoost spoke; an educated, clipped, English hockey stick kind of accent, slow, but elegant, cultured but contrived.

"Yes, we have my dear, Mr......"

She paused for an uncomfortable moment, then looked as if she were trying to remember something, a real name perhaps, then failed, then continued.

"Mr. Elephant was a guest of yours at the New Years Eve party at Bell Street last year, you recall don't you Eloise my dear ?"

Mrs Van Hoost called everyone 'Dear', at nearly fifty; she felt it was mandatory address for anyone under thirty, or for her husband. Almost in the same fashion as Gonda used the phrase 'Lady Wife'.

They were both wrong.

Eloise replied.

"Of course I remember Mother".

She smiled warmly at him, and gave her hand demurely, unexpectedly, she continued, leaning forward slightly in her seat, tilting her head slightly, and slightly easing the grip on her parasol, allowing it to spin slightly.

The whole world changed slightly as she spoke.

She enquired, and continued with perfect pauses and enunciation.

"But I don't think I've met this young man before".

She looked the younger, slightly shorter, slightly thinner, slightly more youthful looking, slightly more handsome, slightly more attractive man, square in the eyes; and asked; demanded.

"Can you introduce us please?"

She nodded to The Elephant. Before he could answer, Dykka interrupted.

"This is the Banjo King!"

He said, and smiled, not realising his rudeness.

Nor caring.

Eloise turned to the younger man, and asked, in all seriousness.

"Are you a musician then?"

Everyone laughed, even the young man, and Mrs Van Hoost, (though the young man with a hint of embarrassment): everyone except Eloise laughed. Then he replied; in a modest attractive voice with true tones, and almost no accent.

Eloise thought it beautiful.

"No Miss Van Hoost; a 'Banjo' is railway slang for a shovel. They call me 'King Banjo', (not Banjo King), over at the sidings, because I can fill lorries and tenders with coal quicker than anyone else. My shovel is my instrument."

Now she also laughed.

Dykka interrupted again, telling all present that the race was about to start.

Mambo returned with his bosses betting slip, and resumed his position next to the car.

"Come on!"

Said Dykka excitedly; again too loud, again too brash.

"Let's get over to the finishing post, and watch all that lovely money come in".

65

As she dismounted the car, the young man lent her an arm for support as she stepped down from the running board. As she moved; her head down, and the sun licking the back of her white neck, and without looking at him, she asked.

"So what is it then, your name?"

As her foot touched the grateful ground, she raised her head, and looked deep into his desire. Her lips parted slightly, and he saw the moistness of her tongue.

"Well?"

She asked again.

"What is it?"

In monotone dullness, his reply seemed to drain the chiming grandstand bell tower of all it's clanging, of all its movement, as the words struggled to form. His world seemed to stop with such a jolt that it would have hurled him like a twig in a storm into oblivion, had he not scrunched up his toes enough to just hang on to God's golden Earth.

"It's Yuris".

He managed.

"Yuris Androskewowicz".

"Well I'm very pleased to meet you Yuris Androskewowicz".

Eloise replied without needing a second hearing of his surname, and she shook his hand, shook it in the fashion of a man., she then said, without any prompt.

"My name is Eloise, with the emphasis on the 'S', it's a hard 'S'; not a soft 'S', everyone seems to get it wrong. Hard; you will remember won't you?"

Then she was gone.

Into the crowd.

Rushing, giggling towards the winning post.

He watched her move.

He watched the swish of her dress rub her thighs.

He watched the bare skin of her forearms shimmer between her gloves and her sleeves.

He watched curls of her hair undress her ear as they rose and fell in the gentle breeze.

He watched her for no other reason other than that she was there.

After an age.

After about twenty paces.

She looked back at him and smiled, and then turning in a full circle, she carried on into the crowd, and was swallowed up.

Yuris stood alone, like an island in the central enclosure, with everyone else rushing in waves to track edge rails to view the race.

"Fuck the race!"

He thought silently to himself.

It was a one and a half mile flat race, with the horses shimmering in the rising heat. Their dark hyde's caking with sticky whiteness.

Yuris, remained where he was, his eyes did not move from the top of Eloise's parasol, which he could only just still make out in the distance.

The eruption of the crowd into whoops and jeers jarred him back. Like fight nights without the blood, snot and shit.

As the crowd dispersed, and broke up like late ice at Odessa, into various pockets, all chattering and jibbering, some holding hats aloft, others tearing up betting tickets and stamping them into the ground; Yuris was aware of the tannoi announcement spilling into his head.

"First, by a short head, at twelve to one, Gomers Flash, second at even money, joint favourite, last years winner, Kerasons, and third, at nine to two, Windward Boer Boy".

Yuris decided that the central ring was not the place to be when Dykka came back, he did not like losing, and he would be in a foul mood. A mood where he would do and say things and regret them later, but later would be too late to make amends, and Dykka would view it as weakness or an apology. He didn't do either.

Yuris glanced at Mambo the chauffeur, and shook his head, almost secretively from side to side. He could see from the chauffeurs, (almost jet black, almost purple), face, sweating in the sunlight; that if he could; he too would have been heading out of the centre ring; and away from Dykka Van Hoost. Poor Mambo however was stuck there.

The dice was already cast for Mambo the chauffeur!

As he walked away, Yuris pulled from his pocket, his ten shilling betting ticket, and studied it for a second as he went. 'Ten bob to win, Gomers Flash' it said. He grinned broadly; then looked around sharpish; to make sure Dykka hadn't seen him start to laugh. He studied the betting ticket once more, before sliding it back into his trouser pocket.

"That's twelve quid and ten bob to come back; that's a hundred and twenty five coal tenders, I don't have to fill!"

He thought to himself.

Yuris smiled again, this time not worrying too much who may have seen him, and started heading back to the betting ring to collect his one hundred and twenty five tenders full of the hard black stuff.

As he walked, taking the long way back to the betting ring, towards the grandstand. Yuris was sure he could hear Dykka, screaming and cursing, in the distance behind him.

He smiled again.

He began to run.

He began to laugh.

He began to skip and dance.

Laughing loudly like a small boy as he went.

Springing The Box,
'The Bowls Inn',
Penyrheol,
Caerphilly,
South Wales.
A Saturday in March 1972.

It sat, alone on Jimmy 'C's dining room table for five nights and five days.

Christlike and un-blasphemed amidst the desert of oilcloth and doyley's.

Orange as the sand that Spartacus new, it's black and incandescent livery evoking salivating images of Tawny port, glugged with Stilton or Gorgonzola, amidst the fresh crunch of toasted perforated wheat squares with delicately rounded corners.

The 'Jacobs Biscuit Tin', was a design icon, fit to grace any gourmet restaurant, or Royal table. It befitted and behoved well, the pride of place it had received on Jimmy and Mrs. 'C's back room dining table, in their modest two up, two down, one stuck on, and one out the back terraced house in High Street, Senghenydd.

Jimmy had been working 'afternoons' this last week, at the British Airways Test Beds in Nantgarwr, where he was a fitter and turner. 'Afternoons' were that shift between 'Days', and 'Nights', two p.m. until ten p.m., which was not quite convenient enough to allow a life either side of work hours. It was back in the days before daytime telly, so unless you were a 'Mary Mungo and Midge' fan, you were fucked as far as telly went. Fortunately Jimmy 'C' was a bit of a golfer.

He had a mixed bag of seven unmatched irons, a putter, two unmatched woods and an extendable telescopic aluminium pole thing with a grabby thing on the end and a twisty thing in the middle, (which he had made himself), for retrieving golf-balls out of bramble bushes.

He played, (when shifts and weather allowed, and when the shifts of others coincided), at 'Castle Heights Golf Course', on top of Caerphilly Mountain. It was a municipal course, and you paid by the round. It was not 'hoity toity', as Jimmy used to say; as he extolled it's socialist credentials, over its private members, snobby, conservative competitors; where they evidently still used slave labour to trim the fairways, and shoved little orphans up chimneys in the clubhouse to clear out miss-hit 'Titleists'.

His golfing butties' were primarily, Spinksy, and my Father, Harold, known as 'H', because he absolutely detested the name 'Harold'; a fact I could never quite understand, as I quite like the name myself. Indeed, I had tried in vain to persuade my wife to call our first child after him, but she also seemed to dislike the name; so we eventually settled on 'Clare'.

My father also worked shifts, but at 'Canton Diesel Sheds' in Cardiff, for 'British Rail'. He too was a fitter, and had forgotten more about engines than most people ever knew.

This particular day had become, (by slow filtration of shift changes, bad weather, and mis-matched sleeps), a Saturday. But a Saturday when Jimmy 'C', and my Father coincided (shift-wise), on 'nights'. Spinksy was off anyway, because he had, (what the politicians call), a 'white collar job', in the Draughtsman Department of the Council, and so he had weekends off. My Father and Jimmy 'C' on the other hand were 'blue collar workers', who apparently didn't need weekends off.

Anyway, the three of them had arranged to meet up, at the 'Bowls Inn' at Penyrheol, at one o'clock, for a couple of pints, and to suss-out Stalin's Box.

The Bowls, (then), was a bit of a rough and ready pub, just in front of the public playing fields, and tinkering at the foot of Penyrheol Council Estate.

Today, it's a Tesco Extra.

Most importantly, to all three of them, it was next to Frankie Chiverton's bookies shop, an establishment to which all three made regular contributions, both canine and equine, (dogs and horses to you).

In reality the arduous process of buying the 'Sporting Life', studying each race, the form, the weight, the going, checking the 'nap of the day' etcetera; all over a couple of pints of 'Brains Dark', and a fag; was a social, more than technical exercise. The reality was, that each of them would have saved a considerable amount of time, mental torment and money, if they had just walked into Frankie Chiverton's bookies shop on a Saturday, slapped a crisp ten quid note on the counter, never bought a 'Sporting Life', never wrote out a betting slip, and walked straight back out again.

However today was a bit different.

Betting selections made, slips written out, and donations contributed; the three men sat in the Lounge Bar, (instead of their more usual 'Men Only', Public Bar. Where they always occupied the centre table in front of the elevated telly, to watch 'Grandstand', on the B.B.C., and to commiserate with one another as their racing selections lost one by one), to ceremoniously open the box.

In the 'Lounge Bar', (corner table, with upholstered dark red floral fixed seating, with cheese and onion rolls under a plastic thing on the bar top), they sat. With three pints of 'Dark' in front of them, three 'Benson and Hedges King Size', whisping in the ashtray, and the box betwixt them, they fair hummed in anticipation.

As the fag smoke rose, reminiscent of the scene in 'Doctor Zhivago', with the steam locomotive close up juxtaposed with a smouldering match clutched by Omar Sharif; the selotape was, (almost ceremoniously), removed from around the 'Jacobs Cracker's Tin'.

Thinking about it, it may have been Peter O'Toole in 'Lawrence of Arabia', not 'Doctor Zhivago', but it was definitely a David Leane jobby with Omar Sharif.

As Jimmy 'C' peeled away the ageing selotape with the dexterity of a neuro surgeon, scrumpling the sticky mass into a small ball and discarding it into the ashtray; my uncle Bryn entered the Lounge Bar.

"They told me next door you were in here".

He said, ('next door' could mean either in the bookies, or in the Public Bar, it was not made quite clear which). He gazed momentarily at the box.

"So this is it then!"

My Father had told him of the funeral and the biscuit tin, during a conversation the day before.

Bryn had only returned home on Thursday, and was staying, as usual with my Nanny and Bampy Ford, at their house, his old home, in Ilan Road, Abertridwr. He was, (and still is thankfully), my mothers brother.

Bryn was a merchant seaman, working in the subterranean engine rooms of 'Shell Oil' tankers. He had once given me a flag off one, which I kept, hung on my bedroom wall, in a place of honour, above my beds headboard.

I dreamt of all the winds of all the world it had fluttered under.

My Uncle Bryn represented to me all the excitement of the world wrapped up in a single human being. He had been to Hong Kong, India, Australia, and most exciting of all; America: the home of Batman, Kwai Chang Cain and Elliot Ness, and gleaming flashy cars with radios in them.

Bryn could talk about things that all my other grown up relatives had only seen on telly or in newspapers.

He had even been to Vietnam, and Merthyr.

Once, when I was a little boy, no more than seven or eight, when his ship had been docked in Cardiff, he took me to see it, and we had actually gone into the engine room. With all its gantries and steel stairs, turning things, buzzing things, and

71

whirring things, and things that left oil stains on your daps and elbows, it was the most exciting thing I had ever seen.

He had called one of his shipmates a 'fucking blonky', to this day, I have no idea what a 'blonky' is, but for the next couple of weeks I used the expression at every conceivable opportunity. I used it in the street with my mates, on the bus, in the swimming baths, and in the playground of 'The Twyn Infants School' at Caerphilly. All my friends were 'fucking blonkys', as were the school teachers, dinner ladies, lollypop man, and anyone else I deemed suitable. It became **MY** expression and I loved using it, until Miss Long, my teacher, heard me use it in assembly and belted me round the swede.

She kept me in at playtimes for three days. My 'fucking blonkying' days had come to an all too premature end.

When Bryn had got himself a pint, he joined the others around the glowing box.

'Cracker Tin, Cracker Tin, burning
bright, in the forests of the night.'

The Railway Sidings,
Pietermaritzburg,
South Africa
June 18th 1924.

It was about three weeks after the 'Railwayman's Cup' and Dykka was still licking his wounds.

This day, he had sent for 'The Elephant' and 'Banjo', and the three of them now sat in his office, overlooking the railway yards, at 'Dykkas Sidings' at the back of Pietermaritzburg Station.

His office was on the first floor of the rather shabby, 'Old Stockyard Building'.

"I've got a good one coming off for you".

Dykka said, standing in front of his oversized desk, puffing on his cheroot, and waving his arms as if to demonstrate the meaning of the word 'Big'.

"The Van der Kyper mines in Rhodesia, have got a champion. They call him 'Crusher Hohner'. He's a Kraut, and very popular up there. The Van der Kyper brothers are paying him one hundred pounds a fight".

'The Elephant', looked sideways at his brother, both were sitting in comfortable chairs in front of Dykka, and both knew that they were getting twenty pounds a fight, at the moment, which in itself was very good money.

Dykka was paying the likes of 'Banger' Smutz, (and the others in his stable of 'fisters'), anything between, three and five quid a bout. The Darkie fighters were only getting fifteen bob a match, and only fought for nigger crowds, so the betting was sparse, and there was no real money in it.

Dykka made his cash off his Darkies on the tobacco and booze he sold at their fights. He kept about a dozen black fighters, and although 'The Elephant' had trained against them, Dykka would never put them into a proper match against one of his white fighters. If he did so, and; if, (heaven forbid), the nigger won, Dykka would lose all his credibility within the social, (and business), circles though which he navigated.

The racial demarcation lines were stark, and strict, and could only be crossed at ones peril.

"How much is in it for us?"

Asked 'The Elephant'.

Dykka paused, more for effect than for deliberation, then said.

"The Van der Kyper brothers have put up a purse of five hundred pounds. That's two hundred for me, for all the organisation, a hundred for the loser, and two hundred quid for the winner".

He smiled, puffed at his cheroot, and pointed it at 'The Elephant', and then he added.

"And, that; will be you!"

He smiled, that wide Dykka smile that said, 'money'. It also said, 'be careful because there's a lie in here somewhere'. He took a puff on the cheroot, then, as he exhaled, went on with.

"Get some good bets in, you should be about six to four, or even seven to two with Fat Malcolm; you could end up with over five hundred quid if you play your cards right".

Dykka smiled again, held his arms wide again, puffed on his cheroot again, exhaled again; and asked rather pointlessly again.

"Well, what do you reckon?"

It was not Dykka who had to do the fighting, and it had not gone un-noticed by 'The Elephant' that he had set the odds with Crusher Hohner as the favourite.

Dykka went on to explain that he would hire the parade ring over at Scottsville Racetrack to be the venue, and they would hold the fight on a Saturday with a dusk start time, for maximum drama. He was animated as he strutted around the office, explaining that he would have proper bookies boards up, and he would light the ground with the headlights of twenty of his lorries set in a circle, and he made a circle in the air with his arms, and all the while, those huge teeth were beaming.

Chattering.

Lying.

'The Elephant' asked what Dykka knew about his opponent.

It was clear he knew nothing, (or at least nothing he wanted to share), other than how much he got paid, how much the betting would bring in, and how much he could charge as entry fees to the fight. Dykka summed up with;

"But he's probably some over the hill Kraut with a belly full of sausages and a fat hausfrau up there in Rhodesia".

He smiled that wide Dykka smile again, all those teeth ringing, hanging like piano keys.

There was nothing to discuss anyway, Dykka knew it, and so did the brothers. This was the deal they signed up for. Dykka was their paymaster, and like it or not, they were lumbered with him. They had a good life and spare cash: and they liked it.

As the two men left, being not much the wiser. They passed Gonda Vischer who was now sitting, (and waiting), in the vestibule. He was reading a newspaper, cross legged and looking relaxed. They all acknowledged each other by way of slight nods of the heads. As Banjo opened the vestibule door, Gonda, (almost as if he had just caught the tail a passing thought), raised a hand, and said:

"Banjo, see if you can find Old Cedric in the coal sidings, and tell him to put the Lesotho wagons in bays eight and nine, and not in bay ten. Bay ten is still choc-a-bloc with Dykkas cut from the 'Rhodesia Railways' tenders. See if you can get them loaded onto Dykka's trucks, by the end of the day. They've got to be off to Port Elizabeth by this evening. If you can finish them there's an extra two quid each in it for you".

Banjo acknowledged the request, and Gonda went back to his newspaper, (for a brief moment), before Dykka appeared at his office door, and called him in.

Despite his fame, (He had now been Dykka Van Hoosts top fighter for going on two years), 'The Elephant' still worked in the coal sidings with his brother, and they could still out-shovell, and out-earn any other crew on the tenders, and the lorries.

As Banjo and 'The Elephant' walked down the stairs from Dykkas office, to the ground floor, they came across Mambo, sitting on the bottom step smoking a thin roll-up.

They knew that Mambo, as well as being Dykkas some time chauffeur, also doubled up as a bit of an odd-job man for him; doing some fairly dirty stuff in the 'Nigger Neighbourhoods'. Like collecting rents from Dykka and Gondas' flee infested tenements, and delivering shit whiskey, thinned with iodine and water, to the shit-hole drinking clubs.

Everyone knew that Mambo took a skim off everything he collected for Dykka and Gonda; but it was a very small skim, and if it meant that Dykka could avoid going to his properties in the 'Nigger Neighbourhoods', then it was probably worth it. In any event, Mambo knew that if he got too greedy, Dykka would not think twice about sending some of his so called 'White Boys' around to cut Mambo's black bollocks off and make him eat them. It was a simple, (but effective), method of control.

The two men exchanged a few sentences with Mambo, who they quite liked. Banjo asked him if that was Dykkas tobacco he was smoking?

"Not fucking likely man; I like my teeth where they are, that shit he stretches his baccy out with, makes your fucking teeth fall out. You should see the old niggers down Fattelau and Maleens; not a tooth left in their fucking heads".

They all laughed, but tried to keep the noise down, 'The Elephant' asked him what he was doing here today, and if he had Dykkas Austin Twenty, so they could cadge a lift across to Old Cedric on the other spur of the sidings? Mambo continued smoking; and, while still casually crouched on the bottom step, he said.

"No such luck; if I had his car today, I'd take a trip across the tracks and fuck the daylights out of one of my bitches, and I'd do her in the back seat of his pride and joy. Maybe I'd even shag her on the bonnet, holding onto his golden fucking horse, while she screamed in delight".

Again, they laughed, Mambo dabbed his roll-up out on the floor at the foot of the stairs, while Banjo and 'The Elephant' lit fresh cigarettes from Banjo's tin. Mambo's timing was perfect, and contrived, and Banjo felt obliged to offer him a fag. Mambo reached into the small tin, which had the words 'Golden Virginia' rusting away on the lid. He took two, placing one behind his ear, and lighting the other one, from a match struck by 'The Elephant'. He sucked in a long drag, from Banjo's roll-up, then carried on.

"I don't give a fuck what he wants. All I know is there's fifty quid in it for me, and it's something to do with those Indian fuckers down Durban way. Those cunts are nothing but trouble. There's no Prozzy business from them, and the bastards don't drink, or smoke, there's no money in the cunts; you know what I mean?"

The two men nodded. Prostitution and booze were big parts of Dykkas business, and he made next to nothing from the 'Wogs' as he called them. Wog ships even haggled over the price of Dykkas coal. As he had complained on more than one occasion, saying:

"For fuck sake, it's stolen coal anyway, and is half batt. What the fuck do these Wog cunts expect?"

Pietermaritzburg society was strictly striated, the 'Whites' at the top, with the 'Niggers' underneath, and the 'Niggers' and the 'Whites' both complaining about the 'Wogs'. The 'Chinks' kept themselves to themselves, and only ran the rickshaws which nobody else wanted anyway.

This whole arrangement made no difference to the two white coal shovellers. They were used to societies with stark divisions, Reds or Whites, Bolsheviks, Loyalists, Jews or non-Jews. Quite frankly, they, (nor anyone else for that matter), gave a toss.

The brothers' view was strictly pragmatic, just get on with it, make some money, bend some rules, break some others, and don't loose any sleep over it.

They told Mambo, (jokingly), not to get caught fucking any white women, shook his hand, finished their fags, and went about the unfolding eventuna of their day.

The *'Cok Guzel Denizala Baligi'*:
And the flight from Odessa.
The first time he had seen the sea.
Early in the morning.
April 12th, 1919

Karem Tortruk, was a swarthy, stocky Turk.

He spoke Russian with a thick accent, and managed to get only three words in five correct. His hand gestures, grimaces and inflections generally seemed to fill in the gaps in his vocabulary. He could, however count in Russian with practiced perfection, and knew, and could pronounce, without imperfection, the words for 'gold', 'silver', 'money' and 'women'.

He was the Captain, and part owner, of the Steam Ship *Cok Guzel Denizala Baligi*, translated, (very roughly), as "Beautiful Black Sea Salmon".

The vessel was only 1,800 tons, and had seen better days. It's prime function now was to make money for Captain Karem Tortruk, some of which, (not very

77

much, and only enough to keep them quiet), he sent to Paris in the form of 'Bearer Bonds' drawn on British Banks for his owner partners. His accounts were as rusty as his hull, and his entries, as twisted as the courses he plotted across the Black Sea.

The *Cok Guzel Denizala Baligi* was registered in some obscure port, and most of its papers were forged. It ran mostly from Odessa, or the Odessa second port of Kushner. This was summer 1919, and most of Captain Tortruks' cargo these days was human.

Odessa itself had changed hands several times in the last two years, and each change brought fresh custom for The *Cok Guzel Denizala Baligi*. Odessa was the end of the road.

After Odessa there were no more towns to run to.

After Odessa, there were only the waves, the indifferent waves that could not care less whether you were a 'Red' or a 'white', Russian Orthodox, Muslim, or Jew.

After Odessa was The *Cok Guzel Denizala Baligi*, or any one of dozens of other ships that made their livings from these desperate cargos'.

After Odessa there was brutality, loneliness and disease.

After Odessa there was hunger, fear and more darkness than all the sunlight in heaven could chase away.

After Odessa there was usually a cold lonely death.

Like the waves upon which he lived, Captain Karem Tortruk did not care either. If you had the fare, you became a passenger, if not; you more than likely became a casualty.

In late 1917, Odessa had been occupied by the *Ukrainian Tsentaina Rada*, their latest conquerors. The complexion of their ideology left the towns population, (like the waves that lapped its ports), indifferent. They had generally become 'Pink', a local Rabbi had said, since they had flipped so frequently between 'Red' and 'White' occupation.

But now it was the 'Reds' who were at the gates. Once sympathetic to, (and supported by), the Jews of Russia, the 'Reds', like the 'Whites', and like the Czars before them, had come to distrust the Jews. They had all relied on Jewish wealth to buy their bullets, shells, trucks, trains and horses; and when the Jews decided to stop giving, they had all decided to take.

Taken or given, no matter, the result was the same; the result was all that what mattered.

Across the Black Sea, across the narrow straits, the Turkish Revolution blazed.

Kamil Ataturk was the backlash of the Allied partition after the Great War. An Independent Turkey, born of the Ottoman Empire, and the bad luck to have picked the losing side in a global conflict, was squealing into life on the opposite shores of the Bosporus.

Captain Karem Tortruk viewed all these tortured, natal screams of international flux; through the puffs of smoke from his Virginia cigars, and over the rim of his, several daily glasses, of Highland Malt Whisky.

To mix an unfortunate metaphor; the Cross which Karem bore was his own uncomfortable allegiance to Islam.

In Catholic terms, he had 'lapsed'. In reality, and in simple terms, he had never really been up for it in the first place.

Karems' religion was money.

As he stood on the bridge of the *Cok Guzel Denizala Baligi*, armed White Guards tied off the mooring ropes around the rusting cast iron capstans of the dockside. As he looked down, his Boson, (an elderly Greek, wizened, but fit looking, and with skin the colour and texture of cracked leather); barked orders to the guards as to which rope to put where.

The guards were soldiers, not dockers, and most were ignorant, (which was good), and some were new, (which was bad), and all were scared, (which was dangerous).

Karem recognised some of them from previous trips. They knew the ship, they would have told the others, and they would know the rates. There was nothing worse than having to explain the, 'arrangements' to a new mob.

One twentieth of the take to the guards; that was the going rate, by the time Karem had fiddled the arithmetic it was nearer one fiftieth.

As ever, the dockside was teeming, five or six other ships stood moored at the jetties. Karem recognised most of them, and they all operated on the same basis as the *Cok Guzel Denizala Baligi*. It was a business, and while it lasted, Karem would carry on short paying guards, and over charging 'customers'.

There was no time for overnight stays, or brief forays ashore. Karem took a large pull on his cigar, and shouted over the bridge rail, to his boson below.

"Set up my table and the green chair; and a sun umbrella, it's like a furnace today. Guns to Vradesh and Stannoy; and Ublis with the rifle up here on the bridge. Then, and only then, secure the gangplank. Get four of those guards", (he gestured at the White Guards on the key side), "at the bottom. No more than two people up the gangplank at a time".

Arris, the Greek boson, touched his cap in acknowledgement. He knew the drill, and did not need to be instructed, and he had already allocated the pistols before they had docked, but he also knew Karem was thorough, and would reprise his usual orders.

Karem would not move from his bridge rail vantage point until he had seen for himself the satisfactory organisation of his instructions. After about fifteen minutes, and numerous clarifying adjustments shouted from the bridge, Karem was satisfied.

"Lower the gangplank, Arris; I'm on my way down!"

Karem flicked his cigar butt over the rail, and watched it sail down to the mob on the dockside. Like kids with sweets, they fought over the one inch stub, wrestling with each other until the dog-end was neither visible nor relevant.

Karem laughed, his usual gruff low laugh, and walked through the metal door from the bridge gallery back into the wheelhouse. As he continued through the rat-run corridors and down the steps which would eventually lead to the main deck, (where Arris awaited him), he took off his grubby white cap, its cracked and chipped black peak dulled from age; he wiped the thick greasy sweat from his forehead with his equally grubby neckerchief. He would remove his threadbare blue jacket once he had arrived at his gangway top, and his table and green leather chair.

Below; in the sceptic bowels of the sweating mass of bubbling puss, that was the dockside throng, a small group of three protected their ever shrinking space.

They had been there for five days and five nights, shit, piss, blood, and vomit slewed around their ankles. The sweet, but pungent stench of corpses rotting in the sub-tropical sun hung thick in the air. All that fell to the ground never rose again, trampled by others into the filth that massed there.

The group of three guarded a leather canteen of water each, which draped like a noose around their necks. The two boys, each in their late teens or early twenties, clutched a ragged Hessian sack between them. Both wore tattered shirts of thick wool, too heavy for the climate, and watched all with eyes, as wide and tired as a summer moon.

Karem exited one of the oval metal doors, stepping out onto the metal plating of the deck, which was painted in a flaking pale green, with odd arrows here and there, hand-painted in whatever colour seemed to have been hanging around at the time. He walked over to Arris, swinging his jacket over the back of the green leather chair as he traversed it.

"Three hours today, not a second longer", (he wagged a finger at his boson), "That French-Algerian freighter over there", (he pointed at a large ship about 300 yards away at one of the other jetties). "It must be 15,000 tons; it'll be a magnet for the Russian Fleet. I don't want to be within twenty miles of it when they spot her".

From his observations from the bridge gallery, he had calculated from it's depth to Plimsoll Line, that the big freighter was still eight to ten hours away from fully laden and ready for departure.

Captain Karem Tortruk; for all his failings and shortcomings as a human being, was a consummate sailor. An excellent and intuitive navigator, a capable helmsman, an accomplished and clever engineer and a delicate cook.

He was also loathsome in most accepted applications of the word.

He had however, and in strange contrast, earned the justified respect of all his crew.

He had done what any pseudo piratical ships master needs to do in these trying times, that is; firstly: pay them, on time, and in full: secondly satisfy their lust for booty, in the form of additional payments, in cash or in kind; bullion or loot, silk or jewellery; or if there is nothing better, alcohol and women will do. And lastly; be brutal when the need arose, cut out any 'bad apples', either in the crew, or the customers, and get rid of them without debate.

81

He had weeded out such apples on many occasions, from 'both sides of the gangplank', as he liked to say, that is crew, and customers.

During the Great War, Karem had been a Second Officer, In the Imperial Navy, having served on the Turkish Battle cruiser SMS Groeben, (seconded from the German Fleet). He had been mentioned in dispatches by Fleet Commander, Admiral Wilhelm Souchon; in recognition of his:

> *'extreme gallantry, and cool head, during*
> *the Battle of Imbros, and again when the British*
> *Fleet was thwarted in it's blockade of, and attack on*
> *Istanbul, in 1915'.*

An action, incidentally, which precipitated the disastrous Dardanelle Campaign.

A favourite story of Captain Karem Tortruks' was his part in the sinking of the Flagship of the Russian Black Sea Fleet; the Dreadnought, The *Imperatritsa Mariya*, when, moored with her sister ship, The *Imperatritsa Ikaterina Velikaya*; Karem had swum over two miles from a Turkish submarine, with three colleagues, and planted limpet mines on the hulls. This allegedly happened in the port of Varna, Bulgaria, during a ships re-fit.

Unfortunately, according to Karem, his compatriots all foundered in the swelling sea, and only he, and his three limpet mines reached the ships alive and completed his mission.

It is an undeniable fact, that the The *Imperatritsa Mariya* was sunk in Varna harbour, on the 20th of October 1916. It is also true that she was dispatched by a series of explosions. But the Russian story is that they were caused by an electrical fault in the magazine. But it was a good story, and Karem liked to tell it. The truth is probably somewhere between the two.

Depending on how drunk he was, it was sometimes at this action at Varna that he sustained his injuries, and sometimes when the SMS Groeben, hit one of their own mines in the exit from the Bosporus, in early 1917. In any event, Second Officer Karem Tortruk, (as he was then), had lost an ear, a thumb, a kidney, and a testicle.

Fortunately all elements for which he had a spare.

Once seated in his green leather armchair, he drew a new cigar from his shirt pocket, and lit it with a gold engraved lighter, which he then placed on the table in front of him. A large whisky was placed before him, by a particularly dirty and scruffy member of his crew. Without a seconds thought, and scooping up the glass in his thumb less hand, he threw the spirit in the mans face, followed by the glass itself, which left a raging cut above the left eyebrow.

Karem sprang to his feet; he knew he was against the clock, and that made him agitated, and ill tempered. Not because of any logistical pressure, he could handle that; but because he knew that three hours, instead of his usual four to four and a half in port, could seriously reduce his takings.

"Another one; now; in a clean glass, served with clean hands! Now!"

Karem screamed at the man as he scurried away like a ships rat.

"Now! Now! Or I'll leave you in this shit-hole with a bullet up your arse for company!"

The crewman was back within two minutes, scrubbed and cleaned, hands and face washed, a bandage over his eye, and a clean blue shirt on, with sleeves rolled up to the elbows. The glass of whisky was placed on the table, in a crystal glass, freshly shined and polished. No glances or words were exchanged, and then the crewman left; glad to be still on board, and glad not to have a rifle round up his arse-hole. Two very real possibilities just a couple of moments earlier.

In truth, the man looked not much dirtier or cleaner, no scruffier than anyone else on board the *Cok Guzel Denizala Baligi*, even Karem Tortruk himself. It was just one of those, 'wrong place, wrong time' kind of things. But it demonstrated to all present, (if any further demonstrations were ever necessary any more), how the times in which one lives dictate the values by which one must live.

Or possibly die.

The Captain, now seated comfortably, took a long puff on his newly lit cigar, and rolled it in his fingers, holding it occasionally next to his ear, his one good ear. This was done only for effect; he had no idea what he was listening for.

He then took a large swig of his whisky and some dribbled down his chin, he made no attempt to wipe it off, but let the sun evaporate it. Placing the glass back on the table, and glancing to his right, (to make sure the metal storage lockers were lined up behind him); he shouted to Arris, who stood on the other side of the gangway opening, less than five paces away.

"Let the customers up….. no more than two at a time don't forget!"

Springing The Box. The rummage continues.
The 'Bowls Inn',
Penyrheol,
Caerphilly,
South Wales.
The same Saturday in March 1972.
A few pints later.

Jimmy 'C' removed the top.

Like a 'Jack in the Box', the cramped contents exploded from their confinement, spewing over the table top.

Papers, letters, clippings, photographs, tickets and cards of all descriptions seemed to expand exponentially to fill the available space atop the table.

And.

Lonely in the bottom of the tin, six or eight coins, a mixture of silver and copper, accompanied by a small shiny curve of grey wood, polished and flat on the concave side, and polished and rounded on the convex, no more than a half inch long in total.

Years upon years of Stalins' detritus had been crammed, cajoled and squeezed into the tin box.

Each of the four observers picked up random bits of paper or old photos, then, scanning each item cursorily, returned each to a different section of the table. Then they picked up other random pieces, which were then in turn treated with ever repeating, and ever increasing shuffling.

Any order that once may have existed within the box, decayed in minutes.

This process continued for possibly half an hour, and two pints, or more; with bits being passed around, items being discussed, possible 'why's? What's? Where's? And 'who's?' Being bantered about like a game of ping-pong doubles, with bits of paper being pinged and ponged; ponged and pinged, hither and yon.

Eventually; and largely none-the-wiser, and another pint or two later, the four men sat in front of several small tumps of seemingly un-related cuttings, letters and the like.

"Well; I don't know about you, but I haven't got a fucking clue".

Said Jimmy 'C' to no one in particular, and downed the remainder of his third or fourth pint of Dark.

"I think some of the letters might be in Russian?"

Uncle Bryn hypothesised, and downed the remainder of his pint too.

"The photos are quite nice".

Mused my Father, and downed the remainder of his pint too.

"Looks like a load of old crap, if you ask me!"

Said Spinksy with some conviction, then, after another swig of Dark, continued with.

"It's a scrap book in a box! Nothing else! Shove it back in the tin Jim, and stick it under your bed like Stalin did, until you snuff it; then get Gerty," (Jimmy C's wife), "to dump it on some other bunch of poor sods at your funeral, then they can waste a perfectly good Saturday too".

He too then downed the remainder of his pint, put the empty glass on some of the papers that were still scattered across the table, and asked.

"Same again all round then, four more pints of Dark?"

It was not really a question, and everyone gestured to, (or lightly touched), their glass as an indication of assent.

While Spinksy and my Father went to the bar, for the drinks, my Uncle Bryn started to collect, and bundle up the little piles of documentation, and return it to the Jacobs biscuit tin. Jimmy 'C' scooped up odd photos and handed them to Bryn.

They chatted idly about the stuff they had exhumed from the box, and pondered further, (but with only half interest), the contents as they continued to stuff them, (somewhat unceremoniously), back into their metal container. Though; in fairness to him, my Uncle Bryn, (as he packed the documents and trinkets away), could feel unexpected questions forming around the polished innards of his skull.

'Who were the lads in the photos?

And the old lady?

And the crowd by the horse; who were they?

And the young woman?

What did the Russian writing on the letters mean?

What did the fading scrawl on the backs of some of the photos say?

Why were the old newspaper clippings kept?

What did they say about some robbery?

What's that bendy bit of old wood?'

Old South African railway tickets, sketches, of trees and mountains, things drawn on the backs of old brown paper bags, the sort you get from sweet shops; bags that previously held sherbet dips and barley sticks, and those paper flying saucer thingy's.

'Was any of it relevant?'

My Uncle Bryn found himself asking a million simultaneous questions of himself.

Postulating occasional answers and occasional dismissals.

Or was Spinksy right; was it all just a bewildered collection of memorabilia, a passing thought of a dying old man?

It all appeared a random hotchpotch of ephemera.

Random mementos.

Random irrelevances.

Random junk.

'A load of old crap!'

As Spinksy had so succinctly summarised it.

Bryn's head continued to whirr, spin and buzz, like all of those machines in his ships engine room.

'And what about those coins?

He quizzed further to himself, South African again, and some others that looked like Australian with a picture of a Kangaroo on one side and The Queen on the other; and others with funny writing on, and a picture of someone no-one recognised?

As he tried to close the lid of the box, (which now seemed to have five times the amount of stuff in it that it had when it was first opened), Bryn turned to Jimmy 'C' and said.

"You know Jim, there must be more to this lot than just junk, otherwise Stalin would have binned it a long time ago, but he left you a message on the tin, a message with no come-back for him, a message which he felt was important".

Bryn touched the paper that was still stuck on the biscuit tins side, and read aloud.

"For my friend Jimmy when I'm gone".

Bryn emphasised the word 'Friend', he knew it would strike home; he had placed his arrow well.

He paused, then continued.

"I think we should give this stuff to Dilwyn Amethyst!"

Bryn paused again.

"Let me take it with me, and I'll call up Dilwyns' tomorrow, and fill him in on it, see if he can come up….."

Bryn was cut short by Jimmy 'C', who interrupted him.

"Dilwyn knows about the box, he was at the funeral; and Ellis and Maldwyn were there. I showed them it; course we were all a bit pissed by that time, but they know about it".

Jimmy then turned towards the bar, and shouted to my Father to get him a cheese and onion roll, and a bag of Pork Scratchings, while he was there.

My Father raised a thumb in acknowledgement.

Imperial Japanese Navy Submarine, I-21.
The Coral Sea.
New Years Eve 1942.

In the tranquil midnight stillness, somewhere alone in the warm vastness of the Coral Sea, the Japanese giant type B1 submarine, I-21, blew main ballast and broke surface.

Her Captain, Kanji Matsumura, had not celebrated the New Year.

The last day of December, 1942, had slipped by almost un-noticed aboard the I-21, melting seamlessly into the first day of January, 1943. He had been too busy, thirty feet below the silken ocean top; squinting through his periscope eyepiece, and searching for what he desperately needed: supplies.

He was first out onto the conning tower, the standing remains of the sea water, drenching his head and shoulders, as he flipped the hatch, and climbed the metal exit ladder. The nightscan red film binoculars, which were slung around his neck, swayed across his oil stained shirt, as he moved; and his thin canvass jacket, hung still, and limp about his shoulders, in the breathless night.

"There!"

Whispered his number two, hot on his heals into the humid black air. Matsumura turned; there was no need to raise his binoculars. There, to the west, less than 2500 yards away, loomed the vast silhouette of the Imperial Japanese Navy Ship 'Kumano'. A heavy cruiser of 13,660 tons, complete with 3 reconnaissance and torpedo aircraft, fifteen, 155mm main guns, four, 40mm heavy anti-aircraft guns, and no less than fifty; 25mm rapid fire light anti-aircraft guns.

Just for good measure she also boasted substantial armour plating, and twelve excess bore, 565 millimetre torpedo tubes.

She also had four large diameter, five blade propellers, which could push her through the waves as fast as anything else afloat, of comparable size.

With a ships compliment of eight hundred and fifty well drilled, and committed, Imperial Japanese Navy regulars, She, and the other three 'Mogami Class' heavy cruisers in the Imperial Japanese Navy Southern Fleet, represented an awesome display of fire power.

But although an impressive, (and welcome), sight in the loneliness of The Coral Sea, of more interest to Captain Matsumura, was the two vessels she shadowed. They were the light, Yugumo Class destroyers; 'Kazagumo', and 'Naganami'.

They were 2,500 tons each, lightly armed, with only 100mm guns. Each had a crew of two hundred and twenty five men.

But, most impressive of all to Captain Kanji Matsumura, they were both chocked full of fresh torpedoes, fuel oil, spare batteries, canned fruit, artillery shells, medical supplies, Saki, soap, clothing, and everything else the monster submarine would need for the next two or three months.

These supplies; along with his fresh orders from Admiral Takeo Kuritai; Commander of Imperial Japanese Navy Cruiser Division 7, (a position he had held since the Battle of Midway, in June 1942), was all Matsumura had dreamt of for the last two weeks.

The I-21, had become attached to Kuritai's division some months earlier, and Captain Matsumura, had developed a genuine appreciation of, and respect for the Admirals strategic abilities, his foresight, and, most of all, his courage.

Matsumura had captained the I-21, under many divisional commanders, and had been attached to many sections; from Subron 1, before the attack on Pearl Harbour, under Admiral Zinjin Katori, and a little later under Vice Admiral Sato Tsutomu.

He had, (most recently), been under the command of Vice Admiral Komatsu, since May 1942, a secondment he had not particularly enjoyed.

But, contrary to this former position, he had now grown to enjoy greatly, the new found freedom which Admiral Kuritai's, style of command had allowed him. His Commanders open ended orders, permitted Matsumura to self judge attack opportunities. And he wanted to keep things this way.

He had always been a successful attack Captain. He had persued, engaged, and very nearly sunk, the United States Aircraft Carrier 'U.S.S. Enterprise' in late December 1941. And did catch and sink the large U.S. freighter 'Montebello', off Point Aguello, California, on the 23rd of that month.

In May 1942, the I-21 had also engaged the 'U.S.S. Yorktown', but had to withdraw, after heavy air attacks from a squadron of American, Douglas TBD Devastators. Captain Matsumura, had, also in that May of 1942, torpedoed and destroyed the American Liberty Ship, the 'U.S.S. John Adams', and the Greek heavy freighter, 'Chloe'; in the western Pacific.

But in these actions, he had been attached to hunt-packs, relying as much on luck, as intelligence.

Now: under Admiral Kuritai, he considered that he could instigate his own contacts, plan his own attacks in advance, and with more certainty. And also; (in line with Kuritais' own expressed desire).

'Keep the enemies heads down.'

Under these earlier free ranging orders from Kuritai, he had shelled the Australian port of Newcastle, in June of 1942, destroying many factories, and substantial sections of the dockyard.

He had also shelled Sydney harbour twice, causing absolute mayhem in Australia's second city.

He had persistently harried Australian shipping all along her south-eastern coast, and reduced merchant convoy sailings by twenty percent.

He had already forwarded to Admiral Kuritai, a request that he should be allowed to continue his work in Australian waters. And he had also sought special permission to organise, and command, (along with Captain Ito, his midget submarine force first officer); a daring attack in the heart of Sydney Harbour.

Matsumura had estimated that in this attack, at least five capital ships, and several merchant vessels could be destroyed. And, with their sinking, put huge sections of the harbour beyond use for many months, if not years.

Captain Matsumura, now hoped and prayed, that Admiral Takeo Kuritai, would, by way of the eagerly awaited orders, for the first time, really cut him loose upon the enemy. The orders were as important to Kanji Matsumura, and Kateo Ito, as any of the supplies.

Both men had formulated their plans in pinpoint detail.

Both men now awaited the envelope from Admiral Kuritais' Chief of Staff.

Both men wanted the honour of the planned attack.

Matsumura knew that the re-loading would take at least six hours, and that the sunrise was against him. Full or not, he would order the disconnection of the pump lines, (and the cessation of re-stocking), fifteen minutes before sunrise. Then five minutes before it, he would order a crash dive.

The night would pass all too swiftly.

But the Commanders would be granted the orders they craved.

<u>The Amethyst Brothers.</u>
<u>And their Historical Society.</u>
<u>Abertridwr,</u>
<u>South Wales,</u>
<u>1972.</u>

Dilwyn Amethyst, his brother Ellis, and Maldwyn Somerset, (a bus driver with Caerphilly Urban District Council, and in charge of a single decker green and cream liveried 'Foden' forty two seater, running between Caerphilly, Llanbradach, Ystrad Mynach, Tir-Y-Birth, Aberbargoed and Fochrhiw), collectively constituted:

> **'The Aber Valley, Historical, Socialist, Classical and Non-Conformist Christian Society'.**

The only organisation in South Wales, with more words in its title, than members on its books.

Dilwyn was the President, Ellis was Vice President, and Maldwyn, his forty eight inch waist trousers, his Jack Russell Terrier; Tango and his P.S.V. license, (Maldwyns, not Tangos'), was the research department.

Today; Dilwyn, Ellis and Maldwyn could well be termed; 'Geeks'.

They were all a bit funny looking, Dilwyn and Ellis were non-alike twins, both skinny and ginger with glasses like 'Corona' pop bottle bottoms, and, although nudging forty were still spotty. Ellis habitually wiped his nose on his jacket sleeve, (always the same jacket, incidentally, green check with brown leather patches on one of the sleeves, yes, and I did say one of the sleeves). He and Dilwyn were frugal, and lived with their Mother in the last house on the left, up the four terraces in Senghenydd.

They had never married, and bought all their clothes from the Oxfam shop in Saint Mary Street in Cardiff. Hence the sleeve patches.

Both of them were Librarians, one in Abertridwr; in the Council Library by the Welfare Ground, and the other in the Council Library in Caerphilly, by Morgan Jones' Park.

As both libraries were owned and run by the Council, the two Amethyst twins used to switch seamlessly, and at a whim, between Aber and Caerphilly branches. Life did not get much more exhilarating than the expectation of surprise at never knowing for certain which of the Amethyst boys would stamp your library card when you collected the latest Alistair MacLean.

Dilwyn was six foot five inches tall, with a pencil moustache, and well kempt; and with a slow deliberate gait. Ellis was four foot ten inches with a full beard and hair down to his shoulders, a nervous tick, and a left leg that was one and a half inches shorter than his right. Dilwyn looked like a ginger Basil Fawlty, with the facial features of Douglas Fairbanks Junior, and Ellis looked like a Hobbit on 'Wizz'.

However, both of the Amethyst brothers were clever little tinkers.

Dilwyn held a Doctorate in Classics from Aberystwyth University, spoke Latin, Greek, Chinese and a little Welsh.

Ellis, had done his Bachelors Degree in Contemporary History at Swansea University, and then completed a Masters in European Humanities at Bangor.

Maldwyn, could drive anything with four wheels, and had a certificate for swimming a width underwater at Caerphilly Baths.

'The Ninth Mission Hospital'.
Grubakor Hill,
(Overlooking the Red Sea port of Suakin),
The Sudan,
East Africa.
Christmas 2013.

Sister Lubia Brezhnitzen was sixty eight years old, and had been in the Sudan for forty of those sixty eight years.

It was a swelteringly hot day of over forty degrees in the shade, the corrugated tin roof of the hospitals white-washed wings would be untouchable to bare skin. Huge and aged fans spun foolishly in every office and every ward.

The nursing sisters in their blue and white habits scurried between beds, wards and corridors distributing medication, care and solace to the sardine crammed patients.

Swatting flies as they went.

The doctors continued to fight their losing battles at every bedside and in every operating theatre. Occasionally victories would be trumpeted, and consistently, defeats would be accepted in their pitiful mundanety.

The hospital complex was large, but ill equipped. Like most hospitals in the Horn of Africa.

Sister Brezhnitzen was the nursing manager and felt the shortcomings acutely. But without her order, and its efforts; and her efforts, there would be no hospital here at all.

As she looked out through her window, down upon the empty jetties of the port of Suakin, (a few miles downhill of her), she could see the remains of the rusting hulk which had sat on the shallow sea bed ever since she had arrived here all those years ago.

She had watched it slowly decay, colouring the sea a sad ochre with its rust, and black with its leaking oil and coal dust. Mingling streaks of the colours conjoined as they stretched their skinny fingers miles out into the Red Sea. She would have thought by now that it would have all been gone, washed away, but every day the thin slick streaks re-appeared.

All that could be seen now of the dead old monster were some lifting jib crane masts, which broke the surface at odd angles; and a row of smashed windows of the bridge and wheelhouse, which peeped above the lapping waves.

She had never found out the vessel's name.

Though deep down she knew.

The gentle beep of her desktop computer told her that she had an e-mail, and she turned her chair to face the screen, and swizzled and clicked her mouse.

It was from her orders Australian Mother Superior, based in Darwin.

It was drafted in jubilant tones, and informed Sister Brezhnitzen that an anonymous donation had been received by way of a bequest.

A bequest in the sum of five hundred thousand dollars. It had been bequeathed with the specific requirement that all the money should be spent on satisfying the needs of The Ninth Mission Hospital, at Suakin.

The e-mail asked that Sister Brezhnitzen draft a detailed list of all the items she would require, (up to that value), and to send the list to the Mother Superior, (by e-mail), within the next seven days.

The response would be with The Mother Superior within twelve hours.

Sister Brezhnitzen turned her chair again towards her window, and again looked down upon the rusting hulk.

She clasped her hands, and said, over and over again, at least twenty times:

"Thank you God".

"Thank you God".

"Thank you God".

The Amethysts take the brief,
March 1972.

Bryn put the box in front of him, and said to Jimmy 'C',

"Leave this with me then, and I'll keep you posted".

The four men spent the balance of Saturday picking losers, and spilling pints. Eight quid over the bar of The Bowls Inn, and thirty two quid to the Frankie Chiverton retirement fund.

On Sunday morning, Bryn, (as promised), called to Dilwyn and Ellis' mothers house, and duly delivered the box. Bryn handed it to the brothers in the back kitchen, over a cup of tea and a toasted current bun; and a brief explanation of the previous day's discoveries, or rather, the lack of them.

Dilwyn and Ellis said that they would give it a, "good sort through" over the next few days, and get a "research list" drawn up for Maldwyn, who was off work for a couple of days with Piles. So he had some time on his hands. The seat of a Foden forty two seater had not been designed with upper-most thought, to the suffering of those afflicted with severe haemorrhoids.

At some time during the second cup of tea, and the third current bun and just as Mrs Amethyst was pulling the boiled eggs out of the breakfast saucepan; an argument broke out between Dilwyn and Ellis. The argument was intense, and pertained to the relative purpose, in terms of power and wealth, of the Silver Mines at 'Laurean', outside Ancient Athens, and its relationship to, and influence on the participants of the Peloponnesian war in the fifth century B.C. Aegean.

Bryn decided it was time to leave, thanked Mrs Amethyst for the tea and toasted buns, and said his goodbyes without Dilwyn or Ellis even noticing.

Get out of Gaol, but not quite free.
(Or 'Jail' if you prefer),
KalgoorlieBoulder,
Western Australia.
January 13th 1943.

January 13th, 1943 dawned; as every other day in Western Australia Penal Work Camp 18, with the arrival of the agonising sun, and the usual stream of abuse from Top Sarge Fuzzy Dolenz.

Except today's tirade did not culminate with the customary,

'Get to work you lazy bastards!'

Or,

'Let's be having you, don't you know there's a fucking war to win!'

But uniquely, with;

"Now! Everybody in the centre of the compound in four nice neat fucking ranks. Those of you who cant count to four, that's one less fucking clout than my boys," (referring to his prison guards), "will fetch you, if your not standing straight in thirty fucking seconds. Now: fucking mooooove!"

His voice rose to a crescendo towards the end of his command, to the point that the last five words were screamed out at the top of his voice, and only barely comprehendible.

The cons all ran at the double toward the centre of the compound, where, with some unwelcome coaxing from the guards and a couple of foot of hardwood Ironbark club, they formed into four, fairly unequal rows. The armed guards in the compound, surrounded them at a reasonable distance, and the sentry guards in the towers, made sure they were noticed, as they barked aloud the instruction:

"Line up! Line up!"

Then swept the parading cons with their rifle sights.

Fuzzy Dolenz strode to the front rank, facing the cons, from about five paces distant. He yelled.

"Now! You bunch of idle no good cunts; the Warden wants to talk to you this morning. You will listen, you will shut the fuck up, and you will only move if I tell you to move. If you need a piss! Piss in your pants. Anyone twitches, and they'll have a 303 round up the jacksy!"

He took three paces backwards, and looked left and right at the columns before him. Pausing for long seconds, and studying for any signs of dissent.

He then took off his bush style hat, and, holding it up in front of his eyes, and moving it around the perimeter fence, using it as a shade against the sun; he surveyed the sentry towers, and the patrolling guards on the 'Free-Side' of the fence.

Once he was satisfied that all was in order and secure, he shouted to the gate sentries; who stood waiting for his command, a good hundred or so yards away.

"Let them in Mr. Fellowes!"

He shouted, as only men who command other men can shout.

The double gates were flung open, and Mr. Fellowes, a guardsman in his mid forties, with a small beer belly and warts; waved in through the gates, two dove grey Prison Service pick up trucks, which had been waiting on the 'Free-Side'.

Each truck bore the coat of arms emblem of Western Australia emblazoned on the doors, and the bonnet; (two rampant kangaroos, on either side of a black swan), with the motto, *'Cygnis Insignis'* written below each, and 'Prison Service of Western Australia', written above in blue.

The first truck pulled up in front of the columns of scruffy convicts, slightly to the right, and about five yards behind Fuzzy Dolenz. A plume of dry, sandy dust hung around it, churned up by its tyres, and then slowly settled, like a puddle of melting vanilla ice cream.

From the cab of the pickup truck, and from its bed, five guards jumped out and lined up, on bended knee, with rifles at the shoulder, pointed at the cons. In the back of the pick up, low down, and crouched, two further guards, manning a Vickers 303 General Purpose Machine Gun, again trained their muzzle on the ranks of convicts.

Once these preparations were complete, and Sergeant Dolenz was completely satisfied, he walked over to the second truck, and, leaning through the drivers' window, he spoke to the passenger.

"All right Mr Summersby, we're ready when you are now Sir".

He tapped the windscreen and turned back to face the prisoners.

Warden Frank Summersby, (as he liked to be called, although his true title, and pay rate, was 'Deputy Warden'), got out of the truck. He walked to the rear, where two guards lifted a pair of wooden steps into place for him to climb onto the bed of the pickup.

He was a slight man, in his early forties, mousey and, grey haired, and with an unsightly scar in the centre of his lower lip. He was clean shaven, and wore round wire rimmed spectacles; he had thin, drawn features. He puffed on a filter tipped cigarette as he mounted the steps, and never once glanced at the rows sweltering prisoners.

Though each one of them studied him intently.

Not anticipating his announcement, but rather each wondering where he would flick his dog-end, once he had finished his fag.

His shoes were black and covered with the dust that settled on everything in the compound. He wore dark blue trousers with turn-ups, which habitually collected the dust, and were a bugger to clean out. His shirt was white and short sleeved, his tie was dark blue, the same as his trousers, (Government Issue), and done up tight to his top button. Fuzzy Dolenz, had never seen Frank Summersby with his tie slackened, and top shirt button undone. In fact, he had never seen Warden Summersby sweat.

Well, apart from that once.

That 'once' that they never spoke about.

The Warden flicked the remains of his cigarette without any consideration. Clearing his throat, he drew from his shirt pocket, a single folded piece of flimsy yellow paper, unravelled it, and began to read. He exchanged no pleasantries with the guards, or Sergeant Dolenz, he had no wish to indulge in any social interaction with any of them. His manner was that of a schoolmaster who expected subservience and obedience from his charges, with no debate, no discussion, and above all no questions.

He began to read, aloud.

> "His Majesties Government, and the Executive of the
> Prison Service of Western Australia, instructs, that
> any inmate, volunteering today, for 'non-combatant'
> war service, in the Australian Mercantile or Royal
> Naval Marine, will be granted a full review of their
> remaining sentence, upon cessation of hostilities.
> Volunteers will be accepted immediately, whereupon
> you will be conveyed to the nearest designated
> receiving centre. You have five minutes to apply."

Warden Summersby folded the paper neatly, pushed it back into his shirt breast pocket, and walked down the wooden steps. He turned briefly to Fuzzy Dolenz saying;

"Take details of any who apply, and get them on the trucks".

He pointed at three, dark green, canvass covered military lorries parked up randomly beyond the gates.

"There's a Major of Marines over there, with a couple of dozen squaddies; make sure he signs for them; and make sure he handcuffs them to the rails inside the trucks; we don't need any jump-outs".

He did not wait for a reply from Dolenz.

He got back in the passenger seat of the pickup, waved a finger at the windscreen, and the driver started the vehicle, and drove out of the gates.

"Is that a pardon if we sign up then Sergeant Dolenz?"

Asked one of the cons in the front row. Fuzzy Dolenz turned smartly on one heel; and screamed in his usual fashion, walking up close to the man's face as he yelled.

"I told you horrible cunts, no fucking questions! You heard the Warden; he was quite clear; you lot should have been paying attention, you ignorant wastes of human organs!"

He stepped even closer towards the con who had spoken, their noses nearly touching. He still shouted, and the man could smell Fuzzys' early morning eggs.

"You've got four fucking minutes now! Make your minds up, I don't give a fuck myself, it's either the rock pile, or the fucking Japs, both will kill you in the end!"

He turned again.

"Donovan!"

He shouted, without looking in any particular direction. A guardsman, evidently Donovan, trotted forward, shouldering his rifle as he ran;

"Yes Sarge?"

He said, as he pulled up in front of Fuzzy Dolenz, and stamped his right foot, and stood to attention.

Sergeant Dolenz looked him up and down, exaggeratedly, and with a look of mock disgust on his face, he leaning forward, and in his best condescending voice, said, (quietly so the cons could not here);

"Your not in the fucking army lad, your in the Western Australia Prison Service, behave like it, and be proud of it".

He turned about to face the mustered prisoners. Looking along the rows, he continued; this time at full volume, so all could hear. His vocal range was indeed impressive, from merely belittling and belligerent to absolutely threatening and terrifying.

"Now, Guardsman Donovan, take any of these worthless cunts that fancy accepting his Majesty kind invitation, to get blown to smithereens by Johnny Jap; and foxtrot the bastards in a nice neat line over to the gates!"

He spat on the floor, and trod it into the dirt with his boot. He turned back to Guardsman Donovan and instructed;

"Get a clipboard from the office, and write up the names and numbers of all them that are off; then get that Marines Major to count them, and sign for them, give the paper back into the office; then get the rest of these cunts back to fucking wooork!"

Again, his voice rose to a scream, as he stretched out the last word for effect.

The prisoners, (who were not renowned for their patriotism), generally took the offer with the large pinch of salt, that both the Warden, and Fuzzy Dolenz had expected. Those with less than two or three years to go remained silent, and collectively decided to carry on breaking rocks, and ticking and chipping their time away.

Those with families on the outside largely decided to sit tight, on the basis that a monthly visit may well be better than several lonely years at sea.

Some even decided that life under the Japs may be better than life under the Australians. It is worth remembering that Penal Work Camp 18 was in no way, a representative cross section of Ozzy society.

In any event, the vast majority would clearly be returning to the rock pile.

All in all, only eighteen of the inmates accepted His Majesties offer, the other one hundred and ninety had decided that His Majesty could go and fuck himself.

Prisoner number 89855812 was the first to volunteer, although no guarantee of Pardon or Parole, the deal at least provided a chance to get out of the sun. And the thought of all that water, (even if it was infested with Jap submarines and battleships), would be a welcome change from this dust choked cauldron.

"Fall in over there!"

Instructed Guardsman Donovan, gesturing to his right.

"At the double!"

He barked, not satisfied with Prisoner number 89855812's progress.

As he trotted, Prisoner number 89855812, made a slight detour, of one or two paces, and, smartly bending down as he ran, he retrieved the fag-end flicked away by Warden Summersby, and deftly parked it behind his left ear.

The Amethyst-Somerset Dimension.
The Aber Valley and Cardiff,
South Wales.
March 1972, (ish).

Maldwyn Somerset; (despite his affliction, and his portly appearance, his languorous manner, swarthy complexion, and an unfortunate stammer, and a propensity towards flatulence, {both of which incidentally, surfaced in moments of extreme excitement or anxiety}), was as quick brained, and sharp witted, as anyone you would ever meet.

Like Dilwyn and Ellis Amethyst, Maldwyn had never married. He had always been overweight, and, (unlike Dilwyn and Ellis), had been unfortunately let down by the state education system. Having been condemned to Secondary Modern obscurity, by his failure to turn up for his eleven plus exam due to mumps and an infected varrucha.

At school, he had excelled at everything even remotely academic, and failed miserably at sport, and anything socially interactive, in all their guises. However, as a Secondary Modern kid, the opportunity for 'O' levels, 'A' levels, University, and Academia, had been substituted, (for Maldwyn), with courses on 'how to build a canoe', and 'how to cook bacon without splashing yourself with hot fat".

Maldwyn therefore left school at sixteen, and went straight into a job with the Council, planning bus routes and making tea. Then, after a few years sorting out their logistical routing problems for crap pay; Maldwyn persuaded them to train him up as a driver in which position he could earn an extra two quid a week, and the rest, as they say is history.

He now spent his days conveying passengers to and from the same drab destinations up and down the wiggly Rhymney Valley. Its roads snaking along the banks of its black river of the same name, which flowed, (opaque from the coal silt, sludged from the washeries further up the valley), to discharge at some point in a brighter future, into the violence of the Bristol Channel.

Most evenings, (on a Monday to Thursday), between the hours of seven thirty and ten, Maldwyn could be found in the public bar of the Panteg pub, on the square in Abertridwr. On a Friday he frequented Senghenydd Rugby Club, and on a Saturday, the Castle Hotel, or The Piccadilly Inn in Caerphilly. Often ending up, leaning against the bar in the Checkmate Club, above 'Woolies', up the top of Caerphilly town centre.

There were only two other places in Caerphilly where one could secure alcohol after eleven at night, (stop-tap); they were, The Camelot Club, on Castle Street, and The Corbett's Club, at Pwll-Y-Pant.

Both of these establishments required smart jackets and ties as entry pre-requisites, and therefore precluded Maldwyn, who, even after his best endeavours at dressing-up, still looked like a sack of shit tied in the middle.

He was a creature of habit, and his main habit was that he could drink an inordinate amount of beer at a single sitting, without ever becoming incoherently drunk. Unless, that is, some fool, (like at Stalins funeral), started buying him Johnnie Walker. In which case, he turned into a stuttering, mumbling, vomiting, sweating lump of fat.

Not-withstanding his shortcomings, Maldwyn spent every spare minute reading, he always had a 'History of this or that' stuffed into one of his pockets, and the last thirty odd years and several thousand paperbacks, had crammed his head with an Everest of knowledge. But, more importantly, he had one of those minds that sparked questions from each book he read, and prompted new ideas for him to explore. He had a bloodlust for research, and, like a vampire, he sucked the hidden information from source material of any description.

On Saturdays and Sunday mornings he caught the train from Aber Junction to Cardiff Queen Street, with a Woolworth carrier bag full of corned beef and Branston Pickle sandwiches, a flask of Nescafe, three bars of Curly Wurly, and a notepad full of blank timetable sheets. These sheets, (surplus to requirements, and borrowed, {permanently}, from the Bus Depot on Mill Road, Caerphilly), were ideally suited for note taking.

As they were self carbonised, and, as long as you pressed hard enough with the pen, they made an automatic copy on the sheet below, high-tec early seventies, this kind of stuff.

He also had a tight bundle of various coloured Biros, (from the same supplier), wrapped together with a thick red elastic band.

His destination was always, either the Welsh Central Library, on 'The Hays' in Cardiff City Centre, or the University Library, in Column Road. The latter of which was open to the public at weekends.

The students of University of Wales, Collage Cardiff were usually in bed all day on a Saturday and Sunday, so the University library was usually the quieter of the two locations, and Maldwyns' favoured destination.

This particular Saturday, he had been tasked by Dilwyn and Ellis Amethyst with finding all he could, about the following:

An Australian Merchant Vessel, the 'SS Iron Knight', and a Royal Australian Navy Ship called the 'H.M.A.S Waterhen', circa 1942 to 1945.

The Amethyst boys had also given him an A4 envelope with a load of black and white, crinkled and cracked photos of old ships; and had said simply.

"See what you can get on them an' all, while you're at it".

Also, they had asked for any information on, Yuris Pavel Androskewowicz, Itzhak Lev Androskewowicz, and Marta Araka Androskewowicz; anything on Yaris Ladros Akpaganaths, and the Russian towns or villages of Greniko and Gwalikin Palatinsk.

They had said that should keep him busy for the weekend.

Like everyone else, they underestimated Maldwyn.

Cutting from:

The Newcastle Herald Newspaper.

The following, is a copy of an incomplete clipping, found in the Jacobs Biscuit Tin. The date had been written on the top of the clipping in faded pencil.

On the 22nd of March 1972, my Uncle Murray, in Kalaroo, Perth, Western Australia; received a copy of it, along with some other documents, sent via air mail by Dilwyn Amethyst, from Abertridwr.

Enclosed with the selection of photocopies, was a short one paragraph letter, asking Murray, if he could check out his local library, (or anywhere else he thought fit), just to see if he could shed any light, (from local sources), on anything in the bundle.

My Father, (at the request of Maldwyn in particular), had subsequently phoned my Uncle Murray and dictated a list of a dozen or so items to him, which Maldwyn had asked if he could check out further from Australian sources.

The old newspaper clipping read:

'From our previous articles.

The SS Iron Knight sank in less than two minutes after the second torpedo hit.

The H.M.R.S. Le Triomphant, rescued some fourteen survivors, from a single lifeboat some six days later.

After hospital treatment all bar two, have been discharged, a third man is currently still, 'in safe keeping', at Newcastle Police Station.

Captain Iestyn Tynsdale, and Midshipman Alexander Hawks, have each been awarded the Sea Gallantry Medal, in recognition of their outstanding seamanship in maintaining the lifeboat on station, in the days before the rescue.

Both men, including some crewmen with military experience, at their request, have now been accepted by, and, re-commissioned back, into the Royal Australian Navy for active service.

Before leaving for a well earned, one week leave in his home town of Toomawoora, and still with seven stitches in his calf; Captain Tynsdale paid tribute to his crew. He said:

"I am looking forward to taking up my new duties at Port Keats, and I am very pleased that some of the old crew from the Iron Knight will be coming with me. I cannot give any more information about those duties for obvious reasons, but I could not wish for a better ships company".

Talking about the rescue, Captain Tynsdale paid special tribute to one crew member, saying.

"There is one man, to whom, I personally owe, special thanks, he was only aboard for a fortnight or so before the sinking, but in that time he proved himself to be a stirling member of the crew. He saved my life. We were in the water, pitch black for five hours, both of us severely concussed, and me with an injured leg, and having lost a lot of blood. He kept me afloat for those five hours, until we found the lifeboat. He never let me go once. I want that man with me on my next posting, and I'll go on record with that formal request today".

When this reporter asked for the mans name, Captain Tynsdales response was short.

"I'm not sure of his real name, but we all called him 'Stoko'. He could shovel coal, or, 'The

105

Hard Black Stuff', as he called it; faster than any
man I've ever seen".

Off to sea,
The port of Albany,
Western Australia,
January 15th, and 16th, 1943.

Prisoner number 89855812 had been jostled and bounced around in the back of the lorry, for over 5 hours. He was handcuffed to the centre rail between the two rows of bench seats, with his back bent against the canvass cover drape. The Marine Major had allowed the prisoners only one stop so far, for a piss break, and nothing more.

Any re-fuelling had been done at the roadside from jerry cans, and there were two armed marines for every one prisoner in the back of each lorry.

His cigarette end still languished behind his ear. Occasionally, one of the marines would poor some water into his mouth from an aluminium canteen, which hung from the top rail in the back of the lorry. The water was always warm, and tasted slightly bitter. Prisoner number 89855812 was fairly sure that the marines had pissed in it, as they drank from different canteens, slung from their belts. But it was the only game in town, and it was furnace hot, so he always drank.

The port of Albany was just about the southern most point of Western Australia, clinging to the oceans edge like an infant on a tit. The buildings were generally weather-beaten and sun-scorched; as, (ever increasingly), were the inhabitants, indeed the more scorched and grizzled they became the nearer they got to the docks. The inhabitants and the buildings that is.

106

As the lorrys drove through the suburbs, Prisoner number 89855812, could see, from the flapping drapes of canvass at the back of the truck; small shops, bars, filling stations, a hotel, a school, some churches.

They passed school-kids on their way home, fellers digging up roads, people washing cars, and walking dogs. It was a world Prisoner number 89855812 could barely remember; and there were women, pretty women, even the ugly women looked like pretty women. In truth, even the dogs looked like women.

After a couple of miles, the scenery changed by osmosis to ramshackle clusters of warehouses. The cars metamorphosed into dock vehicles, with shipping company liveries and names on them, every one of them with working dents and scratches. Fork trucks with sweaty loads and sweaty drivers criss-crossed behind the lorries. And the women turned into dock labourers with dungarees and heavy gloves, with crow-bars slung over their shoulders.

It seemed to Prisoner number 89855812, that this place was a prison where the other inmates could go home at the end of a shift.

He realised that he could not.

It dawned on him like a shark attack, that nothing was going to change for Prisoner number 89855812.

Gradually, the waft of salt air burrowed into his nostrils, and he found saliva bubbling in his cheeks at the faint odours of fish that undressed on the early evening air.

The lorries drew to a thundering halt, forcing the occupants to drive one foot into the bed to prevent themselves being hurled sideways. Almost instantly the back canvass drapes were flung wide open from the outside.

"Everybody out! One line in front of the lorries!"

It was a marine corporal, with a forage hat and a crisp uniform. He hadn't been in the lorries, he was too clean.

Too sharp.

Too military.

Too dry.

The marines in the lorries, un-cuffed the prisoners from the centre rails, and re-cuffed them, hands in front. As they jumped down from the lorry backs to the tarmac, some stumbled, all squinted against the late afternoon sun.

"One line! One line!"

The corporal repeated, as he walked along outside the lorries.

"One line! One line!"

After some organising, a line of some description began to form, kaleidoscope-like the jigsaw of blue and buff uniformed souls danced, and re-configured. Eventually a jagged, almost hand drawn line of blue clad prisoners evolved, backed up against the lorries.

As Prisoner number 89855812, looked along it, his eyes slowly growing accustomed to the brightness; it became clear that more lorries had joined their little caravan, the nearer they had come to Albany. There were now a dozen or so, parked up at the roadside, at differing angles, and differing degrees of neatness.

The jagged, thin blue line must have been about fifty or sixty prisoners long.

There seemed to be a couple of hundred uniformed marines, all with rifles, buzzing with chit chat, and mulling, willy-nilly around the sweating, dirty, and uncomfortable; wavering blue line. Rifles at the ready, half watching, half thinking about other things: beer, women, pork sandwiches, motorcycles, home, Yanks shagging their girlfriends; or getting killed by the Japs.

The crisp shiny corporal continued to march up and down the rank of prisoners.

"No one move, no talking, and stay exactly where you are!"

As he moved, he repeated himself, probably every ten yards or so…..

"No one move, no talking, stay exactly where you are!"

After a few moments, he walked back down the line. He stopped for a second, just adjacent to Prisoner number 89855812, the man next but one to him, was just pissing himself, and a large puddle was appearing at the end of his left leg. The prisoner was impassive, and seemingly oblivious to the absurdity.

The shiny corporal looked at him, and tutted.

He then turned on his heel, and facing away from the prisoners, and addressing a small group of Majors, standing about ten paces away, flipping through and comparing clip boards: he said to them;

"All present and correct Sirs; awaiting allocation".

He stamped his shiny boot, and marched towards the Majors.

A group of Majors, a bunch of Majors, a gathering of Majors? Prisoner number 89855812, tried to work out if there was a collective noun for Majors; he settled, in his own tongue, and in his own head; for:

'A complete cuntfull of Majors'.

The 'Cuntfull of Majors', began to collect themselves into a little nest, stepping out their fags on the tarmac as they turned towards the melting, thin blue line.

'Oh no!'

Thought Prisoner number 89855812;

'Here comes another fucking speech".

Before the most senior Major of Marine Cunts, could start; a rumpus blew up at the far end of the line, the end farthest away from the dockside.

A prisoner had decided that a chance had presented itself.

An escape.

Sensing the newness of the marines, their semi attention, their half interestedness; the man had decided to make a sprint for the street corner, and then disappear into the warren of alleyways between the tatty warehouses.

From there, he had decided, he could make new life for himself, as a baker, or a bus conductor, a miner, or a logger; get married, raise three fine boys, retire, go fishing at weekends, have friends over for Christmas dinner, and organise family holidays, go camping in the hills and the like.

The prisoner was a lithe aborigine, no more than twenty five years old; with wire tight curls and skin the colour of wet coal, he was bandy, and ran with an awkward gate. But he was fast, fast as a warm wind off a cool hillside. He was within ten or fifteen yards of the street corner.

Within ten or fifteen yards of being a baker.

The new marines were taken by surprise, the aborigine was right. But he had misjudged the distance to the corner, misjudged his own speed, misjudged the newness of the soldiers, and misjudged the Major Cunts.

"Stop that Abo!"

One of the Majors shouted, and pointed down the street.

The volley was deafening, and echoes bounced between the brick and glass facades of the streets adjacent buildings. Other prisoners covered their ears, and instinctively crouched.

At least thirty of the marines swung their Enfield rifles, aimed and fired. The Abo disintegrated; hit almost simultaneously by thirty odd rifle rounds from comparatively short range.

Hands, feet, fingers, arms, sections of skull, rib-cage, individual vertebrae and lumps of quivering flesh, glided through the air in a vapour of red haze. The Abo had been turned into a pile of red sludge in a milli-second.

Even at this distance spatters of blood hit those prisoners and troops at the street end of the column of trucks. Some prisoners were sick, others jeered, yelped and swore.

The marines were generally silent.

"Get these men into the muster hall!"

One of the Major Cunts was shouting to the shiny corporal.

"Then get a detail to clean up that mess".

He pointed down the street, where dockyard workers, passers by, and civilians had come out of their offices and yards to see what the commotion was about.

The prisoners were double paced into the muster hall, and untidily lined up in three rows, each leading to a desk where an official looking finger in a dark suit, (not military), sat with a pile of important looking port documents in front of him.

Troopers, between each line kept the prisoners in order, pushing from both sides with their horizontal turned rifles.

As each prisoner arrived before them, the fingers allocated them to ships and duties, and gave a flimsy piece of pink paper to the next pair of marines who queued in other lines, (their own lines), the marines lines, at one hundred and eighty degrees to the desks, behind the fingers, and opposite the cons lines.

110

Two marines would then double march each prisoner, the prisoner corresponding to the pink sheet, across the muster hall, taking him under the arms, and slinging their rifles over their shoulders. Then they would shuffle each con; their con, their private charge, unceremoniously, out of the small personnel door at the back of the hall.

This noisy metal door led straight out onto the concrete dockside, and banged and slammed noisily and continuously in the soft breeze.

"Next!"

The fingers would shout, as each prisoner was processed, and the following man would step up to the desk. They never once looked up. They didn't need to, as the marines behind them read aloud the numbers on each prisoners shirt, as he approached the fingers.

The allocation paperwork in the muster hall was completed in double quick time.

There would be questions about the Abo, and that was now top of the Major Cunts lists.

But at the end of the day he was an Abo, and a con, and this was wartime. A few letters, a new file, a phone call, a couple more letters, and it would all be 'fucking history', as the squadies had said as they had shoved the cons into the muster hall.

They were right.

"Prisoner number 89855812!"

Called out a marine from behind one of the desks. The finger, scanned his documents, moved some files, thumbed down a list or two, picked up a fresh flimsy pink form, wrote on it briefly with a bright red fountain pen, stamped it with a loud rubber hand stamper, handed the form over his left shoulder; and shouted.

"Prisoner number 89855812; SS Iron Knight; Pier five, Birth twelve: Stoker: keys to Captain Tynsdale".

Then without a pause.

"Next!"

Instantly Prisoner number 89855812 felt the hands of two burley marines under his arms, and he was out the door, running, and being dragged along to Pier

111

five, Birth twelve. His tired feet scuffed as he ran, his marines, pulling, tugging and pushing him. As he arrived at the gangplank, he stumbled, but was soon dragged up, and shoved along the steep wooden gangway.

Uncomfortable memories surfaced in that moment, but he dismissed them in the same instance. There may be time for such thoughts one day, but not today.

Not now.

As he glanced up, he saw three men in loose white shirts, and white sailors peaked caps.

Such caps are always grubby, particularly on merchant vessels, and those aboard the SS Iron Knight were no exception. The hauling of Iron Ore was after all, a grubby business.

At the top of the gangplank, Prisoner number 89855812 noticed that two of the ships officers had holstered revolvers at their waists. The guns did not match, and the holsters were not designed for the guns, this was not a military ship, it was a work ship, a floating Penal Camp 18.

'No change after all'

He thought to himself; as he, his handcuffs, his keys, and his piece of flimsy pink paper were handed over.

The marines got a signature, retrieved the paper, and left.

Maldwyn and the Haemorrhoids.
(Sounds like a 70's heavy rock band),
A Saturday in early April 1972.

Maldwyn had arrived at the Welsh Central Library at just after nine forty five a.m.

They opened on a Saturday at ten a.m.

He was in the habit of eating his first sandwich of the day whilst sitting on the impressive entrance steps, as he awaited the opening time; (the Rhymney Valley line, British Rail, train timetables, not quite coinciding with Cardiff library opening times).

The building itself was early twentieth century, pseudo gothic, constructed of dressed granite stone, dark and glistening in the ever-present dampness of South Wales. Its huge rectangular Renaissance style windows made from shellac'd Welsh oak, each window festooned, (and perched above, on its lintel), with carved gargoyles. The parapet wall topped, like St. Peters in Rome, (except not with Saints), with life sized statues of the civic dignitaries who ran Cardiff at the turn of the nineteenth to twentieth century.

The building stood directly opposite the entrance to the indoor market, (formerly a women's prison).

The early morning fishmonger's smells of cockles, mackerel and lava bread, as thick as new boiled tar, wafted across to Maldwyn, making him contemplate the indulgence of another corned beef and Branstone Pickle sandwich.

The Castle spire clock chimed ten, and as if by some divine intervention to limit Maldwyns waistline, the library entrance doors opened.

Maldwyn had decided to go firstly to the Central Library because they had an excellent array of old newspapers on micro-fiche, and a selection of machines on which to install, and roll them, allowing cross referencing, by running two or three machines simultaneously.

They also had a part time, second floor archive assistant, (who came in at noon on a Saturday), called Dmitri, who lived in Splott, a suburb of Cardiff. According to Maldwyn, Dmitri was something of an expert in the Diaspora of Russian Jewry post 1917.

"Could be useful?"

Maldwyn had commented to Dilwyn.

Dmitris' Great Great Grandparents were themselves Russian and had come here in the 1880's to work on the docks. Maldwyn had collected such snippets of information via years of idle chit chat with the library staff during his weekend *sojourns*.

No information was ever wasted on Maldwyn Somerset; everything was mentally filed away for future use.

Most important of all, he knew that Dmitri was an active member of the small ex-pat community of the Russian Orthodox Church here in Cardiff, and that, (like all his family), spoke fluent Russian. Maldwyn also knew that Dmitri had an avid interest in his own family history, and the history of the local Russian Orthodox movement, in which he was a prescient participant.

Maldwyn went to the main desk on the ground floor, and claimed three yellow coloured, numbered paper slips from Anton, (the desk clerk), to reserve machines one, two and three until two p.m. He also collected a pink piece of laminated plastic card, with a 'fee paid' endorsement on it, to allow him access to the micro-fiche archive.

Maldwyn knew all the staff at the library by first names, as they knew him.

He exchanged his usual inane banter with Anton, (which neither party really neither liked nor required, but somehow felt obliged to exchange), and then Maldwyn went about his business. Rummaging in his carrier bag, he retrieved small bits of paper from various pockets, and scrutinised each of them, he then organised them into some sort of allusive and abstract order; an order which would have been totally unfathomable to anyone except Maldwyn.

After viewing one such remnant, he looked across the counter to Anton and asked;

"Can you also ring the University Library for me, and ask if they've got a full set of 1939 to 1949, 'Jane's Merchant Ships', and the same period in 'Jane's Fighting Ships'?"

Anton, like Maldwyn, knew that the Central Library had no copies of 'Jane's'; but that the University Library would almost certainly have them.

"Will do Maldwyn", replied Anton, and gave an efficient smile; Maldwyn was already walking away towards the lifts, as Anton shouted after him cordially:

"I'll give you a shout later to let you know. If they have, shall I ask them to pull them for you?"

"Definitely!"

Responded Maldwyn with his usual brevity.

"Tell them, I'll be over at about three-ish. I'll be up on the second floor here till then, so if you can give Lauren a buzz up there to confirm they've got them that would be great".

He juggled his required slips from Anton as he walked away, shoving some of them into his carrier bag of accoutrements, and others into seemingly hap-hazardly selected pockets.

He then took the lift to the second floor.

Stairs were anathema to Maldwyn in anything except domestic dwellings; especially when his piles were playing up.

Thinking about it, it could have been years of sitting on the cold library steps on weekend mornings that could have caused Maldwyns rectal discomfort in the first place; and all as a result of an inconsistency between train timetables and library opening times.

Isn't fate cruel!

As the lift 'dinged' to announce its arrival at the second floor, and the doors opened automatically, (like the bridge doors in the original series of Star Trek), Maldwyn tucked his carrier bag under his arm, shoved his last remaining authorisation slips in the back pocket of his baggy arsed jeans; and began unbuttoning his long, and poorly fitting overcoat. As he exited the lift, he waved an acknowledgement to a short dumpy woman behind a small counter, a little to his left.

"How are you today Maldwyn?"

She asked with the condescension usually reserved for the very old or mentally infirm, and not really expecting an answer.

However; unexpected or not.

She got one.

"Horrendous piles, thank you Clarrissa", replied Maldwyn altogether too loudly, "Got two sani-pads down my pants, just in case".

There was no reply from Clarrissa.

By the time Maldwyn shuffled round the corner, further along the corridor from the lift, a stunned silence seemed to have enveloped her.

The sort of hovering, settling silence that washes over someone who has momentarily realised that they have only been in work for five minutes, but, already their day has descended into abject, absolute, dissolute and irredeemable mountains of shit.

Had Maldwyn turned around he would have seen Clarrissa, open mouthed, and holding a sagging ginger nut biscuit over her smouldering tea cup. She had on her chubby face the kind of look you expect to see from pigs in abattoirs just after the stun bolt has knocked them senseless.

Clarrissas' ginger nut, which she was dunking happily in her first cup of tea of the day, disintegrated, fractured and plunged into the hot liquid, leaving only a small morsel clutched between her thumb and forefinger. The ginger nuts dive was an uncomfortable belly flop in Olympic terms, no twin pike double somersault followed by a delicate entry; it was a real bomber. Its splash sent droplets of sticky glutinous ginger all over her paperwork, and spitting up the front of her fresh, and newly cleaned, white blouse.

As she paused, she pondered for a fleeting second or two, the possibility, but, at the same time, the total pointlessness of a reply. Finding nothing even remotely suitable as a response; (and time never being on the side of a hot, tea soaked biscuit), the last vestigial remains of the ginger nut also plopped, noisily, and messily into the tea cup. Wiping the splashes from her once pristine blouse, she uttered the single word:

"Twat!"

She did so in the barely audible, but potent tones that only librarians can produce. Whether she was referring to Maldwyn, or the ginger nut, we will probably never know for certain.

But my money would be on Maldwyn.

In this instance, (incident), is encapsulated the fundamentals of why Maldwyn Somerset, was, (and would, more than likely, remain so), a bachelor.

Even more fundamentally, it demonstrates why, he, and the Amethyst brothers, (although shipwrecked in a sea of relative normality), had inevitably found one another, and clambered aboard the same metaphoric life raft.

Once he had set down his carrier bag, and overcoat, placing one item on each of the chairs in front of micro-fishe monitors two and three respectively, (to discourage unwelcome interlopers); Maldwyn laid out neatly, (next to each of the

116

first three monitors), the yellow 'Reserved Slips', he had collected from Anton earlier. He then padded off to the micro-fishe archive vault enquiries desk.

He knew exactly what he was looking for, and, waving his pink 'fee paid' card at Lauren, who stood, shuffling papers, behind the public counter enquiries desk, he said:

"South Wales Echo, and Western Mail, from January 1st 1942, until December 30th 1946 please. Also, Department of Health and Social Security Records for the same dates".

1972, was well before the Data Protection Act, and back in the days when the world wanted to get everything on micro-fishe.

"Micro-fishe" was the new word, (or words), all 'Pseudo Governmental Organs of Repression', (as Maldwyn and the Amethyst brothers liked to refer to them); fought with each other to get the biggest banks of micro-fishe screens, and the biggest micro-fishe cassette archive libraries known to man. The D.H.S.S., was no exception, and strived valiantly to lead this charge; spending fortunes in getting every living souls details onto innumerable copies of plastic micro-fishe cartridges. They then scattered them to every corner of this sceptered isle, so that any 'Herbert' or 'Wilson' with a library card, could find out anything he wanted to, about you and me.

Now-a-days, it makes front page news, and item on the B.B.C., if some 'Dick-Sweet' from Swannage, (with nothing better to do), finds two sheets of paper left on a train seat, containing details of some poor nobody's vasectomy.

If, by some quirk of fate, one miserable morning, you, (the reader), should find such a stash of accidentally lost official looking documents; try this:-

Instead of scrambling for your mobile, to phone the Daily Whatnot, or Sky News, just pick up the offending papers, tear them to shreds no bigger than a postage stamp, and throw them in the nearest fucking bin, and carry on with your life.

Lauren, jotted down Maldwyns requirements on her metal spring bound notepad, smiled at him, and disappeared through the double doors behind her, into the archive stores.

He could not help but glance at her rear end as she walked away, the curvature of which was accentuated by her leather skirt, and knee high boots, with heels that made her sway as she walked. She swayed in a way that only women in leather skirts and high heels can sway, like a gentle, well polished pendulum, just a little too long for the clock it served.

'Oh!'

He mused to himself.

If only he was twenty years younger, thinner, better looking, a bit taller, with more hair and less spots, (and remotely interesting), he may stand a chance.

But he doubted it.

Within seconds she returned, her perfect teeth, perfect hair, perfect eyes, perfect breasts, and perfect skin beaming at him.

"There you go Maldwyn, give me a shout if you need anything else".

Her tones were dulcet, and her Cardiff accent rich with obscene vowels.

'Oh! If only.'

She handed him five micro-fishe cartridges, all piled neatly, and in date order.

Maldwyn took them clumsily, (a crap gypsy fortune teller could have predicted it), and they began to escape his grip.

He juggled with them for a split second, like a T.V. amateur juggler, who is really a baker, or a plumber, but entered as a contestant, in one of those talent shows where most of the contestants haven't got a talented bone in their entire gene pool, and winds up with zero on the 'Clapometer'. If it was ancient Rome and not 1972 the feckless entrant would have been hauled off to the nearest log and shagged to death by rampant Hippopotami or the like.

Then, inevitably, Maldwyn dropped them, three on the counter and two on the floor, he then accidentally kicked one of the cartridges he had dropped on the floor, and it careened towards the monitors, as he tried unsuccessfully to mitigate his Kak-handedness.

As he collected the cartridges off the desk, he attempted a smile at Lauren. It was one of those smiles you see from people in asylums for the criminally insane, as they try to shove star shaped plastic shapes, into bus shaped plastic holes.

When he bent down to retrieve the cartridges he had dropped on the floor, he felt something pop in his anus, and a sharp pain shot from his arsehole to his bell-end.

Maldwyn let out a dog like yelp, and gave silent thanks for the two sani-pads in his underpants. Rising, somewhat carefully, (and almost like watching something in slow motion), he turned and smiled gingerly towards Lauren. Noticing the incredulous look on her face, felt obliged to make some explanation.

"Fucking piles!"

He explained, through grimaced features.

Lauren nodded politely, and escaped through the double doors as quickly as her leather skirt and high heels would allow.

Maldwyn walked, (like someone with a Hoover stuck up their bottom), back to monitor station one, and sat, (extremely gently), down.

He wished he had not tendered an explanation to Lauren, and construed that, (in ideal circumstances); the phraseology could have been improved.

With a pinched look on his face, Maldwyn poured himself a cup of Nescafe from his flask, and extricated another corned beef and Branstone pickle sandwich from his carrier bag. He also placed in front of him, his bundle of pens, and timetable notepads.

As he chomped on the sandwich, he shoved, (with unnecessary force), the first cartridge into monitor one; this being the earliest 'South Wales Echo' micro-fishe. Leaning uncomfortably across the table length, and holding his sandwich between his teeth, he then inserted the earliest 'Western Mail' cartridge into monitor two, and the 'D.H.S.S.' cartridge into monitor three.

He dropped small dollops of Branstone pickle onto the table top as he moved, then picked them up, as spare hands became available, and popped them delicately into his mouth. Piles or no piles, Maldwyn Somerset was not a man to waste Branstone Pickle.

He toyed, momentarily with opening one of his 'Curly Wurly's', but decided it was probably too early.

"It's never too early for a Curly Wurly!"

Maldwyn said quietly to himself.

As an afterthought, he wrote the entire short sentence on top of one of his timetable note pads, along with a second note to himself, to send it off to 'Cadburys', as a possible slogan they could use, in return for a lifetime supply of 'Curly Wurly's'.

However, like a Naval Officer, with rum, Maldwyn would not eat chocolate until the sun was over the Yardarm, and unlike Oscar Wilde, resisted the temptation.

Unusually for Maldwyn, (and generally rare in most attempts at historical research); he struck gold almost immediately, or at least after about an hour, which is virtually the same thing.

It was a small 'stop press' item in a back page entry in the South Wales Echo, late evening edition of 9th February 1943.

It carried a brief eight line entry, (amongst other 'stop press' entries of unassociated losses), concerning, His Majesty's Australian Navy convoy ref. OC8. The small article confirmed the loss; by Japanese torpedo, of an Australian merchant ship, the 'SS Iron Knight', in the early hours of February 8th off the coast of New South Wales.

In a flash, and piles not-withstanding, Maldwyn had changed seats to monitor number two, flinging his carrier bag onto the floor by the chair as he moved. After some frantic flicking of switches and spinning of knobs, he found what he was looking for. There it was, on page 8, of the 'Western Mail', early morning edition, of 12th February 1943. Not a large article, but concise, measured, quite detailed for that time, and, (most importantly to Maldwyn), the first secondary source confirmation of an item that the Amethyst boys had found in the Jacobs Biscuit Tin.

Maldwyn knew in that instant, that the box had just graduated from a "pile of old crap", (as Spinksy had apparently said), to a historical 'Primary Source'. The article went:

> *On February 8th at 2.30 a.m., Western Australia time, the Australian merchantman, the SS Iron Knight, a 4812 ton iron ore carrier, was sunk by a single Japanese torpedo, 18 miles off shore of the port of Newcastle, New South Wales. Japanese radio claims that the submarine I-21 fired the torpedo.*

It was the kind of brief report favoured by reporters during the Second World War, supposedly factual, without compromising secure information. The crucial piece of data however, that the article did not give; was casualties. Maldwyn resolved to investigate further, and would go to the 'Nationals', a more arduous search, but now with a good starting point, it may not be as long drawn out, as it may have been.

Setting aside his earlier embarrassment, he returned to the counter where Lauren now sat again, filling in inventory slips. She stood up as Maldwyn approached; before she could speak, he started, and jumping in before any more embarrassment could engulf him.

"1943, February and March editions of the 'Daily Mail', please".

He made every effort to avoid eye contact, and she immediately scurried off through the double doors. She returned a few moments later with a single cartridge and, without speaking handed it to Maldwyn; though she did smile courteously. And so it was that the awkwardness about Maldwyns arsehole appeared to be all forgiven and forgotten.

However; one could rightly assume that any chance Maldwyn may have had of a fuck with Lauren, was well and truly blown out of the water.

He ejected the D.H.S.S. cartridge from monitor three, and inserted deftly, the 'Daily Mail' one. He searched immediately for the second week of February editions. He found what he needed in the 'Foreign Correspondent' section, on page 15, of the 16th February 1943, evening copy. It consisted of nothing more than a two inch column, which re-iterated the information given in the 'Western Mail', but then finished with:

> ..... *A Royal Australian Naval ship collected*
> *yesterday, from a life boat at sea, some fourteen*
> *survivors, from the recent sinking of the Australian*
> *merchant vessel SS Iron Knight. Thirty six crewmen,*
> *including the First Officer are now feared lost.*

Maldwyn then scanned dozens of national newspaper micro-fishes for anything else he could find on the crew of the S.S. Iron Knight. He was like a ferret after a rat, this was what he loved. He was whirling wheels on the micro-fishe machines, scurrying for books on the miles of shelving, zipping between floors in the lift; and, all the time, scribbling vast amounts notes.

For someone with no formal training, Maldwyns note taking was superb. He had the handwriting of a dyslexic Orang-utan, but his referencing, abridging and indexing, was an absolute joy.

People in Oxford or Cambridge would pay armies of research assistants, hundreds of pounds an hour for someone with Maldyns skills: and the Amethyst boys had him for two tins of 'Fray Bentos', and a loaf of 'Hovis' every Saturday.

Bargain!

The SS Iron Knight.
And his arrival;
Port of Albany,
Western Australia,
January 16th 1943.

The SS Iron Knight was a metal ore freighter of 4812 tons displacement. It spent its repetitive life skirting the southern and eastern shores of Australia, hauling the raw materials of warfare, primarily Iron Ore and Zinc, to and from ports, to the north of Sydney, in New South Wales, all the way around to Perth in Western Australia.

She was built in 1937 by Lithgow's at Port Glasgow on the Clyde in Scotland. She was a single stack twin screw, steel plate cargo vessel with no frills. Her crew of fifty was made up of solid merchantmen; experienced seamen who knew their way around a deck winch, as well as a whisky bottle.

Her engineers were real fitters who could fix things at sea, change bearings in a swell, and free lumps of seized metal with ball-pane hammers, wooden blocks, and sledges. She was a real ship, a proud ship; her cleats were clean, her decks swabbed, her rust spots scraped, and patches of red lead primer were slapped on any welds, anywhere, that showed the slightest salt blister.

Her Captain was Iestyn Tynsdale, a third generation Australian of Welsh descent. A tall, gaunt man, clean shaven and immaculate. Always with a carved Meerschaum dolphin head pipe wedged in the corner of his mouth. His only flaw, (if there has to be one), was the yellow/brown teeth common to addicted pipe smokers. His tobacco was Navy Rough Shag, which he bought in pressed strips, which he then rubbed himself between his rough palms before smoking. He kept it in a leather pouch in his trouser hip pocket complete with a lettuce leaf to stop the 'Baccy' drying out.

Captain Tynsdale had seen action in the first War; having served as a Royal Navy Flag Officer under Admiral John Jellicoe, and Rear Admiral Hugh Evan-Thomas.

He was wounded at the Battle of Jutland in May 1916, and still carried a slight limp of remembrance in his left leg.

Now that the New War was underway, he revelled in regaling his petty officers with tails of the Last War.

In fairness he had quite a distinguished War record, and if one needed to find one word to describe Captain Iestyn Maurice Tynsdale D.S.O.; C.G.M. & Bar; the would be, 'Decent'.

He had a reputation for directness, fastidiousness, and fairness, and had nothing to prove. He was 49 years old, married, with two daughters. His wife and children lived at the family home in the inland city of Toowoomba, Queensland.

The medal ribbons he wore on his pressed white shirt, needed no explanation in naval circles; but for the uninitiated, the purple one, sided on both edges with narrower blue stripes, was the 'Distinguished Service Order'. The other, a wide light grey stripe, flanked by two narrow black edge stripes at either side, was the 'Conspicuous Gallantry Medal'.

The latter, he had received for his actions in the Battle of Jutland, Sub Lieutenant Tynsdale, as he then was, had been aft in the Royal Navy dreadnought, H.M.S. Warspite of the 5th Battle Squadron, under Rear Admiral Hugh Evan-Thomas.

He had been in command of the rear turret of a pair of twelve inch guns, when a shell from the German Battleship, SMS Seydlitz plunged into the deck just in front of them. The explosion had disabled one of the guns, and killed two of the gun crew. Tynsdale and two other men had suffered shrapnel wounds to the legs, but had continued firing the remaining single rear gun, for a further two and a half hours, before being relieved, scoring two hits on the SMS Seydlitz in this time.

The former award, his D.S.O., he had never spoken of, and when asked, by anyone: he had refused point blank to do so.

Captain Tynsdales first Officer was a softly spoken New Zealander, named Cyril De Venneray, capable, athletic, experienced, and in his mid thirties. He now stood beside Tynsdale, facing Prisoner number 89855812; slightly side on, with his right hand gently unclipping his side arm holster flap. He allowed his thumb and forefinger to stroke the grip of the Browning HP 9mm, and made sure that Prisoner number 89855812 saw the movement.

On Captain Tynsdales left, and two paces back stood Midshipman Alex 'Greener' Hawks, a smart looking, self assured twenty something; who you knew, (just by looking at him), would be capable of anything in years to come. It was an undeniable certainty, that, somewhere down the line, Midshipman Alex 'Greener' Hawks, would absolutely definitely, and irrefutably, make a name for himself, at something. Even if it was forging twenty dollar bills.

Both of Tynsdales' teenage daughters, although they had only met Greener once, had fallen madly and secretly in love with him. His natural 'Hollywood looks', (as De Venneray termed it), and the superb tutelage that both men had received from Captain Tynsdale, over the past two years and eight months; (not only in Seamanship, but in simple good old fashioned honourable behaviour); marked Greener out now as a man, and not the remains of a boy.

At his side, hung an open topped, white webbing holster, containing a polished wooden handled Webbley Mk IV, 0.38 revolver. A less sophisticated weapon than the one De Venneray had caressed earlier; but either one would 'kill you stone dead', and make just as big a hole in your future, thought Prisoner number 89855812.

As the two marine privates galloped noisily down the gangplank to the concrete wharf below; Captain Tynsdale, without hesitation, unlocked the convict's handcuffs. He held them up slightly, and pocketed the key.

"Shouldn't be needing these again".

He said matter of factly.

In truth it was a mixture of an order and a question; but he bracketed the sentence with a forthcoming half smile.

Indeed; in those few words, and two small and limited gestures, the Captain had gone some way to changing the prisoner's earlier perspective of his situation. He had left him considering the possibility, (at least), that this could be a better place than that from which he came.

The Captain had also made it clear that infractions of the rules, (rules that Prisoner number 89855812 had yet to learn), would not be tolerated. Yet he had done so without the screaming barracking of Sergeant Fuzzy Dolenz, and without the necessity of the brutality of the Major Cunts and their Marines.

The place had definite possibilities.

Captain Tynsdale turned towards Greener, and said in plain speech.

"Midshipman Hawks; take three hands and escort our new 'Third Stoker' to his quarters, introduce him to any of the boiler room crew that are back aboard yet, and issue him some new number '8' overalls from stores. Show him the 'facilities' while you're about it. Then make sure he gets a good meal and all the hot tea he can drink".

He then turned back towards the prisoner, and in a low, pleasant tone, said, again almost as an order, but not quite.

"Get some sleep, once you've been kitted out, fed and watered. You'll have a busy day tomorrow, you're on the five a.m., shift, and we sail with the tide. You'll remain below decks until we're three miles out, or whenever we're approaching harbour."

He looked his new Stoker straight in the eyes, and with no malice said.

"That's the rules, that's the conditions you put your hand up for. They won't change".

Tynsdale then offered his hand to the prisoner, after all he was closer to a civilian than a sailor, and did not warrant a salute. After some hesitation, Prisoner number 89855812 took it.

Greener had gathered together a group of seamen that were stowing tarpaulins further down the deck, there were three of them; then he and the sailors, without further discussion, took the prisoner away.

"What do you think?"

Asked the Captain of his First Officer, as they watched the group of five men walk along the starboard covered way.

De Veneray replied with his usual conciseness.

"I think we need a stoker Captain; and he looks like he's used a shovel before".

Both men laughed, and Tynsdale clapped his First Officer on the back, puffing billows of pipe smoke into the dusking sticky air.

"It'll be right!"

He said, taking another puff.

"It'll be right!".

Dmitri and the names.
The Dykka and Gonda Articles.
Cardiff,
South Wales.
A Saturday in early April 1972.

Dmitri caught up with Maldwyn, somewhere on the first floor between 'Heavy Oil', and 'Japanese Naval Ranks'.

"You wanted me Maldwyn ?"

A broad Cardiff accent dripped in library soft tones into his ear, as he turned, Maldwyn dropped some of his note pads on the floor, fumbling, he smiled, then replied.

"Ah; Dmitri, my old mucker".

Maldwyn rummaged in his pocket for a scrap of paper which he had written the names on earlier. He handed it, somewhat ungainly, and in the fashion of a circus contortionist to Dmitri. He completed this handover, whilst simultaneously balancing books, notes, and a sandwich, and trying to stand on the notepapers he had dropped earlier.

Once stabilised, he continued;

"Where do these names come from? Somewhere over you're ancestors neck of the woods I think. But I'm hoping you night save me a bit of time like. If you can shed a bit of light see".

Maldwyn, went straight to the point, with no idle time passing, no chit-chat or niceties.

He had no time,
His head was full of ships and funny names,
Of wars and dates and many things,
Of torpedoes, Russians and Australians,
Of Africans
But no Kings.

The world of social skills had completely by-passed Maldwyn Somerset, like a small village isolated by a new motorway.

He smiled affably, some corned beef snuggled between his teeth, and all his running about, excitement, and piles, had made him more sweaty than usual.

"I'll be up on the top floor, by the micro-fishe machines, if you could just jot down a couple of notes, and pop them up to me; be appreciated, know what I mean".

127

Dmitri, who was only about thirty, looked at the paper, then back to Maldwyn, with a degree of astonishment at his sheer cheek. But he could see that Maldwyn was animated about something today, and so, Dmitri resigned himself to the fact that if he wanted Maldwyn off his case, then it was easier just to do as he had been asked.

He glanced down at the paper and replied, in as cheerful a fashion as he could muster.

"I'll make some phone calls to some of the Church elders, and see what I can dig up".

He turned and walked away between the isles of books. Maldwyn shouted after him, ignoring the 'Keep Quiet' signs that peppered the library building:

"I've got to be gone by two-ish, so if you could pull your finger out on that Dmitri, that would be appreciated 'Butt'".

Dmitri kept walking, and raised an acknowledging hand without looking back. If Maldwyn had seen his face, he would have seen Dmitri, silently mouthing the words.

"Fucking Twat!"

As he turned the corner at the end of the isle. Like the attendant with the ginger nuts earlier, and given the choice as to whether or not Dmitris' exclamation referred to Maldwyn or not. I think that, (again), my money would be on Maldwyn.

Maldwyn passed the next hour or more pulling reference books from shelves, skitting through micro-fiche cartridges, requesting more, then skitting through them, making notes, cross referencing, drinking coffee, and eating corned beef and Branston pickle sandwiches.

He had also gone through the first of his Curly Wurly's, which he dunked in his coffee, which melted the surface chocolate to a semi viscose material, and softened the interior toffee core; this made the whole thing, 'All lovely', as Maldwyn termed it.

He had already exceeded his original brief concerning the ships, and Dmitri was on the case with the names. Maldwyn had drawn a blank on the

D.H.S.S. records with nothing flagging up. So he had decided to give his mind some free reign, and do some digging on the South Africa sources. Maldwyn was thumbing through the old notes he had made at his first sit down with Dilwyn and Ellis, after Uncle Bryn, had delivered them the box.

He recalled seeing some old railway ticket stubs from the, 'Cape Government Railways Company'. He checked his notes, and, shuffling through his timetable pad, Maldwyn found his starting point. His notation, as ever was perfect, clear, and concise.

Three tickets, singles, from Pietermaritzburg station, Natal Province to Port St. Johns in the Eastern Cape. The tickets, he had noted, were One Day Singles. This meant that they were bought on that day, and had to be used on that day. Maldwyns notes told him that the day was July 12th 1926, and the tickets cost eight shillings and thrupence each.

Now it is at moments like this, that Maldwyn Somerset is worth his weight in Curly Wurly's. Within minutes he was thumbing through glossary's of newspapers and their owners, checking out the total population of Pietermaritzburg in the 1920's, pulling together maps of railway networks in South Africa at the time, and generally undoing the nuts and bolts of the society he was investigating.

Inside half an hour, he had already handed Lauren a scribbled request for a few more micro-fiche cartridges, and now; as she handed them to him, across the counter; he was about to click into top gear. Eric Hobsbawm and Karl Marx had nothing on Maldwyn and his corned beef and Branston pickle sandwiches when it came to speedy research.

As he sat at micro-fiche monitor number one. The luck of his day, (or was it skill), continued. As his first cartridge yielded, what he later described to Dilwyn and Ellis, as:

"Screaming fucking gold-dust".

Maldwyn had requested local newspapers for one week either side of the date on the railway tickets. He had opened a fresh page in his bus timetable notepad, and had already made a coffee cup ring on it, with a small blob of melted chocolate to the left of it. But it didn't matter to Maldwyn, he was already scribbling furiously with a green biro, and underlining, 'special bits', as he called them in red.

Dates he underlined in blue, and names and places he circled in black. Source references he wrote at the bottom of each page, in the relevant colour to that to which the source referred. That is, blue for dates, black for names and places, green for general information, and red for specifics, or particularly pertinent items.

On the screen in front of him, Maldwyn, had displayed, a page of 'The Natal Witness', daily newspaper, dated July 13th 1926. The day after the train tickets in the box. There was a stop press item, stating:

Stop Press, 12.28 a.m., July 14th 1926
Pietermaritsburg Natal Province, South Africa.
Pietermaritzburg Local Magistrate; Mr. T.A.
Jackson Jakeseni, and Town Clerk, Mr. W.T.
Williams, confirmed, just after midnight, that the
bodies of two men, had been discovered at a lodging
house in the Port Napier district of town, near the
Eastern Railway Terminus. Natal Police captain,
Raymond Dospar, and South Africa Mounted Rifles,
Police contingent Major, Dieter Umbarstek,
confirmed that witnesses say that three people were
seen in the vicinity, a day or so previous, and that
two of them seemed to be helping the third man, who
may be injured. The police also said that one of the
people they are seeking, may be a woman. There is
no further information regarding the dead men at
this time.

Maldwyn had also discovered an article in the 'Eastern Province Herald', dated 15th July 1926. It read:

Captain, Raymond Dospar, of the Natal Police Force, confirmed that the bodies of two men found in Pietermaritzburg on the 14th of July, just past, were those of local businessman, Mr. Jan Dykka Van Hoost, and former Cape Government Railways Executive, Mr. Gonda Vischen.

South Africa Mounted Rifles, Police contingent Major, Dieter Umbarstek, said that Mr. Van Hoost had been shot twice in the head, and once in the chest, and that Mr Vischen had been stabbed repeatedly in the face, chest and abdomen.

He also said that the hunt for the perpetrators had been extended as far as Durban, and the Eastern Cape, and that the authorities were seeking three people in connection with the slayings. There is evidence from witnesses at the scene and surrounding areas, that, although dark, one of the suspects is probably a woman.

The search continues.

Maldwyn found no less than sixteen other newspaper entries concerning the crime, in papers from Johannesburg to Cape Town. Articles ranging from a one inch column, to quarter page *'exposes'* of Mr. Van Hoost, and Mr. Vischer, and their respective business dealings, both legitimate, and otherwise.

The Van Der Kyper Brothers,
The 'Big match'
Mambo, the Indians, Eloise,

131

And when it all started to go wrong.

Pietermartzburg,

July 1924.

Crusher Hohner arrived at Pietermaritzburg Railway station on the 18th July 1924. It was a Saturday and quarter to one on a hot afternoon.

There to meet him, from the 'Rhodesian Trans African Railways' steam locomotive 'R.T.A.R. Cecil Rhodes', from Bulawayo, was Mambo the chauffeur. Standing to attention, and in full regalia, on platform three awaiting his charge, he looked every inch the Darkie flunky.

The train was resplendent in its dark red, black and gold livery, with its name emblazoned in raised cast iron letters on its nose and curved sides. Jets of steam whooshed from it, spilling over the platform; and the bustle of black porters with white caps and green jackets hummed, as they dragged their trolleys of luggage from platform to platform to outside world.

Mambo had already grabbed a porter, and kept him close for fear of his escaping to a more generous customer. The porters were all from the 'G.W. Hollins Cartage Company', (who ran the station porters, and kicked back to Dykka for the privilege); Mambo pressed a shilling into the man's hand to ensure his commitment. The shilling had been provided by Dykka Van Hoost for this very purpose; and Mambo was above carrying bags on railway stations.

He enjoyed his authority over the porter.

As the steam cleared and the passengers began to disembark from the carriages, the unmistakeable frame of Crusher Hohner flickered into view from the carriage immediately behind the locomotives tender. It was a first class carriage, and Crusher had revelled in having an entire compartment to himself. He had stretched his heavy feet across the thick upholstery. He had kept his boots on for the entire journey, and had scuffed the weave of the seats mercilessly.

As was his reputation.

Mambo, who was about thirty yards away, gestured towards him, and turning to the captured porter and his trolley, said simply:

"Bags!"

He nodded towards the newly disembarked giant. Crusher did not move, but acknowledged Mambo's gesture with the merest hint of a nod of his head. The porter ran towards Crusher. Mambo did his best to walk, 'in an official and dignified manner', as Dykka had instructed him, at his office some days earlier.

As he approached Crusher, Mambo realised just how big this man was. 'The Elephant' was big: tall, wide, and hard; but this man was immense. Mambo had never seen such a man, he was, (Mambo estimated), at least six feet eight inches tall, with a face that would fit snuggly in a box, clean shaven with short cropped blond hair, and covered with skin that looked as though it had been stretched over him at a Tan-Yard.

His clothes, a plain dark suit with white shirt, and blue tie seemed to struggle to contain his body, and his hands, each the size of one of Banjos' coal shovels, hung loosely at his sides, with knuckles that looked as hard as the 'Hard Black Stuff'.

Once Mambo stood before him, and could see that the porter was trollying Crushers luggage; he clicked his heels, and saluted, as Dykka had instructed. Crusher smiled, more to himself than anything else, then said, looking down at the chauffeur; simply, and in a broad Afrikaans accent:

"Take me to the Hotel, I need a bath".

Mambo saluted for a second time, turned and led the way outside to Dykkas car and the hotel.

The porter followed five paces behind Crusher.

As they walked through the station, everyone looked at Crusher, men jealously, women admiringly, others greedily. Many already knew who he was, and why he was here.

Outside the station, two cops stood by Dykkas' car. Like Mambo, they too were under instruction. They would make sure that Crusher got safely to his hotel, with no delays, and no accidents, at the end of the week, as always; they would each collect one pound from Dykka, and another pound from the offices of Gonda Vischer.

Across town, in an expensive restaurant on Loop Street, opposite their suites at 'The Imperial Hotel', The Van Der Kyper Brothers sat at an overdressed corner table with Dykka Van Hoost, and Gonda Vischer, eating under-dressed crab.

Dykka was in his usual tweeds, complete with diamond tie pin, and eternal cheroot. The other three men wore sombre dark suits with suitable shirts and ties. All smoked, and the ashtrays were beginning to fill with shop bought, imported, 'Players Navy Cut' cigarette butts.

"I hear this Srinivasa Sastri is causing you
sleepless nights Dykka."

Said Louis Van Der Kyper, the elder of the two brothers. He came directly to his points with accuracy and bluntness. Dykka looked at Gonda slightly uncomfortably; he had not expected such a plain approach.

"No one causes me sleepless nights!"

Dykka heard himself reply, but mentally cursed himself for this fruitless show of bravado.

Bernard, the younger Van Der Kyper seized on the moment, leaned forward across the table, and rejoined with:

"Then why the fuck are we here? You think we'd come all this way to watch two gorillas smash the shit out of each other?"

Bernard was as direct as his older brother, but somehow, (Gonda thought), lacked his siblings finesse.

Dykka bit back.

"You've got your own problems with the Wogs, same as us! It's not just Sastri. He's the tip of the ice berg, he may be the appointed 'Indian Agent', but it's the others. Fuck me, they've even started importing tobacco!"

He pointed at the Players Cigarette butts in the ashtrays.

"And they don't even fucking smoke. And I hear that when you ship your ore north from Bulawayo, they don't go in your rail trucks anymore, they go in wog trucks, on lines run by wogs, guzzling coal that they don't buy from us anymore, because they get it from more fucking wogs. The biggest fucking mistake this country made was not shooting that cunt Gandhi when we had the chance!"

Gonda tried to take the heat out of the situation, and interjected, stating that all their businesses were beginning to suffer, and that the general consensus both in South Africa and Rhodesia was that the Indians were becoming a, he paused seeking the right phrase. Then, failing, finished with:

"Pain in the arse".

And that they were here tonight to, he paused again, and failed again, he concluded with:

"Do something about it".

Despite Gondas poor delivery, his sentiment hit home.

The men all nodded in agreement, and Louis beckoned to a waiter for another bottle of '*Perrier Jiouet*', and to clear away the entrée dishes.

The Austin Twenty had parked outside the 'Norfolk Hotel', where Dykka had arranged a front room with a private bath for Crusher. The hotel was only a stones throw from the Railway Station, and the car ride, escorted by the police van, and the two officers; had taken less than ten minutes.

Mambo, had completed his duties well; and had got Crusher fully ensconced and comfortable, and explained food, drink and training arrangements to him; and all by one thirty p.m. He told him that he would call in every morning at ten a.m., to see if there was anything he needed, and that the car, (and he), would be at Crushers full disposal.

Crusher had thanked him politely, and gave him half a crown.

Mambo decided, that, based upon his first hand, close up experience of the big Kraut, that Crusher would,

"Beat seven colours of shit out of The Elephant."

Mambo had over fifty quid saved up, and decided that he would risk twenty of it, on a big bet on Crusher. He resolved to drive to Meleens, and put the bet on with Fat Malcolm Mpopo. He would get better odds there, as it was a strict 'Nigger Neighbourhood', and they would probably never get to see Crusher in real life, and certainly not see the fight. But there had been a lot of people at the railway station, and the cops had big mouths, so Mambo knew the word would spread quick about Crusher, and his gargantuan appearance. Mambo, could not wait, he would collect his money now, and drive to Maleens, and get the bet on, before anyone else could get the word to 'Fat Malcolm' about Crusher, so that he could slash the odds.

"It's not just Srinivasa Sastri"

Said Louis Van Der Kyper, his voice had a slightly effeminate edge which made Dykka inexplicably uncomfortable. Louis stopped speaking as the waiter distributed the Lemon Soles, asparagus, and boiled potatoes with parsley, and topped up their Champaign flutes. Once the waiter moved away, he continued.

"It's the I.A.C. that's the root of the infection, they campaign tirelessly with our respective governments, and in London as well for heavens sake, for the removal of what they call, 'Unfair Laws'. Every bloody street corner in Africa will have an 'Indian Chamber of Commerce' on it by 1930 at this rate. It really must stop".

He took a drink of his Champaign, puffed his cigarette, put it in the ashtray, picked up his silver fish knife and fork, and began eating.

"Mmm!"

He exclaimed.

"This sole really is delicious".

Dykka addressed him directly, and confirmed that the, so called, 'Indian Delegation of Unity' meeting of all the 'Indian Commerce Organisations', and the 'Indian African Congress Presidium', were still meeting in Pietermaritzburg, over the 25th to the 28th of June coming. The fight between Crusher Hohner and The Elephant, was scheduled for the 27th; the Saturday.

"So the dates are all set, the same as discussed at our last meeting?"

Asked Benard, seeking confirmation.

"It's all set".

Confirmed Gonda, tucking into his fish course, and swilling a little too much champagne.

"The big night is the 27th, they've booked the Constitutional Hall, on Church Street, from ten in the morning until nine thirty in the evening, there'll be speeches, resolutions, commendations, all sorts of shit. The night of the fight; absolutely perfect for us, exactly as we discussed, nothing has altered".

Dykka interjected with;

"And they couldn't have picked a place further from the 'Dorp Spruet' if we had asked them!"

"The 'Dorp Spruet'?"

Enquired Louis.

"The River man! The River!"

Answered Dykka sharply.

"If there was ever a fire in that Constitutional Hall, the fire brigade would be using buckets, and pissing on it to put it out. Either that or they'd need hoses a fucking mile long."

"Oh dear, what a shame"; replied Louis, with a wry grin, and continuing with his meal. He turned to Gonda and said;

"This really is a very fine restaurant you know Mr. Vischer, far better than anything we have in Bulawayo".

"What about Crevitt, Mousafan and Tandis, we want nothing left to chance; you must feel the same about Sastri?"

Asked Bernard Van Der Kyper, speaking a little too loudly. He looked directly at Dykka.

"You know that's all arranged".

Dykka replied.

Feeling that he now had the upper hand; he pressed on.

"Our man from Jo'Burg comes in on Thursday, one of my lorries is bringing him up overnight with his kit, he'll be staying with Mambo, (one of my men), out of town. Out of sight. After it's done I've arranged a freighter transport for him from Maputo in Mozambique to Zanzibar, all good blokes, all reliable, all mine".

Dykka took a mouthful of champagne before continuing.

"My man will need picking up at Bulawayo Station, and taking to the coast, that's a three hundred mile trek, so you'll need a reliable truck and two good blokes".

"Leave that end to us", Bernard said, taking a noisy slurp of his champagne. His brother Louis gave him a distasteful look, disapproving his coarseness.

"We've also got the guys fixed up at Beitbridge Tunnel, hole ready dug",

Bernard finished off with, dribbling some champagne down his chin.

They all laughed.

"Sounds like absolute clockwork".

Louis interjected, and laughed again, raising his glass in a mock toast, they all reciprocated.

Dykka took the opportunity, as it presented itself, (and taking advantage of the good mood around the table), to remind the Van Der Kyper brothers of the costs, a thousand pound to the man from Jo'Berg, plus two hundred quid to the Captain of the freighter, and at least another two or three hundred for backhanders to the port harbour-men etcetera to look the other way. Not to mention the transport costs from Jo'Berg up to here and back.

Louis interrupted him, and said:

"Of course Dykka; do forgive us, I almost forgot, we did discuss it previously, I trust this will suffice for the moment as our share".

Louis put down, (reluctantly), his cutlery, and, reached inside his jacket pocket. He slid across the table to Dykka, a certified cheque for two thousand pounds.

"This includes the purse money for the fight, we'll square any balance if there is one, after the event. I trust this is satisfactory gentlemen?"

He looked at both Gonda and Dykka in turn. They acknowledged, and Dykka raised his glass once more, in a silent toast to the Van Der Kyper brothers, and their joint ventures.

Dmitri and the names.
Cardiff,
A Saturday in early April 1972.

As he spun the monitor control knobs with his left hand, and made notes with his right, and held a half eaten sandwich between his teeth; Maldwyn was conscious, (out of the corner of his eye), of Dmitri approaching him clutching a sheet of paper.

Maldwyn took a bite of the sandwich, and placed the remains on the table in front of him. Dmitri looked at it a little disapprovingly, though the subtle rebuke went straight over Maldwyn's head.

"These names, you've given me, they're not Russian in the true sense of the word", Dmitri said, "and certainly not Russian Orthodox."

He paused.

Maldwyn took another chomp of his sandwich and replaced it on the table top. He then asked Dmitri to carry on, spitting bits of sandwich on him as he asked. Dmitri gave another wasted disapproving look and continued.

"But you were right in thinking that they were kind of, 'our neck of the woods', as you said."

Dmitri paused again and looked at Maldwyn before continuing.

"My grandfather, who I've just spoken to on the phone, is sure they are *Y'hude Ashk'naz* , Ashkenazi Jews."

Maldwyn made notes as they spoke, and Dmitri ploughed on.

"My Grandfather and his sister-in-law seem to think that the type of name, suggests Crimean Jews, or at least Black Sea regional origins".

Maldwyn became animated, and banging the point of his pen on his timetable note pad, (making deep green dots on it), he said, getting progressively louder as he spoke.

"That explains it! That explains it!"

"Explains what?"

Dmitri asked, a quizzical look on his face, framed by his long curly locks.

Maldwyn looked up at him from his seat, and continued, somewhat disjointedly.

"Two villages, Greniko and Gwalikin Palatinsk, here in my notes from Dilwyn and Ellis; I checked them earlier, downstairs, in an old atlas you've got on the first floor. The two of them are only a kick in the arse away from Odessa, on the Black Sea".

Maldwyn laughed out loud.

The laughter of someone for whom previously abstract and random Kaleidoscope images were beginning to come together to form hazy, but discernable pictures of a real life. Suddenly, Maldwyns animation plunged into silence, a look of machinery whirring, crept across his face, a look of bits of jigsaws dropping into place. Furrows appeared on his brow like a newly ploughed field in the rain. He returned to his notes, and thumbed through furiously. He stopped dead, holding his notes, and moving his head as he mentally read.

He looked back up at Dmitri, it was one of those Maldwyn moments when he had found previously unrelated number two's and had just made them equal four's.

He burst out with,

"I'll bet this photo, the Amethyst boys have got of a Turkish ship, is more than just an unrelated photo, I made notes on it the other day".

Maldwyn continued to rifle through his pad, while he continued to ramble.

"I'll bet that ship lugged in and out of Odessa, on the Black Sea. It was as much a Turkish Lake after the First War, as it was a bloody Russian one!"

He paused as he found the note he was hunting for.

"Here it is!"

He tried to say the name he had written down, he stuttered, and spat as he tried to get his tongue around it.

"The *Cok Guzel Denizala Baligi*".

"The beautiful salmon", said Dmitri.

Maldwyn looked at him as if he gone suddenly insane.

"What!"

Maldwyn asked, his face in a contortion of painful enquiry.

"That's what it means"; continued Dmitri.

"Or at least something like that. I did a module in Turkish at university; as you said, it's almost my neck of the woods".

Maldwyn, reached out and took Dmitri's hand, and shook it vigorously, and thanked him, and spat on him again, unintentionally. Dmitri acknowledged Maldwyns appreciation with a tortured smile, the kind of smile a serrated knife makes in a rotting carrot.

As he turned and left, Dmitri wiped his hand on the side of his jeans.

The Afternoon of 6th June 1944
D-Day.
Aboard the H.M.A.S. Waterhen.
Three miles off the Normandy coast.

Captain Tynsdale and First Officer Greener Hawks re-read the telegram order from the U.S.S. Saratoga. Both men stood on the bridge of the H.M.A.S. Waterhen in full battle dress with steel helmet, life vest, and side arms.

They had been assigned to mine sweeping and artillery support detail for the British and Canadian landings at 'Sword' and 'Juno' beaches. But the landings had met with lighter than expected resistance, and they had been ordered south, (along with every other gunned vessel that could be spared), to support the American landings at 'Utah' and 'Omaha' beaches further south along the coast.

"We're just about where we are supposed to be now"; said the Captain, and he pointed to the headland about three miles away.

"That's got to be *Point Du Hoc*!"

Greener Hawks nodded his head in agreement, his British design steel helmet wobbling as he did so, and he adjusted the chin strap to make it more secure.

"Ten thousand yards, and forty five degrees, Sir, guns are ready, and maximum range. We should drop the shells about two miles inland; well clear of the Yanks, and blocking up any Kraut withdrawals or reinforcements".

Greener turned back towards captain Tynsdale, and added, (almost apologetically).

"It's the best we can do from this range, and we're already being targeted by the shore batteries, any further in and we'd be easy pickings for those Kraut SIG 33 150's".

Captain Tynsdale, thought for a moment, and re-read the telegram order once more. At that moment two shells screamed overhead, and splashed, a hundred yards or so further out to sea, both men ducked.

The noise all around was deafening.

Incoming shells from the German shore battery exploded in the sea all around them; and Allied shells from the large capital ships, ten miles further out to sea, whistled over the Waterhen, heading a further ten miles inland, to disrupt and destroy German armoured brigades, making their way to the coast.

"Give the order to fire Number One, and keep firing till we run out of shells. Run up and down the coast at half ahead, and zig-zag as she goes. Let's not make it too easy for the bastards".

Captain Tynsdale folded the order and shoved it inside his life vest. Greener Hawks acknowledged the order with a casual salute, and left the bridge.

Inside two minutes the Waterhen's small guns were firing at maximum rate, and at maximum range. Every man aboard did his job silently, efficiently, and in solemn and well intentioned prayers for his own survival.

In the engine room, the mechanics busied themselves with ensuring that every moving part was oiled and running smoothly. This was not the time for a mechanical breakdown: as, 'dead in the water', would mean exactly that. Stoko's job was to control the flow of fuel oil to the boilers, and make sure that the pressure was maintained. If the Captain called for full speed, he had to make sure it was available, with no delay. Captain Tynsdale, and First Officer Hawks had learnt from experience that Stoko, and the rest of the engine room crew, could be relied upon when the chips were down.

The Waterhen continued her traverses up and down the *Point Du Hoc*, promontory, firing as she went for a further three hours. She had also, and against better judgement, moved about half a mile closer to shore to create a creeping barrage between two and two and a half miles inland.

All around them American landing craft cut curving wakes towards the beaches, making sharp turns as shells burst in front, or to the sides of them. Occasionally, one would take a direct hit, and the air above it would fill with a fine red mist, shards of metal, droplets of fuel oil, and a profusion of body parts. Those men that survived such a direct hit, generally drowned under the weight of their packs, or were mowed down by the next landing craft on that line.

The 'Officer of The Deck', clambered into the bridge, soaking wet from the spray of the ever nearing explosions. He said to the Captain, shouting above the deafening shell bursts.

"We only have ammunition for another fifteen minutes, at this rate Sir!"

Tynsdale responded immediately.

"Get her back as we fire, let's get out to maximum distance, then find the Exeter, and the auxiliaries, and re-stock."

He turned to the Communications Officer who was also on the bridge, and shouted above the din;

"Make to the Saratoga, let them know what we're doing, and ask for fresh orders for our return".

As the Captain turned away, back towards the Deck Officer, there was a massive explosion less than fifty metres to starboard. Every window on the starboard side of the bridge housing, burst into a thousand pins of razor sharp plexi-glass, filling the bridge with flying shards. The Communications Officer who was closest to the windows was killed immediately, literally sliced into a hundred small pieces, reduced to a gelatinous lump, quivering on the deck plates. The Deck Officer and Helmsman were badly cut about the back of their heads, and hands; but had been facing to port at the time of the blast, and were on the port side of the bridge; their wounds, though bleeding profusely, were superficial.

Captain Tynsdale, however had been facing to starboard, and standing, almost directly behind the Communications Officer; whose body had shielded him from most of the flying shards. But, as the Communications Officer had disintegrated, a football sized cloud of plexi-glass pins had passes through the Comms Officer, and hit the Captain full in the face. He had been blinded instantly, with all the soft tissue of his cheeks and his eyeballs being destroyed by the shotgun glass. His hands raised in reflex to his face as he flew across the bridge with the blast wave, coming to rest, completely unconscious against the grey steel of the binnacle housing.

On the deck, and at the starboard rail, First Officer Greener Hawks looked out to sea, at the still settling debris.

A German shell, a 150mm, had hit a landing craft square on. The vessel must have been carrying additional ammunition, as well as troops in to shore.

He could see men in the water, maybe five, or even eight. He recalled his own feelings after the sinking of the old Iron Knight. He looked up, and saw the decimation unfolding in the bridge house, medics, and deck hands, were streaming towards there, clambering up the metal staircases, and hoop ladders.

Against all standing orders, and using the deck pipes to the engine room, Greener ordered:

"All stop!"

Shouting at the top of his voice; he then ordered his midshipman, who was standing behind him, to get up to bridge and throw the wheel ninety degrees to starboard. The midshipman, acknowledged, gave no salute, and ran off towards the bridge. Returning to the deck pipe, Greener yelled

"Half astern slow!"

Then, almost immediately, he screamed once more into the deck pipe.

"All stop!"

Without any further delay, he turned towards the stern of the ship, and still shouting, and to no one in particular, issued instructions to get the side clambour nets over to starboard. Then returning to the deck pipe, screeched,

"All spare hand to the main deck, lend a hand on the starboard side railing; at the double".

Within seconds the first of the below deck crewmen, were topside at the starboard rail. As they arrived at his side, Greener turned towards the front gun turrets, and cupping his hands around his mouth, screamed as loudly as he could:

"Keep those guns firing!"

He then turned aft, and yelled the same order. Grabbing Stoko, by the arm, and pointing over the side, he told him to take two or three men, or whatever could be spared, and get the men in the water up the clambour nets as quickly as possible.

Leaning over the guardrail, Greener screamed at the men in the water to swim for the clambour nets. This instruction was not required; those that could were already making their way towards the Waterhen kicking at the sea with all the strength they could muster.

The tension on deck was as hard as the Captains Ironbark cane. The entire ships company knew that a stationary vessel would attract the attention of every German shore battery within range. The Waterhen, had already drawn this attention, and she was being straddled by shells from several batteries already.

Stoko was at the bottom of the clambour net, with one leg up to his thigh in the sea, above him was three other crewmen, helping the survivors up towards the guardrail. There was one man left foundering in the swelling waves. He was a young man in his early twenties, and, unlike the other survivors who were all Yanks; this man had a British steel helmet still strapped to his head, and a full pack strapped to his back. He was about fifteen yards away from the ships side, and clearly struggling. As he went under for the third time, Stoko released his grip on the clambour net, and allowed himself to fall the five foot into the cold sea. He also, (in these eternal seconds), recalled fleetingly his time in the water after the sinking of the Iron Knight.

As he broke surface, Stoko scanned the heaving skin of the water, and saw the British tin hat bobbing in the light salt swell. He swam towards it as quickly as he could, remembering sharply as he went just how difficult it was to swim in boots and heavy overalls.

As he reached the man, he sank again. Stoko reached down beneath the surface, and grabbed the mans webbing, swearing him back to the deafening air. He turned the soldier onto his back, put his arm across his chest, and began kicking back towards the clambour net. From the guardrail high above him, he could see the First Officer, leaning over the rails, his mouth moving silently against the background horror. The soundless mouth told him to hurry up. He could hear nothing above the shell bursts, and aircraft flying overhead, and the engines of the hundreds of other landing craft and the myriad of ships in the water; but Greeners message was clear enough.

As Stoko reached the clambour net, the other men who were hanging there took the soldier from him, and hauled him up. As he passed the man over him, Stoko saw that he wore the uniform of a British Officer, a Major in the Royal Welsh Fusiliers. Under his battle dress, and at his neck, Stoko could see he wore the black vest and white dog collar of a Chaplain, and on his lapel he wore two small gold crosses.

The officer was completely unconscious now, and had to be manhandled aboard.

As Stoko's hand touched the clambour net, Greener Hawks, returned to the deck pipe, and shouted as he had been shouting all day it seemed;

"All ahead full!"

He glanced over the side to make sure Stoko was on his way up the netting, and yelled, again to no one in particular;

"Get that netting stowed, as soon as that man's aboard!"

He then turned to the bridge, where the Midshipman was leaning out of one of the shattered windows; and, again cupping his hands to his mouth, shouted up at him,

"Hard to port Mr Fielding, hard to port!"

Within a few moments the Gunnery officers had informed Greener that the ammunition was exhausted. He, shouted again to the bridge, his rasped voice hoarsening with every word, to instruct Mr Fielding to head out to sea at full speed, and that he would give him the course towards the Exeter, and the auxiliary supply ships once he had sorted things out on the main deck.

Mr. Fielding needed no second instruction, the wheel was swung to starboard and the bow pointed towards the horizon. A huge and thankful wake bubbled furiously behind the H.M.A.S. Waterhen.

Half an hour later, she was well out of range of the shore batteries, and the whole ship had breathed a sigh of relief that could have been heard in Darwin.

The Captain had been tended to by the ships medical team, (both of them), his wounds were washed, bandaged, and morphine administered. This was all that was available.

He now slept.

The Deck Officer and the Helmsman both wore heavy dressings on the back of their heads, and hands, and were struggling to drink large mugs of steaming cocoa.

The British Officer, had regained consciousness, and been given some dry overalls to go with his cocoa. He had explained to Greener Hawks, that he had responded to a request from the American Ranger Division for a temporary replacement Chaplain, after their own had been stricken with appendicitis, two days earlier. He explained that he had been in Felixtowe visiting relatives the week before embarkation. So his Commanding Officer had made it clear to him, that he was the obvious choice, (given his location), and that he was that 'volunteer', and had in fact already been 'volunteered' to help out 'The Yanks in their hour of need', as he had put it.

"You can imagine my gratitude", the officer had said, and smiled at Greener over the rim of his steaming tin mug.

Both men shared a momentary escape in this whisp of humour.

The Deck Officer and the Helmsman would return to duty in two days time. Captain Iestyn Tynsdale would be blind for the rest of his life, and return to his wife and Family, in Toowoomba, New South Wales three months hence.

The young British Officer would prove to be a worthwhile saving.

He would go on to be attached to the American Rangers for the next eight months.

He would earn a purple heart from the American Government, and a Military Cross from the British.

He would be there at the crossing of the Rhine.

He would be there at the entry into Belsen concentration camp.

He would try not to change. Try to hold on tight to his humanity.

He would fail.

His young wife, a W.A.F. corporal, posted to the South Coast of England after the war, would be killed in a freak railway accident in 1962. They would have no children.

His wartime experiences would haunt the young man deep into old age.

147

The young mans name was Major Iolo Pugsley.

The night of the big match.
Pietermaritzburg.
July 27th 1924.

Her arms strained beneath her under the weight, she arched her back, and her kneeling thighs quivered as she tried not to collapse. She bit down, not hard, but firmly on his fingers as he played them over her sweet red lips. She was conscious of the sounds of her own ecstasy as he thrust into her from behind, resting occasionally his heavy frame, across the fineness of her cream white shoulders. Her perfect hands clutched, and crumpled the sheets beneath her, her eyes closed, mouth opening, noise emanating, bedstead rattling. She felt his hands grip her waist and pull her back, her elbows buckled and she slumped forward burying her face in the bedclothes, she bit at them to muffle the noise of her own delight.

Then; it was over.

They both slumped in a shattered, sodden exhausted heap onto the mattress, into the mattress, through the mattress.

The dishevelled sheets soaked them up.

"My God!"

She said in exhaled pants, speaking more to herself than her partner; the sweat glistening on her marble skin.

"Where does it come from? My God, where does it come from?"

At Scottsville Park, the atmosphere was electric. 'The Bloody Elephant' and Banjo, sat in the back of one of Dykkas canvass covered lorries.

'Banger' was there too.

He had been called in by Dykka for few days, to set up the punch bags and weights in the Norfolk Hotels' Courtyard, for Crusher Hohner to train on, and to do some sparring with the Rhodesian if he wanted.

The night of the fight, Dykka had told him to be at Scottsville Park, to generally help out and be a 'water man'. Dykka had promised him three quid for the night, and a quid a day for making himself available for Crusher.

'Banger' was now working as a warehouseman for Dykka in a bootleg booze, and tobacco thinning yard just outside Durban Docks. Dykka was paying him One pound and five shillings a week, the same as the 'Darkies' in the yard. 'Bangers' younger black wife cleaned the offices and toilets, for seven shillings and sixpence a week and he thought she was getting fucked by the Yard Manager, a cousin of Gondas' named Silvo.

Banjo thought that 'Banger' looked like shit.

He had lost weight, and now looked like a fifty year old white man that had gone to seed. Saggy, and with bones showing, but still a lump of a man for all that.

Banjo thought his young wife probably deserved all the fucking she could get.

He and 'The Elephant' had heard that 'Banger' hadn't had a fight for over a year, and that the last one he had, left him in bed for over a week. And that bloke, a Dutch feller from Ulundi, was a cheap slugger who 'The Elephant' had flattened in under three minutes, eight or nine months ago.

They both felt a bit sorry for 'Banger', and had given him a quid from each of them, just for some betting money for the night.

Outside the lorry, they could hear the crowd, and the bookies shouting odds. 'The Elephant' and 'Crusher Hohner' were on last; they reckoned it should be about nine o' clock. There were at least a dozen other bouts which Dykka had arranged, every one designed to make him money in fees and bets.

The three men sat in the covered lorry, and smoked some roll-ups. 'The Elephant' had a bucket of water between his boots, and a tin mug in his hand. He was trying to drink the entire bucket before 'Bell Time', then he would 'take a long piss', as Banjo had said, just before entering the ring of headlights.

"Then wash your hands in the piss before the fight starts. Krauts hate the smell of piss", Banger had said.

In the failing light of the late afternoon, the shabby rooms of his lodgings in the Port Napier district of Pietermaritzburg looked more drab than usual. Standing naked at his solitary chest of drawers, he poured himself a large Scotch, and drank it

149

greedily, he poured another, and, sliding a second glass in front of himself said, without turning around;

"Want one?"

He felt the sweat trickling down the taught valley of his back. He looked up, and stared blandly into the small wood framed mirror hanging on the faded blue floral wallpaper before him.

"No thanks", replied Eloise, still lying on the bed, naked, her eyes half closed, and gently touching her breasts as she felt the rise and fall of her own breaths.

Mambo turned and gazed at her.

He knew she was trouble for him.

He knew she didn't give a flying fuck for him.

He knew one day he would be sorry.

He knew he couldn't stop himself.

He drained his second large glass of Scotch, in one draft, and returned the glass to the top of the chest of drawers, and walked the two paces to the end of the bed. With no discussion, he gripped her ankles, and raised her legs, high in the air, and back towards her, she made no resistance, just uttered a slow breathless,

"Yes; do it now, again".

She inhaled sharply as he entered her, forcing her legs back further, he leant forward and squeezed her breasts. Thrusting and forcing for all he was worth, swearing and spitting as instinct captured them both. His hands made pink imprints in her thighs and calfs as he held them, sometimes lifting her to force deeper into her wet loveliness, sometimes moving her left or right. Her climaxes, as always, came in torrents, her head shaking, her nipples stiffening, her mouth opening and closing, her tongue flicking in and out, in and out. Mambo leaned further forward and put his hand over her mouth to silence her delight.

As she subsided; he withdrew, and crawled up the bed on his knees, she took him in her mouth, her neck moving back and forth, back and forth, faster, faster, faster.

Then.

Then she took him all, swallowed and licked every salty drop, rubbing the remnants across her cheeks and breasts. She looked up at him, smiled, ran her tongue across her lips and teeth. Mambo collapsed next to her, panting, glistening and exhausted.

Breathless, she said;

"I think I'll have that whiskey now".

An hour, and several Scotch's later, Mambo said that he had to leave, as he had a job to do for 'her father'. He knew the expression annoyed her, so he used it all the more.

"He's not my father!"

She said in mock anger, she knew Mambo's game and played along.

Mambo told her, (as he threw his clothes on, not washing); to sit tight until it was properly dark outside, then leave by the steel fire escape stairs at the back of the building.

The instruction was unnecessary, as she knew the routine by now; she would avoid the buildings warren of corridors, and when she stepped out onto the steel stairs, she would not close the window behind her, this to avoid any noise.

Always watching for others.

Always hugging the shadows.

She always wore a hooded coat for her meetings with Mambo, and she raised the hood before leaving his rooms.

The walk home by the unlit back roads, and cutting behind the 'Norfolk Hotel', and the Rail Tracks, took less than twenty minutes.

Once home, she would go through the 'Orangery', and take the kitchen stairs to her room, where she could bathe, wash her underwear, and dress in peace.

The atmosphere outside the covered lorry was getting boisterous; they could hear bets being placed, odds being screamed between bookies, cheers and foul mouthed abuse being hurled at the lower ranked bouts. The air was thick with the odours of the fights, the odours of the cattle yard, the slaughterhouse. The mixed sweet cocktail of blood, sweat, vomit, tobacco, and spilt booze and gore, all fused with the exhaust fumes of Dykkas trucks; parked in a large circle, their lights on to illuminate the formed arena; their engines running to keep their batteries alive.

And all around them, in between them, on their running boards, on their bonnets, their roofs; clamboured the spectators. A liquid mob of venom, and bile, salivating, for ever more gruesome a spectacle, for ever more blood. Men, women, all dressed up, all flashing their money, all enjoying the mock secrecy of this gutter-life; this other world.

"There must be a huge crowd out there", 'The Elephant', said to 'Banger'. He then asked him what odds he'd got?

"Two to one" said the old thumper.

"I hope you bet on me", said 'The Elephant', and laughed, a little bit nervously.

'Banger' laughed too, and replied with,

"It's your fucking money. It would be rude not to".

Then, in more hushed tones, he leaned forward on the bench seat, and while rubbing some goose fat into 'The Elephants' eyebrows and ears, he said:

"Just remember what I told you, watch that left boot heel. It's a dead give away, only an old fister like me would spot it. It's hard to see, but it's always there, very slight. It's like he can't help it, it's part of him. When that heel twists in the dirt, you know there's a big right hander coming, then, just before he throws it, he drops that left guard, only for a split second. I tell you he can't help it".

'Banger' stood up, crouching his head in the covered back of the truck, and demonstrated the action to watch for.

"That's when to let one fly, when you see that left drop a bit. You might still catch the right, but that's a chance you take".

'Banger paused a second, and held up his right fist, before continuing, his voice deepening.

"And I tell you, that right is a fucking monster; I seen him enough round at The Norfolk to know, seen what it did to the punch bags. Fucking monster!"

The canvas back flap of the lorry was flung open. A man in a tall black hat and a red jacket stood there, and waved a silver topped cane at 'The Elephant'. Behind him were two small coloured lads, each with a Railwayman's lamp held high in their hands.

"You're up next lads!"

The man spoke with a thick Scottish accent, full of authority. None of them had seen him before. They guessed that Dykka must have brought him in from Bloemfontein or Durban as a 'Ringmaster'; it was after all a big occasion.

"Two minutes": said Banjo, and snatched the flap back, closing it tight, he gave the Scott a look that brooked no argument. He tied the chord on the canvass flap, and turned to 'Banger' and 'The Elephant', his brother. He said, in low tones.

"Now, take a good piss in the bucket, you've had enough to drink".

As he "took his piss" in the galvanised noisy bucket, he asked Banjo if he'd got their own bets on. Banjo confirmed that he had, as he wiped 'The Elephant's' back with a damp towel, and said that he'd managed to get nine to four with 'Fat Malcolm' over at Maleens.

'Banger' told 'The Elephant' not to forget to soak his hands in the piss. Banjo told 'Banger' to 'fuck off!'

It appeared that Crusher was favourite everywhere.

The Escape from Odessa.
April 12th, 1919.

The two boys and their mother edged towards the bottom of the gangplank, they had been jostling and jostled for at least an hour, and were still a good thirty yards from the beckoning gangplank.

The heat and the foul stench had become unbearable. There was no respite, no refuge. Dead bodies stood; bolt upright in the throbbing crowd, unable to fall to the ground. The very act of breathing became an act of will, rather than a natural process. The weak and solitary, unable to lift their arms in the crush, were strangled deliberately from behind by the strong, willing to risk all, and commit any crime, subvert any moral behaviour; merely to escape the solid earth.

The two boys used all their strength to create occasional space around their mother, occasional space for fresh air, for occasional total lung-fulls of breath, for an occasional additional heave towards the gangplank; one step, maybe two.

153

An hour later, and they were within five good paces of the foot of the gangplank, to their right, and draping over their mothers shoulder, was an old woman, in a thick fur coat and a brown velvet hat. She looked rich, or had once been rich, a lifetime ago, before this cataclysm.

Before this experiment.

Her face was was a pale blue; her eyes open but empty, bulging as if startled, but sad. The blood capillaries in her cheeks were plain, like a map, popped purple etchings on a blue background. Her lips were dark, nearly black, and pushed part open by her swollen tongue. She was dead, strangled or suffocated, crushed or deliberately squeezed from this life.

Who cared?

The younger of the boys could see her wealth; she would not be here without the fair. She was alone, and escaping, buying her way out of this inferno with everything of value she could carry; just like the boys, and their mother, with their Hessian sack. He wriggled and squirmed, eeling his arm about the womans stiffening corpse, inside her coat, searching for pockets, bags, pouches; then: in the clammy deadness of her wrist, his hand fell upon a small silk smoothness, tied to her arm by a thin soft chord. The boy pulled and tugged at it in the tiny space, the cramped invisible space below the heaving purulent crowd. He twisted the chord, and yanked it, his finger nails stripping the ripening skin from the old ladies hand and fingers. He struggled and sweated, sweated and swore; it took nearly half an hour, edging closer to the gangplank, and willing the swelling corpse not to slip below the human ocean as it moved; but eventually the fine chord snapped, and his numbing hand closed like a clam around the silk purse.

He did not know what was inside, nor would he until he could stretch and pace and leap and spring up the wooden slats of the gangplank.

"Two at a time! Only two at a time!"

He heard someone shouting. It was Russian, but not the Russian he knew, this was stilted, difficult, harsh and unpleasant.

He was close enough now to hear the guards swearing at the crowd.

Close enough to smell the scent of the sea, stringing subtle flavours near foul odours.

Meshing them.

Mixing them.

Melding them within the brutal stench of this moving graveyard.

Another fifteen minutes, and they were at the gangplank base. The boy and his brother were heaved from the crowd by five White Guards, and shoved onto the bottom of the gangplank; his brother ahead of him carrying the hessian sack, his feet slipping at the surprise of freedom, he stumbled, striking his elbow on the timber foot rail, he felt a yelp fall from his lips, the pain was intense, the kind of pain dreams spring from, the kind of pain that lasts forever deep in your skull.

Rifles criss-crossed behind the boys, barring the gangplank to others.

"Up here, quick as you can, no dawdling!"

The boson yelled at them, in a Russian thick with an accent they did not recognise. It was him the younger brother had heard earlier.

In seconds the boys were at the gateway at the top of the sloping planking, with one foot each on the deck.

"Not so fast, you pair", said the Boson.

The two seamen with the guns, Vradesh and Stannoy stood behind Arris, and between him and Karem's table; each pointing their revolvers at the boys. "Fare's please", said Arris, and laughed.

The same laugh he had laughed four or five hundred times already today, after the same request he had made to each of Karem's 'customers'. The boys handed him the Hessian bag, which he emptied onto the table, again as he had emptied hundreds before this day, and thousands over the previous months, from dozens of ports.

On to the table fell two large Synagogue candelabras made of silver, a small golden lectern about six inches square, and a gold crucifix with an onyx base with Hebrew writing carved into it.

"This'll do said Karem", and handed the *fare* to the sailors standing behind him, and filling the now creaking lockers.

Arris leaned across the table, and put his face within a hands breadth of the Captains face.

"That big freighter's starting to make steam Sir".

He nodded across the jetty. Karem turned his head, his thick neck dripping sweat from its folds. He rose quickly to his feet, leaned across the deck rail, and shouted down to the guards, waving both arms aloft at the same time.

"No more! No more!"

He gesticulated towards the bow and stern of the *Cok Guzel Denizala Baligi*.

"Cast away the lines" he shouted in Russian, to no one in particular.

He turned to Arris; and said, this time in Turkish:

"Make steam, and prepare to get us out as quick as you can; make sure we are in front of that big bastard".

He pointed towards the freighter, whose both funnels were now beginning to puff clean pale grey smoke high into the pure blue sky. He turned back to Arris, and, again in Turkish commanded;

"Tell the wheelhouse to watch him", he pointed again at the freighter. "Watch him like a bloody hawk, if he turns left at the breakwater, we turn right, make sure they know", he pointed now up at the bridge, "I'll fucking skin them if they balls this up!"

There was now urgency on the deck, orders being barked, and arrangements being made for embarkation. Information spread like plague, and all hands ran here and there, pushing befuddled passengers out of their way as the ran. Karem, for all his agitation and instruction, had not failed to notice the Senior White Guard and three other Guards each bearing rifles and side arms, marching briskly up the gangplank. Again he turned to Arris, and this time, in Greek, (he and Arris being the only Greek speakers on board), said, in almost a whisper,

"Give them this box".

Karem pointed to a large rusty red coloured locker amidst the other lockers behind his green leather chair.

"And this one too", he kicked a small black one to the side of his table.

He paused for a split second; and changed his mind:

"No, just the red one, it's enough, we are not full, there's no time to anti-up properly; if they grizzle too much give them the black one too. But only if they grizzle. Just get us out of here in front of that".

This time he pointed an angry finger in the air, jabbing towards the big steaming freighter, and stretching to tip toe for emphasis.

"Sir, Sir, please!"

The boys interrupted Karem.

"Our mother, she is still at the bottom of the gangplank".

Karem only had eyes for the freighter, and ears only for Arris. The White Guards were on the deck, and arguing with the Bosun about their payment. Karem could see that Arris was losing the argument.

"Give them this too!"

He shouted to Arris, and kicked the small black locker one more time.

This time louder.

This time harder.

He began to move away from the table. At the foot of the gangplank the boys mother had realised what was happening and was screaming at her sons. They continued to protest to Karem. He turned to face them.

"No more! I said; this is only enough for two".

He gestured at the contents of the Hessian sack which was still being stowed in the lockers.

"How about this?" said the younger of the two boys.

He was holding up the small silk purse by its broken chord.

Holding it up close up to Karems' face.

Holding it up in front of the Turks greedy eyes.

The Captain snatched at the small bag with his hand, the one with a thumb missing, and began opening it with the other. The older boy looked incredulously at the younger. The younger boy prayed as he had never prayed before that the effort for the purse was worthwhile.

Karems' fat sweaty face took on a glow, an inner glow not caused by the glistening sweat, a glow powered by greed. He tipped the purse out into his thumbed hand, and snatching up the eyeglass which was always on his table on these occasions, began to survey the two inch diameter egg-shaped cut and faceted emerald. For a brief moment the puffing, steaming freighter was chased from his thoughts.

His silence confirmed the stones pedigree.

"Will this buy one more ticket?" the younger boy asked, pointing at the stone.

Karem held the emerald up towards the sun, and amidst the carnage he enjoyed, for a brief moment, the small sunbeams, like bright dancing men skitting around the beautiful objects cuts and angles.

Regaining his composure, Karem slipped the emerald back into its silk purse nest, and dropped it delicately into his shirt breast pocket, and buttoned it down. There would be no locker box for this trinket, nor any shares for anyone else. The Captain walked to the edge rail, and shouted down at the guards who were still at the bottom of the gangplank.

"One more; that one!"

He pointed at the boy's mother. The two boys leaned over the rail too, and also shouted, making sure the guards heaved the right person onto the gangplank. They did, and she ran up the slatted slope to her sons.

"Thank you Sir, Thank you!" she said to Karem.

Arris was still arguing with the White Guards on the deck; Karem intervened, and taking the Senior Guard gently by the arm, he said, in Russian,

"There are five cases of good Moscow Vodka in the deck store over there, and a gallon tin of caviar. If I throw all that in, plus the two lockers, will that do it?"

The Guard stroked his chin for a second, and then agreed.

"Good!" said Karem.

Then, (and in Greek), he instructed Arris to get some hands, get the vodka, get the caviar, get the lockers, and get these "fucking Russians off my ship".

He then told his Boson to get the gangplank dropped and get underway as quick as he could.

As the White Guards cast the *Cok Guzel Denizala Baligi* off from the jetty, its single funnel belched and burped into the clear blue sky. Its pair of small propellers made revolutions for eight knots towards the breakwater; and Captain Karem Tortruk, now in grubby white peaked hat, and tatty naval officer's jacket, waved at the White Guards who were already dispersing the remaining would be refugees, and distributing the bottles of vodka between themselves.

By the time they were approaching the breakwater, Karem was in front of the freighter, (just), and had returned to his bridge. He had hoped to be a little further ahead of the big steamer by now, but the argument with the White Guards over their cut had delayed the Turk.

He stepped over the raised foot-well threshold and walked back into the wheelhouse towards the binnacle. Turning to the helmsman he reminded him to watch the freighter, and to remember his orders about direction.

"Wait for her to turn first", Karem said, looking aft through the rear viewing porthole.

He took a cigar from inside his coat pocket, and one of his bridge crew lit it for him. Moving across the bridge deckplates to the forward windows, he looked down upon his customers, each jostling for sleeping space on the deck below. He imagined the repeating scenarios unfolding there as five hundred odd passengers gave thanks for their salvation; then fought for use of the eight toilets on board.

They had all paid for passage on a boat they did not know, with a fare they had not agreed, to a destination, of which, as yet, even their Captain was undecided upon.

Karem smiled to himself, and chewed at his cigar, making the end wet. The customers would soon enough learn to shit over the side. It had not, after all been a bad day, he patted his shirt pocket. He had made good time; he had beaten the big freighter out of harbour. He had short changed the White Guards, as he always had, the gallon can of caviar had a small puncture in the bottom and was on the turn; and the vodka was not 'Good Moscow Vodka', but crap 'Riga Vodka', already thinned with turpentine.

All in all, not a bad day at all.

Maldwyn, an unexpected visitor,
and the Beautiful Salmon.
Cardiff,
Later in the afternoon,
after his discussion with Dmitri.

The same Saturday in early April 1972.

By the time Maldwyn had walked up St. Mary Street to the University Library, at the Junction of Column Road and Cathays Terrace, it was just after three p.m. He had eaten all his sandwiches, was down to his last Curly-Wurly, and probably had only two cups of coffee left in his flask.

As he entered the ground floor foyer area, the middle aged woman there, greeted him, in her usual fashion, and with a broad smile. She genuinely liked Maldwyn, and made idle chit-chat with him as she busied herself behind her counter. Then, handing Maldwyn a small bundle of paper slips, she said:

"I've had the girls pull all the stuff Andre asked for earlier. It's a fair few volumes, so I've had them all put together, and in chronological order, on one of the big tables overlooking St. Anne's square, at the back of the first floor."

She then leaned, (somewhat surreptitiously), across the counter top, and lowering her voice to a whisper, said.

"I've also put a white paper bag up there for you, with a Cornish pasty in it; from Ferrari's; The Bakers". She winked, turned away and went about her work.

"Ta"; replied Maldwyn, and took the lift to the first floor, without further discussion.

"How's the Piles Mal.?"

The woman shouted over as the stainless steel lift doors swished open.

"Bleeding and itching like a bastard, to be fair, got two sani-pads in today, and squirting germolene up every time I go to the toilet".

As he entered the lift, Maldwyn held the doors open for a young female student, clutching a bundle of books to her chest. She nodded her head from side to side, and said; through gritted teeth, and with the look of someone who was about to projectile spew.

"No thanks; I think I'll take the next one."

"Suit yourself", said Maldwyn.

The first thing he wanted to find was anything on the 'Salmon'. He poured himself a coffee, shed his overcoat, set out his timetable notepads and coloured pens, scratched his arse, (with no consideration for any other surrounding patrons in the library), and set about his Cornish Pasty.

It didn't take Maldwyn long to pick up the scent of the *Cok Guzel Denizala Baligi*. Like all good researchers he focussed on the items he needed.

He knew from the scraps of English notes in the box, and dates scribbled on the backs of some of the photos'; that anything before 1919 was not really relevant. And, also time was against him today, as he had spent a bit too long in the Central Library.

He needed to be heading back home reasonably early tonight; as there was a good 'turn' on in Caerphilly Social Club, and he didn't want to miss the start. A magician of some sort, called 'Mr Mephisto, and his beautiful assistant Nicole'. He had tried to talk Dilwyn and Ellis into coming along, but they had declined on the grounds that there was a very good programme on B.B.C.2, concerning the 'Phoenicians', with Joan Bakewell. They both had the hots for Joan, and Ellis had a poster of her on his bedroom ceiling.

The Amethyst brothers had also suggested, based on past experience, that 'Mr. Mephisto', would probably turn out to be, as Ellis had put it;

'A right grizzly old wanker with a bent wand'.

Not really much of a theatre critic was Ellis, but he could make a salient point when circumstances required.

Dilwyn had however commented on 'Mr. Mephisto', that, 'There was a name to conjure with'. He was a dry old stick on his day was Dilwyn. Anyway; Maldwyn had to be on the five forty five p.m. bus from North Road, to Caerphilly. So he was against the clock, and was beavering away like a fat sweaty beaver.

Turns out, that the *Cok Guzel Denizala Baligi*, was an old rust bucket by 1919. She had been built at the tail end of the 1880's, and had managed to stay off the 'Maritime Standards' registers by plying her trade in parts of the world where strife and conflict allowed her to hide. Her trade incidentally, (which Maldwyn had gleaned from the coded inclusions in Janes' Merchant Ships for various years); was the illicit transport of human beings, primarily refugees.

By early 1918 She was zig zagging across The Black Sea, with forays through the Bosporus, sometimes as far south as Athens and Crete. If no port would allow her to dock; She anchored off shore, as close in as possible, and delivered her cargo via row-boats to the nearest convenient beach.

Maldwyn knew that by early 1919, things would have been getting very difficult in The Black Sea, with the Russian Revolution blazing on one side; and the Turkish Revolution simmering on the opposite coast.

He discovered from the records that the ship had been attacked and boarded by an Imperial Russian Navy vessel in the early morning of April 13th 1919, approximately twelve miles from the Bosporus straits. There were casualties arising from the incident, '*including a number of fatalities*', it had said in the 'Jane's' entry.

By absolute ferret like research, and cross referencing between Janes' Merchant Ships, and Janes' Fighting Ships records, Maldwyn managed to winkle out the names of the ships involved, in the incident, the dates and places etc. He then sub-checked, as far as he could, death registers, along with any *Cyrillic* translations he could track down. But the Russian Revolution destroyed many records just by its very nature.

This type of thing is not un-common, in conflicts, indeed over forty percent of the First World War British Military Records were destroyed in the *Blitz* of the Second World War. But Maldwyn knew his way around this kind of problem, and could think; 'Outside the Corned Beef sandwich', as Dilwyn liked to say.

He had located a very good Journal Entry, on The Russian Imperial Navy Battle Cruiser, '*The Czareavitch Alexai Romanov*', (a front line vessel of the Russian Black Sea Fleet), which contained a translation of the Captains Ships Log entry for the incident. This; along with, (and, more crucial to Maldwyns research); a list of the casualties.

The information for this casualty list, having been garnered by the boarding Officers of *The Czareavitch Alexai Romanov*, from other passengers aboard the 'Salmon'.

Maldwyn's notes related that the Russian Warships Captain, Boris Lev Anroskov Tupalin, had sighted the *Cok Guzel Denizala Baligi* at dawn on the morning of 13th April 1919. She was showing no navigation lights, and when challenged by morse lamp to stop and be boarded, She had turned sharp starboard, (approximately 80 degrees), and increased speed in an attempt to outrun *The Czareavitch Alexai Romanov.*

The *Cok Guzel Denizala Baligi* being less than a dozen miles from the straits, and knowing the Russian Ship would not venture beyond The Black Sea; had clearly decided to try and make a run for it. However the Battle Cruiser was far superior in terms of speed and manoeuvrability, and chased down the smaller older vessel in only a few miles.

As ever, Maldwyns notes were well presented, (apart from the coffee and Cornish pasty stains), and superbly referenced and verified. Clear, concise, detailed, succinct, and above all accurate.

He then set about the Janes' and dug out every snippet he could regarding the H.M.A.S. Waterhen. He had managed to obtain a 1943 detailed register of the full ships company, names, dates of birth, previous postings, ranks where appropriate etc.

He noted with some excitement the inclusion of 'Androskewowicsz Y', and a rating by the name of 'Akpaganathos', as entries on the list. The former, (in the column marked 'Duty/Rank'), was simply listed as 'Engine Room'. The latter as 'Able Seaman First Class'. The former; like a half dozen or so other entries, showed the SS Iron Knight, as a 'Previous Posting'; but this was asterisked, and the footnote description of this legend said simply, 'Merchant Vessel'. The one thing that did set the 'Androskewowicsz Y' entry apart; was the inclusion, (underneath the name), and written by hand, the reference 'W.A.P.S. 89855812'.

It took Maldwyn literally fifteen minutes, eight books, and two Journal entries in Criminology Publications, to discover that 'W.A.P.S.' stood for 'Western Australian Prison Service', and that all Prisoners in that system, were awarded an eight digit reference number. Somewhere, there must be an inmate record, or log; but he knew it would not be on the shelves of Cardiff University Library, however diverse its material.

He set this aside for different research methods, and a discussion to be had with Dilwyn and Ellis regarding a proposition he had in mind. The proposition consisted of roping in Murray and Wilf Swayzee from Abertridwr, who had emigrated to Australia a decade or so earlier.

In any event the day was spinning by, and it had already gone four thirty p.m. So Maldwyn decided to spend what time he had left, (before the attractions of 'Mr Mephisto, and his beautiful assistant Nicole', became too much to bear), in searching out the movements of The H.M.A.S. Waterhen, and its War record.

About an hour later, as he tabulated his findings from the cross checks from the 'Janes', with port records, convoy reports, dry dock repair logs, and individual Officers Filed Logs, etc. All of which built up a chronology of the Waterhen's movements, duties and actions, from 1943 until 1946, Maldwyn came across a familiar name, in an unexpected place.

It was in fact in a copy of a half page, badly typed, citation request. Prepared by an Acting Captain Hawks, (a name Maldwyn also recognised from his diggings on the SS Iron Knight), now of the H.M.A.S. Waterhen, but it wasn't that name that had peeked Maldwyns interest.

The document was signed, (as a receipt), and witnessed by a Second Officer, (whose signature was illegible, but whose rank and ship were printed below his scrawl); the document was handed over aboard the British Destroyer H.M.S. Exeter.

The document was dated June 6th 1944.

The Black Sea.
April 15th 1919.

The Imperial Russian Navy, Black Sea Fleet vessel; *The Czareavitch Alexai Romanov* had shadowed the *Cok Guzel Denizala Baligi* for over three hours, and had now positioned herself so that the Turkish ship would be silhouetted against the rising sun. As the morning broke the horizon, Captain Tupalin ordered his Communications Officer to 'make to' the *Cok Guzel Denizala Baligi*, by morse lamp, to 'heave to, and prepare to be boarded'.

The *Czareavitch Alexai Romanov* was under orders to prevent from travelling, sieze or destroy any vessels which were suspected of 'ammunition running', or being used by 'The Reds', in any way.

Whilst Karem Tortruk displayed sublime indifference to the political complexions of his customers, he had no doubt that he had aboard, fleeing Red soldiers, as well as fleeing White ones. He certainly had a selection of small arms, purloined from both sides.

Such a mixture, may well, in the eyes of the Imperial Russian Navy constitute assisting one side against the other, and result in the arbitrary seizure of his ship, and everything on it. In theory, he could even be shot as an enemy of the state, by the Whites, or as an enemy of the Revolution by the Reds, and he knew all too well that summary executions were a daily occurrence around the Black Sea regions.

But, this was the nature of the business he and his crew had chosen, and they all knew the risks.

He yelled to Aris for a ships position, and an estimate as to how far to the straits.

"Too fucking far!" replied the Greek Boson.

"At least twenty kilometres", he shouted.

For the first time, Karem heard genuine fear in Aris' voice.

Captain Karem Tortruk, who was not renowned for his patience, but was for his seamanship, thought for a moment, and looked out to port, out over the bridge walkway rail. The night was still, and the sea calm, and he calculated that they probably had about two hours of reasonable darkness, or half light before the sun sprang full above the horizon. He decided to make a run for it. Turning into the bridge housing, he shouted at the wheel man.

"Hard a' starboard!"

Then turning to Aris, demanded,

"Full ahead!"

He then turned back to the wheelman, and said, calmer now:

"Hold that starboard turn to about ninety degrees; keep it there for two minutes, count to one hundred, slowly if you need to. Then put the rudder amidships".

Turning back to Aris, he said, in as steady a voice as he could muster;

"Collect up all the ships weapons, and throw them over the side, if they catch us with any of that, we're dead".

Aris went to say something; but before he could get any of the words out, Captain Tortruk cut him short; and loudly this time.

"Just do it Aris!"

Karem returned to the bridge rail, picking up a pair of binoculars as walked, and pushing them tight into his eye sockets, he said, to no-one in particular, and in hushed, almost pensive tones.

"Sixteen guns, could be two hundred and twenty millimetres each, and another eight, at, looks like could be ninety or a hundred and ten millimetres, and machine guns on her upper works. She's a big fucker".

He dropped the binoculars from his eyes and allowed them to hang loosely from his neck; turning to the wheelman, who was now pulling the *Cok Guzel Denizala Baligi* hard over to starboard; he said.

"Well, I don't think we'll out-fight her".

There was an attempt at levity in his voice.

It failed.

Over the next half an hour Karem altered course almost at two minute intervals, playing a dangerous game of chess with *The Czareavitch Alexai Romanov*, struggling to creep into the diminishing darkness. He knew that the Russian Warship was trying to keep him against the sun, as an easy target, but also always in view. If the big ship wanted to sink the *Cok Guzel Denizala Baligi*, she would have been at the bottom of the Black Sea by now. She wanted to check her out, before deciding the Turkish vessels fate.

Karems' thoughts were for the safety of his cargo.

His lockers.

He didn't give a fuck about his passengers, his customers.

The Russian ship persisted with her morse lamp demands for the *Cok Guzel Denizala Baligi* to heave to and be boarded. Karem Tortruk persisted in his erratic changes of direction, hunting for that moment of darkness in which the warship would turn the wrong way, and an opportunity of escape may present itself.

166

After two, long, desperate hours, and now with the sun tangenting the horizon, and a carpet of brightness spewing over the sea, the two ships were within three hundred yards of each other. The Captain of the Russian Battleship, had demonstrated his seamanship, and now with a sudden change in his previously repeated morse lamp demands, he upped the stakes; he added the morse for:

"Or we will open fire".

Captain Karem Tortruk, took down his grubby white hat, from the hook in the wheelhouse, and placed it, (with some ceremony), across his sweating, shiny, and equally grubby forehead. He walked out onto the bridge gangway, and looking down, he saw that most of his 'customers' were now thronging on the main-deck below him. All looking out towards *The Czareavitch Alexai Romanov*, her Cyrillic name plate clearly visible on her prow, her huge battle flag and the ships name clearly demonstrating her allegiance.

As he stood on the gangway, Karem saw Aris, who was striding up the metal steps towards him, taking two steps at a time.

"Did you see the morse lamp?" asked Aris pointing at the big ship.

"I did", replied the Captain, an air of resignation in his words.

"Tell the engine room all stop, I think this particular trip may be shorter than we…….."

He was cut short.

The Russian Warship had fired two shells from its 110mm forward turret. The first, with a low trajectory, screamed into the water and exploded in the sea about twenty yards in front of the *Cok Guzel Denizala Baligi*, sending cascading sprays of saltwater high into the air, and splashing down on the foredeck like thunderbolts from the Ancient Gods. Aris and Karem stared forwards eyes and mouths wide open.

The second shell, either by accident or design, careened through the portside foredeck guardrail, smashing an area of about three yards long to smithereens; sending splinters of cylindrical metal tubing hurtling through the air ripping to shreds any 'customers' or crew that happened to be in the vicinity. The shell carried on in a split second along the foredeck, exploding the metal deck plates as it went, and shattering into a thousand pieces the anchor winch housing, decimating the chain and sending the anchor, unattached, plummeting to the sea bed with a monstrous, roaring splash. As the shell hit the starboard guardrail, a micro-second later; it exploded; ripping a three metre diameter hole in the deck plates and the bow and side plates of the *Cok Guzel Denizala Baligi*. The ship bellowed in agony, and wailed as knives of flame spat from the gaping wound. Coin sized slivers of baking metal pattered into the sea like miniature dancing men. The slivers that bounced across the deck at whining speed, removed hands, eyes, fingers, scalps, the flesh from thighs or buttocks. In some cases they removed the lives completely from those 'customers' whose geography on the deck just made them a little more unlucky than their neighbour.

On the bridge gangway steps, Aris, and Karem Tortruk, were laying face down on the plating, ducking for dear life in a reflex action. Karem looked up, and at the top of his voice, screamed into the bridge housing;

"All stop, all stop!"

Both men staggered to their feet, their ears ringing with the clanging, banging, metallic explosions. Karem leaned over the gangway guardrail, and yelled at the Russian Warship, (somewhat pointlessly).

"We surrender! We surrender! Don't shoot, please don't shoot any moooooor......."

As he yelled, he saw the third and fourth gun flashes from the forward turrets of the 110mm canons.

"Oh my God!"

He screamed as the first shell hit the water less than thirty metres to port of the bridge, and the other thirty metres to starboard. Again the air was filled with sea spray, ranging from fine strand-like whisps to globules of water the size of a man's head; all of which crashed noisily onto the gangway, and in through the bridge housing doors. Karem was on his feet again, waving both arms in the air, and shouting.

"Stop! Stop! Stop!"

The sharp rattle of machine gun fire, split the air, its intensity multiplied by the echo's bouncing between the steel hulls of the two ships, which by now were less than one hundred metres apart. The machine gun bullets hit the water, like the ends of leather whips, then, as the gun muzzles rose with the light swell, they hammered into the side plates of the *Cok Guzel Denizala Baligi*; rising ominously above the Plimsoll line, not piercing the thick plating, but shattering portholes as the spitting muzzle passed them.

Each impacting round sent chips of rusting metal from the side plates and rivets in all directions, all at screaming, rattling, piercing bullet speed. One such fragment, the size of a mans fist and thin as a cigarette, skittered skyward up the side of the *Cok Guzel Denizala Baligi*, and removed the left arm of Aris Kristapoulis at the elbow, an arm which had been inadvertently extended beyond the bridge gangway guardrail. A fountain of bright red blood left a shining diagonal stripe across the dirty white shirt of Karem Tortruk, like some sick impression of an expensive Champaign bottle. Aris slumped forward, into his Captains arms, and both men crashed to the floor.

The firing stopped, and, after a brief moment the world returned to silent semi normality. A voice broke the retreat, a voice speaking in Turkish, poor quality Turkish, and with a thick Ukrainian accent. The voice was distorted further by the megaphone it emanated from.

"Do we need for fire shoot again?"

There was a pause.

"This is Captain Tupalin; of Imperial Russian Naval vessel *Czareavitch Alexai Romanov*. You have thirty now seconds to confirm me you surrender, and you accept allow that we will to board you vessel, after that seconds, we will remove us to safe way distant away, then accept allow you five minutes less for to abandon you ship, and then we shoot fire to sink you vessel……", he paused. "You now not have less twenty seconds!"

Karem shuffled off the screaming, bleeding Aris, who was laying on top of him, and across his chest; and pushed him unceremoniously onto the deck plating, where he continued bleeding, and screaming.

Rising to his feet, and leaning through the bridge house door, Karem saw the wheelman crouching behind the binnacle, shaking like a leaf in a gale. He demanded:

"Where's the fucking morse lamp?"

The man gestured to a small wooden cupboard above the doorway through which Karem was leaning. He stepped inside, and reached up, it was locked, he turned back to the wheelman.

"Key? Where's the fucking key?"

The wheelman shook his head, still quivering in terror. Karem took the binoculars from around his neck, they too were splattered with Arris's blood, and he began to smash them against the small wooden door above his head, after three or four or five good blows, the door split at its hinges and crashed away from its frame. Karem threw the binoculars at the wheelman, cursing him in Turkish, Russian and Greek, they struck him on the bridge of his nose, splitting it like a ripe banana. Karem heard the wheelman yelping, but did not look back; he rummaged frantically for the morse lamp. As his hands fell upon it, he snatched it down from the smashed cupboard and ran out of the bridge, and onto the gangway, stepping over the wriggling, writhing, spurting, swearing Aris as he went to the guardrail. He began signalling, immediately:

"We surrender!

We surrender!

We surrender!"

The reply came back via the megaphone, again in broken Turkish.

"I am send two boats. Put down you boarding steps on starboard. We have more machine guns point on you. Next we will shoot fire on deck. Get all crew bodies and passenger bodies to deck, not one bodies to be underneath".

Karem understood that the Russian wanted all personnel 'customers' and crew, on the main-deck. He turned back inside the bridge to the wheelman, who was now on his feet, but leaning against the binnacle, his face streaming with blood.

"Yublis!"

He pointed at the sorry looking wheelman.

"You worthless dollop of spunk! Get down below, and get some of the hands together; make sure there is no one below decks, get everyone topside. Find Akra and Sumiel in the boiler rooms, and tell them to lower the boarding steps on the starboard side".

He looked down at Aris, who was clearly in excruciating agony, and now lying in a pool of blood that was wider and longer than himself. Turning back into the bridge housing, he shouted to Yublis, who was now exiting through the port-side door.

"And see if there's a doctor amongst the 'customers'; or a nurse, or both, just get someone up here now!"

As he spoke, he was removing his belt, from around his portly tummy, waist is the wrong word, it had been many years since Captain Karem Tortruk had possessed a waist.

He knelt beside Aris, who was now slipping into unconsciousness. Karem slipped his belt over the pulsating stump of Aris' bicep, and pulled the belt as tight as he could, wrapped it once more around, and tied it off. The pumping blood withdrew to a trickle. Karem pulled Aris towards the guardrail, sliding him across the slick of blood beneath him; and, lifting the stump upwards, tied the remaining tail of the belt to a low rail to keep the stump vertical, to further minimise blood loss.

Eventually, Yublis returned to the bridge, with a small Jewish looking man in his fifties, and a fat peasant woman. He said the man was a doctor, and the woman was a midwife. He also said there were other doctors, and some 'proper nurses' down on the main-deck, but that they were busy, and it was 'carnage' down there.

The old fat woman looked strangely offended given the circumstances, that Yublis, who was himself Russian, did not consider her a 'proper nurse'. The man carried a large cracked and creased black doctor's bag, and looked the part. He was already kneeling beside Aris and examining the remains of the arm.

Karem turned to Yublis, and said:

"You stay here with these pair; make sure they get everything they need".

He looked at Yublis, with his huge split nose, and blood all over the lower section of his face; his eyes had also now both began to swell and blacken.

The incongruous thought, briefly assuaged him, as to how much like one of those multi coloured blue, red, purple and black monkey things from South America with coloured faces, Yublis now looked.

Karem paused, then added, turning to the fat old woman, and gesturing with his thumbless hand towards the multi-coloured Yublis.

"See what you can do for this thing once you have sorted out my Boson".

Karem retrieved his cap, dusted it off, (another rather pointless exercise), and placed it on his head. As he walked down the bridge house access steps, towards the main deck, he glanced at the two small launches, (each with about a dozen sailors on), making their way across from the *Czareavitch Alexai Romanov.*

He prepared himself for the worse.

Mrs. Amethysts front room,

The Four Terraces,

Senghenydd,

South Wales.

An evening in early April 1972.

The front room of Mrs. Amethysts house in 'The Fours', had, (over a period of twenty years), become the third biggest library in the Rhymney and Aber Valleys.

Dilwyn and Ellis' accumulated collections of periodicals, reference books, journals, and non-fiction works, lined almost every available section of wall space; save for doors, windows and fireplace. All piled off the floors, stretching three quarters of the way to the ceilings.

There was not a single shelf in the entire house. Books were piled on the treads of the staircase, on the boys' bedrooms window cills, and even on two small tables in the downstairs bathroom. A room which, (as a recent addition); nestled beyond the kitchen, towards the back yard, the coal shed steps, and the disused railway cutting of the old 'Barry Line'.

Mrs. Amethyst drew the line at books in the kitchen, and she guarded her territory with the ferocity of a tiger.

The boys, being librarians, had all their stuff filed, (or piled), in subject and date order. And, in the centre of each wall, hung on a nail, by a monster crocodile paper clip, (the size, and weight of which would break your toes if it were to fall on your foot); was the wadge of papers which were the index for that walls documents.

This process was repeated all over the house; and, strangely enough, it worked a treat.

If the Amethyst boys needed anything, they knew instantly where to go, and could find it in seconds.

The front room, was originally two front rooms, but like most terraced houses in the early seventies, they had had it 'knocked through into one', with the improvisational use of a cut down length of old railway track as a girder, and some neatly applied bricks and plaster, usually nicked from one of the Councils yards.

In fact, it was my Uncle Charlie, and my Uncle Stan, from Nantgarw Road, who did the job for Mrs Amethyst. I think they also did the downstairs bathroom, but I am not a hundred percent sure.

In the corner of the room was Mrs A's, twenty four inch, 'Bush' black and white telly, with slatted wood surround and silver and black push buttons. The room was nicely carpeted, in thick, dark brown sculptured Axminster. Complimented by a very comfortable 'Laura Ashley' floral design covered, three piece suite in mauve; (mauve being the new chocolate brown), all clustered cosily, around the telly. In the back half of the room was a large, rectangular, old oak dining table, with tea cup rings on its top, and four heavy chairs, (almost matching, but not quite), perched around it.

This particular evening, Mrs Amethyst had just settled down to watch 'Callan', starring Edward Woodward. It was her favourite T.V. series, and she always felt a bit sorry for Lonely, because Callan was always getting him into trouble, or thumping him. She had her cup of tea on the coffee table in front of the settee, and a 'Princes' crab paste sandwich on a small plate on her lap.

Dilwyn and Ellis sat on either side of the large oak table, with the original contents of the box, in neat piles between them, a pile of A4 photocopies, and two 'East Light' lever arch folders also rested there. They both had spring binder note pads in front of them with a selection of rubbers, some 'Tipp-ex', a paper punch, and an old Tupperware box full of multi-coloured paper-clips and elastic bands. In the centre of the table crouched a small, old, green glazed pottery jug with raised yellow daffodils on it; snuggled in its hollow was a profusion of pens, pencils, and rulers which peeped over its chipped rim. There was also another heavy duty big old paper

173

punch, which Ellis had rescued from the bin in Caerphilly Library, and which Maldwyn Somerset had got one of the fitters at the Bus Depot to fix for them, this one could punch about twenty sheets at a time, whereas the other one would only do singles. Ellis reckoned the Council used to employ two 'Fat Birds', (as he put it), just to sit on the arm of the punch when holes were needed.

Mrs. Amethyst was watching 'Callan' and munching her paste sandwich; and the boys were sitting at the table, jabbering away between themselves; scribbling and arguing, as ever.

Occasionally one of them would flit around the room, check the hanging reference crocodile clip, then scuttle to a pile of books or papers, then rummage until he retrieved the item he needed.

Mrs. Amethyst would shout at them, as they flitted by, to:

"Stay out of the way of the telly!"

Then all would settle down again.

"Maldwyn did well on the weekend, down in Cardiff"; said Ellis, without looking up from his note-making.

"Not bad", replied Dilwyn, also not looking up.

Dilwyn held up a small folded piece of white card, about four inches by six inches.

"I did some checking on this, the other day".

Ellis glanced at him, and Dilwyn carried on.

"This feller Dykka Van Hoost, the one in the article Maldwyn found in Cardiff. Well, he owned one of the horses in the big race on this here race card!"

He waved the card at Ellis, then continued.

"May 28th 1924, Scottsville Racecorse, Pietermaritzburg, South Africa. I even found a photo of the horse, 'Kerasons' it was called".

He took the photo from one of the other neat piles, and passed it to Ellis.

"Apparently, he was a real thoroughbred. I've got a copy of a receipt here", (he pointed at the table, a general sort of point), " from the 'Jockey Club of Great Britain', dated November 1922, which confirms that he was sold to this Dykka Van Hoost, and two other blokes, whose names I don't have anything on yet; for two thousand five hundred guineas".

Dilwyn looked directly at Ellis and paused, waiting for a compliment on his efforts, he got an approving nod, before proceeding.

"The other thing," (he paused again, and adopted something of a supercilious tone), "is, that this Gonda Vischer, the other bloke in the newspaper article Maldwyn dug up; was the sponsor of this big race; and also this Mr. Van Hoosts business partner. I checked it all out at Companies House in Cardiff, cost me a quid for the copy records, they arrived in this morning's post".

Dilwyn held up another sheet of A4 paper, like Bobby Moore holding up the World Cup.

Dilwyn then proceeded with a discussion of shipping costs of the time, and how much it must have cost to get the horse from Britain to South Africa. And that consequently, this information, plus the Companies House discoveries must, "proffer the conclusion", that Mr Dykka Van Hoost, must have been a, "man of some substantial means".

"Excellent!"

Said Ellis, acknowledging his brothers efforts again.

He then stumped in with his own little triumph.

A triumph he had been itching to deliver.

He started with:

"I think I know who the young girl is in the photo".

He delicately extricated a small three inch square photograph from one of the piles on the table.

"Seriously!?"

Exclaimed Dilwyn, prompting his mother to shout a loud; 'Shoosh', from across the room. As the boys were interrupting, her enjoyment of tonight's episode of 'Callan', and apparently 'Lonely' had just got a right hammering off two drunk Irish fellers.

"Seriously?"

Dilwyn asked again, this time quieter. In fact the Amethyst brothers from this point on, toned down the entire volume of their discussion by about a third.

"I scraped the back of the photo, lightly with a razor blade", began Ellis.

"I did it once in 'Uni' with an old First World War print of a Royal Field Artilleryman called Gunner Billy Bray, seated on a big grey horse, he was. The photo itself was very grubby, and had been in someone's attic for years, but I managed to......"

Dilwyn interrupted him.

"Yes, yes I know the technique, a light scrape, and then a delicate wash with some 'meths' and cotton wool, then scrape again etcetera etcetera, get to the point".

Ellis pursed his lips for a moment, annoyed that Dilwyn had disrupted his self glorification; he paused for another brief moment, made a tutting sound, then carried on.

"Anyway, before I was so rudely interrupted, I was saying, that I found the faint remains of something on the back of the photo, written in thick, but faded pencil."

Ellis referred to his notepad;

"It said:

'Eloise Hunter, February 12th 1931, 3
copies, eight shillings and ninepence'.

"I also found; once cleaned, a small stamp, underneath the pencil marks; it said, Ronald Murray & Murphy, Professional Photographers, 219, Leichardt Street, Brisbane, Queensland, Australia".

Dilwyn interrupted again, but at the same time acknowledged Ellis' work.

"Hunter", he said: "that's a new name in the pot, where the..." (He leaned across the table, so his mother would not hear, and mouthed the words), ".....where the fuck did that come from?"

Mrs. Amethyst, with almost a combined fifth and sixth sense, turned her head to one side, and hissed,

"Do not use language in this house....if your father was still alive he'd skin the pair of you!"

She went back to 'Callan'.

Ellis tittered.

"That's not all".

He now grinned broadly.

"I then checked the births, marriages and deaths records, at Somerset House, in London, just on the off chance like. And guess what I found dated 20th October 1922?"

He did not wait for an answer…….Ellis explained at some length that he had phoned Somerset House from Caerphilly Library, and spoke to a woman there, who he had once been on a three day, 'Archiving and Referencing' course with, at Bishops Castle in Shropshire. This, about three years ago, and they had, 'kind of', (as he put it), hit it off, and kept in touch.

For a brief moment, Dilwyn tried to imagine what this long distance woman must look like, then, after slightly frightening himself by the possibilities, indeed probabilities; he dismissed the thoughts from his head, forcing them out with a tight squeeze of his eyelids.

He returned his attention to Ellis, who was carrying on regardless.

"The marriage took place at": Ellis held up another piece of paper, this time, a long piece, about eighteen inches in all, and narrower than a normal piece of A4; "The Register Office, The Old Marylebone Town Hall, Westminster Council House, 97-113 Marylebone Road, London"….. Ellis leaned across the table again, and said, somewhat unnecessarily secretively; "Tin-Tin photocopied it for me, and posted it".

Dilwyn marvelled for a moment that Ellis would know anyone called 'Tin-Tin', or indeed, that anyone would call anyone else such a name, given the countless alternatives that were available. He exhaled, and shook his head very slightly, so as not to aggravate his brother. Ellis, continued; passing the certificate across the table to Dilwyn, as he pressed on with his delivery.

"Look at the names, of the bride and groom, 'Dykka Van Hoost', and 'Vienna Sunday Hunter Schmeizer Cutter-Kleist'; and I'll bet the witness is one of the other blokes that bought the horse with Van Hoost".

Ellis looked directly at his brother and watched as the pennies all dropped. Dilwyn, smiled, and started filling in the gaps. He then took up the story himself.

"They were over here buying the horse, the witness *is* one of the other names", (Dilwyn cross checked it against the 'Jocky Club' receipt document as he spoke).

"They're all South African citizens"; (he picked up from the information on the marriage certificate, and pressed the relevant 'written in' box with his finger).

"They must have combined the wedding, into their trip; all the dates fit……."

He paused, then, sat bolt upright, and together, they both said, almost in unison.

"Eloise Hunter is, or was Eloise Van Hoost. She's gone to Australia and changed her name".

Ellis stood up, slowly, and walked over to his jacket, (the one with the awkward patches that matched his brothers). It hung on a hook behind the kitchen door, and had his name written in the inside collar label, in red biro, and in his mothers handwriting.

He drew from the inside pocket, another piece of paper, in fact two sheets; which 'Tin-Tin' had acquired for him, from the 'British and Commonwealth Office' in Perth, Western Australia.

Without unfolding them, he handed the documents to Dilwyn, with, (it must be said), some ceremony. As he did so, he enlightened Dilwyn, as to their origins, and 'Tin-Tin's' assistance, in obtaining them.

Dilwyn looked at Ellis slightly quizzically, but said nothing, he unfolded the papers, like a small boy unwrapping a delicate Christmas present; and read, silently to himself.

After a good two or three minutes of quiet prescient assimilation, Dilwyn returned his attention to Ellis, who still stood, impassively now, opposite him across the table. Dilwyn asked, in low tones.

"Are these what I think they are?"

"They most certainly are!" replied Ellis.

Dilwyn looked again at the documents, and flipped the single stapled appended page; without looking up, and with little regards for Mrs Amethysts sensitivities: he concluded:

"I'll bet Bethany Harrington knows fuck all about this!"

"Language!"

Yelped Mrs. A.

The night of the big match.
Pietermaritzburg.
South Africa.
July 27th 1924.
8.35 p.m.

Mambo sat in the old lorry, with the lights off, parked down a narrow alley between De Keet Street and Church Street.

He had collected the truck a few days ago from Dykkas yard outside Durban Docks. He had driven it up when he brought 'Banger' back for the big fight. He had journeyed down to Durban in the back of one of Dykka's 'Baccy Wagons' as he called them.

Mambo was still a bit tired from the trip, (not to mention his exertions with Eloise). He had, (as he put it, when pleading for some extra cash from Dykka, at his office, some days earlier), had to drive to Johannesburg from Durban, and then back to Pietermaritzburg.

"That's over three hundred and fifty, mumpy, bumby fucking miles, with two of the most boring cunts in the world".

Mambo was referring to 'Banger' and his other passenger, the one acquired at Johannesburg.

He had continued with, as if to emphasize his argument further.

"And collecting some Skinny, miserable, Irish feller, who didn't say five words the entire journey, from some shithole in Jo'berg, is a real killer in the dead of night Boss!"

Mambo had paused to see if his protestations were making any headway with Dykka.

He went on.

179

Mambo didn't give up easy when money was at stake.

"And then, the skinny bloke insisted on sitting in the cab with 'Banger' and me, like a fucking morgue Boss, all the way back, like a fucking morgue."

Dykka had enquired as to the lodgings for the 'Skinny Irishman'.

Mambo had told Dykka that he was outside Maleens at Mambo's sister's house. Sinetta, Mambo's sister, was a whore and a drunk, but she did some business for Dykka on the prostitution front sometimes, and had once fixed up some young Zulu girls for one of Dykka's Railway customers. He didn't like her, but then he didn't really like Mambo either.

"Write down the address".

Dykka told him, and gave Mambo a pencil and a piece of paper. He did as he was told, and gave the address back to Dykka.

"I don't know who this guy is Boss, but he's as miserable as………"

Dykka cut Mambo short.

"You don't need to know who he is! Neither does your fucking whore of a sister, nor any other cunt. I'll see to the rest of it!"

He held up the paper with the address on. Dykka dug his hand hard into his trouser pocket, and pulled out two five pound notes, and tossed them on the desk.

"Here's an extra fiver each, one for you and one for that shag tart bucket of spunk Sinetta; for your trouble!"

Dykka knew that Mambo's sister, Sinetta, would be lucky to see a quid out of the money, but he didn't care. He then took out his wallet from inside his jacket, and peeled of another five 'fivers'.

"Here", he said, "here's half the fifty I promised you for the job on Saturday. Don't balls it up".

He had asked Mambo if he had got everything he needed from Durban, and if Silvo, Gonda's cousin, had shown him how to use the '*Bang Bangs*'. Mambo had confirmed he had everything, and that Silvo had sorted out everything that was needed.

"Piece of Piss Boss!"

Mambo had said.

Dykka had nodded his approval, and then, finally, he had asked about the lorry itself.

"It ran like a bag of shit".

Mambo had told him.

Dykka said it didn't matter, as it only needed to last a few more miles. And that Mambo was to keep the lorry on the waste ground behind his lodgings at Port Napier, parked up tight behind the old Railway signboards. No one went there, and Dykka and Gonda owned the derelict site anyway.

In the darkened cab of the lorry, time dragged its leaden heels.

Mambo was puffing on a one inch length of remaining roll-up, with a two inch length of ash bending from it; and swigging at the remains of the bottle of Scotch from his rooms. As he leaned across the steering wheel of the aging truck, and remembering the cargo under the tarpaulins behind him, he dabbed out the fag-end on the dashboard, flicked it out of the wound down window, and took another hefty pull on the Scotch.

The clock tower above The Constitution Hall told him it was eight thirty five p.m. The expected 'G.M. Holloway Cartage' company taxi had just been waved off from outside the hall, with the three departing delegates aboard, and headed for the Railway Station.

He had watched Sastri, his wife, and four or five other people, all dressed smartly in suits and best sari's; wave until the taxi disappeared around the corner at the end of Church Street.

Mambo then watched in silence as the small group of Indians climbed the entrance steps to the double doors, chatting as they went, and with a lot of back slapping and hand shaking went back inside the Hall. Above the doorway, hung a large banner with black letters, at least two feet high painted on it. It said;

'*Natal Indian Congress & Natal Indian
Association Annual Meeting*'.

At either side of the steps stood wooden billboards, each about six feet by four feet, with a paper sign pinned on each, the one on the left stating in bright red letters;

'Ban 'The Class Areas Bill', and, 'D.F.Malan; Out!,Out!,Out!'. And the one on the right demanding; 'Support YOUR Indian African Congress', and declaring, 'The I.A.C. is YOUR voice'.

Dr. Malan, was the South African 'Minister for the Interior', and the author of 'The Class Areas Bill'. An item of legislation the Indians viewed as an illegal limitation of their rights to commerce. An item of legislation which, incidentally, had the whole hearted support of Dykka, Gonda, and the White Business Community of Natal; and the more distant White Business Community of Rhodesia, represented by the Van Der Kyper brothers and their interests.

Through the opened doors of the Hall, Mambo could see that there remained a large number of delegates still inside, mulling around, drinking tea from china cups, and nibbling on cucumber sandwiches. He could hear the gentle humm of their conversations, both in English, and the rich dialects of India; wafting in through the opened window of his lorry, with sallow indifference on the still night air.

"Fucking Wogs".

Mambo muttered to himself.

It was now eight forty five p.m. by the clock tower dial, and Mambo's instruction was to sit tight until five past nine.

This being fifteen minutes after the departure of the 'Rhodesian Trans African Railways' overnight train to Bulawayo. On which, by that time, (and well on their way north); should be the three bains of the Van Der Kypers lives, 'Crevitt', 'Mousafan' and 'Tandis', the Rhodesian activists for Indian rights: the occupants of the earlier 'Holloway Cartage Company' taxi.

Church Street was not too busy after nine o'clock at night. The Coolie Rickshaws which still buzzed around the streets of Pietermaritzburg didn't run late. And the big night over at Scottsville Park had whittled down the Saturday night revellers from this side of town.

It was now just before nine, and Mambo reached under the passenger seat of the old lorry. He withdrew; (quite gingerly), a little coconut sized cluster of three British Army, First World War 'Mills Bombs' hand-grenades. They were lashed together with fencing wire, and with a burn fuse, about a foot long attached into one of the grenades. He placed them gently on the seat beside him.

182

Mambo, had in the back of the covered lorry, the better part of two hundred and fifty gallons of petrol, in five, forty five gallon steel drums.

He jumped from the cab, and went to the back of the lorry, clambering over the tail gate, and through the canvass flap, he went inside. There he took the caps off each of the metal drums. He dropped them carelessly to the floor, where they tinkled to a standstill among the other debris. The floor of the lorry was littered, five inches deep, with old nuts and bolts, railway track chairs and clamps, bits of pipe, and shards of metal of all descriptions. The lorry was a huge fragmentation grenade, weighing the better part of ten tons.

Mambo gave each of the drums a violent shake, allowing some petrol to spill out over the top and sides of each, and cascade down, onto the metalled floor. Within seconds the back of the lorry reeked of petrol fumes. Mambo jumped out, and without adjusting the canvass flap, ran back to the cab, once in the driving seat, he patted the 'Mills Bombs' gently, and started the engine. It was five past nine.

He engaged the gear stick, and drove the truck, (as quietly as he could), out of the alley-way, across Church Street, and made a sharp left turn, to park outside the doors of 'The Constitutional Hall', at the foot of the entrance steps, with his two drivers side wheels mounting the pavement. He put the handbrake on, and left the engine running, he struck a match, lit the fuse on the 'Mills Bombs', and jumped from the cab, closing the door behind him.

Church Street was quiet, half a dozen pedestrians taking the evening air, mostly courting couples, and all further along the road out of the way; a couple of Coolie Rickshaws and the usual compliment of stray cats and dogs. It was as empty as he could have hoped for, and most this street life, apart from one of the Rickshaws was far enough away to stand a fighting chance.

Inside the Hall he could see the Indian multitude, the open entrance doors would suck in the fireball like Eloise sucked in his cock.

He knew he had about thirty seconds; he walked behind the lorry, and crossed the road to the alley, the stench of petrol assaulting him as he crossed behind the lorries tail gate.

He was nearly sick.

As soon as he entered the alley-way, and without really knowing it, Mambo found himself sprinting for all he was worth. He was sweating, bucketfuls of sweat, thick smelly sweat, scared sweat. His heart was pounding like a steam hammer, fit to burst open, and tear his chest apart, like the canvas cover of the old lorry that would shortly be torn apart. His legs were spinning like the wheels already turning and whirring on the Bulawayo Night Train, his hot breath condensing in the cooling night air.

His head was full of her.

Gundhar Crevitt, Kanmachand Mousafan and Sachin Tandis sat in their carriage at the back of the Bulawayo Night Train, sharing their views on the conference they had attended; each man had removed his jacket, and loosened his neck tie. A black waiter had brought them a large pot of tea and a selection of cakes and scones' for the journey. It would be a long trek, but they had a compartment to themselves, and a water closet at the end of their carriage.

Mousafan was already complaining that Sastri was concentrating too much on South Africa, and not devoting enough attention to the rest of 'Commonwealth Africa'. They would spend the entire night in animated debate, fuelled by tea and sweet desserts. At least until they passed the Beitbridge tunnel, about fifteen miles over the Rhodesian border.

If the 'Rhodesian Trans African Railways' steam locomotive 'De Crup' kept to time, they should enter the tunnel at about one thirty in the morning.

On the Gwandia road from Bulawayo, a Van Der Kyper ore lorry bumped over the uneven ground towards the Beitingar Junction, just beyond the first railway bend after the Beitbridge tunnel. It was pitch black as the driver heaved the truck onto the dirt road below the curve in the tracks. They stopped at a suitable spot, close to the cusp of the curve as agreed. It was isolated, and less than twenty yards from the railway lines, clear and gravelled to their right towards the tracks, and dense overgrowth to their left.

Perfect.

It was just after nine o'clock.

'The Elephant' looked down at his boots as he walked towards the ring of light; Banjo had put his lucky strings in them. The ones he had laced up the night he beat 'Banger', in the warehouse at Dykkas Sidings.

The noise assuaged him, there must have been a thousand people in the parade ring. As he passed a bookie, he noticed on his blackboard that he had cut the odds on Crusher Hohner, and that 'The Bloody Elephant', was chalked up as moving out to three to one.

Banjo and 'Banger' were behind him. 'Banger' stepped out of line, and, tempted by the odds, put another ten bob on 'The Elephant'. Though touched by the old fister's faith, 'The Elephant', for the first time in a few years now, was the underdog.

It made him nervous.

He didn't like it.

As he stepped between the front wings, of two of the ring lorries, he could see why the odds were changing. Across the circle of light, about thirty yards away stood Crusher Hohner. He must have been eight or nine stone heavier than 'The Elephant', and a good six inches taller, wider and thicker in every direction.

If 'The Elephant' had had any money left in his denim trousers at that moment, he would have handed it to Banjo, and told him to "stick it all on Crusher".

If he had not 'taken a big piss, in the back of the lorry, he could well have pissed himself now.

Inside his head, the world grew silent. He concentrated as he had never concentrated before, he tried to remember every blow he had ever thrown, how fast he could be, how smoothly he could move. He thought of David and Goliath, thought of his mother, thought of every boxing lesson Mr. Switch Rillington had given him.

He saw the Scottish Ringmaster speaking to the crowd through his megaphone, he heard nothing, he saw the Grandstand clock face, lit up by the moon, it was just after nine o'clock.

As he looked down and brought his jaw back to level, he saw Crusher hurtling towards him. The bell had clanged, and he hadn't even heard it. In a second the big German was on him, over him, and a straight, lightning swift, left hand sledge hammer with 'The Elephant's' name on it was screaming towards his face. He bent his right knee, stooping sharply to avoid the blow, he had not been quick enough, and, although deflected, the giant fist caught 'The Elephant' high on his left cheek. He felt the cheekbone shatter, and his eyesight distort slightly as the bony socket holding his left eye in place, split and cracked. He was low, almost crouching, the pain bellowing in his skull. Then, through the dancing forearms of his own guard, he saw it, as clear and blurred at the same time as ice in ice cold winter water. Even his untrue eye could not disguise Crusher's mili-second of mistake. The heel twisted in the grass of the parade ring, (just as 'Banger' had predicted), and, as he glanced upwards, 'The Elephant' saw the left hand drop, just a fraction, and open to the side.

Mustering all the strength he had, and all the skills he had learned, 'The Elephant' threw his scything right hand, and felt the third and fourth knuckles of his hand smash as it collided with the leading point of Crusher Hohners chin.

The guaranteed right hand 'monster' of Crusher's own blow was falling back, and loosing trajectory, as it connected with the collar bone of 'The Elephant'. Apparently the crack could be heard, above all the din, at the far end of the Grandstand as it snapped clean in two.

As Crusher Hohner's mammoth frame hit the turf, people who were there, would say that a man could see the ring of lorry headlights, lift, as the ground shook under the impact of the huge Krauts fall.

'The Elephant' looked up once more at the Grandstand clock face; it was not even five past nine. The crowd; now, really was silent. His eyeball had filled with blood, and the world looked pink and twisted, his cheek felt fluid, and mushed, and Banjo and 'Banger' were studying him with gawping faces.

"He's dead!"

Clanged the Scottish Ringmaster, then repeated it, then, somewhat belatedly screamed for a Doctor, kneeling over the silent, still, dead, Crusher.

Dykka would have Crushers' corpse of the grass and into one of his lorries in minutes. His body would turn up in a week or so at some road junction in Kokstad or Kwa Dukuza or some other God forsaken Hell-hole. The right palms would get crossed and he would become a drunken road accident, or a heart attack. The Van Der Kyper brothers would square up any family problems back in Rhodesia.

This was the sort of thing that happened all the time in this game.

Banjo pulled a bundle of betting slips from his pocket, and pressed them into 'Banger's' hand.

"Go and collect the money for me, there's some tickets for these fuckers here".

Banjo gestured to the forest of tall thin 'Bookies Blackboards' and coloured fancy signs, stretching skywards for the nights stars between the lorries.

"But the big ones are from 'Fat Malcolm', over in Maleens."

He leaned forward to 'Banger' as if to re-enforce some implied importance.

"You're on ten percent of everything you pull in".

'The Elephant' interrupted, his voice slurring.

"Twenty percent! Twenty percent!"

Twenty percent of the winnings was a good deal for the advice from 'Banger' which had probably saved 'The Bloody Elephants' life.

"O.K.; o.k., twenty percent", said Banjo, he pointed a finger at 'Banger', "but that's after we get the stake money back, and the Rickshaw fare to Maleens comes out of your end".

'Banger' nodded and smiled, he let go of 'The Elephant's' arm, and ran off into the crowd sorting out the betting slips as he went, and seeking out the unsuspecting bookies.

As if as an afterthought, Banjo shouted after him:

"And if 'Fat Malcolm' gives you any trouble cut his fucking nose off".

'Banger' was a wise choice to send to 'Fat Malcolm'; although out of the fight game; he was still a horrible individual who one wouldn't intentionally cross. He would think nothing of cutting off 'Fat Malcolm's nose, or anything else, and he wouldn't double deal 'The Elephant' because he knew that Dykka viewed 'The Elephant' as his own investment, and if 'Banger' crossed him, it would be like crossing Dykka himself, then Dykka's White Boys would be on him like flies on shit.

'Banger' was safe hands.

Banjo shouted after 'Banger' for a second time, nearly allowing the disorientated 'Elephant' to stumble to the ground.

"Banger'! Eighty eight Greyling Street, out towards Victoria, if we're not there when you get back; Wait on the stairs; Flat 'C'".

'Banger' turned as he walked away, and, walking backwards, shouted above the general hub-hub that he knew where the brothers lived, and that he would be back before midnight.

Banjo sat his brother on the front bumper of the nearest lorry, and began washing him down from a galvanised bucket and the pile of rags he always had around his shoulder on these occasions.

He kept one eye on 'Banger' doing the rounds of the Bookies. Banjo smiled, he saw that 'Banger'was not one for queuing, and he pushed to the front of every line, and nobody argued. Within minutes 'Banger' had collected the local winnings, and Banjo saw him running across the centre oval, toward the Scottsville Park main gates, and the exit onto Milner Road, where he would probably still get a Rickshaw, or maybe even a taxi at this time of night. Banjo smiled again, and returned his attention to his brother.

He had started cleaning up the wounds, there were only two cuts, and neither would need stitches, (just). He had packed them with Vaseline, and was just setting about massaging the broken eye socket back into position, (the broken collar bone could wait until last, it only needed pulling back, and a figure of eight bandage across 'The Elephants' back); when, suddenly! The sky lit up in the darkness, and the loudest bang that God could create threw the air to the ground and pressed the crowd beneath it.

Banjo lay across his brother who winced with the pain of hitting the grass with such force. High above the Grandstand Roof, and about a mile and a half to the north east of Scottsville Park, rose a column of bubbling smoke and fire, so thick that it looked like a liquid full of strawberries and clinkers.

The people in the parade ring could feel the heat on their faces.

Fights broke out as some of the Bookies tried to make for the gates without settling their slips.

Banjo gazed at the swirling tower of pink smoke, as the wind picked it up as it climbed, and made twisting tortured stretched out shapes of it: like barley sugar sticks high above the districts of Pietermaritzburg. Wherever that was; he was glad he wasn't under it, and whatever it was, he knew it was not a good thing.

Half an hour later, the smoke still hung thick as palace curtains in the air, and ash fell like winter snow in the hills above Odessa. Banjo and his brother had rags across their mouths and noses. Fire engine bells clanged and sang in a dozen different keys, as they came and went from all directions. The people in the Park had generally stayed put, not really knowing what else to do.

Someone had said.

"It's the Wogs over at the Constitutional Hall; they've blown the bloody place up!"

By now, the clock on the Grandstand roof was chasing ten o'clock, and Banjo had strapped back his brother's shoulders, and had stuffed as much cotton wool as he could above the top teeth gums of his mouth. This, and the wadding he had forced up one nostril, was done to stop the bits of cheek bones from falling inwards, and healing to form a big crater in the side of his face.

Tomorrow morning, (if the world was still here); Banjo would cut a two inch slice in the fatty part of his brothers cheek, and shove two coins high up inside, to keep the bones healing towards the outside, to try, (as best he could), to keep the shape of his face.

He would boil the coins first in salt water to try to stop any infections, either that or decent whiskey.

The boarding of the *Cok Guzel Denizala Baligi*,
The Black Sea,
The morning of April 15th 1919.

Lieutenant Leonid Ilyich Brezhnitzen of *The Czareavitch Alexai Romanov* of the Imperial Russian Navy, Black Sea Fleet, introduced himself as he stepped onto the littered deck. Human remains, blood, entrails, shards of metal and random lengths of cable lay strewn from the forward anchor winch, as far back as the boarding gate.

Crewmen fought a small fire in the bow. They were winning.

"Who is in command here?"

He demanded.

Karem Tortruk stepped forward and made a poor attempt at a salute, and began to remove his cap, holding it by the peak. He answered in poor Russian.

"I am; my name is Capt......."

Lieutenant Brezhnitzen struck him across the face, hard with the back of his hand. Karem fell to the deck, still clutching his cap. Brezhnitzen gestured at the carnage before him.

"This; this is your fault, I could have you shot, you could have stopped when we first signalled!"

Brezhnitzen gestured to two of his men to hold the Captain; they dragged him to his feet with little consideration. He then shouted to the gathered 'customers';

"Is there anyone else here who speaks Russian?"

Every hand went up; he turned back to Kerem, and slapped him again. Brezhnitzen knew exactly what kind of ship this was, he had seen them many times before, and had sunk more than one.

"I want a list of all those killed; who will volunteer to collect this?"

He glanced around the gathering throng.

The Doctor, who had been treating Arris the Boson, was walking down the bridge steps, his Doctors bag in his hands.

"I will lieutenant, and gladly so", he said as he arrived on the main-deck.

He walked over to the gangway gate, where the rest of the Russian sailors had now boarded, and were congregating about the deck, awaiting instructions.

He turned to Karem Tortruk, who was still being held by two of Brezhnitzen's men. He remarked, almost casually:

"Your Boson is dead, he lost too much blood, and the shock; anyway he's dead".

He waved his hand dismissively before continuing.

"Your helmsman though will be fine, my nurse is cleaning him up".

190

The Doctor called some people over from the gathered crowd on the deck, and asked them to collect the names of all the dead, and write them down, and give it to the Russian Officer. He then turned to Brezhnitzen, and asked if they had any medical facilities aboard *The Czareavitch Alexai Romanov*. The Officer confirmed that he had the Ships Doctor and two of his staff with him on the deck. He stated that he would avail them at the Jewish Doctors' disposal.

The Navy medical team and the Jewish Doctor then left the deck and went below.

Brezhnitzen instructed some of his other men to form details from the crew and the passengers to clean up the mess, and to find the Ships Engineer, and bring him to the Captains quarters.

He then looked back to Karem, and said simply;

"Now, you take us to your cabin, I want your logs, your crew list, and your registrations; if you have any?"

As they marched Karem away, Lieutenant Brezhnitzen said quietly to one of his men, who was reasonably close at hand:

"Throw the bodies over the side".

He nodded towards the steps to the Bridge gangway.

"That goes for the Boson too, and make sure his name is on the list of casualties. Do it as quietly as you can. No time for niceties, no services, no ceremony, just get them off the ship. Then get the steam hoses running and clean these deck plates. I'll send you the Engineer once I've finished with him".

The Russian sailor acknowledged the orders with a proper salute, and went about his duties.

"Mama! Mama!"

The two boys cried as they ran along the deck walkways, flitting from side to side, shouting up steps as they passed, and in through open doorways, occasionally looking over the side rails.

"Mama!"

They continued to shout, until they arrived at the bow of the *Cok Guzel Denizala Baligi*.

The elder of the two brothers bent down near the guardrail, or rather its twisted remains, just beyond the decimated anchor winch housing. There on the deck-plates he found a piece of his mother's blue and yellow headscarf, scorched and bloodstained, but unmistakably hers. As he looked around him, he realised he was surrounded by the offal that was once human beings, once his mother. He turned and held the remnants of the scarf out towards his younger brother.

No words were necessary.

No tears were shed.

The boys were already beyond tears.

In the Captains quarters, the Russian's found a young Turkish boy, no more than fifteen. He nervously offered them tea. Karem said something to him Turkish, and the boy sat down in a small chair in the corner of the cabin. Brezhnitzen needed no further explanation of this relationship; and struck the Captain once more across the face.

"Pig!"

He spat in the Captains face.

"No one is supposed to be below decks, you heard the orders. Do you want us to shoot you, because it would be no problem, no problem at all?"

Then, regaining some of his composure, Brezhnitzen asked sharply:

"How many passengers are aboard?"

Karem Tortruk, had to admit that he could not be certain, this admission earned him another slap; his lip and nostrils were now bleeding.

"Where are your Logs?"

Brezhnitzen demanded next.

Karem told him that they were in the top drawer of his desk. The desk was old with a polished but stained top; it had one wide drawer, set in the side facing the Captains green leather chair.

It was locked when the Lieutenant tugged at it, he did not ask for a key, merely gestured to one of the two sailors still holding the Captain. The man released Karem's arm, walked to the desk, and unlocked the drawer with three clouts of his rifle butt.

The desk edge and drawer face splintered, and the locks escutcheon plate fell to the floor.

In the drawer Lieutenant Brezhnitzen rummaged through some bottles of pills, a small silk pouch, some pens, a pair of spectacles, until he found two things he needed. Firstly, the Ships Log, which he dropped with a thump onto the desktop, and secondly a small bore Webley revolver.

Holding up the pistol, he said;

"This is another reason I have to shoot you!"

He dropped the gun on the desk, next to the Logbook.

There was a knock at the door, and one of Brezhnitzen's men stood there with an oily fat individual, quite short, and abnormally ugly.

"This is the Ships Engineer, Sir, his name is Gorkin; he speaks Russian".

The Russian Navy sailor pushed the man into the cabin.

Brezhnitzen took up the conversation.

"Can you confirm that this vessel is still sea worthy? And is there anyone aboard, apart from this 'Pig'", he gestured at Karem, "who can navigate this Ship?"

The Captain made to say something, the inevitable slap across the face silenced him.

The Ships Engineer began to speak, he spluttered as he spoke, and a small shower of spittle flew in all directions, delivering his words.

"The engine room and boilers are not damaged. We have plenty of chain below decks, and we can rig a replacement anchor. We can winch by hand if we have to".

"And the navigation?"

Asked Brezhnitzen once again.

The man thought for a moment, then confirmed that the only other person on board that was capable was 'Boson Arris'. Gorkin confirmed that Arris was a very capable seaman, and was Captain Tortruks 'First Officer really'.

Lieutenant Brezhnitzen stroked his chin for a few seconds, and turned to Karem.

"Is that the 'Boson' the Old Jew spoke of on deck, the one that 'bled to death'?"

Karem nodded in affirmation.

"Arris is dead?" asked the Engineer.

No one answered him.

"Get him out of here", said Brezhnitzen to the sailor that had brought Gorkin to him; "Take him up top, and get him and his engine room crew to rig the steam hoses, and get things cleaned up".

He stepped forward as they were about to leave, and looking directly at Gorkin, and stooping to be eye to eye with the fat oily man, he added.

"Any nonsense, shoot this one", and he prodded Gorkin in the chest.

Gorkin's jaw dropped as quickly as the anchor had plummeted earlier to the bed of the Black Sea. The guard threw him out of the cabin with unnecessary violence, and seemed to take some pleasure in his tormenting. Gorkin knew the guard would shoot him without a second thought, and suspected he may enjoy it.

He made a silent vow to do the best steam cleaning job that had ever taken place aboard a ship.

Anywhere.

The Lieutenant returned to the desk, and opened the Captains Logbook.

"You sailed from Odessa I see; who was in charge of the City when you left?"

He looked at Karem.

"The Whites", he said, "you lot".

He was trying not to offend, trying to stay alive.

"The Reds had it before, but the Whites took it back, it goes back and forth".

He then added, attempting some ingratiation.

"The Whites are better than the Reds they let the people go, the Reds are all thieves".

Karem hoped that his Russian was up to the task, and that he had not said anything insulting by mistake.

The Russian Naval Lieutenant walked from behind the desk and stood directly in front of Karem, his two sailors holding the terrified Turk upright.

"I want the names of the Russian soldiers you paid to allow your ship in and out of Odessa".

194

Brezhnitzen knew the way this trade of human cargo worked. He loathed it, and he loathed the people who profited from it.

Karem stuttered as he said that he had no names, it was just a standard arrangement with whoever held the port. It was the truth, and yet he longed to be able to say something else.

"So you trade with The Reds as well then?"

The Captain of the *Cok Guzel Denizala Baligi* knew that he had just signed his own death warrant. He was sweating now, sweating like the pig he was.

"No, no, I mean The Reds force me to, they make me, I have no choice, I have......."

This time two slaps silenced him, and then a sharp hard punch to his right eye. He heard himself scream.

There was another knock to the cabin door; it was the Doctor from *The Czareavitch Alexai Romanov*, along with one of his medics, and the Old Jew.

"There's Typhus on board", he said simply, "I've instructed my medics and some of your men to isolate the infected passengers towards the stern of the ship on this deck. Everything forward will need steam hosing. There's next to no medical supplies aboard, it's a bloody disgrace!"

Another slap came Karem's way, his face was now a mixture of reds and purples with small rivulets of blood here and there, and everywhere covered with a greasy film of sticky sweat.

The Russian Naval Medical Officer, Brezhnitzen and his Ships Doctor arranged that they would send one of the launches back to *The Czareavitch Alexai Romanov* for medical supplies, fresh linen, whatever food could be spared, along with as many drums of fresh water that could be brought over.

Lieutenant Brezhnitzen instructed the Doctor, that he wanted all his men off 'This bucket', within one hour, he then told the Doctor to make the arrangements. As the medic and the Doctors were leaving the cabin, Brezhnitzen asked:

"You; Old Jew, do you know how to treat this?"

The small Doctor turned and replied.

"I do; with the right supplies, I can possibly stop the spread".

He paused for a moment, then, almost as an afterthought, but with the certainty that comes with the chill arrival of winter, there is the comforting knowledge that a summer will follow eventually.

"The ones that are already infected: most will die, the younger stronger ones may have a chance, but they will probably die too".

He looked at the Lieutenant in silence, for what seemed an age, no further words were exchanged.

Then he left.

Karem took another beating, this time one fuelled by absolute rage. He slumped between his two guards. Brezhnitzen said, with tempered emotion.

"If there was one crewman on this hulk who could read a chart, I'd have shot you by now!"

Karem knew the Lieutenant meant every word, and he gave secret thanks for Arris's demise. The Russian continued.

"I will take your Log, I will make my report, and if I hear that you do not deliver these people to a safe port, I will hunt you down Captain Karem Tortruk, and I will execute you. Personally! Like I should be executing you today".

He turned to his sailors, and told them to let him go. They did so immediately, and he dropped to the cabin floor like a sack of soaked lentils.

Brezhnitzen turned to the young Turkish boy sitting in the corner.

"Where is his loot?"

The boy pointed to a small louvered door in the opposite corner of the cabin. Again the lock was smashed off with his sailor's rifle butts, and the door flung open. Inside Brezhnitzen found the lockers that had been spread around the deck at the loading in Odessa.

He turned back towards Karem.

"I am not going to open these, or throw them over the side, you can keep it. But you return half of it to your passengers when they disembark. The other half is yours and your crews, to make sure you do as I have instructed".

He bent down, leaning over Karem, whose left eye was now black, and closing with the swelling bruise.

"Do you understand?"

He shouted at the top of his voice.

When Karem failed to answer immediately, the Russian struck him hard on top of his head with a clenched fist.

In the fashion of a hammer.

"I understand! I understand!"

Rumbled Karem.

Lieutenant Brezhnitzen rose, and straightened up. He told the prostrate Captain that he would explain the arrangements to his crew, the Old Jew, and representatives of the passengers. He also told him that he would expect a telegram signal from his port of destination, (wherever that would be), to confirm their arrival, and also, he would expect confirmation from the Old Jew that all the arrangements had been honoured.

Before he left the cabin, he told Captain Karem Tortruk, that if, after today, he ever saw him again, it would be for the express purpose of taking his life.

He turned to the young Turkish boy, and told him to clean up the 'mess on the floor', (referring to Karem), and to have his Captain back on deck in ten minutes.

Lieutenant Brezhnitzen returned to the desk one last time, and picked up the Ships Log, and the Webley revolver.

The Russians all left, without closing the cabin door.

The knock, and the Nuns,
April 1972.

It was about a week or so after Maldwyn's first *sortie* into the Cardiff Libraries, and just before the meeting at the Amethyst house, where the Historical Society had formulated the list for Harry 'H' to give to Uncle Murray in Australia.

Dilwyn had just come home from work, and was about to start writing up some notes about the contents of 'Stalin's' box, but firstly he was punching some photocopies, (he had found out during his day a little more information on the Japanese submarine I-21, and was collating it for the files). He had also decided to

197

make up a further, and separate file of 'Australian Items', as he had now begun to call them.

He had already decided, independently of the others that an Australian connection would need to be made, for additional research, and that my Uncles Murray and Wilf, in Perth, would be ideally placed.

Mrs Amethyst was in the back kitchen, with faggots and peas on the stove, and bread pudding smelling delicious in the oven. All should be ready in about half an hour, by which time Ellis should be home.

Ellis, incidentally, this very day, and from his own shelves at the 'Caerphilly Public Library', had been researching, (as far as he could), the New South Wales port of Newcastle, and its Police Force of the 1940's.

He had also arrived at the inescapable conclusion that they needed more, 'on the ground' help with the 'nuts and bolts' of what had happened to 'Stalin' in Australia. He would discuss it with his brother later that evening over tea, which his mother had promised would be faggots and peas, and bread pudding with custard for afters.

Yum, Yum.

Ellis was due home slightly later than Dilwyn, as today was his turn at the library in Caerphilly, and Dilwyn was working more locally at the library in Abertridwr.

'Land of the Giants' had just started on the telly, and Dilwyn was half watching it, as he punched, annotated and filed documents.

There was a gentle knock at the front door. Mrs Amethyst said, peeping around the scullery door; that if that was Ellis, and he'd lost his key again, this time he could pay for a new one. Dilwyn volunteered to answer it.

As he walked across the living room, something made him look through the front window, prior to going into the passage to the front door. He flicked the net aside and saw a fairly old grey coloured 'Morris Thousand', parked in front of their house.

"It's not Ellis Mam, there's a car out the......"

He glanced to the right towards the front door.

"Hell's bells!"

He said, turning towards the kitchen.

"It's a couple of Nuns, blue and white ones!"

Mrs Amethyst hurtled from the kitchen screaming, as she wiped her hands in her pinny.

"Oh no, something's happened to Ellis!" she squealed.

Dilwyn entered the passage and took the two steps to the front door, his mother two inches behind him, a look of terrified anticipation on her face.

"It's not our Ellis is it?" she asked, a quiver in her voice.

The elder of the two Nuns, a kindly looking lady with clear framed glasses, and well into her sixties; looked bemused for a moment, then smiled a proper benevolent Nuns smile; like Deborah Kerr in 'Black Narcissus'. After a short pause, some facial bewilderment, and some mental acrobatics, the nun realised Mrs Amethyst's concern, she continued smiling, but broader now, then said; in a lovely Northern Irish accent, full of treacle, full of wind and sunshine.

"No; no my dear lady, there's nothing wrong, we're actually looking for Mr Ellis Amethyst", she paused again, then, looking at Dilwyn said, "and, of course his brother Dilwyn, who I assume is yourself young man", she nodded at Dilwyn.

Mrs Amethyst invited both of them in, and as they walked into the living room, and Dilwyn shut the front door, the older, Irish Nun explained that they were from St. Winifred's Hospice in Cardiff, and that they had been sent here, after visiting Bethany Harrington. Mrs. Amethyst offered both of them a cup of tea, and a toasted current bun, which they accepted. Dilwyn ushered them to the settee, as they sat down, the older Nun said;

"Ah, 'Land of the Giants', I think the little spacemen are so clever, how they make hatchets and such out of huge matchsticks, and bits of massive razor blades. Who thinks these things up?"

Dilwyn turned the television down slightly, and as he sat in the other armchair, and whilst his mother was in the kitchen, he asked quizzically;

"You said Bethany Harrington?"

"Oh yes", the Nun began.

She explained that 'Stalin' had spent the last eight days of his life at St. Winifred's, and had passed away in their care. Except she didn't call him 'Stalin' she called him 'Mr. Androskewowicsz'; and with perfect pronunciation it must be said. She explained that she was Mother Superior Anunciata Devlin, a qualified nurse as well as a Nun. She then introduced the other Nun, come nurse, (who was a good deal younger at around thirty five), as Sister Lubia Brezhnitzen.

She explained, at some length, (while Mrs. Amethyst delivered and distributed the teas and buns, and individual small plates to eat them off, and paper serviettes, these were after all nuns, no ordinary visitors), that Sister Brezhnitzen, had something for them. Something which, by rights was to have gone to Bethany, but which she had, earlier that day, asked if the Nuns would deliver to the Amethyst brothers.

The younger Nun handed Dilwyn, an A5 sized, fairly thick 1972 diary, made of green plastic, with the name of a double glazing company, from Ely, emblazoned on the front in gold.

Dilwyn had not even noticed her holding it, but now as she handed it to him, he noticed that she also had a hard cover notepad in her hand as well, a black one with a red spine. She did not pass this over.

Dilwyn took a sip of his tea, and put down his cup, then opened the diary. After thumbing a couple of pages, he looked back to the Nuns, saying:

"I can't understand this, it's in Cyrillic script, and handwritten; Ellis might have a chance, but I don't know…"

Sister Brezhnitzen interrupted him, saying, in a quite delicate voice, and with no trace of an accent, just delicate and perfect.

Dilwyn found himself drawn to her.

"I have already translated the document for you it was only about thirty pages or so. Here take this", and she handed him the notebook.

She explained that 'The Diary' as such, was not really a 'diary' of 'Stalin', but it was used by him as a notepad. It was something that had been given to the hospital by some workmen, who were replacing some window frames, and had never been used. She went on to say that 'Stalin' had asked for something to write in, and so this had been given to him. He had used it merely to write up some remembrances.

Sister Brezhnitzen explained that her Great Great Grandparents were Russian, and that they had left Russia after the Revolution. They had fled to Prague in the early twenties, from where they again fled in the late thirties, this time to London. She herself had been brought up in Shepherds Bush in London, amongst many ex-pat communities including many Eastern Europeans and Jews. She explained that she spoke Polish, Czheck, and Russian, as well as English and Hebrew, and was in fact learning Welsh.

She stated that she had enjoyed translating the notes, and it had allowed her to, "Keep her hand in".

She then went to great lengths to say that she had not shown the 'diary' or its translation to **anyone** else; she glanced at Mother Superior Devlin, and concluded with;

"I just thought that it should be returned to Miss Harrington; as I had seen her visiting Mr. Androskewowicsz many times, and they seemed very close".

She commented that the name above the Stalin's bed at St. Winifred's had not read 'Androskewowicsz', but that the translation went some way to explain that.

She went on to tell Dilwyn that the Mother Superior was teaching her to drive, and that the 'Morris Thousand' had 'L Plates' on, and that delivering the book gave her an opportunity for a lesson. After all; this was a good fifteen mile round trip to Senghenydd, and then back to Cardiff.

The two Nuns finished their teas, and current buns, and made polite chit-chat as to how 'Stalin's' funeral had gone. Mother Superior Devlin asked if the television could be turned up slightly, (which it then was), and after 'Land of the Giants' the two Nuns left. Dilwyn saw them out.

As they got in their car, Sister Brezhnitzen said, he could phone them at anytime, if he needed any more assistance, and that, given her own ancestry, she was always interested in the stories of; "other refugee families".

Dilwyn watched the car disappear around the corner at the end of the 'Four Terraces', then rushed back inside, desperate to read the translation before Ellis got home.

The night of the big match.
Pietermaritzburg.

201

It would take all night and all the next day to douse the Fire at the Constitutional Hall. Water had been a problem with the 'Dorp' running low for the time of year, and Church Street being so far away from it in any event. They had set up a human chain of buckets, but, quite frankly, as Dykka had commented, 'They might as well have pissed on it'.

There had been some survivors, all horrifically burned, and taken to the 'Victoria Hospital' in Pretoria, by ambulance, fleets of cars, lorries and vans, anything really that could be mobilised. None of Dykka's lorries were provided. In some cases the survivors had to be moved by special train to the 'Suffi Hospital' at Bloemfontein.

Pietermaritzberg's own hospital simply did not have the facilities or expertise for this kind of disaster. The whole of Church Street would be closed for months, the facades of every adjacent and opposite building had been blackened by the smoke, every pane of glass for two hundred yards in any direction had been blown to pieces.

As far as Felix Vischer the Fire Chief could work out, the death toll was somewhere between sixty and one hundred and twenty.

Felix was Gonda's brother.

The horribly disfigured Sastri had been found near the rear fence of the Constitutional Hall; he had either been hurled there, by the explosion, or had staggered there before collapsing. He had been found alive, but was dead on arrival at the 'Victoria Hospital'.

He had been strangled in the back of the truck which was transporting him, by one of Dykka Van Hoosts, 'White Boys'. A service for which Dykka had haggled over, concerning the fee to resolve this unexpected problem. He eventually settled the matter in agreeing a sum of twenty pounds cash, and half a case of Scotch. This discounted rate on the basis that, as Dykka so economically put it.

"The fucking Wog would have probably died anyway".

Felix Vischer stated for the newspapers, two days after the horror; that the explosion had been caused by a 'Gas Main'. His statement had said:

'A gas leak, probably from a fractured pipe, damaged due to settlement as a result of the drop in level of the Dorp Struet'.

Gonda had arranged for some of his Railway workmen, to dig random holes up and down the length of Church Street, and in the vicinity of where the Constitutional Hall used to stand; and for them to look 'official' as they dug them.

Over the next fortnight, he would have them excavate a dozen or more sections of pavement and roadway, stand around, drink some tea, look 'official', (as per Dykka's request), and then fill the holes in again.

It took a week for the stench of petrol to disappear.

A month later, and the Horse Racing season was back in full swing. The Pietermaritzburg skies were blue again. Work had started on re-building the new Constitutional Hall, which was to be re-named the 'Railway Workingman's Institute'.

In the Parliament, Dr Malan's 'Class Areas Bill' had been made law. And the 'Wogs' as Dykka put it; 'Were back where they belonged'.

My Uncles; Murray and Wilf andThe Slaughtermen.
Perth,
Western Australia,
July 3rd, 1972.

My Uncle Murray, and his brother Wilf, (who I never referred to as my uncle, but obviously is), had received the final package from Jimmy C, and the Amethyst brothers about a week ago. They had not given it much attention, because the 1972 summer Olympics were on the telly, and, like everyone else in Australia, they had been staying up until the wee small hours, watching the games.

The time difference between Munich, West Germany, and Perth, was about eight hours, so the days became kind of squashed up between, work, sleep, the Olympics, and the day-to-day stuff that occupies most of us.

The whole thing, of course, got squashed up even more by the 24 hour news coverage of the terrorist attack on the Israeli athletes.

My Uncle Murray, and my Auntie Flo had emigrated to Australia back in 1965, and his brother Wilf, and his family had followed them about two years later. They were all 'Ten Pound Pomms'. Though my Auntie Flo never failed to correct those Ozzy's who called them 'Pommy Bastards'. They were 'Welsh Bastards', or 'Taffy Bastards' and proud if it, and she made sure everyone knew it.

My Father and Jimmy C had phoned Murray a couple of weeks before, to brief him up about Stalin, (who he and my Auntie Flo had known before they emigrated. Them having lived on the Graig Stretch in Abertridwr, and being regulars in 'The Windsor', which was also Stalin's local). They; (Jimmy C and my father), had also filled Murray in, (as best as possible over a bad phone line), about the box, the funeral, Maldwyn and his piles, the Amethyst brothers, Bethany Harrington, my Uncle Bryn, submarines, Russia, Jewels, the Japanese, Cardiff Docks, the Germans and Spinksy etc.

But now, at last, international sporting events, and news coverage prevailing; Murray and Wilf were ready.

It was a bank holiday weekend, so both of them had the Friday to the Monday off work, and the timing seemed perfect. Despite the general consensus of the families 'Down Under Contingent', (as Jimmy C called them), being largely in agreement with Spinksy's statement that it was all 'a pile of old crap', they had agreed to the expedition, albeit a bit tongue-in-cheek.

Murray and Wilf had decided that they would make it a fishing trip and take in the Sanford River, if Spinksy turned out to be right. But that they would also take along a bottle of champagne, just in case he turned out to be wrong, and barking up the wrong Coolabah tree.

The Sanford River was a good sixty or eighty miles further north of where they were heading, but apparently the fishing was good, the beer was cheap, and the camping was easy. But their primary target, (so to speak), was Mount Magnet, and its neighbouring towns, a sheep and cattle stock region about three hundred miles north east of Perth.

My Auntie Flo, and Bills wife Irmantrude had made a bucket load of sandwiches, cheese and onion mostly, with some chicken, some ham, and a few sardine and tomato paste. They had bottles of squash, and tap water, a case of Swan Lager, a couple of packs of Golden Virginia tobacco and Rizzla papers, boxes of England's Glory matches, a paraffin primus stove, a two man tent, two shovels, toilet rolls, mess tins, plastic mugs, two picks, a general tool box, some overalls, and a couple of changes of clothes. Plus of course, half a dozen fishing rods and equipment, wellies, and a magnum bottle of cheap sparkling wine from the local supermarket, which could double as champagne in the unlikely event it, would be required.

The two men loaded the gear into the back of Murray's Ford Taunus estate car, or 'Station Wagon', as he now referred to it. Wilf, had a pick up truck, or 'Ut', pronounced 'Yute', in Australian, which probably would have been better suited; but one of the wheel bearings was shot, so they had decided to take the station wagon. Hughie secretly hated the Yute; it was old, heavy, uncomfortable, unreliable, and ideally suited for the back roads of Oz.

Much better, and more practical really than the Taunus.

But the Taunus did have air-con and a radio, which probably gave it the edge.

It was early July 1972, just scratching autumn in antipodean terms, as the two men kissed their wives farewell on Murray's front porch, and set off on their long weekend of male freedom. In their rear view mirror, Flo and Irmantrude were already planning their girls long weekend of freedom, no sports, no cooking, no washing and no cleaning; of watching, 'The Brothers' on T.V., and re-runs of 'Peyton Place' and the 'Forsyte Saga', and sipping cool glasses of white wine without bloody men.

"Free at last".

Flo said, as she waved goodbye and the Taunus turned the corner at the end of the cul-de-sac.

"Thank God, we are free at last".

Responded Irmantrude; echoing and mimicking the famous civil rights speech of Martin Luther King. They both chuckled.

The two women went back inside the house, and put the kettle on.

"I'll bet their missing us already Wilfy boy" said Murray, and slapped Wilf on the thigh. Despite having only lived in Australia for only seven years, Murray spoke Oz like a Perth native. Wilf, who still retained his Welsh Valley drawl, replied:

"Four days without us, they'll be counting the seconds. Now they'll see exactly what we do for them, you watch, they'll treat us like Kings when we get home; like Kings".

Both men laughed, and Murray concluded that the trip, whatever the outcome; would, in any event, work well in their favour on the matrimonial front.

For the next ten or fifteen minutes they tried to work out between them how to make coffee without one of those 'percolator thingy's'. Eventually they decided, (as it was a 'boys long weekend'), they would probably just stick to drinking lager; and concluded that they would need to buy some more on the way. Wilf also expressed some concern that the girls had not made enough sandwiches. They would therefore need to get some crisps as well.

The *Cok Guzel Denizala Baligi,*
Across the Aegean and the Mediterranean.
A Saturday in August 1919.

Karem Tortruk, his crew and his 'customers' had spent the better part of four months shuffling along the Mediterranean coastline, begging for safe haven at each port they had come to.

Each port refusing them in turn.

The typhus outbreak had been all but eradicated, all-be-it with the loss of over eighty 'customers' and nine crewmen, all of who's corpses had been cast over the side with a difficult mixture of Christian, Muslim and Jewish ritual.

The Old Jewish Doctor had done a magnificent job with the meagre resources at his disposal, relying mostly on the medical supplies provided by the Imperial Russian Navy, and the frequent use of the ships steam hoses as a sterilising tool. His fat old nurse had not been so lucky, having contracted the disease only five weeks ago; she had in fact been one of the last to die.

The ports they had attempted landings at, had, in the main, been helpful, and, (although refusing any docking), had ferried supplies out to them. Largely free of charge, but sometimes forcing Karem to dip into the lockers which the Old Jew now kept tabs on.

This almost affable conveyance of this 'Plague Ship' was not however universal. *The Cok Guzel Denizala Baligi* had in fact been shelled, by port artillery batteries on two occasions, once at Piraeus in Athens, and again at Haifa, the former forcing the ships about turn, but occasioning no damage. The latter hurling a 60mm shell through her hull just above the water line, and well aft. It had killed eight of the infected.

They had been quarantined there.

The hull had been poorly repaired, and in even moderate seas the welded plates sprung and allowed in water, the bilge pumps managed, but only just.

Against his better judgement Karem had attempted a landing at Alexandria in Egypt. He knew of its unenviable reputation for theft and corruption.

However, it had been a long haul around the Eastern Mediterranean, and they had been turned back thirty miles off the Maltese shore by a British Destroyer. The British had replenished *The Cok Guzel Denizala Baligi's* fuel, water and food supplies, but offered her no further assistance. Indeed they had escorted her the next fifty miles south to ensure she did not attempt to come about.

The authorities, (if that is the right word), at Alexandria had inspected the vessel, and had at last, and after some exchange of documents, (and the conveyance to the officials of an entire locker of booty), provided Captain Tortruk with a 'Certificate of Sea Worthiness'.

An Egyptian Certificate, ostensibly worthless in any other country, or at any other port. But at least it stopped him from being impounded, or even worse, sunk where she lay.

The Cok Guzel Denizala Baligi was anchored up about a mile off shore. The provision of bribes, (Karem was discovering), would only take him so far in these southern potentates, and it was made clear that none of his passengers or crew would be welcome ashore, indeed they would more than likely be captured and shot without any discussion.

It was however suggested by an Egyptian Port Officer, that the Suez Canal might provide Captain Tortruk with the best opportunity of disembarkation. The conversation took place in Karem's quarters, with him sitting at his desk, his Turkish Cabin Boy serving tea, and with three Egyptian soldiers, each with a rifle, standing at attention behind the seated uniformed Port Officer.

The Port Officer, a swarthy individual with a dark moustache of pubic hair and pockmarked skin, said;

"A set of passage documents through the canal will cost a considerable sum Captain".

He patted the breast pocket of his uniform and explained that he had all the necessary papers with him, and that only the ships name needed to be entered on them.

He explained to Karem that the Sudanese port of Suakin was less than one thousand two hundred miles away, and that the 'Officials' there, (he laughed as he used the word), would be more than amenable to unloading his stricken vessel of its human cargo. For, as he put it:

"Of course, the right price".

The Port Officers smile revealed two rows of yellow/brown teeth; he smoked heavy tar cigarettes profusely and did so now in Karem's quarters.

"How much for these 'Passage Documents'?" asked Captain Tortruk, in his worst broken Arabic.

If nothing else the arduous journey from Odessa had taught Karem, and most of his passengers for that matter, a smattering of virtually all European and Asian languages. Some collected from the crew, others collected from the 'customers' and various boarding parties; and none of them, absolute.

The Port Officer leaned forward across the desk and said, in equally poor English, so that his guards could not understand;

"Three more of those metal chests you paid me with for the 'Sea Worthiness' Certificate."

Karem became apoplectic at the charge, making it clear that such a fee was extortionate, even when the entire negotiation was one of degrees of extortion. The Port Officer knew that Karem had little choice, though he could in theory just up anchor, and carry on around the Mediterranean and take his chances.

Since the encounter in the Black Sea with the Imperial Russian Navy, (during which *The Cok Guzel Denizala Baligi* had lost her anchor and deck winch), the ships anchor had been makeshift, replaced by a selection of buckled deck plates welded together, and with a large hole burned through them to take a chain. It had become a symbol of the ships deteriorating condition.

Karem needed a solution to this purgatory he found himself in. The Suez Canal transit papers seemed to offer him a way out, a route to a different world, a world away from the Prison of the Mediterranean. He heard himself say, again in broken language, this time English:

"I give you two lockers, and I pick the lockers!"

The Port Officer considered for a moment, scratched his chin with a hand which also held a cigarette, and replied;

"I'll take two, agreed, but we will pick one each".

Then, lowering his voice to a whisper, and reverting to Arabic, the Port Officer added,

"And I want half an hour with your Cabin Boy".

Without even so much as a glance in the Turkish boy's direction, Karem said. "Done!"

He stood up, leaned across the desk, and shook the Port Officers hand.

He left the cabin, and the Port Officer gestured to the soldiers to go with him. In the corridor outside his quarters, Karem Tortruk heard the 'snick', as his door locked from the inside.

He headed for his bridge house, escorted by his enforced guards, where he would plot his course to the Sudanese port of Suakin via the Suez Canal. His plotting would take him half an hour, then he would return to his cabin and choose two lockers with the Port Officer.

He was already considering which ones he would try and palm him off with.

Any thought of the thirty minutes his Cabin Boy would be enduring, would never enter Captain Karem Tortruk's head.

The night of the big match.
Rhodesian Trans African Railways.
The Bulawayo Night Train From Pietermaritzburg.
July 28th 1924.
01.15 a.m.

Blissfully unaware of the events unfolding over two hundred miles behind them in Pietermaritzburg, the three middle aged Indian rights 'Delegates' were still discussing the salient points of their three day *sojourn*.

Tea and cakes had been delivered with exemplary regularity, and the conversation had been educated, informed and stimulating. And they had pulled the compartment blinds down, so not to be disturbed by fellow passengers and waiters, mulling back and forth in the corridor outside.

In fact, they were the only occupied compartment in this carriage. The other five compartments, each with eight seats in, had all been fully booked, and tickets sold to various individuals. However, in the event, none of the seats, (save one, three compartments back), had been taken up by their due travellers, though all seats had been fully paid for.

The tickets, in the event, had been burnt in an ashtray in Dykka Van Hoosts' office, by him and Gonda, over a couple of large whiskeys. The ticket stubs, had already been delivered to the train 'Conductor' when the nine fifty five p.m. 'Bulawayo Night Train' had stood at platform five at Pietermaritzburg Station. Given what was intended, the last thing they wanted was a few dozen nosey passengers dishing out statements to the Railway police in Bulawayo Station.

The entire carriage had to be empty for the purpose, but had to be full if investigated.

210

The 'Nigger Waiters' and 'Conductors' were provided under a catering and administration agreement, between the 'Rhodesian Trans Africa Railway', and one of the Der Kyper's business's. They had all, according to Louis and Bernard, (in their phone discussions with Gonda), been well 'greased' as they termed it. They would take their brakes at the 'Right Times', and confirm, (if asked), that the carriage had been 'Full', and that the three 'Indian Gentlemen', had left their compartment, and disembarked at Baitingar Junction, the first stop after the Rhodesian border.

A station which is conveniently un-manned after ten p.m.

The three men had already begun drafting their notes for their next meeting with the Rhodesian Governor General. They had been formulating their arguments against the legislation, (which they knew he intended to implement), along the lines of Dr. Malans proposals in South Africa.

At around ten past one a.m., Sachin Tandis, looked at his pocket watch, which he had removed from his jacket when he took it off some time ago. The watch rested, with its cover open, on the seat next to him, along with some books, and his notes from the conference.

The train was just entering the one mile long Baitbridge tunnel.

"Still a good way to go yet 'Gents'. You'll have to excuse me for a moment while I make use of the Rhodesian rail networks excellent and very modern 'Water closet'", he said.

The others smiled and indulged the banter.

As Tandis slid back the half glazed polished wood door of the compartment, a small, wizened, wisp of a white man, in a fawn coloured suit, stood in the door way. Before Tandis could ask the man to 'excuse him', Tandis was heading towards the corridor floor with a fractured skull, and minutes to live.

The small man had struck Tandis with a heavy 'blackjack'. The favoured weapon for circumstances where death was required, but the spillage of blood was to be avoided.

As had been the brief in this instance.

The weapon of choice was a dense packing of heavy lead balls, like fishing line weights, sealed in a thick black rubber sleeve, thicker at one end, and a good foot long. In the right hands it would deliver a punishing fatal blow, and seldom break the skin.

With three more swishing, slashing, strikes, delivered as he stepped through the compartment door, Crevit and Mousafan, were despatched with the same efficiency. The blackjack was returned to a specially stitched pocket inside the slight man's jacket.

Then, with an abnormal and impressive display of strength, he dragged each man to the caboose at the back of the carriage, and dumped each unceremoniously on the metal smoking platform. He then returned to their compartment, collected their cases from the overhead racks, their books, notes and jackets, and the pocket watch, distributed these into the men's cases, and took them also to the caboose.

The 'slight man' stood next to the bodies on the smoking plate as the train exited the tunnel. He was to count to one hundred and fifty before throwing them off, this should place them in just about the right place after the bend.

As he got to 'one hundred and twenty five', he hoisted Tandis up, and rested him over the guardrail, at 'one hundred and forty eight', he heaved him over the side, and into the darkness. At 'one hundred and sixty five', Mousafan went over. As he jerked Crevit upright, and bent him forwards on the rail, the 'slight man' heard him groan, regardless he placed a hand under Crevit's thigh and pushed him over the guardrail, as he went, and even in the nights blackness, he saw Crevit's eyes open in terror, and his hand try to catch the moving metal baluster.

The three suitcases followed swiftly.

The 'slight man' closed and locked the caboose door, and returned to his compartment.

Within fifteen minutes, the three bodies, their suitcases and belongings, had been collected from the heavy stoned and gravelled border between the railway line and the dirt road. The stoned area had been checked for any blood or skin, or bits of broken suitcase or clothing, and any offending articles, had been collected, and thrown into the jungle overgrowth on the opposite side of the dirt track, to be consumed for ever.

As the Van Der Kyper brothers men threw the three Indians and their belongings into the 'hole', and began the task of backfilling it with the previously exhumed earth. Crevit still moaned and groaned, and his eyes opened once more, just before the first shovel full of dirt hit him in the face, and filled his mouth to muffle his final scream.

The first 'Rhodesian Indian Activist' group, still, to this day, remain somewhere on the far bend of the Baitbridge tunnel north bound railway track.

Sandstone,
Western Australia.
November 6th 1932.

Malakye Wylachi, (junior), was born on the 10th of October, 1915; he was first son, but second child of Corine, and Malakye Wylachi. Their first child, a girl they had named Tryfa, had died of some unpronounceable disease when she was three. Her mother, Corine, had followed on five years later from a much easier to pronounce disease.

The Wylachi's were third generation Australians, and had settled in Sandstone, a small original prospector's town almost mid-way between the Indian Ocean Coast, and the Great Victoria Desert.

Their business was sheep. Sheering them, breeding them, selling them and butchering them.

Malakye, (Senior), had no other family to speak of, save for his two younger brothers, who he had effectively raised, and now employed. His parents had both died in a cholera outbreak at the turn of the century, along with his youngest brother and two sisters. Malakye had only survived because he had been on Roustabout with friends from two neighbouring farmsteads, and his two other brothers Stanforth and Mordichae; they had been searching out new grazing territory, and collecting up any woolly-backed stragglers.

Today, was his birthday, November 6th, 1932, he was fifty four, and looked every hour of it.

'Old Man Mal', as he was known in Sandstone; was heading for the Shillington Arms, with his son Mal Junior. They had just got off the train from Mount Magnet, at Sandstone Railway Station, having sold twelve thousand head of sheep at the stock auctions there.

Approximately three quarters of their herd.

Their trucks would not be back until tomorrow, with the new breeding Bulls and cows that they had bought with some of the money they had made. Also, their Drovers and Stockmen were coming back with the trucks, so the rest of today was a good day to celebrate his birthday. There wasn't much else to celebrate in Sandstone; for its dwindling population, (now under three hundred souls), had been hard hit by this new decade of the 1930's.

Old Man Mal, would not spring for train tickets for Drovers or Stockmen, they could rough it for a couple of days, the three trucks had to come back anyway, and train travel was expensive.

The Great Depression, as people were already calling it, had hit Western Australia like a steam locomotive full of wet wool. Livestock prices had nose dived, and land, especially agricultural land, had lost something nearing sixty five percent of its value.

Malakye Wylachi had seen three out of his five nearest neighbours get foreclosed by the banks, and ship out to become street cleaners, or trolley car conductors, or factory day hands, in the big cities to the south. But he was a 'clever old coot'; as Dunder MacFall, the owner of the Shillington Arms, had called him; and by selling watering rights to the dug wells he had made on his spread, he had managed to make some money over the last few years, and stave off the problems that had seen off some of his neighbours, (and his competitors).

In fact, he had made enough money to buy back from the banks, the Landsdown Fields spread, and the Rumney Flats Farm, that stretched all the way up to the small town of Coolanar Hill, north of Sandstone.

He had recently struck a deal with a Milk Tanker Transport company in Paynes Find, (about thirty odd miles to the east), to pump and collect milk from him, starting next winter. And he had also, (on this current trip to Mount Magnet) agreed a discounted deal with a small abattoir there to butcher his cattle and sheep. At the

214

moment, he was shipping them to Mount Magnet Stock Yards, (who charged him a holding and processing fee per head); and then paying rail freight on top, to ship them on, to the nearest abattoir in Wandina on the coast, for slaughtering by others, then onward shipment by rail or sea to the cities of Perth and Fremantle further down the coast.

It seemed to Malakye, that he was getting further and further away from the money end of the livestock industry. He had vowed to do something about that, and he had made a start.

Malakye Jnr., was seventeen, tall, thick set, fit, athletic, and, if anything, quicker off the mark than his old man. He was good looking; handsome even some might say, with a shock of thick black hair and piercing blue-grey eyes. But he had suffered, since birth, with a hair lip, which had, in a strange way, made him more self reliant, and gave him an almost imperceptible, but curiously endearing, very slight lisp.

Truth to be told, it was he, and not Malakye Snr., that had negotiated the discount deal with the small abattoir in Mount Magnet.

"Two chilled ones please Dunder, and make 'em long"; said Malakye Snr. as he entered the single fly-screened door of the Shillington Arms daytime bar.

"And two Scotch and Sodas' too", added Malakye Jnr., "and you can make them short".

The three men laughed casually, and exchanged the obligatory pleasantries, while Dunder prepared the drinks.

The daytime bar of the Shillington Arms was spartan, it had a stained and flaking old timber counter, with three jugs of water standing on it, none of which matched each other, and at least two of which contained dead flies or wasps. Against the counter stood half a dozen bar stools which may have once matched each other, but which now, after years of breakages and botched repairs, only bore a passing resemblance to one another. The floor was timber floorboards, patina'd by years of beer spills, spit, and fag end burns. There were five tables, all tired, and scratched, two round ones, two rectangular ones, and one of some other shape, which may once have been square.

As the drinks appeared on the counter, Old Man Mal dropped a scrumpled five dollar bill onto the bar-top, next to them.

"Keep 'em coming 'Dund', until this is gone".

There were half a dozen or so other men, dotted around the bar; Stockmen, judging by their bush hats, worn dungarees and scagged and torn shirts. The Wylachi's knew them, and acknowledged them, but there was no friendly interaction, no discourse, no exchange of banter or information. In fact, there was an uneasy tolerance between them all, an accepted discomfort. Dunder made an attempt at easing the potential tension.

"I see the Brisbane Bandolero's have struck again, right here in W.A. this time".

Dunder reached behind him to the glasses shelf, picked up some fairly tired looking newspapers, (though they were only two days old). The papers were, 'The Geraldton Guardian', a coastal regional daily, from up the coast north of Perth, 'The Countryman Western Mail', a local Stockmans Weekly, and 'The Kalgoorlie Miner', an irregular periodical published in Paynes Find, and specifically for mine workers.

Dunder tossed them casually on the bar, sending a small puff of dust into the arid air. The Wylachi's picked them up in no particular order. Like all barmen, Dunder carried on, unsolicited;

"Trucker-Bowman's dockyard payroll, apparently. Down in Albany; shot the payroll clerk in the chest, dead in his chair behind his desk while he counted the money. Found him in a pool of blood, still sitting there, a ten dollar bill in each hand. The only cash they left; they reckon they got away with over eighteen thousand bucks. Drove over a dock gate security man as they made their getaway, bust both his legs, and shot his mate in the arse. These lot don't fuck about!"

Old Man Mal thumped one of the papers on the counter, and only half jokingly said, as he cut Dunder short.

"Is there any point in reading these papers, Dunder? I mean you should have been a fucking reporter,
Instead of a barman".

Dunder took the hint, not that it was a hint, more of a direct instruction to 'shut the fuck' up really. He turned back towards the glasses shelf, mumbling as he turned:

"I'll get another set of drinks for you guys".

Mal Jnr., was reading the front page of the 'The Geraldton Guardian', as he swigged back the last of his first long beer.

"Fifteen robberies in the last year, over four hundred and twenty thousand dollars so far it says here, twelve in New South Wales, a couple in Queensland, and now the first ones in W.A.".

His father said in reply, as he thumbed through the racing pages in 'The Kalgoorlie Miner', and checked the Perth stockyard prices in the 'The Countryman Western Mail';

"Well; as long as they stay down south, they shouldn't bother us up here, that's the main thing, eh Dunder?"

He pushed his empty whiskey glass back across the bar, for a third re-fill. The barman picked it up, and retorted:

"Oh, you want something now, Mr Fucking Nice Guy again.

Malakye and Dunder had known each other for over thirty years, they knew each other well enough to be downright rude to each other, with neither of them taking offence. In fact the two men genuinely liked each other, and were probably one another's best friends, if not only friends.

"Just pour the fucking drink Dundy, and get one for yourself".

One of the other Stockmen in the bar had stood up and walked over to the counter, and put his empty beer glass on it, its froth still kissing its sides.

"Get me another chilled one while you're at it sport" he said.

Then, leaning against the flaked wood bar-top, and facing back towards the other men in the room, he said; (in response to Old Man Mal's comment about the robbers staying down south):

"Yeah; we got enough of our own robbers up here!"

He tapped Old Man Mal on his shoulder, whose back was towards the Stockman.

"Stolen any more farmsteads this month Wylachi, you've already pinched Matt Landsdowne's spread, and the Rumney place".

"That's enough!"

Shouted Dunder, and turned towards the bar.

"No more booze for you Ticker, you've had enough!"

Old Man Mal had not turned around, and continued reading his racing reports, Mal Jnr., interjected.

"Ticker, you're a waste of fucking human organs, if you spent more time tending your place instead of boozing the clock around in here, perhaps you wouldn't have the problems you've got".

'Ticker' St. Thomas was the owner of 'The Sainted Tee' dairy ranch, between the Landsdown and Rumney spreads. He was a boozer, a loudmouth, and a troublemaker. His land was ideally located to join up the Wylachi parcels into one huge spread, and Old Man Mal, had been refusing him access to the dug wells for the last month or so, because 'Ticker' could not pay the fees.

It suited the Wylachi's to see The Sainted Tee in trouble, and Old Man Mal knew the spread was only worth anything to the Wylachi's, as it was surrounded by their land, and needed their water to work.

'Ticker', was so called because he was a 'clock watcher', fifteen years ago, he had been a Stock Hand at the Wylachi place, and rumour had it that it was Old Man Mal, who had originally coined the nickname. He had only lasted there a few months, and had acquired The Sainted Tee when it was left to his wife, after the death of her father.

It was called the 'Forrow West Farmstead', in those days, and was a well run stock and dairy farm, with its own wells. 'Tickers' wife had died about three years ago, and he had crawled inside a bottle in the Shillington Arms, and had stayed there ever since. 'Ticker' had no children. The spread had gone downhill, and so had 'Ticker'. He had borrowed money against the farmstead, and had drunk most of it, and invested little if any.

It came out during the next few minutes at the bar, that 'The Northern Highway And Railwayman's Bank', in Payne's Find, had called in 'Tickers' mortgage, while the Wylachi's had been away in Mount Magner.

218

'Ticker', and his fellow drunks, clearly blamed the Wylachi's for his current misfortune. Everyone needs to blame someone for bad-luck; it is the nature of mankind, and the nature of bad-luck.

Despite Dunder's best barman type protests, the mood in the daytime bar was getting darker, and uglier, and a few of 'Tickers' drunken mates had risen from their seats and were joining in the argument.

Old Man Mal placed his newspaper on the bar-top, finished his beer, leaned across to Dunder and said;

"Get my whiskey ready, I'll be back soon".

He turned, and walked outside.

'Ticker' followed two paces behind. Old Man Mal would not start trouble in Dunders bar. It may be a dump, but it was the only beer serving dump in town, and Dunder was his friend. He would feel obliged to pay for any damage caused, and he had better things to spend his dollars on.

Mal Jnr. evidently did not inherit the same scruples. As two of 'Tickers' mates passed by him, he struck the second man across the shoulders with one of the heavy wooden bar stools, and for good measure booted him full in the face, as the man hit the planked floor. Mal Jnr.'s thick hobnailed working boots made the man's nose and lips explode in a cascade of blood, skin, snot and bits of teeth. As the man in front turned around, Mal Jnr., stamped, hard on the spine of the now prone man whom he had hit with the stool, and, springing forwards off him, drove his forehead, twice, into the standing man's face, Mal Jnr. had his hands around the man's throat, and was shoving his big, calloused thumbs hard into his adams apple. As the man's eyes bulged amidst the smashed nose and cheek bones, Mal Jnr. brought his right knee viciously up, repeatedly into the man's genitals. After not many seconds, when the man lost consciousness, Mal Jnr., dropped him like a sodden tampon, and let him fall, limply to the floor, next to his mate.

Mal Jnr. walked outside, just in time to see his father plonk a straight right hander, with his immense sheep grabbing fist, onto the lazy chin of 'Ticker' St. Thomas.

'Ticker' crumbled like the derelict worm eaten structure he was, folding to the boardwalk outside The Shillington Arms. Old Man Mal stood astride him and lifted him forward. Although still dazed, 'Ticker' was squinting at the sunlight, eyes rolling, but slowly coming around. Without any niceties, Old Man Mal shook him vigorously, like an old but unloved rag doll, his huge hands grabbing 'Tickers' dungarees.

He screamed into his face.

"How much? How much do you owe the Bank on the mortgage, on The Sainted Tee?

He shook 'Ticker' again, this time waving a monstrous fist in front of his eyes.

"Two thousand dollars odd".

'Ticker' managed to blurt out.

"Right!"

Said Old Man Mal, calmer now.

"I'll pay that over to the bank tomorrow, and I'll give you the train fare to Fremantle, and throw in a case of cheap Scotch; I'll also give you forty eight hours to get off my fucking land. That's from the big Ironbark on Cutters lane over to the railway tracks at the back of Coolinar Hill".

He let go of 'Tickers' dungarees, and allowed him to slump awkwardly to the boardwalk. Turning to his son, who was now standing behind him, he said;

"Not the most polite business deal we've ever struck: but not a bad day's work for all that".

The two men, walked back into the daytime bar. As they did so, Old Man Mal, surveyed the broken stool, and the two Stockmen, who were now coming to with the help of a bucket of ice water, delivered, with little finesse, by Dunder.

As they entered, the bar keeper turned to the Wylachi's and said.

"You two owe me a fucking stool, the cost of a good clean up, and the loss of three regular customers. We'll call that twenty five bucks. Your drinks are on the fucking bar, and all of your five dollars is gone, so cough fucking up and I'll have a large Scotch to settle my nerves."

He then turned to the two semi conscious Stockmen, who were now trying, (with some difficulty), to rise to their feet. He walked around the bar picking up splinters of wood and smashed beer glasses from the floor as he went. Reaching for a broom, which stood in the corner, and pointing it at the two struggling stockmen, he continued his tirade.

"And you pair, get the fuck out of here, and settle your dollar eighty five tab, before you go. And if you're thinking about not squaring me up, I'll tell 'Junior' here to collect it for me."

He gestured at young Malakye with his thumb.

Both men reached hurriedly into their dungaree pockets as they staggered to their feet.

Port Suakin.
Western Sudan,
East Africa.
November 6th 1919.

Suakin can only be imagined in Biblical terms of devastation.

The so called port consisted of three of the most dis-used jetty's one could ever imagine, crumbling concrete, rusting exposed re-enforcement, rotten old tyres hanging from their disintegrating walls by ropes that were thick and green with algae.

Beyond the port, and in the near distance, the town itself appeared to have fared little better, rows of tin roofed shanty's puffed smoke in thin grey fillets against the pure crisp blue of the sky. The landscape rising gently into the quivering distance.

There were no clouds, no tugs, no pilots, just a hotch potch of jet black labourers in scruffy grey, (which may once have been white), vests and short trousers. They all seemed to carry rifles across their shoulders. They all smoked, they were all tall, and they all looked the same.

Dangerous.

Karem Tortruk was hanging over the bridge rail, shouting instructions to his helmsman inside the wheelhouse.

"Easy! Easy, bring us up tight but easy!"

He had already issued the 'All Stop' command to the engine room via the voice pipes, and they had been coasting in for the last few hundred yards. An extremely difficult and precarious manoeuvre for a vessel the size of *The Cok Guzel Denizala Baligi*, the slightest mis-judgement in speed direction or distance would careen the ship bow first into the concrete jetty wall, or allow the ship to skid along its side and run aground on the adjacent beech.

"Hard a-starboard now Yublis! Now!"

Karem screamed into the wheelhouse, he then made a quick inspection over the bridge rail before dashing back inside to the voice pipe.

"Full astern! Full astern!"

He yelled into the pipe, then rushed back to the bridge rail.

The ship hit the concrete wall of the jetty with a heavy thump which hurled everyone aboard forward, and generally onto the decks, or into walls or rails.

Karem was on the floor of the bridge gangway, and had cut his hand as he tried to catch hold of a stair tread, (and failed), to break his fall. He struggled to get back on his feet, pulling himself up the guardrail steelwork.

"Shit! Fucking shit! Fucking shit!"

He shouted as he looked over the rail. He could see the buckled bow plates from the bridge gangway, but the damage looked all above the water line, which gave him a small amount of solace.

He once more bundled through the doorway into the wheelhouse, and flung his bleeding fist around the voice pipe.

"All stop! All stop! And get me a damage report, someone check forward, I need to know if we're holed?"

Yublis had been thrown hard against the wheel in the collision, and was nursing what looked like a few broken ribs. Karem poked him in them, hard, and called him a 'Stupid worthless cunt'. He then returned to the bridge rail, and shouted towards the deck.

"Get those ropes over the side, and onto the jetty, forward and aft!"

Karem then turned to the jet black labourers on the dockside, cupping his hands around his mouth, he yelled as loudly as he could, and in broken Arabic, and then in French, and then in English.

"Tie us off! There's an English gold sovereign for each of you, now get it done".

The jet black labourers duly obliged, if there was one language Captain Karem Tortruk was fluent in, it was money.

Within an hour the jet black labourers had each been paid their gold sovereigns. Karem complained that there were only five of them on the jetty when he had called to them to tie the ship off, and yet twenty two of them now each demanded payment. He knew how easily ropes could be cut with a machete, and most of the jet black labourers seemed to have one, and so he duly obliged with the payment. He called them 'filthy thieving black cunts' in Turkish, as he counted out the twenty two sovereigns, and hoped none of them spoke the language.

He was disturbed from his counting by the arrival on his bridge of a jet black uniformed man, in creased grey trousers, a pressed blue shirt with gold bands on the epaulettes, and a blue peaked cap, also with gold bands around it. He wore a side arm, in a black leather holster, and he carried a thin brown brief-case. With him he had two more jet black men in similar uniforms, but with berets on their heads.

Both held ageing Enfield rifles.

"You have docked without permission", the man said, strangely and somewhat curiously, in perfect English.

Karem knew this drill by now, and after not very many minutes the men had agreed a rate for the mooring of two hundred golden sovereigns, (the word had clearly got around that Karem had such coinage on board).

"I need to dump these passengers ashore. How much?"

The Captain asked with his usual consideration.

The jet black official scratched his chin, as the Port Officer in Alexandria had scratched his chin, then he said:

"Two thousand English pounds! For that we will leave the dock gates open for twelve hours, then, you leave!"

"Impossible!" Screeched Karem indignantly, "I must have repairs done, the ship is in no fit state to return to sea, we must repair our bow plates, and secure suppl……"

The jet black official cut him short.

"Two thousand five hundred pounds, and six hours then. Yes or no!"

Unlike at Alexandria Karem had no options here; and the jet black official new it. A price of two thousand five hundred pounds was agreed, which was duly paid across the desk in the Captains quarters, to where the meeting had adjourned.

For an additional three hundred pounds Karem had negotiated a stay in port of twenty four hours, to affect his required repairs. The three hundred was paid to the jet black official personally, and in ten pound notes, which the man folded and shoved deep into his trouser pocket. The balance of the transaction was settled in a mixture of gold coin, English Bank notes, and the contents of two of the smaller lockers. The Captain also secured, (for an exorbitant sum), additional fuel coal and provisions.

As he left, the jet black official reminded Karem of the dock gates 'open' period of twelve hours, after that he said, quite concisely:

"Anyone inside the dockyard will be shot!"

"I don't give a fuck!"

Karem had replied, adding bitterly,

"I just want these fucking Jews and misfits off my boat".

The man turned to leave, shouting to Karem as he walked along the corridor outside the Captains quarters;

"Oh, by the way, the casting off fee for the dockside jetty labourers, is two gold sovereigns a man, you may be surprised how many men it will take to untie your ropes".

He laughed as he and the two jet black guards disappeared up the corridor steps.

It was just after mid-day and the Sudanese Sun was blistering the paint on the elderly deck plates of *The Cok Guzel Denizala Baligi*. At the stern, Itzak and Yuris leaned against the deck rail, looking back out to sea. They were smoking thin roll-up cigarettes and sharing a small dented galvanised bucket full of water. Their clothes were now worn and tattered, and in need of a thorough washing out, their hair was unkempt, and both sported stubbly beards from the ship wide absence of sharp usable razors.

"Take me with you!"

A voice said from behind them, they turned to see the young Turkish cabin boy.

"I can't stay here with that pig".

"Fuck off!" said Itzak, "he's your husband, you married him, you live with him".

He turned back towards the rail, and continued smoking his cigarette.

"I can make it worth your while".

The young Turkish boy said with a hint of desperation in his voice. The conversation was taking place in a mixture of Turkish, Russian and English, but was clear enough.

"What are you going to offer, let us both shag you?"

Asked Yuris mockingly. The two brothers laughed, and continued to look away from the cabin boy.

"The Captain's had steel plates put on the door of the storeroom in his cabin, and three new locks, and he hides the keys so no one can steal from him. So you can't get at the lockers anymore. But he keeps a jewel in his desk drawer, he takes it out sometimes when he's drunk and stares at it. The desk lock is broken. I'm the only one who knows it's there, it's beautiful. If you take me with you, I'll get it for you".

The two brothers turned back around to face him; Yuris rubbed his chin, and asked,

"Can you get us a sharp razor as well?"

Yuris and Itzak both laughed. This time the cabin boy joined in, saying,

"Then you'll take me. Yes?"

"Only as far as the town", Itzak said, "after that you're on your own".

The young boy protested saying that the jewel was worth much more, and that he was a good cook, and could make tea, and read, and speak Arabic.

225

Itzak could take no more and thumped the boy, (what he considered to be lightly), in the chest. The boy slumped heavily to the hot deck plates, wheezing, his eyes bulging. Yuris threw away his cigarette over the side, and dropped the small water bucket. They both pulled the cabin boy back to his feet, fearing that The Captain may see them from the bridge.

Already people were beginning to muster on the deck, and the gangplanks had been lowered. Word had spread; as the typhus had spread that all the passengers must be off the ship by six p.m.

"Alright! Alright! We'll take you!"

Yuris whispered, trying to shut the cabin boy up. He had now started to cry.

"We'll meet you at the metal steps at the end of the corridor outside The Captains cabin. Make it at four o'clock; Tortruk should be busy on deck by then getting us lot off the ship. That should be the busiest time."

Itzak interrupted his younger brother, saying,

"Make sure you wear something to cover that pretty face of yours, dress up like a girl, that should be easy for you, wrap a scarf over your head or something".

Itzak spun the cabin boy around and pushed him away from them, back towards the bridge. As the boy walked away, still rubbing his chest, Itzak said, as loudly as he dared;

"Four o'clock, don't forget, and don't be late, and bring the jewel".

He added as the boy walked away:

"And don't come without that razor either, or I'll stick that jewel, whatever size it is, up your well greased arse!"

The boy left the deck.

The next few hours on board, for Itzak and Yuris, were filled with gathering meagre possessions, hunting out canned food, (and stealing it), finding old beer bottles with glass stoppers to fill with water, and generally making sure they had something to survive on for the next few days. They sought out the Old Jew, and said their goodbyes to him.

He had seen them through the time when their mother had been killed, and he had earned their respect.

The ship was bustling. All over, in gangways and corridors, in stairwells, and at dozens of places around the deck rails, small groups of families and friends were nestling together ready to leave.

Albeit into an uncertain future.

People had been drifting off down the gangplanks for the last hour or more and Captain Tortruk had been overseeing their departure from his vantage point on the bridge. Occasionally he would yell, "Move along there!" or "Hurry up!" in a plethora of languages. Always, and constantly he looked at his watch, he did not want any passengers still aboard when the dock gates closed at six p.m.

Itzak and Yuris had been ready to leave for over an hour, and had debated whether to do so, and to:

"Fuck the little Turk!"

As Itzak had advocated.

"And leave him and his arsehole to The Captain".

Yuris had persuaded his brother that the jewel may be worth staying for, and that in any case he could do with a good shave.

By five minutes to four, the brothers were at the top of the metal staircase looking down onto the corridor walkway that led to The Captains quarters. Beneath the open risers of the steps, and underneath the staircase they could see the shape of a small person. Yuris whistled quietly, and the small shape stepped out into the corridor. The brothers laughed, then tried to smother the noise of their laughter.

"You look very pretty as a girl", said Yuris in English.

"I think I could go for you myself, in that get up", said Itzak in surprising good humour.

The Turkish cabin boy looked up at them from the foot of the metal staircase. His girl's clothes and headscarf would certainly fool any inspection by the deck hands as they left the ship.

"Look, I have them both!"

The cabin boy said, holding up his two hands, he held a brown suede purse in the one with a silk pull chord, and a whale-bone razor with a long clean blade in the other. He had a huge grin across his feminine face.

"Hey! I recognise that", said Yuris, pointing at the suede pouch.

As the brothers looked down at him, the huge grin faded, and the big blue eyes widened, a look of terror replaced the earlier brief elation. The boys spun around; behind them was Captain Karem Tortruk.

"What the fuck is going on here!"

He demanded in Russian as he pushed Yuris against the bulkhead wall, he began shouting:

"Yublis, Stannoy, help! Quick down here, hel….."

His pleas were cut short by Itzak, who head butted Karem hard, and full in the face. He grabbed the Captain by his thinning hair and threw him down the metal steps; he landed hard at the bottom, face up in the corridor holding his smashed nose, still shouting.

In an instant, the Turkish cabin boy had drawn the blade of the clean whale bone razor hard across Karem's throat. He had sliced it clear through to the bone, and although The Captains mouth still moved, no sound emanated except for the bubbly gurgling of the blood which now spurted in all directions. The cabin boy danced his way over and around his Captain to avoid the blood spatters and scurried up the stairs.

The three boys were on deck within a minute, and down the gangplank and on the concrete jetty inside two. Once ashore they ran as quickly as they could in the direction of the moving throng.

Once outside the dock gates the cabin boy discarded his disguise, and the three of them ran for over half an hour through the warren of dusty streets and souks that were Suakin, until they found themselves on the far side of the town; uphill of the port, and looking down on the ship in the distance.

Exhausted, they slumped on a pile of rubble, and Yuris opened, and passed around the water bottles from their hessian sacks.

"Interesting place this!"

He said between puffs and pants, and swigs of water.

"Now all we need is a way out of here".

Captain Karem Tortruk, nor *The Cok Guzel Denizala Baligi*, were ever mentioned again.

Dykka's business goes south,

Pietermaritzburg,

South Africa.

June 1925.

By June 1925, Itzak Androskewowicsz, 'The Bloody Elephant' was working full time with his brother, Banjo, filling locomotive tenders, and lorries with coal, 'The Hard Black Stuff'. But the 'fiddles on the side' for Dykka were drying up, and most of their work now was direct for the Rail Yard, and the Railway Companies. Not so good money, but steady, and mostly legal.

They had done well on the fight with Crusher Hohner, and even with 'Banger's' cut, they had cleared over a thousand pounds; and had, tucked away, in a box under the floorboards at their Greyling Street lodgings, one thousand five hundred and eighty pounds.

Mostly in fivers and one pound notes.

Over the last twelve months, Itzak had returned to the fight game twice. Word had spread quickly that he had killed Crusher Hohner in a match, (mostly spread by Dykka van Hoost); and Dykka could now get two hundred quid per bout for an appearance by 'The Bloody Elephant'. On both occasions the fights were stopped as Itzak's eye socket had opened up, and needed to be re-set. After each fracture Banjo had kept his brothers eye and head, bandaged for over a month. The second match had left Itzak's eye permanently damaged, and he had probably lost at least half of his vision in it.

However, always one for an opportunity, and now fully aware of his brothers infirmity: Banjo had placed various bets, anonymously, (and sometimes with the help of 'Banger' and Mambo), on the 'other guys', as he had put it.

But all that was over now, and Itzak had told Dykka that the wound delivered by Crusher Hohner, had effectively ended his career. His face bore testimony to the brief moment in the ring of lights with the deceased German from Rhodesia. He had two zig-zag blue-red scars on his cheek where the coins had been inserted, left for six weeks, and then removed. His eye, on the same side, was now slightly out of true to the other, and the eye socket bone to the outside of his face had dropped, and not healed correctly. This gave his once taught and angular and certainly handsome features, something of a sad perspective. Anyway, his fighting days were, (all too briefly), over, and he was back on the shovel with his brother full time.

"Not to worry old son, it was good while it lasted".

Dykka had commented.

It has to be said that the two boys, who were now easing past their mid twenties, missed the kudos of the 'bouts'. They still occasionally attended some of Dykkas' arrangements, but they had now become low key affairs, and Dykka was even pairing young white fighters against 'niggers' in open matches.

Even Dykka and Gonda's pet coppers refused to look the other way for these arrangements, and more than once they got raided. The 'nigger fisters' got dragged off to 'clink', and a 'good tuning', as the cops called it.

After the 'Constitutional Hall' incident, the City Councillors of Pietermaritzburg had written to the Central Government in Johannesburg, bitterly complaining as to the, 'perception of lawlessness', and the 'lack of police authority'.

Nothing was ever pursued concerning the explosion on Church Street, and the 'Fractured Gas Main' story was almost universally accepted. In truth it suited the establishment, (both locally and in Johannesburg), to be rid of the awkward 'Wogs', whatever the cause.

The crux of the councillors complaint really, was that the local coppers were utterly corrupt, and that, as City Chief Clerk, W.T. Williams Esq., had phrased it, in his letter to the Governor General:

> '*The Natal State Authority should not*
> *tolerate this fair city being likened to an American*
> '*Wild West Town*'.

This was a reference to an article published in the 'Natal Witness' newspaper, shortly after the destruction of the Constitutional Hall. The article referred to the increasing number of 'Drunken Blacks' that could be found on the streets of Pietermaritzburg, making the area:

'Unfit for decent white citizens to walk their own streets'.

The Androskewowicsz brothers had been in South Africa long enough to know two things. Firstly, no one really cared about 'Wogs' or 'Niggers', the same as no one really cared about 'Hooky Coppers', as Mambo called them. And secondly, and most importantly, 'Wogs' and 'Niggers' should be kept separate, so they could be 'not cared about' out of sight.

Social control was the name of this particular game.

Hence the 'Hooky' local coppers, got put under the control of the Regional Natal Police, in the form of Captain Raymond Dospar, and his enforcement arm, a contingent of the 'South Africa Mounted Rifles', commanded by Major Dieter Umbarstek.

Their true mission was to get the blacks and Indians out of the city, stop them misbehaving, and generally crush all public displays of criminality. Truth be told, this was the fuse that Mambo lit that dark night a year ago, on Church Street: he just didn't know it.

Life for Dykka Van Hoost and Gonda Vischer, was about to change very quickly. The blacks shoveled Dykka's coal, drove Dykka's lorries, thinned Dykka's 'baccy' and whiskey, and spent the money Dykka paid them, on Dykka's smokes and booze, and lost what was left on bets at Dykka's fights.

Dospar and Umbarstek even stationed armed A.M.R. Police in the railway sidings, at the request of the Railway Companies, and the local Council. Dykka couldn't even steal 'The Hard Black Stuff' anymore.

As for Gonda, three quarters of his loaders were blacks. He paid them in whiskey, tobacco, and counterfeit notes bought from Dykka, at half face value. Now he would have to pull in 'Dutchies' or even worse 'Irish', they would demand payment in full, and in real money. He would also have to buy 'The Hard Black

Stuff' from legitimate mines at the going rate; instead of the thirty five percent rate he paid Dykka, his business partner.

This first whistle of these winds of change, which had started as a sullen breath in Church Street, in June 1924, would end for Dykka Van Hoost and Gonda Vischer, as a hurricane in the tenements of Port Napier, Napierville, Pietermaritzburg in July 1926.

For Banjo and Itzak, the gusts would blow them clear across to the other side of the World.

My Uncles; Murray and Wilf andThe Slaughtermen.
Perth,
Western Australia,
July 3rd, 1972.

The journey northward along Highway 95, The Great Northern Highway, out of Perth, passed with good humour and high spirits, the two brothers exchanging jokes and reminiscences about 'the old country'; a country of only seven years ago, but a lifetime away. Australia had been good to both of them. Wilf was a Supervisor with the Perth Highways Inspectorate; and Murray was a Logistics Manager with W.A. Water. Both men, and their wives had become 'Dinky Dai Ozzys', as my Auntie Flo termed it, enjoying the outdoor life, revelling in the sunshine, the sea food and the beach culture.

A giant hand had plucked them all from the dank misery, and slag heaps of the South Wales Valleys, and plonked them into paradise.

On their way to Mount Magnet, and with fairly open roads, Murray and Wilf had made good time over the first hundred miles or so of their journey. They passed through romantic sounding places like the Upper Swan, Muchea, Chittering, Bulls Brook, Bindoon and Yarawindah.

Needing a grub break, and a toilet, Murray pulled the Taunus in at a general store, and petrol station, in the town of New Norcia, the first main town they had come to on route '95', The Great Northern Highway; in reality, the only northern highway.

The petrol pump attendant greeted them cordially, with the mandatory, 'G'Day', and asked what they needed. Both Murray and Wilf got out of the car, and stretched their arms in an exaggerated manner.

"Fill her up with standard", replied Murray, and said he would pay at the counter inside the shop, Wilf asked if there was a 'loo' inside. The filler-man answered that there was, and that they should ask 'Tildy' for the key. As they walked towards the shop, the filler-man shouted that 'the dunny's round the back'.

In the shop, Murray and Wilf collected two cases of lager, a selection of snacks and crisps, some more toilet roll, (you can never have enough on a camping trip), some bars of chocolate, and a newspaper.

As they approached the counter, and laid out their purchases, Tildy, an Aboriginal lady of ample proportions and a floral pattern dress, added the items up on scrap of paper with a broken red biro.

"That'll be eight dollars seventy please fellers, plus the juice."

The filler-man poked his head around the door of the shop, and said;

"Eighteen bucks for the standard gents".

The attendant then returned to his plastic chair, under the canopy between the two solitary petrol pumps.

Murray and Wilf paid their account, made use of the 'dunny', returned the key to Tildy, said their goodbyes to her and the filler-man, and drove back onto highway '95'.

As they drove the entire six or eight hundred yards of route '95' that snaked through the middle of New Norcia, a sign on the right, at one of the side road junctions caught Bills eye, it said, 'Frederick Armsby Boulevard'.

He cricked his neck backwards through the passenger window to double check. It was, as his first glance had suggested, 'Frederick Armsby Boulevard'. He turned to Murray, who was driving, opening a bottle of squash, and unwrapping a bar of Cadburys Bourneville Dark, all at the same time.

"Where's the package?" Wilf asked.

"Under your seat", replied Murray, displaying fantastic multi-tasking, with only the slightest dribble of dark chocolate escaping from his lower lip.

Wilf rummaged under his seat, and found the A4, mottled grey lever arch folder, which Jimmy C, and my father had sent to them by airmail. All this at a cost of over £9.00, which they had subsequently split between my Uncle Bryn, Spinksy, and the Amethyst brothers each party picking up a £3.00 cut.

Maldwyn had been let off contributing because he was still on the 'sick' with his piles, and Bryn would have to cough up his end at a later date, as he had by this time, returned to sea. Maldwyn though, it must be said, did chip in the folder, courtesy of Rhymney Valley Urban District Council, Department of Transport.

Wilf foraged through the file, then like Archimedes leaping from his bath, began to gesticulate in the fashion of a lunatic who had just discovered that fires were hot.

"I bloody knew I'd seen it, here it is!"

He pressed a finger hard against an A4 leaf of paper, as if it were attempting to escape from the file. The piece of paper had a photocopied newspaper clipping stapled to it. Wilf carried on, still quite excited about his discovery.

"Here he is Frederick Armsby; Police Constable Frederick Armsby!"

He looked over at Murray, and gave out an exaggerated laugh.

"Ha, Ha! We're only on the fucking trail, Ha, fucking Ha, roll on Mount Magnet Murray boy, roll on!"

"Read it out Wilf, read it out loud, let's here it", Murray asked.

Wilf replied to Murray that he thought he had already read the file. Murray said he had only read the important bits for the trip.

"For purposes of navigation like", he expanded.

Wilf called him a 'knob', only half jokingly, and decided that he would use the road time to reprise the file from cover to cover.

"Come on Wilfy, read it out", repeated Murray, still munching his Cadburys Bourneville, and now trying to open a bag of Smokey bacon crisps, drive, and drink squash all at the same time.

Without speaking further to his brother, Wilf, (who hated being called Wilfy), began to read aloud:

*The gunfight took place on the
lower slopes of Daggar Hills, to the
west of the drover's town of Coolana
Hill, W.A.*

*Police had been in pursuit of the gang
for several days before. They had come
close to capturing them at Walebing,
and later, at Bindi-Bindi, where they
had managed to evade the Police by
using a stolen sheep truck to make their
get away.   In another incident at the
railway station in Payne's Find, a train
guard had been wounded with a
shotgun, and subsequently lost an eye,
after trying to stop the gang stealing
the sheep truck from the stockyard car
park opposite the station office.*

Murray interrupted him:

"They were a bunch of tinkers Wilfy boy, proper tinkers!"

Wilf replied, a little dryly;

"I should co-co Murray".

He smiled and continued his reading.

*Police Chief Gilbert Van
Der Faisey, sixty two, of the New
Norcia Constabulary, said that
Police Constable Frederick
Armsby, aged twenty eight, died at
the scene of the gunfight at
Coolanar Hill, after being shot in*

*the throat by one of the gang. He
leaves a widow, and five children.*

*Police Chief Van Der
Faisey said that Constable Armsby
was, "an extremely brave officer,
and a credit to the Western
Australia Police Force".*

*Two other Policemen were
wounded during the shootout, at
Wylachi Stockmans Station near
Coolanar Hill. Neither men are
thought to be in any danger, and
are expected to make a full
recovery.*

*Police Chief Van Der
Faisey said that the full resources
of the W.A. Police Force, were
being brought to bare, and that,
"no stone would be left unturned,
and no effort spared in capturing
any remaining members of this
murderous armed gang, and
bringing them swiftly to justice".*

*The Police Chief also stated
that the man presently in custody
had been charged with armed
robbery and murder. He also
confirmed that three of the gang
had been killed at the Stockman's
Hut, during the shootout, and a
further man had died at Cutters*

Lane during an attempted escape
of the remaining gang members.
The Police Chief reminded
the public that any men that may
be still at large, if indeed there
were any others, were to be
considered armed and dangerous,
and should not be approached.
Anyone with any
information should contact their
local Police Station.

"Bugger me!" said Murray, more seriously now, "they sound a right handful".

Wilf nodded in agreement, still studying the photocopy, he then said,

"Maldwyn's written something on the bottom of the paper here, it says, 'Pithara and Nugadong Chronicle, August 6th, 1933', he's put his initials after it; M.S.".

Wilf continued reading the file, as Murray drove.

For the next fifty miles they exchanged observations on snippets of information, which Wilf would read aloud from the file. They pointed out roadside signposts to each other whose names they had found in the documents; Waddington, Bindi-Bindi, Milling, Wubin, and Payne's Find.

The expedition morphed, in the space of fifty miles of black tarmac, from Spinksy's, 'pile of old crap', to real people with real names and real lives, and real stories.

They mused that some civic dignitary had proposed the naming, of 'Frederick Armsby Boulevard'. They imagined his widow and five little kids, back in the 1930's, unveiling the street plaque nameplate. And tearfully receiving a cheque made up from all the donations of the citizens of New Norcia. And maybe old Chief Van Der Faisey saying a few words to the gathered crowd.

They wondered if any of the little Armsby children had stuck around in New Norcia, or even if there were any Armsby's still living thereabouts. And if there were, did they know what had happened to their Great Grandfather, or whatever relation he was to them.

The file had just become real, and the expedition, had become an adventure.

The African Railway's
From The Sudan to South Africa,
October 1920 to July 1921.

Mr Cyril Switch-Rillington was formerly of His Majesties Royal Engineers. A Major, but not from a privileged background.

He was that rare breed who had served with distinction throughout the entire duration of the Great War, and never picked up so much as a scratch. He had been in Damascus under General Allenby.

He had later been seconded to water supply works for the British army in Khartoum, when a letter had arrived announcing the untimely death of his wife, that was about six months ago. The circumstances had persuaded him to leave the army, resign his commission and take a job with the 'British East Africa Trading Company', to build a railway line from the mis-named, and land locked city of Port Sudan, (north of Suakin), all the way to Bulawayo.

The work was to be completed in various chunks and stretches by numerous gangs working simultaneously. The intention being to join each section with those adjacent, and eventually create one continuous railway line, stretching from The Sudan in East Africa to Bulawayo in Rhodesia, and thence connecting with lines onwards into South Africa.

The stretch of tracks traversing South Sudan to Juba, then through to Kampala in, (what is now), Uganda had already been completed. But stations were still being built, along with maintenance depots, signal boxes, watering and coaling points, turntables and the like, and other service buildings which still being erected. Indeed all the necessary paraphernalia of the workings of a railway system.

It was this portion of the works; the paraphernalia, which Mr. Switch-Rillington was now overseeing. All the vast and varied ancillary structures which needed to spring up along the respective sections of line.

The construction of the railway lines from Kampala to Mbeya in Tanzania, and the section from Mbeya to Lusaka in Zambia were already well under way by others. And the final stretches from Harare to Lusaka, and Harare to Bulawayo, both in Rhodesia, were being undertaken by the 'Trans African Railway Corporation', and were destined to link up, by the middle of 1922, or earlier.

All in all, (as Mr Switch-Rillington was in the habit of calling it), with his usual, and infectious, enthusiasm.

"A magnificent adventure!"

He had first come across Itzak and Yuris Androskewowicsz at the Sudanese town of Aljammalab on the eastern shore of the struggling Nile. The town slumped like a tired pilgrim on the banks of the shrunken river at this time of the year. It was October 1920 and the small settlement was almost crushed beneath the weight of its sagging palm trees. It was harvest time.

He had seen the two brother's clambouring like anaemic monkeys through the thick palm fronds. They were working at the date harvest, earning food, tea and lodge and little else, other than knowledge of Arabic and the Qur'an.

The first time they, in turn, had seen Mr. Switch-Rillington, he had been astride a huge chestnut gelding, and dressed in beige jodhpurs, a green shirt with large pockets, and a well worn pith helmet. He carried a short brown whip, but did not use it.

"You two up there!"

He had shouted:

"You white chaps; do you speak English by any chance?"

Yuris had looked down, he was standing astride a pair of buckling palm fronds about twenty feet in the air, but he seemed and felt wholly secure in this precarious position, practice had made him so. The Englishman, (for he could be nothing else), held up his hand against the Sun. He said nothing more, merely awaited a reply, he controlled the giant horse with the gentlest movements of his hand on the reins and the deft heels of his riding boots against the animals sides.

"We do Sir", answered Yuris.

"Can you use a pick and shovel?"

It was a blunt question.

"Anyone can use a pick and shovel Sir".

Yuris came back with.

"No they can't!"

Said Switch-Rillington sharply.

"Just as not everyone can climb palm trees and pick dates!"

He told them that he had just completed the final commissioning works on the railway turntable at Al Manaqil, about thirty miles south west of Aljammalab, and that he was camped about two miles upstream towards Al Douiem.

"I'll pay you fifteen shillings a week, that's each, plus tentage and grub. The work train moves south from Kosti tomorrow night, and we'll be in Kampala in a week to complete the terminus there. Be at my camp tomorrow morning if you think you're up to the job, you can't miss it just follow the river, two miles upstream, when you get there ask for me".

Without waiting for a reply, and without giving his name, Mr Switch-Rillington pulled the chestnut gelding around and galloped off, southward along the shoreline. As he went he waved, and without looking back shouted;

"And bring some dates with you, I love dates!"

The two boys climbed down from their respective palm trees, and stood on the ground watching the chestnut gelding disappearing into the distance. Both of them wore only cut down trousers and boots to protect their feet from the sharp frond spikes, they had their shirts tied around their heads against the beating Sun.

"Looks like we're going to Kampala little brother", said Itzak, "and I think we'd better start speaking English full time".

"Kampala it is then. Wherever the fuck that is", replied Yuris, his English having improved dramatically on the journey down the Red Sea.

They gathered up their belongings from the mud shanty they had been staying at, and said goodbye to Sharif and Aouda whose dates they had been harvesting.

They all wished each other well, and Aouda gave them water and bread for the journey, and a sack which he told them to fill with dates from the drying pile. He offered them no money, for they had none until their dates were shipped downstream to Khartoum to be sold.

In a strange way, the brothers would miss the date fields, the poverty, the sense of belonging.

They would not take the Turkish cabin boy with them, he was weak and even the date harvest had proven too much for him. He had been sick for a few weeks now, and was coughing up blood. Aouda's wives had been caring for him in an old mud shanty on the outskirts of the town. Yuris and Itzak decided that they would pay him one last visit before their departure.

The shanty smelt of rotten meat and sweat, and next to the single cot was a large beaten old bucket, half full of sick, blood and phlegm. The cabin boy was covered to the shoulders with a thin muslin sheet, and two fat women in black burkha's sat outside, fanning themselves with palm leaves.

The boy's eyes were wide open and terrified, bulging from his sweat polished face, he, like the two women, and the two brothers knew that death was only a few footsteps away; hiding in the shadows of the room.

Yuris knelt next to the bucket, and told him they were leaving to work on a railway, at some place called Kampala. Itzak leaned across him and, with little finesse, tore from around the boy's neck the small suede pouch which was tied about him by the silk chord. The boy could not speak, he was too weak, but his eyes cried out.

The two boys left the shanty, and headed upstream.

As promised, they had found the campsite with ease, and, despite darkness beginning to fall, they had successfully searched out the man on the chestnut gelding. He introduced himself as Mr. Cyril Switch-Rillington, and had also pointed out some of his 'team' as he had called them, as he showed the brothers to a billet tent for the night. The boys had given him the dates, and he had seemed genuinely grateful.

There were at least twenty tents in the camp, and half a dozen old green lorries, one with a horse box attached to its tail.

"Those are to take us all down to Kosti tomorrow to pick up the work train", he had said as they walked past them.

The brothers would sleep well.

The journey to Kampala aboard the work train had been exciting, the food had been good, bread with boiled chicken most days, and beans every morning and hard boiled eggs at bedtime.

The carriages were crammed with railway workers, Irishmen, Dutch, Scots, Welshmen, some Frenchmen and a Spaniard. They slept on wooden bunks with old, but good, British army mattresses on them. There was always a bucket of tea boiling at the stove in the middle of the carriage.

The boys played cards, and games of dice for cigarettes, they laughed, and made friends. The men were hard, rough, foul-mouthed, humorous and good company. In the evenings they would sing songs, the Irishmen vying with the Welshmen for the best tunes. Occasionally the Spaniard would try to sing a song from his country, the rest of the carriage would boo and jeer, then they would all laugh again, even the Spaniard.

Mr Switch-Rillington ran a good 'team'; they showed him respect, and if he said 'jump', they jumped. His carriage was forward, just behind his chestnut gelding, and he had a small office in there with maps and drawings on the walls. Yuris had taken food and tea to him there sometimes, and now and again, particularly of an evening, he would come back to one of the workers carriages and join in with the singing. He had a beautiful voice, and his rendering of a song called 'Keep the home fires burning, brought many a tear to the eyes of Irishmen, Welshmen, Scots, and even the Spaniard alike.

The carriage at the back of the train was full of 'Darkies', as the workers called them; they ate only beans and rice, and did not wash.

The workers carriages had latrine rooms with toilets that emptied directly over the tracks. The 'Darkies' carriage had a pile of straw, and a drum of disinfectant. If you leaned out of the windows of the other carriages you could see them shovelling the spent straw out of the door as the train went along, and there were shit stains along the side of the 'Darkies' carriage.

Mr. Switch-Rillington's chestnut gelding travelled at the front of the train in the stores carriage, and an ex-British army corporal named Kennedy looked after him. When the train stopped to take on coal and water, Mr. Kennedy would get off and make the 'Darkies' climb out of their carriage, and with long handled brooms make them clean the shit from the sides of the train.

Mr. Kennedy was not fond of the 'Darkies', and often called them lazy.

As Switch-Rillington had said, the journey to Kampala had taken about a week.

An unfolding tale.

If this entire story represents a human body.

Complete in its entirety with, skeleton, organs, blood, flesh, eyes, teeth, sinews, muscles, emotions, memories, regrets, ambitions. Then the box was nothing more than an ossuary full of unconnected bones, no cartilage, no skin, no flesh.

Its lungs were the souls beneath the prints, hidden in the clippings, the faded letters, the old coins. They made the box breath.

Its eyes were those of others, some inside the scraped skull bone hollows of imaginings. They saw, once; and they wept, some of them, most of them, all of them.

Its veins, its flooding pipes of blood as red as the fallen Nile are the whispered 'maybe's' of someone's dreams. They still flow. Trickle.

Its memories are all there. One need only look, smell the aging paper and stroke the scribbled script.

Its genitals are in the bitterness of all of its desires.

Satiated.

Its brain, sliced and diced, looked at in the coldness of the years, is in the deciphering, the digging, the mistakes.

But its heart!

Its heart is in the small curve of her thigh.

The small curve of "all that's left" Ironbark.

The book from the young blue and white Nun made Dilwyn cry. It took him five hours to read it all, the lines and the in between the lines. It plugged the gaping gaps like warm moist cotton wool into aching ears. It made him think. It made him feel. It made him sad and lucky all at once.

They were Stalin's words.

Elis and Maldwyn read them too, and they were not as brief tomorrow as they were today.

They were not the same, and went back to the box with different eyes.

They would not share it all.

They couldn't.

Only Sister Lubia knew, and she didn't know it all.

The African Railway's.
Kampala to Bulawayo and beyond.
Learning to play the Banjo, and to use his fists.
October 1920 to July 1921.

The work was hard, backbreakingly hard, the shovels were too short for Itzak and his tall frame, and they made him bend so much that he looked like a man in a cage which had been made just too small for him to stand upright in. They worked ten hours a shift, sometimes they stayed in a new station for two days just benching up some drains or finishing some work to a roof or a platform. At other stops they stayed a month throwing up complete waiting rooms or ticket offices. Occasionally they would stay at lodging houses, but only in places where the stations were big enough.

Amongst the 'Micks' and the 'Taffs' as the Irish and Welsh became called there were painters, bricklayers, masons, carpenters, and track layers. Itzak and Yuris were the lowest of the low, 'General Labourers', 'only a kick in the arse above the niggers' as Mr. Kennedy used to say.

244

Mostly they stayed in makeshift camps at the trackside; with the train pulled up in a siding close by. Now and again another train would arrive at their site and unload materials, bags of stinging lime that burnt the skin from your palms, but made your knuckles as hard as the Hobbs of Hell. Knocking up 'Bankers of Compo' was Itzak and Yuris's main job, knock it up, then barrow it to the bricklayers and the masons.

Sometimes they would get to strip timber planks down into thin laths for the plasterers to lay on to. Or they would hump and shift stone flagstones for the masons to lay in billiard table flats along the new platforms.

They enjoyed the work.

Of an evening there would be singing and drinking, and once a month, Mr. Switch-Rillington would arrange a whole Sunday off, and he would organise sporting competitions.

There would be one and two hundred yards dashes, or a one mile run. One of the Dutch carpenters broke his ankle once doing a long jump competition; but no-one let on to the big bosses. If ever they came to a job site, the rest of the crews would cover for him; they kept him fitting skirtings or floorboards for a month, anything so that he could sit down while he worked.

Sit down to let his bones knit.

Anything on the ground.

After that he was known as 'Limpy the Dutchman'.

Mr. Switch-Rillington was a real athlete; he would take off from the campsites each morning for a five mile run, always carrying a full pack and a rifle. Yuris considered that the Railway Company had been very lucky to have Mr. Switch-Rillington, he was thorough, industrious and conscienseous without being a pain in the arse. He got the most out of the men, and instilled a pride in them for their finished work. The quality of the stations, even in the small signal boxes which they occasionally built was as good as any swanky hotel you could find in Cape Town or Alexandria.

He gave the crews a camaraderie within themselves, which Yuris thought came from his time in the British army. The brothers had grown to like and respect Mr. Switch-Rillington, and secretly, (they thought), he had grown fond of them.

Around the evening campsite fires, amidst the singing, smoking, swearing, drinking, eating, farting and joke-telling; Mr. Switch-Rillington would tell them of war, and the army. He would not have Germans in his work crews, it was his only prejudice, he even allowed the 'Blacks' to join in the singing, but he would not let them camp in the same billets, nor share the same railway carriages.

He had told the brothers that he had been a regimental boxing champion in his younger days, and he had showed them boxing gloves which he had been awarded as prizes after successful bouts. He taught Itzak to box. He had made him fast, and his long arms made the punches hard and painful to the recipient.

Once, on one of the sporting Sundays, at a place called Mpanda on the Tanzanian-Congo border; Mr. Switch-Rillington had allowed, (for a fee of sixpence), anyone to put on a pair of his boxing gloves and have two swipes to try and hit him. Many had tried and failed, and one big Welshman, a former coal miner from a place called Cilfynnydd, managed to land one good right to the jaw, but Mr. Switch-Rillington had stood firm.

Eventually he had shouted at Itzak to have a go. He had refused saying that he didn't earn enough to throw sixpence away on such foolishness.

Mr. Switch-Rillington persuaded him by promising Itzak a shilling for every blow he landed. Being cajoled, the older brother pulled on the gloves, and both men, (stripped to the half), danced around the campsite fire. The bobbing and weaving lasted no more than five seconds, then Itzak threw his first punch, a short left which struck Mr. Switch-Rillington under the heart, the second blow was almost simultaneous and connected with the Crew Master just below the right eye.

Mr. Switch-Rillington woke up in his tent about fifteen minutes later, with the crew doctor mopping his brow, and pouring brandy down him. When he had recovered he sent a big black labourer with a message to Itzak, saying 'Well Done', and with two one shilling coins for him.

On the eight months of work-stops, campsites and train travel between Mpanda and Lusaka, north of Rhodesia, Mr. Switch-Rillington devoted considerable time and effort to Itzak Androskewowicsz. He would take him on his early morning runs with him, and after the working day had finished, he would have some Blacks set up a staked ring with ropes nailed between them. In there he would spend hour after hour teaching Itzak combinations of punches, and skipping and how to block the blows of opponents. But most of all, he taught Itzak how to be fast, faster than he was anyway, faster than the wings of a humming bird.

The big Welsh miner from Cilfynydd had called him something in Welsh that he said meant 'wasp', because he darted and jigged so much, and so quickly.

By the time Lusaka had been and gone, Itzak's body was showing the results of Mr. Switch-Rillington's training. He was wide with a deep chest and a thick neck, his arms were like sackfuls of cricket balls, hard and lumpy, as were his thighs and calfs, and his hands, already like tanned leather, (from the lime), were massive and lethal. His eyes were alert, and his belly was harder than an ungrateful wife.

Mr. Switch-Rillington had completed the 'finishing off works' as far as Lusaka ahead of schedule, and everyone including Itzak and Yuris had received a bonus. The brother's share was fifteen South African Pounds each.

A veritable fortune.

The Railway Companies had offered Mr, Switch-Rillington another three months work, to upgrade the so-called 'jump off stations' between Bulawayo and Pretoria in South Africa. He had accepted and offered the extended work to about thirty of the transit crew, and five of the 'Darkies'. Mr. Kennedy and the chestnut gelding also came along.

As did Itzak and Yuris.

One evening at a large sidings yard in a town called Mokopane, about two hundred miles south of the Rhodesian border, and three hundred north of Pretoria. Mr. Switch-Rillington's crew met up with the crew of Rudolf Holcroft, he was an old friend of Switch-Rillington, and another first rate engineer. He was also a boxing fan and an old slugger in his own right, but he was a good bit older than Mr. Switch-Rillington, and probably in his mid forties, he was spreading a bit around the middle, but was clean-shaven and had an affable face and manner. He also had a Frenchman in his crew, (a stone mason), who he had known since half way through the Great War; the man was a boxer.

With the consent of both, a bout had been arranged for the Sunday evening before each team moved out, Itzak to be heading south with Mr. Switch-Rillington, while Mr. Holcroft's crew would then be moving west.

Each Crew Master had put up a ten pound stake, and the winning boxer was to take the whole twenty pound purse.

There was to be ten, three minute rounds.

The evening was presented with some ceremony, with torchlight and lantern parades for the boxers to the ringside. Darkies mulled through the crowd of workers from the respective crews, passing out whiskey, cigarettes and beer, all supplied by the two Crew Masters. Odd little betting circles formed as if by evolution, and money changed hands.

The boxing gloves were provided by Mr. Switch-Rillington.

The bout lasted precisely one minute and twenty eight seconds. The Frenchman lost two teeth, the sight in his left eye, and one hour and twelve minutes of consciousness.

Itzak and Yuris collected their twenty pounds winnings, and later apologised to the Frog about his eye. He took the apology in good grace and the brothers shook his hand. Itzak wanted to give him a fiver out of the winnings, but Yuris told him not to be so, as he put it with some economy,

"Fucking stupid".

The next few weeks were busy; the powers that be were pushing to get the whole of the Trans-African railway line open ahead of schedule. Mr. Switch-Rillington's crew were at KwaMhlanga, about thirty miles or so east of Pretoria, they had been assigned to the overhaul of a large steam locomotive turntable, and the construction of a new signal box two miles further along the track towards Pretoria.

It was the first day of August 1921.

The day had been like every other day, Mr. Switch-Rillington, had taken his morning run, Mr. Kennedy had issue the work schedules to each gang, and the work had been done. The arduous day had quietly died, tools were packed away, and the mess of the bundles of toil had been cleared to dump pits and store sheds until tomorrow. The men were walking back to the campsite to wash, eat and rest, and the Sun probably had, at most, two hours of daylight left in it.

As Itzak and Yuris cleaned up around the turntable, and collected up the small tools of the tradesman in two large wheelbarrows, they waved to Mr. Switch-Rillington who was astride his chestnut gelding and cantering off towards the lush bush lands for his late afternoon ride. It was his habit, exercise himself in the morning, work his day, exercise his horse late afternoon and early evening, then exercise Itzak until eight p.m., then food, then singing, talking, and joke telling, then whiskey, then bed by ten thirty. It was a regime that worked, and which yielded results.

It was Mr. Kennedy who first raised the alarm, moving from tent to tent, in the hope of finding the Crew Master. It had turned seven, and darkness had settled across the land, only the camp fires, the animal torches and the billet lamps flared against the night.

"Have you boys seen Mr. S.R.?"

Kennedy asked as he poked his head into the entrance flap of the brother's tent.

"No", they both replied, and immediately collected up their shirts and went outside, concerned for their friend, as was Mr. Kennedy.

Within minutes the entire campsite was alive, crawling with men, shouting men, searching, worried men. Mr. Kennedy organised them all, including the Darkies to fan out towards the edge of the bush lands and take lanterns and torches with them, and to call for Mr. S.R. as he called him.

"No one go past the bush line mind, not after dark!" Mr. Kennedy had instructed, and everyone obeyed.

For three hours the gangs buzzed around the tree line, shouting, and waving their torches and lanterns.

All at once there was an almighty rustling in the scrubland, bushes moved, and the crunch of foliage being heaved apart and mashed underfoot gathered sound and momentum.

The chestnut gelding burst from the scrub, screaming as he galloped, knocking some of the tradesmen and labourers off their feet as he passed by. One of the Darkies was trampled under hoof in the blackness and was very badly injured. Mr.Kennedy managed to catch a hold on the geldings bridle as he sped by, and despite being pulled off his feet by the beast he managed to hold on fast, and bring the animal to a stop.

The horse had an ugly wound in its neck, with sheets of flesh hanging down and blood oozing in torrents from the open gash. There were slash and claw marks on its hind quarters and the beasts entire right side was drenched in blood. It let out curdling, withering cries of anguish, pain and suffering.

Without hesitation, Mr. Kennedy drew from the holster which he always wore, a British army service revolver from the Great War, held the muzzle no more than two inches from the animals struggling forehead, and fired two quick and loud shots into the beasts brain.

The chestnut gelding fell immediately to the ground, silent and messy, splattering blood from its wounds and from the gunshots in all directions. Mr. Kennedy stood over the animal, his gun held limply at his side. He was panting heavily, and blood specks spattered his clothes and his face. He looked down at the dead horse.

"Lion!"

He said simply.

"There's a lion out there".

He gestured to the tree line, and, holstering his revolver, he said, almost matter of factly;

"Get this beast out of the way; we don't want to attract any more scavengers."

He waved to the Darkies to deal with the carcase of the chestnut gelding, knowing they would butcher the remains and roast the meat that night over the campsite fires. He turned to the head Darkie, and said, again matter of factly.

"See to your man over there".

He gestured with a nod towards the trampled Darkie who was now writhing in agony on the stumpy thick grass, heavy with tussocks. The man was screaming; the horse's hoofs had landed one on his ribcage, the other full in his face.

"If you can't shut him up, I will!"

Mr. Kennedy said, and patted his revolver holster. He was not renowned as a lover of Darkies.

He then turned around, once, maybe twice, and shouted.

"Everyone; listen up. First light we go into the tree line", Mr. Kennedy pointed northwards, "Mr. S.R. is out there, he may still be alive, get some rest, eat and drink, and those of you who can shoot draw rifles from me at the front carriage over at the siding. No body leaves camp and nobody works until Mr. S.R. is found".

He then turned to some Darkies who were tugging at the corpse of the chestnut gelding, he said to them.

"Get that bridle and saddle off and put it in the carriage; I'll clean it. Tomorrow, you lot cut sticks, and make noise as we search for the Boss. You don't get guns, make sure you bring plenty of water"

He turned away, then shouted a general instruction.

"First light. Be ready! I'll shoot any cunt I have to come looking for to wake up!"

Mr. Kennedy strode off in the direction of the locomotive at the sidings.

The next morning came swiftly. The injured Darkie had died over night, and everyone had gorged, albeit reluctantly on the tender roast chops and steaks from the chestnut gelding.

Everyone had been ready at the crack of dawn, and as the Sun blinked over the horizon the search began. It was an organised search, everyone fanning out, no one out of sight of anyone else, the Darkies beating the undergrowth and whooping to drive any animals in front of them, every third white man carrying an Enfield rifle, those without firearms, like Itzak and Yuris carried picks, bars or shovels.

The search lasted less than an hour, the remains, (if they can be called such), of Mr. Cyril Switch-Rillington were found less than a half mile into the undergrowth. He had been torn limb from limb in a feeding frenzy of carnivorous beasts. Just as the Darkies had gorged on the chestnut gelding, so lions, wild dogs, and now the early morning vultures gorged on the rawness of the Crew Master.

Mr. Kennedy had the Darkies collect up the pieces that could reasonably be carried back to camp, and a funeral service was held at twelve noon. Mr. Kennedy and the big Welshman from the place called Cilfynydd officiated, and read from a weather beaten Bible which had its front cover missing.

The remains were buried in a hole next to the locomotive turntable, and one of the carpenters made a cross, and carved the Crew Masters name across it.

They all sang 'How Great Thou Art', and later, when he was alone in the train's store's carriage, as he cleaned the bridle and saddle; Mr. Kennedy wept like a baby.

The trouble with working for Dykka and Gonda!
Pietermaritzburg,
South Africa
July 12th 1926.

The Napierville district of Pietermaritzburg, was peppered with blocks of rented tenements, three and four stories high some of them. It was a mixed up old area, some properties owned by traditional type Afrikaans with wrinkles and a few shillings tucked away. Others rented to day workers, others to new families on the 'shift' for work, others to Indians, 'Wogs' with ideas of business and mouths to feed.

Mambo had a room in stone a fronted 'step up' there. It was the secret place for Eloise, but just home for Mambo.

Dykka was desperately unloading his property interests as quick as he could unload what was left of his 'Baccy' and 'Booze' business. He was being squeezed by the 'Dospars', as the local cops had now become known, and the City Council had refused to renew his lease on the sidings warehouse behind the Railway Station.

The one bright spot on the Van Hoost horizon, was Bernard Van Der Kyper. After the Church Street fire, and the Baitridge Tunnel business, the Van Der Kyper brothers had put some freight business Gonda's way, and they had all done quite nicely out of it. But that business, like everything now, had tailed off, and Louis Van Der Kyper, was if anything, giving Dykka and Gonda 'The Big Avoid'.

However, during the subsequent business meetings, (after the 'incidents'), between Dykka, Gonda, and the brothers, Bernard, (at some swanky meal set up by Dykka), had been introduced to Eloise. It had been like 'turning a hose of petrol on a raging fire', one of Vienna's few remaining upper crust lady friends had commented.

Dykka had cultivated the relationship, taking Eloise and Vienna with him and Gonda, on fictitious business trips to Bulawayo, and Harare; in order to create opportunities to throw the pair together.

They did not need much throwing.

On one occasion at the Van Der Kyper Mansion in Bulawayo overlooking Makokoba, Bernard had offered to show Eloise the family library after dinner. Dykka, some fifteen or twenty minutes later, had asked the other guests to excuse him, as they drank brandy and smoked cigars in the rapacious dining room, as he wanted to freshen up, before coffee was served.

What he really wanted, was to speak with Bernard and Eloise alone, and brooch the subject of a possible marriage 'arrangement'.

As he approached the large moulded and gilded doors of the library, he paused a moment, he raised his hand, intending to knock gently, but stopped himself. He leaned forward, and turned his ear against the door, and smiled.

He looked left and right, and then, satisfied that he was alone in the hallway, crouched down and peeped through the door lock. Fortunately there was no key in the other side to obscure his view. He smiled again, broader this time, and pressed his eyeball closer to the keyhole.

He saw Eloise, bent forward, spread eagled, across a large polished wood table, with thick books scattered about it; Bernard stood behind her, the trousers of his dinner suit were around his ankles, as were his underpants. Eloise' dress was pulled up over her waist, and her dropped underwear collected over a silver shoe on her right foot. Bernard had his one hand on her cream white hip, and was lifting her other thigh upwards and wider with his other hand, gripping tightly behind the crook of her knee.

Dykka could hear her groans of delight from outside the door. Part of him wanted to stay and see the finale, but he needed to get back to the drawing room, and make sure no one else strayed this way for a little while. He rose to his feet, adjusted his dinner suit tails, and white waistcoat, and walked away, satisfied that an 'arrangement' was probably in the offing.

The Van Der Kyper's were an ideal match, as far as Dykka was concerned. They were 'Old Money'; Mrs Van Der Kyper, the Matriarch of the family, was in her seventies, and spent her time, as the Patron of various Bulawayo 'Establishment Enterprises'. Her primary interest was the 'Eveline High School for Girls', her pet project for the production of future 'Ladies of Quality' as she termed it.

Her husband Duncan Van Der Kyper, a half Scot half Dutch mongrel, had made all the family money originally from railways, freight haulage and mining, and Louis and Bernard now kept it cultivated and growing.

Dykka had not been invited back to 'Makokoba Mansion' for over a year now, and his welcome had declined in direct proportion to the business he did with The Van Der Kyper brothers. But Bernard still corresponded with Eloise, and they met once or twice a month when he was in South Africa, generally either at Johannesburg or Bloemfontein, where the Van Der Kypers had business interests.

The brothers had not been back to Pietermaritzburg since before the Church Street fire, and had no intention of returning. If Dykka and Gonda still carried any hopes of further business with the Van Der Kypers', they were severely misplaced, and the two men would prove to be sadly disillusioned.

However, prospects on the marriage front were certainly improving, and a month earlier, a telegram had been delivered to the Van Hoosts house, seeking permission for Bernard Van Der Kyper to request the hand of Eloise Hunter Van Hoost. The telegram had been drafted by the Old Matriarch, who Dykka knew objected to him. But the intention was now made open to all, and the marriage should improve things for Dykka with the Van Der Kyper brothers, from a business standpoint.

At least he hoped so.

In the same fashion as a drowning man hopes that the sea will turn into a country lane.

At a previous, now distant visit to Makokoba, Dykka had asked where the name came from. Louis had told him that it was named after a Matebele word that they used to call his Father. The word was 'Umakhokhoba', which meant the sound made on the ground by a walking stick.

Louis explained that his father had been a merchant seaman before coming to Rhodesia, and, in his youth, while working on coal transporters from Cardiff, in

South Wales, Great Britain, to Perth in Western Australia, he had developed an infection in the two small toes of his left foot.

The ships surgeon had removed them, fearing a spread of the infection.

When they had subsequently docked in Perth, the ships carpenter had acquired a length of a local Eucalyptus hardwood called Ironbark. He had fashioned from this, for his father, a beautiful polished walking cane. It was in the shape of three platted vines with occasional insects, and a handle carved to the perfect shape of his Fathers gripping fist.

It had been made to glow with a dozen layers of Shellac, and finished with a Whale-Bone shoe. Louis said that his father had carried it until his death, and that it had been placed next to him in his coffin, and buried with him.

Dykka and Gonda had just taken the right hand turn from Langenhoven Road, into Aalwyn Road, South East of Napierville, in western Pietermaritzburg. Gonda drove the Yellow Austin Twenty, as Dykka sat in the passenger seat; he was too drunk to drive. He continued to swig at the bottle of Scotch he clutched in his fuming fist. Spittle and Scotch stained the waistcoat of his ever present tweeds, his tie was loosened and his diamond tie pin peeped over the edge of his lapel. Outside, it was night time, eight or maybe nine o'clock, it was raining.

Gonda was imploring Dykka to calm down, and to let him take Dykka back home, and that things would be clearer in the morning, and that in any event the information may not be true.

"It could all be a big mistake?"

Gonda kept saying.

Across Dykka's lap, rested an 'extra long barrel American Colt 45 Peacemaker', in black gunmetal, with a pearl handle. The car drew to a halt outside Mambo's tenement. Dykka jumped out without discussion, and without waiting for the car to fully stop. He stumbled as he went, falling to the wet pavement and smashing the bottle of Scotch on the ground. Gonda put the handbrake on and got out, he ran around to Dykka to help him up, he had torn his jacket, and grazed the side of his face.

As Gonda tried to lift him, crooking his arm under Dykka's shoulder, he was pushed back against the bonnet of the car; his hand gripped the golden horse head ornament to stop himself slipping along the rain shined metal. Dykka pushed the muzzle of the revolver hard into Gonda's chest, and pulled viciously at the sleeve of his coat with his other hand. He spat the words at him, slurring, angry:

"You, you cunt, I'll bet you knew all along, I'll bet you fucked her too, you'd fuck my dogs if I could stop them barking!"

Gonda had seen Dykka like this before; he had a temper not to tempt. He made placatory gestures, gently raised his hands, and whispered soft assurances that it was all news to him as well. He could not tell where the rain stopped on his face and where the sweat started. The rain was lashing down, and Gonda's sweaty forehead was grateful for it.

"Cunt!"

Dykka spat as he pushed Gonda to the pavement with a splash.

"Where is he?"

He demanded, and pointed the revolver at Gonda again as he lay on the tarmac, his best coat soaking up the water.

"First floor, right opposite the stairs".

Gonda, although lying face up on the pavement, still had his hands raised in submission. Dykka leaned forward and grabbed the lapel of his coat, tearing it as he heaved Gonda to his feet.

"Fucking show me!"

He hissed, spat again, and shoved Gonda through the tenement doorway.

After they had noisily climbed the two flights of stairs to the first floor landing, Dykka dragging the reluctant Gonda behind him, they stood before the entrance door to Mambo's rooms. Without any discussion Dykka kicked open the door, sending splinters of timber jamb flying inwards, and the lock case itself clattering across the floorboards. He hurled Gonda in front of him and threw him into the room, stumbling as he went.

At the small table, in the small room, sat three big men, 'The Elephant', Banjo, and Mambo. The deck of cards they were playing with, scattered into the air as Gonda crashed into the table, and they settled, slowly across the floor, like falling snow. Their whiskey glasses flew to all points of the room and smashed on the floor, or against the walls.

An instant reflex action took root in 'The Elephant', and, not recognising Gonda in the half light from Mambo's Paraffin lamp; he struck Gonda in the face with his huge right hand, he felt the man's nose break and explode into a torrent of blood, snot, and dozen pieces of splintered bone and cartilage.

He heard Gonda scream, as he saw and recognised Dykka standing behind him.

A captured silence descended on them, Gonda was kneeling on the floor, facing forwards, a pool of blood appearing on the ground in front of him, plopping from his crushed, flattened nose. Dykka was waving the monstrous revolver around, and telling everyone to,

"Shut up and stand still!"

And to:

"Get against the far wall!"

They all did as they were told.

He then turned to the moaning and bleeding Gonda, and, whilst keeping his gun pointed at the three men against the wall, he dragged Gonda up by the scruff of his neck, and told him to push the door (or what was left of it), shut, and 'shove a chair against it'. Gonda squealed as he was jerked upwards, but, despite clearly being in substantial pain, he did as he was told.

Dykka took one step towards Mambo, a terrified Mambo, a Mambo who had just pissed himself, and whose slippers were now soaked in his own urine. A large oval piss stain had appeared on the front of his brown trousers, and his thick lips trembled.

"You know why I'm here you fucking nigger louse! You fucking cunt!"

Dykka paused for a second, still swaying, still slurring, Gonda now rested with his back against the door, with both hands held up to his nose, which was still gushing with blood. Dykka carried on:

"Is this the place then, is this where you and her went at it. I know she likes it. Did she pay you, did she fucking pay you with my money, you fucking cunt. When was the last time you fucked her? When?"

Dykka's voice was rising, he asked again, demanded, screamed:

"When?"

Mambo raised his hands quietly, in the same manner that Gonda had done in the street.

"When?"

Dykka screamed the question for a third time.

The two brothers both looked at Mambo, they could see his mind whirring. Whoever Dykka was talking about, an answer would be an admission, anything else, would be a denial, a denial requiring an alibi that would need to be bloody good. Either way, they both knew Dykka Van Hoost well enough to know that Mambo was up to his black cock in thick sticky shit.

"Yesterday".

Said Mambo, in a gasping kind of way.

As the brothers expected from this point, Mambo was in the last seconds of his lifetime. In fact, it is not clear whether he actually finished the word, 'yesterday'.

Two shots cracked out, one hit the wall just to the left of Banjo's shoulder, the other smashed into Mambo's stomach, and he screamed.

Yelled like a gutted pig.

'The Elephant' anticipated that Dykka would loose off the remaining four bullets in the revolver, and once more instinct took over. He lunged at Dykka's arm, forcing it upwards, the gun flinging from his hand. He careened forwards into Dykka's large, but drunken frame, and bundled him to the floor. Mambo had slumped down the wall leaving a stretched stain of blood, downwards behind him. The gun landed and bounced just in front of him; he snatched it up, his face grimaced with the spreading agony. He fired all four remaining shots, as quickly as he could manage to pull the trigger; he had aimed roughly at Dykka, as he wrestled with 'The Elephant'.

Two shots hit him in the head, a third found Dykka's chest; he fell instantly still, and silent.

He was dead.

The two brothers, both with hands raised, froze, motionless, both looking at Mambo, Itzak sitting on the floor next to the dead Dykka, Banjo, crouching, half bent, near the wall, above Mambo, and to his right.

Mambo, mustered all his remaining strength and pointed the gun at Gonda, who was still against the door, looking even more terrified, and in more pain now than five seconds ago, if that was possible. The gun fired its last bullet; it missed Gonda, and smashed into the door frame. Before Gonda could finish his sigh of relief, Banjo bounded across the room to the small stove in the corner, and snatched up the bread knife which he had used there earlier to make sandwiches for the card game.

The card game that was a lifetime ago.

Without any debate or delay, Banjo leapt towards Gonda, and plunged the large knife deep into his chest, then again, and again, when Gonda's hands left his nose to grab at his chest, Banjo stabbed him in the face, in his mouth, in his eyes. He kept stabbing until Gonda dropped to the floor. Throwing down the bread knife, Banjo knelt over Gonda and reached inside his coat. He withdrew a small, ladies type, 32 pistol. Holding it aloft, like some small trophy, he said, as if justifying himself:

"He would have killed us. Definite".

He looked at Itzak. Then they both looked at Mambo.

The Wylachi Spread,
Dagger Hills,
North of Coolinar Hill,
Western Australia.
July 27th 1933.

The Wylachi's stockman's hut, at the base of Daggar Hills, was exactly as it sounded, a timber hut, with a rickety raised porch surround, and roofed with rusting tin sheeting. It had one window to each of its four sides, all randomly sized and salvaged from previous building demolitions in the vicinity. The glass panes were thick with yellow dust, and tracked with occasional darting stripes, where rare rain had sneaked under the veranda.

On its south facing entrance, the doorway was made up of the old original carved Ironbark door from the Wylachi family's first farmstead home.

It had a stylised 'M', in the upper half, and a same style 'W', carved in the lower. This mirror image 'M', and 'W', still formed the brand of the Wylachi herds. In its day, the door must have been quite impressive, but today it had degenerated into a splitting, warped and twisted shadow of its former self.

Malakye Jnr. had spent the night before last at the stockman's hut, along with farm hands Toby 'J', and Linus Sabak, both Aborigines in their thirties, who had worked for Old Man Mal for over ten years. The three men had left their pick up truck at the Wylachi horse ranch and livery, at the Coolinar Hill end of Cutters Lane. From there they had journeyed onwards by horses towards Daggar Hills, riding a large mare each, and bringing two others for pack and spares.

They were on Roustabout, hunting out stray sheep, cattle and odd horses, which may have wandered off from their own herds, or which may have strayed onto Wylachi land from adjacent spreads or from wild herds. These latter elements represented pure profit, as they would be branded, and incorporated at virtually no cost into the Wylachi flocks and herds.

Malakye Jnr., had earned himself a deserved reputation as a keen stockman, and didn't loose animals to either weather or geography. He would also seek out new grazing grounds, and managed efficiently their rotation to maximise usage. He was shrewd, quick, and ruthless when required, and as hard as a barrel full of nails. He was Old Man Mals son, 'and then some', as the locals had come to realise.

Some to their cost.

The land around the stockman's hut was predominantly scrub, suitable for grazing for probably only about three or four months a year. From the slopes of Daggar Hills the hut looked like a spec of dust on the skin of an old fat pig, although it was a good five yards square.

The three men had rounded up the better part of fifty sheep, a couple of cows, and three wild horses. It had been a good trip, so far, and they were aiming to be back at Coolinar Livery by tomorrow night.

This evening they would camp to the east of Dagger Hills, overlooking the railway line to the North of Coolinar Hill, and at the 'Railway End' of Cutters Lane.

The name of Cutters Lane, was something of a misnomer. It had been coined after the Railway Engineer who had levelled the area in error, during the construction of the railway line back in 1905.

His name was Jerome Falmoth Cutter, and Cutters Lane, was in fact over fifteen miles long, and was now an effective dirt track between Coolinar Hill, Sandstone, Dagger Hills, and a quarter the way to Payne's Find.

As for Jerome Cutter, after his mistake, he was shipped off to South Africa by the British Government to work as an assistant designer on Pietermaritzburg Railway Station; where he redeemed himself, and made his fortune.

He married a Scottish immigrant Vienna Sunday Hunter, who tried to be English. They had twin daughters, one of whom died in childbirth.

Cutter himself died in 1916 after a snakebite. His wife inherited his fortune, and rejected his name; she reverted to her maiden name two days after his death, shedding few tears.

Towards mid-day, and heading South West, and down the gentle slope of the Musk Mound of Daggar Hills; Malakye Jnr., spotted a young black stallion skirting the ridge above them, reaching for the binoculars in his saddle bag, he saw that the horse was large, about seventeen hands, and wholly black, with no white flashes anywhere.

"Fuck me; he's a beauty!"

He exclaimed loudly.

Thinking fast, he beckoned to Toby 'J' to take the rains of the pack horse which Malakye had in tow, and said:

"I'm going to get him, I'll have him for myself, and I'll breed from him".

Getting his mount around and facing up the slope, he said to Toby 'J':

"You and Sabak get the stock back to Coolinar Liverey, brand up the 'findies', (the free, new found animals) and fold them back into the herds. Leave the horses with Big Jack at the stables, then take the pick-up back over to Coolinar. I'll catch up with you at Sandstone Farmstead in a couple of days; don't fuck it up!"

Without waiting for any answer, and expecting his instructions to be adhered to; Malakye Jnr., slapped his mare's hind quarter and galloped off up the slope towards the black stallion.

261

Toby 'J' and Sabak, knew that any discussion would be pointless. They also knew that Malakye Jnr. would not accept any excuses, and that by the time Malakye had returned to Sandstone Farmstead the two Aborigines had better have everything he asked for done, and done properly, and the pick-up washed and cleaned as well.

They looked at each other, shrugged, and continued down the slope with the stock. They knew that being a hand short they would have their work cut out keeping the mixed herd together, but they also knew that times were hard, and, old hands or not, if they 'fucked up', the Wylachi's would have two new Abo Stockmen, faster than Toby 'J' and and Sabak, could say:

"Fucking White Men!"

It took Malakye Jnr. over seven hours to run down and rope the black stallion. He had been right, he was a beauty, as black as Grandad Wylachis' Bible, and with a coat as shiny as a Gum Tree in summer, and with muscles as hard as a mature Ironbark.

The stallion would take some breaking, but that would be Big Jacks' job.

Through the chase, Malakye Jnr., had tracked, and ran down the stallion, back eastwards across Daggar Hills. He was now back in those hills, high above the Old Stockman's Hut, and about two miles back to the north. From here, he could look down towards the mid point of Cutters Lane to the west, and the Old Hut to the south.

Overhanging the mid-point of Cutters Lane, was the largest Ironbark Tree one would ever see. It had long shed its summer foliage, and looked like a twisted collection of gallows trees, squeezed into one huge terrifying monster. It had been tortured by thousands of seasons, and stretched into screaming branches by the scorching winds that careened off the slopes of the Daggar Hills in the blistering summer months.

It was both lovely and terrifying.

Bright and dark, all at once.

The sun was sinking down in the west, and he knew dusk would come in the next hour or so. Malakye Jnr. decided that he would camp here for the night, and not bother with the extra couple of miles back to the Stockman's Hut.

He dismounted, and tied the stallion's rope to a convenient rock. He tied his mare to the remains of a Coolabahs stump, about twenty paces away; not wishing to let the two horses get too close to each other. Between the two animals, he set up a small fire of Coolabahs wood and sun dried brush, and surrounded it with stones. He placed a saucepan full of baked beans in its midst, next to his small coffee pot, which he levelled on a flattish stone.

Having unrolled his sleeping pack, and stripped his mare of saddle, rifle, throw over bags, ropes, water canteens, binoculars and sundries; he fed and watered the horses. He then settled himself down to watch the sunset, whilst rolling and smoking some cigarettes, and allowing himself a good sized tin mug of Scotch, all before supper.

The beauty of the night sky over Daggar Hills never failed to satisfy Malakye; it was unpolluted by the lights of the bigger towns like Payne's Find, and Mount Magnet, and resembled a spread of diamonds on a cloth of rich black velvet. He had learned the constellations, and could tell the evolving seasons from their changing positions in the sky. He could recognise the planets as they peeped in and out of the night. For all his harsh bushness ways, Malakye Jnr. was articulate, well read, and at heart, even a secret romantic.

As dusk reluctantly began to give way to night, Malakye's quiet enjoyment of his cigarette and mug of Scotch was interrupted by the distant, low drone of a motor car engine. Against the crippling stillness of the bush nights, the slightest hum carried for miles, and left its wake in the resting air.

Malakye felt the direction of the noise, and immediately turned towards it; he estimated the source at, at least a mile and a half away, probably more. He put down his drink, and slid his cigarette into the corner crook of his mouth, and reached for his binoculars. He stood up and walked a few paces forward.

In the distance, and looking towards the old Ironbark, through the binoculars, he could see a sheep transporter truck, and a large grey coloured Riley car, with all four of its doors, and its boot open. The headlights of both vehicles were on against the creeping darkness, and their engines were running, presumably, (Malakye surmised), to keep the batteries up on charge.

In front of the car and truck, could be seen five men, three of them were digging with picks and shovels, one of them, shovelling like a man possessed. Malakye had never seen anyone dig so fast for so long. The other two men were flitting back and forth to the truck, and the car with torches, and carrying what looked like canvass sacks, and occasional small boxes.

After two hours or more, the diggers clamboured from their hole, which was now a good four or five foot deep, and they, and the other men, began throwing the sacks and boxes into the hole.

A woman stepped from the driver's seat of the Riley, and as she walked over to the men, she took something from her handbag; whatever it was, it was very small, no bigger than her fist, and Malakye strained to see more detail as she scattered her image between the headlight beams.

When she reached the hole, she gave the item, this secret small thing, to one of the men, and he placed it on top of the sacks and boxes in the hole. One of the other men took a canvas tarpaulin from the back of the sheep truck, and threw it over the items in the hole.

The men spent the next three quarters of an hour filling back in the hole, with excavated material, and spreading the surplus around the area so as not to leave a tell-tail tump on the ground.

In the distance, and high above them, Malakye Jnr., needed no guesses as to the identity of these uninvited visitors to Wylachi lands. They had been all over the W.A. newspapers for the last six or eight months, even the descriptions of one of the vehicles fitted.

They had to be the so called 'Brisbane Bandolero's'.

Malakye was sure that the gang would not see his small fire at this distance, nor hear his horses over the sound of their engines, but he allowed his fire to die naturally. He ate his beans and drank his coffee, but discarded his whiskey, as he watched the crowd below, (knowing that he would allow himself no sleep this night), he knew that tomorrow would require planning, time, and effort.

Over the next couple of hours he watched the gang pace out the position of the hole, and sketch the area on a paper which they rested on the bonnet of the Riley. He then tracked them through his binoculars from his vantage point, until, about three hours before dawn. Malakye Junior watched the two vehicles, the five men, and the woman, pull up outside the Stockman's Hut, and go inside. They took from the boot of the Riley, and from the cab of the sheep truck, some rifles, a few suitcases, and a selection of revolvers, and what looked like a couple of cases of beer.

Malakye decided it was time to move out. He saddled his mare, and loaded up his kit. He decided to take the short cut back to Sandstone, down the western slopes of Daggar Hills, then cut across the Payne's Find end of Cutters Lane, and along the railway tracks to the back of Coolinar Hill, and into Sandstone from behind the railway station.

He estimated that the horse-ride would take him a good eight hours with his new stallion in tow. He set off immediately, and would alternate between a good gallop, (when the ground allowed), and a steady trot when it didn't. He would also need to stop for at least half an hour to rest up his mare.

About three hours later, he was crossing the far end of Cutters Lane, and making for the railway tracks. As he did so, and about five hundred yards beyond Cutters; he saw the grey Riley heading parallel to him, in the approximate direction of the Payne's Find junction. He could see clearly, that there was only one person in the Riley; the driver, it also looked like that person was the woman he had seen last night.

He would have no opportunity to see which direction she took at Payne's Find junction. There were at least three choices available, all leading to good tarmac roads.

He kicked his mare on; he still had three hours or more to the town of Coolinar Hill, and another hour after that to Sandstone.

He had no intention of notifying the Coolinar Hills police just yet. He needed to get to the Farmstead at Sandsone, and their phone there. He needed to contact Old Man Mal, who he knew would be at The Sainted Tee today for the first of the winter shearings. He also knew his father had a phone there. It was the first thing he put in once he had thrown Ticker St. Thomas out. He also knew he had trucks there and Mal's younger brothers, Stan and Mordichae.

Malakye Jnr.'s mind was racing as fast as his mare and his new black stallion.

This could be his second gift horse in as many days.

He knew from the newspapers that there was a price on the heads of the Brisbane Bandolero's, and he knew it was ten thousand dollars.

Goodbye Mambo.
Napierville and Maleens.
Pietermaritzburg,
July 12th and 13th 1927.

The two brothers now stood in the apartment rooms in Napierville, facing each other, and less than a live man's height apart.

They were the only ones standing, the only ones capable of standing, Dykka was dead, with bits of his head scattered all over the walls and floor, and a hole in his chest that a fat rat could nest in.

Gonda was awkwardly curled at Banjos feet with at least twelve bread knife sized holes in his face and body. Blood still gurgled from him and made the lino slippery. Banjo had already fallen once, and now had thick red slimy gore right up his one side.

"This is fucking bad!"

Whispered 'The Elephant', almost monotone in his observation of the obvious.

Banjo dropped the knife he was holding, but kept the small pistol, and eased it into his trouser pocket, trying to avoid the wetness.

"We've got to get out of here. Now!"

Demanded 'The Elephant'. Louder now.

"We can't leave him", said Banjo, pointing towards Mambo, "Two dead white blokes and a Nigger, they'd string him up in the street from the first lamp post they came to".

Mambo was in no condition to participate in the conversation. The horrendous damage that a 45 calibre bullet can inflict on the soft tissue and bone of a human

266

being, from six or eight feet, (especially a 'Gut-Shot'), was clear for all to see. Mambo spun around on the floor, making circles in the bloodstains on the lino, both his arms wrapped around his stomach, and his legs were trying to run though he was stuck there. His face was twisted beyond recognition and his eyes bulged, his teeth grated, top against bottom. All the time, as he writhed, he made a terrible screeching noise, like fingernails scratching down a dry chalk board.

"We'll have to take him with us", said Banjo to his brother, "Grab the gun too!"

He pointed to Dykka's long pearl handled revolver that still lay on the floor. 'The Elephant' picked it up, threw on his jacket, which hung over the back of one of the chairs, and shoved the gun in the inside pocket, tearing the lining as he did so.

"Fuck!" he heard himself say aloud.

It took the two of them only a few seconds to get Mambo to his feet. He was screaming and begging them not to move him, at the same time he pleaded with them not to leave him.

Fortunately for them, it was not too late in the evening, and most of the other rooms in the building were still empty.

Rooms that still awaited their occupant's homecoming from the nearby pubs.

Or their return from the brothels or from the gambling huts that littered Maleens, or Falletau.

As they reached the bottom landing, carrying, half dragging Mambo between them, the brothers literally bumped into Sinetta, Mambo's sister who was coming through the entrance door carrying a cake she had baked. She was bringing it around for the boys to eat after their card game, to have with some coffee after their whisky and sandwiches.

She dropped the cake in a squelching pile at the foot of the staircase, and screamed; a scream that could wake the dead, maybe even Dykka and Gonda. 'The Elephant' let go of Mambo and he slumped to the floor, yelping as Banjo tried to hold him up.

In an instant he was on Sinetta, his hand across her mouth.

"Shut up! Shut up! You'll have us all dead woman!"

'The Elephant' explained as quickly as possible, and in as few words as possible, and as bluntly as possible, and without mentioning any names, and certainly leaving out any mention of Dykka or Gonda, some of what had just happened upstairs.

Coming to her senses, Sinetta said:

"I still got Jonny Rickshaw at the end of the street, waiting to take me home; he can take Mambo to the Hospital".

Jonny Rickshaw was a 'Coolie' from behind Dykkas' Sidings. Pietermaritzburg was infested with bloody rickshaws, cheap and dirty, but at this moment very convenient. Jonny Rickshaw was Sinetta's part time boy friend, she gave him the odd fuck, in return, he gave her free late rides from Maleens to Mambo's place and back.

He was a skinny bag of Chinese bones, who spent every day running around the streets of Pietermaritzburg carrying 'fat smerry razy lich cunts' as he called them.

Apparently he had a cock over a foot long.

Outside it was now raining heavily, beating down on the metal fenders and bonnet of Dykkas' Austin Twenty, which still stood in front of the doorway. Mambo was the only one who could drive, and he was in no fit state, and in any case a bright yellow car with a huge golden horse on the bonnet was not exactly inconspicuous.

By the time they had got Mambo to the rickshaw, he was just about unconscious, so was at least quiet. Jonny Rickshaw had panicked when he first saw them, and tried to run off. A cuff around the side of his head from 'The Elephant' had persuaded him to stay, and they all bundled Mambo into the seat. Sinetta jumped in next to him. Banjo took two one pound notes from his shirt pocket, (his shirt was reasonably blood free, and he wiped his hands on the wet pavement to clean them a little, then rubbed them on 'The Elephant's' jacket to dry them), the notes were clean, and he gave one each to Sinetta and Jonny Rickshaw, saying to Jonny:

"Take Mambo and Sinetta to 'Fat Malcolm' the Bookie."

He pulled Jonny Rickshaw hard by the arm, and went on:

"You know where he lives?"

Jonny nodded his head, Banjo carried on.

"Get some whiskey or better still Gin, on your way back to Maleens, and some Iodine if you can find it".

He then reached into the breast pocket of 'The Elephant's' jacket and took out the small bundle of notes he had there, he peeled off two fiver's and handed them to Sinetta.

"Give these to Fat Malcolm, and tell him to sort out Mambo as best he can. He's seen gunshot wounds before. Tell him there's another two of these fivers when we come by later tonight, or tomorrow morning. Tell him to have Mambo ready to move."

Banjo then turned to Sinetta, saying:

"The cops will find out in no time who lives here, that will bring the 'Dospar' cunts to you. You need to come with us as well. Have your stuff ready, just one bag, we'll see you and Mambo at Fat Malcolm's. Forget any ideas of the hospital, or you may as well just take him to the Police Station, your brother's killed two white blokes for fuck sake!"

There was no debate, no discussion. Banjo had taken control of the situation. He knew what was needed, and he was getting it done. 'The Elephant' turned to Jonny Rickshaw, as he was about to pull off, and said:

"And you, you slopey eyed skinny cunt, if you breath a fucking word of this to anyone, I'll chop off that dangly cock of yours and I'll shove it all up your boney arse. Now fuck off, quick as you can!"

Jonny Rickshaw did not need to be told twice, in ten strides he had splashed to the end of the street, and was turning the corner.

The rain had kept the people indoors or in the pubs, and the streets were almost deserted. Banjo and 'The Elephant' kept to the shadows and the lanes, and it took them over an hour to sneak their way back to their lodgings at Greyling Street.

They had decided en-route that they would get the money and the purse from under the floorboards, pack a bag, clean themselves up, get changed, and get over to the Railway Station as quick as they could.

Then they would buy four tickets, third class, for anywhere south; and on as early a train as they could get back from Maleens in time to catch. Third class would have to do, because Mambo and Sinetta, being Niggers, were not allowed in first or second class carriages.

After another hour or so the brothers were ready to leave. They had placed their bloodstained clothes in an old coal sack, and would throw it over the sidings wall into the 'Struet Dump' on the way to the Station. They each had a bag packed and half the money in each of the satchels, Banjo kept the purse in the inside pocket of his jacket. Both of the brothers wore caps, ready against the rain, and against recognition.

As he stuffed the bloodstained clothes into the sack, 'The Elephant' reached into his discarded trousers pocket.

"Nearly forgot this, I lifted it off Dykka, nobody'll notice this gone, for fuck sake the bloke's got no fucking head left".

He held up Dykka's tie pin, the one with the diamond as big as a ladies little finger nail. Banjo smiled,

"Nothing to lose", he said, "may as well make the mo......."

There was a knock at the door of their rooms. Silence; as the brothers looked at each other. Banjo picked up the small pistol he had taken from Gonda, which he had put on the sink drainer earlier.

'The Elephant' had packed the other gun in his satchel, it had no bullets left.

"Who's there?" asked Banjo, a little too hesitantly in reality. He knew it sounded strained, uncomfortable, and he cursed himself for it.

"It's me, Eloise Van Hoost, please, please let me in".

'The Elephant' grabbed Banjo's arm,

"They've found him; them. The jigs up, we've had our fucking chips!" he whispered, sweat appearing on his face, accentuating his scars, and the shadow of his mis-shapen eye socket.

Banjo put a finger to his lips.

"We don't know that!"

He replied, also in a whisper. He knew Eloise could see the room light creeping out from under the door, she knew they were at home.

"Coming!"

He shouted, trying to sound affable. Then, whispering again, he turned to 'The Elephant',

"Pour a couple of whiskies, and shove that sack under the sink, and take your fucking hat off".

He removed his own, and threw it on the solitary settee.

Once he was satisfied that a semblance of normality had been achieved, he opened the door.

She was drenched, she had a coat on, with a hood, but it had not saved her from the driving rain. Her hair stuck like seaweed to a rock across her face, her make up was smeared and had run down her pale cheeks, her green eyes were red from crying, and still, she was the most wonderful thing that Banjo had ever set eyes on.

Even here, even now, he drank her in; and for a moment the world was beautiful again.

She sat on the settee, still in her coat, her stockings wet and wrinkling around her ankles. 'The Elephant' had given her a whisky.

She was distraught and shaking, shaking with fear.

She explained that she did not know where else to go. None of her, (so called), friends could possibly help. She said she was 'desperate'.

She told them that a letter had been hand delivered to their house earlier in the evening, by a man in a smart suit, from the Hollings Cartage Company; he had arrived in one of their sign written taxis.

The letter was addressed to 'Dykka and My Mother', Eloise said, she explained that it was from Bernard Van Der Kyper's Mother, all the way from Bulawayo. It said that they had, 'received information', that she (Eloise), would be unsuitable as a wife to Bernard, and unsuitable to carry the Van Der Kyper name. It said that this was because she was nothing short of a, 'Harlot and a whore, and fornicated with black people'. Eloise said that the letter had referred specifically to, 'Your own families Chauffeur'.

She exploded into tears.

"Dykka's taken a gun, he's gone looking for Mambo, I'm sure he has. I've not seen him; but my mother did this".

Eloise pulled back her hair and turned her head to expose her neck.

271

"She tried to strangle me, it was awful".

She wept again, uncontrollably this time. Banjo gestured to 'The Elephant' to top up her glass, he did so. He made a face to Banjo behind Eloise's back, a face that said, 'We don't have time for this shit!"

Banjo ignored him, and, calming her with his voice, asked her to carry on.

She took a large mouthful of the whisky, and grimaced. She said that she had been to Mambo's rooms, to try and warn him, but saw Dykka's car parked outside.

She said she was scared.

She said Dykka would kill Mambo, and then kill her.

She said she had no where else to go.

She asked what Banjo thought would happen.

For some reason, and to the utter disbelief of 'The Elephant', Banjo relayed the entire evening's events to her, in all their gory detail.

He didn't stop, and she didn't interrupt.

She covered her mouth with both hands, so as not to scream, looked back and forth at each of them in turn, and rocked to and fro on the settee.

When he had finished, Banjo looked into her green eyes which could not open any wider, and said simply.

"You can't stay here now, you know it. Dykka's dead, there'll be no money. The whole of this shit-hole town will ridicule you. Your mother has already disowned you. Everything you ever had is gone. Mambo's taken it away".

Banjo paused.

Eloise still covered her mouth, still rocked on the settee, still had her eyes open as wide as a night time cat.

Banjo grabbed her by the arms, shook her, swore at her, told her how stupid she was, that it was her that had caused all this mayhem; this nightmare. Then he took her in his arms and held her, tenderly, warmly, he kissed her forehead, stroked back her hair from across her face.

"Do you want to come with us?"

Banjo asked.

"We've got plenty of money to start us all off somewhere; somewhere new".

She didn't move, didn't pull away, she lowered her hands from her mouth, and her red lips moved.

"Yes", she said, "Yes please."

"For fuck sake man!"

Said 'The Elephant', and Banjo looked up at him as he stood behind the settee. He knew the look. He drained his glass of whisky, and finished up with:

"Bloody good idea really. Best thing all round probably. I'll grab the bags".

They had called to the Railway Station ticket office, and bought five one way tickets to Port St Johns, but would disembark before the end of the line at East London in the Eastern Cape. There were plenty of ships there, and it was probably where Dykka did least business, so the chances of bumping into anyone from Pietermaritzburg were pretty slim. It was also the first train out tomorrow morning. It was scheduled to leave at quarter past five in the morning, from platform three.

It should be quiet then, at least the brothers hoped so.

The five sided clock, high up in the Station atrium told them it was half past eleven as they walked back outside into the rain.

The night was black.

Black as a dead man's tongue.

There were no rickshaws at this time of night, and a Hollings Cartage Taxi Cab would be too dangerous. Eloise had probably been in every one of them at some time, they couldn't take the chance of a 'Cabbie Boy' recognising her. They would have to walk; 'Fat Malcolm's place in Maleens was a good three miles away.

At night, with Eloise, and in the rain, it would take a few hours.

Eloise was surprisingly talkative on the journey, she told the brothers how long the thing with Mambo had been going on, how she thought once that it was love, but realised soon enough that it wasn't. She used Mambo, as she had used Bernard Van Der Kyper, and she admitted it with no reservations. She said with some bitterness that her Mother had used Dykka, and the long line of husbands and step fathers before him. She even laughed a few times, jumping into puddles, and kicking rainwater over 'The Elephant's' back and legs. After an hour or so, she had once more turned into a happy young girl, and Banjo and 'The Elephant' found themselves laughing with her.

At Fat Malcolm's, they found Sinetta on the porch, she was crying, standing up and leaning against one of the rotten wood posts, she had a quart bottle of Dykka's Scotch and iodine in her hand, it had less than two inches left in the bottom.

She was drunk.

'Bollocks'd' as Itzak had said.

Fat Malcolm came out onto the porch from the rickety door of his shack. He was exactly as his name described; fat as a barrel, with fat legs, fat thighs, a fat arse and a fat face.

He was sweating, and puffing on a fat cigar, which he chewed in his fat lips.

"Mambo's fucked!"

He said with no emotion.

"My Bitch's have been packing that hole in his guts all night, boiled rags soaked in Dykka's gut rot. The cunt's got a hole in his back you could shove Jonny Rickshaws cock into".

He took a huge intake of smoke from his cigar, and as he exhaled he said;

"Anoo, one of my Missus Bitches, have stitched up all the hanging out stuff and the holes, she reckons the bullet might have missed most of the important bits, reckons with some rest he could pull through maybe. Me: I reckon he's fucked".

Fat Malcolm stepped forward to the edge of his porch. Sinetta slumped down on the top step, still crying, still nursing the bottle, still taking the odd pull.

"There was a promise of another tenner", said Malcolm, and held out his hand.

Banjo reached into his trouser pocket, and peeled off two fivers and handed them over. Malcolm's fat fingers closed around them and he shoved them into the top pocket of his white sweat stained shirt.

"Can we get out of the rain here Mal?" asked 'The Elephant', "It's still fucking pissing down you know".

Malcolm waved them up onto the porch.

He gestured at the door and said;

"Get yourself inside if you want to see Mambo; personally, I wouldn't fucking bother".

Sinetta cried now, more loudly than before. Malcolm told her to shut up before she woke his children. Then he noticed Eloise.

"What's this about then?"

He pointed a fat thumb in her direction.

"Nothing to do with you or this!"

Said 'The Elephant'. Fat Malcolm nodded an agreement. The boxer may have been retired, but Malcolm knew that if the mood took him, 'The Elephant' could smash Fat Malcolm's skull like a rotten water melon.

Banjo told Eloise and his brother to wait on the porch, and he went inside to see Mambo.

Anoo told him that the bullet had gone right through which was good, but that he had lost 'buckets of blood', which was bad. She said she had stitched what she could see, inside and out, but that until, or if, as she put it;

"Mambo took some shits or some pisses", she wouldn't know for definite if she'd joined up all the right bits.

Anoo stunk of Dykka's booze, and slurred and swayed as she spoke. The three remaining teeth she showed when she talked, told Banjo that she liked Dykka's sauce; and that she was no State Registered Nurse.

Banjo looked down at Mambo; he was lying on an uneven old wooden cot with a straw mattress under him. He was naked apart from swathes of stripped cotton wrapped around his midriff. The cotton strips were bloodstained, and already flies were crawling on them. Banjo nodded his head at Anoo, and walked back outside onto the porch.

He turned to Eloise and gave her a comforting attempt at a smile, then he put a hand on Sinetta's shoulder and said.

"He's going to be alright by the looks of it, and he's in good hands, but I think it will take a week or so. I don't think he can be moved yet, so I'm going to give Malcolm some money for medicine and to take care of him".

Then, as an afterthought, and to try to cheer her up a little bit, he said to Sinetta.

"I'll square him up for you too Sinetta, you'll be able to stay here for a while that way, and help look after Mambo".

Fat Malcolm was already beginning to protest, as Banjo cut him short, by removing a small bundle of notes from his pocket.

"Come around the corner of the porch Malcolm, and we'll sort the money out with you".

He gestured at Eloise and 'The Elephant' to stay with Sinetta.

"What the fuck are you on about Banjo man, I'm not a fucking hospital. I can't keep a black boy in here with a fucking bullet hole in him. The fucking Dospars would have me strung if they came by!"

Banjo told him to calm down, and said that's not going to happen. He didn't tell Fat Malcolm what had happened in Napierville, because he knew he would hear about it soon enough. For all they knew the bodies could have been discovered already.

He told Fat Malcolm that he was right, Mambo was 'fucked'. Banjo lowered his voice to a whisper, and said; since he was going to die anyway;

"How much?"

He asked, and went on to enquire of the Fat Black Bookie for a price to:

"Get rid of him tonight, before the sun comes up, and to put the body somewhere it would never be found?"

This somewhat surreal conversation may have appeared acutely disturbing to an unaccustomed foreigner, but the reality was, that this was the world that Fat Malcolm occupied. There was no moralising as to the issue, or the question, just a straight forward, 'how much?'

"Thirty five quid", replied Malcolm quietly, "I'll get him chopped up and dump it on the black side rubbish tip of the 'Struet' the rats there will see it off in days. The size of fucking dogs they are, I tell you Banjo man".

Banjo noticed that Mambo had already become an 'it' in Malcolm's mind. He quibbled about the price, saying Mambo would probably die on his own anyway in a couple of days, so twenty five was a fair price.

Fat Malcolm replied with:

"You fucking strangle him then, and I'll chop it up for twenty five".

Banjo sighed, Fat Malcolm continued.

"Look, call it fifty quid, and I'll throw Sinetta in as well".

Banjo stared at him, wide eyed, he frowned, but he also knew Fat Malcolm was right. The Dospars would find out too quick that the rooms in Napierville were Mambo's, and it wouldn't be long before they pulled Sinetta, she would probably be pissed and spill out every name she knew. Banjo's mind was sprinting. He heard himself say.

"Call it seventy quid and do Jonny Rickshaw as well?"

"Done!"

Said Fat Malcolm, and held out his hand, not for a handshake, but for the cash. Banjo reached in his pocket and counted out five tenners and four fivers, and handed them over. As he did so he said, looking Malcolm straight in the eyes.

"Fuck this up, and 'The Elephant' will come and see you, and he'll bring both his fists with him".

Fat Malcolm acknowledged the advice. Banjo knew it was a done deal.

The two men walked back around to the front of the porch. Banjo told his brother to pick up the cases, and beckoned to Eloise to hurry up. As they walked down the porch steps and back out into the rain, Banjo shouted back to Fat Malcolm who was standing behind the crouching, still crying, still drinking, Sinetta.

"Look after them all now Malcolm, and make sure you do a proper job of it".

Banjo turned away, and the three of them walked off into the wet darkness, in the direction of Pietermaritzburg.

All the way back to the Railway Station Eloise never once asked about Mambo; how he had looked, or what would happen to him. She just skipped along the pavements, jumping in the odd puddle, and making 'The Elephant' laugh with bad impressions of Dykka, Gonda and Louis and Bernard Van Der Kyper.

Banjo thought she was nuts, but still the loveliest thing he had ever seen.

The I-21
The Southern Ocean,
Twenty miles off the Coast of New South Wales,
February 8th 1943.

The Imperial Japanese Navy Submarine I-21 moved like a monstrous grey whale beneath the waters of Australia's Southern Ocean. Her Captain, Kanji Matsumura had been shadowing the small convoy for over twelve hours, positioning the B1 class Submarine to achieve the optimum attack position.

He and his First Officer, Lieutenant Ito, had been checking the silhouette diagrams to identify the escort cruisers and destroyers. These would be their prime targets.

They had identified the H.M.A.S. Townsville, and the H.M.A.S. Mildura. They would attack and destroy the Townsville first, then move on to the smaller vessel Mildura, before picking off the rest of the convoy's freighters, who would then be largely unprotected.

Captain Matsumura checked his watch, it was 2.18 a.m. he shouted depth and bearing readings from his periscope dials, and checked the running times for his torpedoes from this range. Once satisfied that he had computed all the possibilities, he shouted the order to fire tubes one and two.

A 'whooshing' sound sang through the vessels hull, and he ordered the helm to come right thirty degrees and increase to flank speed. Lieutenant Ito counted down the seconds to impact. With five seconds remaining Captain Matsumura returned to his periscope observations; as Ito counted down to zero, there was no expected explosion, no towers of flame visible through the viewing lenses.

As Lieutenant Ito continued:

"Plus fifteen, plus sixteen, plus seventeen, plus eighteen", it became clear to all concerned, that the H.M.A.S. Townsville had been missed.

Just as the Captain was ordering the helm to 'come about', and to allow him to prepare for another firing position, and just as Lieutenant Ito got to 'Plus twenty eight' on his count; the Sonar Operator yelled the single word, 'Impact'. The Captain returned to his periscope.

There; behind the Townsville, he saw the massive explosions of his torpedoes. They had sailed under the Royal Australian Navy Heavy Cruiser, and destroyed and sunk, in less than two minutes a merchant freighter, heavy laden with cargo, and laying low in the water.

Thirty six men perished in those two minutes.

Officers Matsumura and Ito would only hear later, from radio reports and from fleet communiqués of their accidental sinking of the S.S. Iron Knight. They would never know, or hear the names of Iestyn Tynsdale, Greener Hawks or Prisoner number 89855812; though it would be as a direct result of this mis-fire, and the survival of these three men, that all aboard the I-21 that night: would die.

My Uncles; Murray and Wilf and The Slaughtermen.
The journey north east from Perth.
Western Australia,
July 3rd and 4th 1972.

By six p.m. My Uncle Murray had just about had enough of bumping the Ford Taunus along dusty tracks that invited diversion at irregular intervals, to wander off the highway. If they had taken one wrong turn they had taken a dozen, and it was getting dark. The careless banter had dried up an hour ago, after they had stopped at a town called Coolinar Hill and asked directions to Payne's Find.

They wanted to go to the latter because that was the last big robbery Maldwyn's old newspaper clippings referred to, and the last place the faded old letter in the box had mentioned, the one signed 'E', and dated 1943. The photocopy in the file was quite sad Wilf had thought when he had first read it:

> *Dearest Banjo,*
>> *Forgive me.*
>> *It has been a long time, and too many things have happened to me, since that last day at Payne's Find to know where to start, and so I won't start, I can't. Please, just forgive me.*
>>> *I send you these mementos of our life together, knowing those days will never return; knowing you will*

279

never be free, and knowing that, in my own way, neither
will I.

   I will not tell you of my life now, but I owe it to you.
You know this, and still you must forgive me.

   You must never hear from me again. You know that
this is how it must be. The few memories in this box are all
we can have, all you can have.

   Forgive me.

   If fate should be kind to you, and one day,
many years from now, you find yourself a free man once
more; NEVER try to find me, for you will not love me
anymore; and I will break your heart all over again.

   Forgive me.

   'E'

The woman they had asked for directions in Coolinar Hill, had managed to get my two Uncles hopelessly lost by explaining a short cut via somewhere called Sandstone. She had given directions, which neither of them wrote down, and which both hoped that the other would remember. They were both wrong.

By just after seven, and after too many wrong turns to count, they came, (by utter chance), upon Sandstone.

It was an attractive little town, the kind of place nobody works in, but that everyone wants to live in, it had a nice main street with quaint little shops, a church with a big old steeple and a crucifix at the top, and a hotel and bar opposite. There were café's, restaurants, even a cinema. All the roads were tarmac and the pavements were laid in herring-bone pattern small clay paviours, in a kind of dark maroon colour. Murray and Wilf reckoned the place was 'Rich Man's Suburbia'.

The woman in Coolinar Hill had told them that the roads in and out of Sandstone were the 'best around', and that the new dual carriageway from there to Payne's Find, that, 'Skirted the Daggars', as she put it, would save them a good half hour or so at this time in the evening.

Tired and thirsty, my Uncles parked up the Taunus on 'Main Street', (it was a main street that was actually called 'Main Street', a difficult concept to grasp for Old World Europeans like my Uncles, and most other people for that matter, except native Australians or native Americans. By 'native' I mean second or third generation immigrants. Not proper natives. Anyway, you know what I mean).

They called into 'The Shillington Arms' for a beer, and maybe a sandwich. The place was quite 'swish', as Murray later recalled, leather seats, a restaurant area to the rear, and a kitchen behind the bar with some sort of serve through hatch.

Above this was an old glass case; screwed high up on the wall, in it were two pistols, mounted so that they crossed each other. One was a short dark coloured thing with a knurled wood handle and a bit of a metal ring of some sort dangling from it. The other was a long black revolver with a shiny pearl handle.

There was a young girl, mid twenties or so, dressed in a black and white waitress uniform, frilly pinny and all. She was taking orders from the customers seated at the light coloured wood tables. The young girls name was, (according to a plastic name badge pinned to her blouse), 'Toraya'.

'Unusual name' Murray had remarked as he gave her their order. She had smiled politely, and explained that the name was a mixture of her fathers name 'Ray', and her mothers maiden name, which was 'Torrance', hence her name, 'Toraya Ballou'.

The bar area seemed to do snacks, while the tables in the back area appeared to be for more formal dining.

There were quite a few people scattered about at the other tables in the bar, mostly couples, some with kids. Murray and Wilf had ordered two cool beers and two hot steak sandwiches with 'fries' from the 'stand-up' menu on their table.

The young girl had brought the beers from the bar, where an "Old Codger", as Wilf described him, had pulled them from a shiny draft dispenser with four nozzles on it, in the shape of the heads of cattle, horses and sheep.

The old man wore a black cotton shirt with 'The Shillington' embroidered on it in white, above the left breast pocket. On the opposite side of his shirt, his plastic name badge said, 'Dunder MacFall'. Murray noticed, (as other uniformed staff flitted by their table), that the old barman was the only one with his full name on his badge, everyone else only had Christian names on them, but he had the full works.

When she had brought the beers earlier, Toraya had said that the food would be another ten minutes or so. Wilf had asked her how far out of town would they need to drive before they could pick up the dual carriageway to Payne's Find. The waitress had explained that they would come to a junction with traffic lights at the end of 'Main Street', and that they should turn left there. That would take them onto 'Wylachi Boulevard', 'the main shopping drag' as she termed it, and then they would see a right hand sign just after the Medical Centre. She said:

"Take that turn, keep straight on and you'll be at the Payne's Find junction in about thirty or thirty five minutes".

She smiled her best waitress smile, and went about her business.

The beers were cool and the sandwiches were hot and satisfying. Both men had commented over their meal, on the name of the shopping boulevard, and that 'Wylachi' had been the name of the 'Stockman's Station' mentioned in the newspaper article about the shooting. They decided not to ask too many questions just in case the map turned out to be real after all.

They would pay their tab, and press on this evening to Payne's Find, (as Maldwyn had suggested); to see if they could find out anymore information about what happened to 'Banjo Anderson' from some local archive sources. Maldwyn was still on the hunt for information about how Banjo was captured after the gun battle with the New Norcia Police at the 'Wylachi Stockman's Station'. After that, they would start their 'Treasure Hunt', as my Auntie Flo had called it, (somewhat sarcastically it has to be said), from the very outset.

Toraya's directions, unlike the woman's in Coolinar Hill, had been excellent. It was creeping up on eight o'clock as the Ford Taunus gunned onto the dual carriageway towards 'Payne's Find'.

"He was lucky not to get hanged you know", Wilf said, as Murray drove.

The file was across his knees, and Wilf held a small torch, by the light from which he was reading and turning pages. He had managed, (from the Perth Central Archive), to get hold of a transcript of the trial at Perth in January 1934 when Banjo Anderson was found guilty of the armed robberies and of murder.

It says here, Wilf went on, reading aloud from the transcript:

> *'The only reason you are*
> *not being punished to the full*
> *extent of the law, Anderson, is that*
> *it has proven impossible to*
> *accurately verify your age. Or for*
> *that matter, much else about you at*
> *all, even to the extent of your own*
> *full name and background.*
>
> > *You have stated that*
> *you are under the age limit for*
> *capital punishment, and whilst I*
> *consider this to be a blatant lie,*
> *given the heinous nature of your*
> *crimes, and your callous lack of*
> *remorse.*
>
> > *The Jury, although*
> *finding you guilty of all charges,*

have stayed my hand in sentencing
you to be hanged, as you maintain
that you are less than twenty one
years of age.

I therefore sentence
you to Life Imprisonment With
Hard Labour. Take him down.

Murray agreed, and went on to discuss with Wilf the Prison Records he had also found at the 'Perth Archive'.

Wilf turned them up in the file.

The prison reference number for Banjo Anderson tied up with the eight digit number Maldwyn had found in the Crew Log of the H.M.A.S. Waterhen, but the names didn't match. One set of documents at the 'Perth Archive' said 'Anderson', the other, from the Royal Australian Navy sources, said 'Androskewowicsz'.

"You know what I reckon", Murray said, "I reckon he told the blokes on the Ship, or at least some of them, what happened to him, all the stuff about South Africa, this woman,", Murray waved a finger towards the file, as he spoke, "everything; and I reckon it was just some slip up, just some cock up on board that some record keeper clerk or something, typed in his real name by mistake".

Murray got quite annoyed with this somewhat abstract idea, and said with some venom in his voice:

"For fuck sake, if that document had got back to the 'Perth Prison Service', instead of rotting away in the 'Naval Records Office' at Sydney, some bright spark could have put two and two together; know what I mean Wilf?"

Wilf did indeed know what Murray meant, if they, that is 'some bright spark', as Murray had said, (and as Maldwyn Somerset had actually done), had winkled out the records, and sieved the sources and

284

connected the name Anderson with the name Androskewowicsz, poor old Banjo could have come home to a rope in Perth Gaol.

As the journey continued, and Wilf flicked more pages of the file, reading aloud pertinent snippets, it was clear from the 'Amethyst Brothers' notes that they had also flagged up this discrepancy concerning the name entries aboard the H.M.A.S. Waterhen.

The Amethyst boys had however noted in the file, that other than the content of 'The Box', and the notebook from Sister Lubia Brezhnitzen, there was little likelihood of any official South African records relating to the Androskewowicsz brothers. And aside from the casualty list from the *The Czareavitch Alexai Romanov* concerning the incident with the *Cok Guzel Denizala Baligi*, their name was unlikely to appear on any pre-Soviet Russian documents.

In any event that casualty list for that encounter only mentioned the death of, 'One Haraka Androskewowicsz', along with some other non-related names.

Wilf read again from the file, then said:

"There's nothing in the list to say who she was travelling with. We only know Yuris and Itzak were on board because the notebook from Sister Brezhnitzen, (her translation of Old 'Stalin's' scribblings), tells us so. I suppose that means the brothers were on their own after she was killed?"

Back in South Wales, Maldwyn and the 'Amethysts' knew that history was littered with such dead ends, missed information and general sloppyness. Given that there was, after all a World War raging all around the H.M.A.S. Waterhen and her crew at that time, in which over one hundred and twenty million people had just died; was there really anyone back then in 1945, with the time or the inclination to chase down this single inconsistency?

Maldwyn had concluded that there would not have been.

Payne's Find arrived like an unexpected rash, dots of streetlights and house lights seemed to spring from nowhere.

285

It was a low level town, spread out and sprawling in the festoons of orange and white glows. It had industrial estates, shopping centres, and grids of streets. It was a large town, bigger than Coolinar Hill and Sandstone put together, and then multiplied ten or twelve times, but it had no high rises, nothing, by the looks of it, over three or four storeys.

The guys were getting tired again, the kind of tiredness that waits in the silent spaces between conversations, or on empty boring stretches of roads, creeping up, then jumping out and frightening you back awake. It had been a long day, with a lot of miles under their belts.

As they drove off the dual carriageway, and followed, (for no apparent reason), the occasional road sign that said, 'Civic Centre', Wilf spotted a 'B & B' at the roadside, directly opposite some traffic lights they had just come to a halt at.

"Looks promising", he had said, pointing towards the neon pole sign that proclaimed in white and red letters, 'Vacancies, Car Park at Rear'.

It looked good to Murray too, his eyes beginning to sting, and already bloodshot.

There would be no camping tonight, no 'Billy Can' tea, and probably no fishing tomorrow. Murray parked the Taunus at the rear of the 'B & B'. He pulled the car into the last remaining space of the five that constituted the 'Car Park'.

He and Wilf got out, stretched an exaggerated stretch, and walked into the small back entranceway of the building. It was accessed via a narrow, crunching gravel pathway from the car park. There was an aging, poorly lit sign above the door which said, 'No admission after ten thirty p.m.".

With self evident gratitude they pushed the door, and found that it opened.

They booked a room with twin beds and a bathroom, with the elderly lady downstairs. She had appeared from her 'back rooms', (presumable her living quarters), to take their reservation at the small desk in the hallway.

She asked whether my Uncles wanted a 'Full English' for breakfast, or just a 'Continental'. Both opted for the 'Full English', and she wrote the letters 'F.E' next to their names in the register. She gave them their key, and said simply:

"Top of the stairs, second door on your right".

She smiled, and disappeared back into her quarters.

The 'B & B' was a bit of a stayover, squeezover kind of place, but felt like the 'Paris Ritz' at the moment.

Murray and Wilf would sleep like babies.

East London,
South Africa.
Then across the Indian Ocean
To Australia.
July 14th 1927.

The journey South by train had been long and uncomfortable, but strangely entertaining. It had in fact been the longest single period, (with nothing to do but chat), that the brothers had ever spent with Eloise Van Hoost. She had made them laugh; her anecdotes were risqué, humorous and pertinent.

She was clever, funny, rain sodden, and still stunningly beautiful.

The trio had waited in the lashing rain for over an hour outside Pietermaritzburg railway terminus, they had waited until five minutes before the St. Johns train was due to leave, and had then moved smartly through the baggage halls and concourse ticketing areas, and along the platform to the third class carriages. They were the only white people seated on the slatted wooden benches of third class.

And the train, and station, was (thankfully), quiet.

The South African sun had now risen on the new world beyond their railway carriage, and was poking its tongue through the long narrow windows. The Elephant was fast asleep, with his feet rested upon the bench opposite, next to Banjo. Eloise too was asleep; she had slumped across The Elephant, away from the window, and now snuggled, like a comfortable child, with her head against his chest, and her hand beneath her cheek. Banjo, who had forced himself not to sleep, found himself a little envious of his brother, and this accidental proximity to Eloise. Then he realised that if the positions were reversed, he would not be sitting where he was, and would not be able to look at her.

He smiled to himself and lit another fag. He glanced out at the golden, honey coloured morning flapping over the lush countryside; then he looked back to her.

The train arrived at East London just after mid-day. They were all a little dryer now, but none-the-less, the previous night had taken its toll, and they looked what they were.

They looked like people running away.

"I'm absolutely starving" said Eloise as they stood on the pavement of a busy road, just outside the railway station.

There were trams scurrying back and forth on the road. The East London lunchtime crowd was beginning to hunt out its coffee shops and restaurants. Banjo turned to Eloise, and said;

"Not yet, that's what we need first".

He pointed across the road. There at the junction opposite, by a tram-stop, was an electrified trolley car, the overhead wires clanking and sparking as it pulled to a slow halt. On its front was a large chalkboard with the words, 'Fort Glamorgan, Esplanade, Harbourside, East London Docks', scrawled on it in foot tall letters.

He grabbed Eloise by the arm, and began to run, she screamed, that small girlish scream, mixed with a little laugh that only carefree young women know how to make. The Elephant followed behind carrying the two satchels.

East London was a long way from cosmopolitan.

Pietermaritzburg was parochial in its own way, but it was a metropolis compared to this place thought Banjo to himself. He could see now why Dykka did no business here.

"What a fucking shit-hole".

Observed The Elephant once they were seated on the trolley car. Eloise laughed again, and Banjo could find no words of contradiction. So far East London would appear to have no redeeming features.

They paid their fares, and Banjo asked the female conductress, (or 'Clippy', as he had heard the other passengers calling her as they shouted to her for tickets);

"Which stop is East London Docks?"

The small black woman, the 'Clippy' in her dark blue uniform had replied, as she hunted in her leather cash bag for some change:

"Last stop Sir, can't go no farther, lessin you wantin some swimming like".

She handed Banjo his change, which he noted was sixpence short. He chose not to make an issue of it, and she went about the two floors of the trolley bus, robbing customers as she did so.

The bus was once blue and cream, but, like most of East London by the look of things, was overdue for a 'tart up', as 'The Elephant' had called it during the journey.

The trolly ride to the Docks had taken about forty minutes or so, the 'Clippy' had shouted, upstairs and down, as the bus had drawn to a halt.

Her instructions were clear enough presumably to the locals, and she had evidently shouted the same sentence thousands of times.

"All's off what's going off, all what's going back town way gets your fares up ready and park!"

As they climbed down the rickety wooden steps of the bus, and out onto the uneven concrete expanse of what was evidently East London Docks, Banjo heard the 'Clippy' shouting as the trolley bus pulled backwards along its tracks, back in the direction of town.

"Ding Dong we gone, Ding Dong we gone".

He surmised that the trolley-bus's bell must be broken, or had been stolen by the 'Clippy' or something.

The other people, who had disembarked the trolley bus at the 'Docks Stop', were quietly mulling away in various directions. Within minutes it was only Eloise, 'The Elephant', and Banjo who remained at the tram-stop. About two hundred yards away, and almost at the junction of the land and the sea, they could see a large, ochre coloured single storey timber building, (there was nothing here over one storey tall), on its corrugated tin roof sat a bright red clock tower, slightly pissed, and leaning to its left. The gold coloured hands on its black and white clock face, said that it was a quarter past one.

Just below the rusty guttering of the buildings sad looking facade was a large yellow sign with large blue lettering. Banjo noted that the colours were (sort of), the same as those of the trolley-bus, and that these must be the East London Council colours, or at least must represent some sort of local administration authority. Whatever it was, Banjo's instincts about this place were shaping up to be right.

East London was the kind of place where the world was only semi-official, and where three people with a bit of cash could sieve through the gratings without making so much as a ripple in a mill-pond.

The sign on the building proclaimed it to be, the 'East London Shipping Office'.

Banjo pointed a finger at the building and waggled it to and fro; Eloise smiled broadly, and giggled a little for no apparent reason. She was clearly enjoying her adventure. 'The Elephant', having realised his role in this troupe, picked up the satchels, and they began to walk.

The area of concrete, (there was no roads as such), which lead to the Shipping Office, was peppered with, (littered with really), wooden planked buildings of various sizes, colours, shapes and descriptions. Smells leaked from them all, oil, tobacco, spices, tar, and animal shit.

Various signs introduced some as public houses, some with rooms to rent for a shilling a night, all the signs said, 'No Blacks'. Others said they were coffee shops, or wool importers, or rope makers; Banjo smiled to himself. It was exactly what he had hoped for; a blank new world.

This dockside village was a free-for-all, sailors from all over the world bustled up and down on it's hard greyness; all of them gazed at Eloise as they passed by.

Beyond the Shipping Office building, they could now see the wharfs, there were at least a dozen freighters moored there of all sizes and descriptions, some with steam up, and smoke billowing from their funnels, either arriving or departing.

Further out at sea, they could see another three vessels, again, either in-bound or out-bound. In any event there looked like plenty of opportunity for escape.

In the hallway of the Shipping Office, the bead and butt panelled wall, with its flaking ochre paint was bedecked with large paper sheets, each held up with dulled bronzed drawing pins. The numerous wormholes all over the walls bore testament to how many previous sheets of paper had been pinned and un-pinned there, how many previous sailings, how many previous lives, over the last decade or so.

Banjo and 'The Elephant' began reading the sheets, each one was a manifest, a ships cargo list, whether in-bound or out-bound, whether full or whether still available to take cargo. It also listed the vessels ports of origin, where they had come from, and, (more importantly to the trio), where it was heading.

Eloise sat on the ageing, dark oak bench that rested against the wall of the hallway, directly opposite the entrance door. She complained about the length of time the brothers were taking in studying the notices, and said that she was still hungry, and would:

"Simply die of starvation if she didn't get some food soon".

"This one!"

Exclaimed The Elephant.

"It say's here that it's got space, it leaves tomorrow morning with the tide at four a.m., and it's a good long journey, it'll give us time to make some plans".

He pressed his huge hand flat against the paper, and turned around to face Banjo, who was checking the sheets on the other walls.

"Where's it going?" asked the younger brother.

He began to walk across the hallway towards his brother. Eloise didn't look up, she was singing to herself, and making shapes in the dust on the wooden floor with the heels and toes of her shoes.

"Australia!"

Banjo read aloud as he squeezed up next to his brother in front of the notice. Reciting each stop off port, each loading and unloading.

The Elephant took up the description, his index finger underling the words as he read aloud;

"Madagascar, some place called The Philippines, then all the way to a place called Christchurch in New Zealand before finishing up in Brisbane Australia".

He turned his face directly towards his brother, his twisted features contorted into what now passed for a grin.

"This is for us Yuris".

He returned to the sheet of paper.

"Look at the dates, it doesn't get into this place called Brisbane until March next year; and it's got good stopovers on the way, time to make some more money, look, it's got three weeks in Manila, wherever that is".

His smile was like a canyon, Banjo could not deny the attraction of the route, nor the joy in his brother's face.

"What's it called; this dream ship?"

Banjo asked. 'The Elephant' moved his finger to the top of the sheet of paper, and said;

"The Merchant Ship West Honaker, I even like the name. It's berthed at wharf eight, its Captains name is Gustav Amberkan."

The two brothers elected to go in search of Captain Amberkan without further delay, after all the ship was due to sail in under fifteen hours time.

In the Shiping Office hallway, at the far end, and set at an awkward angle to the rest of the room was a glass window about a yard square, it had a circular hole cut in its centre. A thick and heavy dark timber frame surrounded it, and beyond sat a series of small desks with lazy looking white men mulling around them with the impression of not doing very much.

Banjo walked up to the window, and, putting his face near the hole in the glass pane, he coughed, an attention grabbing cough, then another, then, after a small a pause a third. One of the men in the office beyond the window was eating a sandwich, and drinking a glass of frothy beer; he looked up at Banjo, and then went back about the business of his sandwich.

'The Elephant' pushed his brother to one side.

'The Elephant's' scarred and now somewhat menacing face and frame filled the window. He poked a stairod of a finger through the hole at the man with the sandwich.

"You!"

He said, the man looked up, he felt the sandwich and beer become less appealing as he viewed The Elephants physique filling the window, filling the hallway, filling his head, gripping his attention.

"Where can we find Captain Amberkan of the Merchant Ship West Honaker?" asked 'The Elephant' without hesitation.

The lazy white man stood up behind one of the desks, carefully putting down the sandwich and his beer, before he spoke. He did not step any closer to the window. He had a small voice, and the features of a weasel.

"If he's not on board, you can try the 'Lazy Arab' pub across the way, if he's not there, then he'll be at the 'Frantic Chaplain Waterfront Hotel' behind the offices here".

He gestured over his shoulder with his greasy thumb.

"There's a touring circus there today, at the back in their skittle alley, you'll probably find him there".

'The Elephant' asked the weasel what Amberkan looked like; he was told he was a big man, fifty-ish with a big grey beard, spectacles, and a smart blue uniform with brass buttons, and a cap to match with lots of gold braid on it. The man added:

"He's not as big as you, I think he's Swedish, or maybe Dutch, anyway, he speaks English, he's big, but not as big as you".

The Elephant thanked him, and told him to finish his sandwich. He picked up the satchels and the three travellers left the building.

Outside, the day was overcast, and the skew-iff Shipping Office clock told them it was after half past two.

"I'm not going any further until we get some food, I've been saying how hungry I am for nearly……..”

Before she could finish her sentence and stamp her foot, which was her definite intention, she was moving again. The Elephant had grabbed her by the arm and she was being pulled across the concrete open area at a small trot.

"Owe!" she had whimpered.

It had no effect on 'The Elephant'. She may be pretty and amusing, but her huge escort was immune to her. The one thing you could say about 'The Elephant', in fact if you had to describe him in just a few words, those words would probably be 'Single Minded'.

Outside 'The Lazy Arab' pub, 'The Elephant' had handed Eloise back to Banjo, and told them both to wait there, and not come inside. He gave his brother the satchels, and went in alone. After about ten minutes he came out with a slight looking man in his forties. The man had on dark blue working trousers, black boots, and a red sweater with the words 'M.S. West Honaker' embroidered across the chest. He wore on his head, a blue naval type cap, it was also dark blue, like his bell-bottom trousers, and had two long black ribbons hanging at the back. He had a nose reminiscent of the beak of a large bird, and so few teeth remaining that one may suggest that he had drunk Dykka's Scotch and iodine at some time in his past.

When he saw Eloise, he removed his cap to reveal the ugliest, knobbliest shaved head one is ever likely to encounter.

"This is Muzzer Elijah Hernandez, he's 'First Mate' on the 'West Honiker', he say's that the Captain has got full holds this trip, but that the rates are shit, because the cargo is cheap stuff, bound for Madagascar".

Muzzer Elijah said, mostly to Eloise, but really as a general introduction.

"Folks calls me 'Cockleshell'; excepting the crew, they calls me Sir".

He smiled; it was an amiable smile, the smile of someone comfortable in his skin and confident in his abilities.

"Captain's over the 'Frantic Chaplain', bettin on the circus, I bets he's losin an' all by now, been there since afore noon 'e have, e's an 'opeless better 'e is, but a lovely feller, an a better man on the sea you'll never find, I been wiv 'im since arter the Great War'.

The three men walked across the concrete expanse back in the general direction of the Shipping Office. Eloise got dragged and let out an occasional and pitiful yelp along the way. As they passed the Shipping Office, its clock said ten past three; and isolated groups of jugglers and acrobats in strange but brightly coloured costumes made efforts to entertain them on their journey, shaking tambourines under their faces to illicit payment.

"Ignore them!" said Muzzer, and occasionally told one of them to "Fuck off!"

"I'm hungry!" said Eloise, at least once every fifteen paces.

By now, they were all ignoring her.

"Oh, wow, a Giraffe!" she said, and laughed out loud as one of the beasts walked by her.

Then she returned to moaning about her stomach, and that if someone would skin it, she would eat the Giraffe.

The Skittle Alley bar of the 'Frantic Chaplain Waterfront Hotel' was really just a low, but fairly large open area with a wooden planked floor with some skittle lanes painted on it, in fading white shipyard gloss.

'Cockleshell' navigated them through the plethora of small, big, and in-between sized tables that filled the hall; for that was what it was, a hall. Each table was surrounded by wooden chairs, and each table strained under the weight of beer glasses, whisky bottles, legs of mutton, immense bowls of boiled potatoes, and trays containing chunks of black bread.

The place was thick with tobacco smoke, and sailors in various stages of drunkenness, and small armies of ugly whores lounged on unknown laps, and shoved their tongues into unknown mouths.

A good way into the room, 'Cockleshell' weighed anchor at a small collection of tables mostly populated by whores, and sailors with the same uniform as his own.

"This is Captain Amberkan folks, a knowd e'd be ere".

'Cockleshell' touched the arm of a big fellow in a smart uniform who was sat with his back to them. He wheeled in his seat as his 'First Mate' spoke. Seeing Eloise he immediately stood up, and took off his cap in respect. He was exactly as the 'Weasel Sandwich Man' had described.

"Pull up some chairs 'Cockleshell', and get these good people some drinks", the Captain ordered.

He then shouted, loudly but to no-one in particular:

"Fresh glasses, over here now!"

295

The glasses miraculously appeared, as did two large pitchers of cool frothy beer.

Amberkan's accent, when he spoke English, was an uncomfortable mixture of Australian, Canadian, and South African. 'Cockleshell's' accent, they would discover later, was Cardiffian.

As he had said, he had been with Amberkan since the Great War, after which, when he had been de-mobbed from the Royal Welsh Fusiliers, he had signed on as a deck-hand on an old Collier sailing out of Cardiff for New York.

In front of Captain Amberkan's table was a large open floor area, about ten yards square, as his new guests and his 'First Mate' took their seats, 'The Elephant', and Banjo noticed that there was spatters of blood on the floorboards.

"So, my young friends what is it that I or my ship can do for you, you are after all not here just to say hello, I think?"

He laughed; a loud natural almost welcoming laugh.

Banjo and 'The Elephant' introduced themselves, 'Itzak and Banjo Androskewowicsz' they had said, straining above the hullabaloo of the room. Captain Amberkan evidently could not here them very well, and from this moment on referred to the brothers as 'The Andersons'.

They chose not to correct him.

They spent two glasses of lager and three roll-up cigarettes explaining that they wanted passage aboard the M.S. West Honiker all the way to Brisbane Australia. None of this seemed a problem to Captain Amberkan who had set a price of one hundred and fifty pounds a head.

Banjo had, over the last twenty minutes, negotiated this down to one hundred and twenty, to include all food, and also he and Itzhak would work on board, doing anything the Captain required for three days of every week at sea.

The sticking point was Eloise.

'Women on board ships are bad luck', Captain Amberkan had said, 'fine enough for shagging on land, but deep down they were lubbers nothing more, nothing less'. He had turned to Eloise after his explanation, and said;

"No offence to you love".

Eloise had nodded and smiled politely.

In the open area in front of the seats and tables, a man in a white leotard with a leopard skin sash and a waxed handlebar moustache was parading around; holding bunches of five quid notes in each hand.

"Any more comers?"

He shouted as he strutted around in front of the tables.

"What's all this about?" asked 'The Elephant'.

"Fisticuffs"; replied Amberkan.

"Fisticuffs good and proper; with money at the end of it. Fifteen quid so far today this posing bastard's cost me. Fifteen of your fucking South African quids".

The Captain stood up and called the man with the exuberant moustache a 'Scheister!'

On either side of the open space formed by the tables two other men walked the crowd, they were holding big straw hats, too big to wear, and shouting at the tops of their voices. They were saying;

"Place your bets! Place your bets! Three to one any challenger against Squasher Flannigan. All Ireland Champion 1921, 1922 and 1923, come on gents, place your bets!"

"I thought this was a circus?" asked Banjo.

"What else would you call it young man?" replied Captain Amberkan.

In an instant Banjo was tugging the Captains' sleeve, downwards towards his seat. 'The Elephant' looked at his brother across the table, his eyes narrowed and he strained to hear the conversation, though really he knew what was going on.

He needed to hear nothing.

He knew what was coming.

After some whispering, the Captain stood bolt upright, swaying a little with the influence of the beers and a day of whisky, but still fairly upright. He pointed one of his thick fingers at 'The Elephant', waggling it like a knarled Chorizo and laughing loudly.

"Him?"

He paused, then laughed out loud; he placed both hands palm down on the table top, and leaned towards Banjo's older sibling.

"No offence Boyo, but I've seen what this ugly fucking Mick has done to three good sea-fairing men so far today. They were men with rope burns and calluses, who could lift a bale of cotton with one hand and a hook. No disrespect lad, but I'd try and save your good looks, what you've got left of them".

Banjo tugged at his arm again.

"What have you got to lose?"

He pointed at his brother.

"Here's the deal. If he wins you take the three of us all the way to Brisbane for three hundred quid. I also replace the fifteen quid you've lost on the bets, and I'll put a hundred quid bet to win on, and split any winnings with you. If it all works out, you get four hundred and sixty five quid, and the pleasure of our company for six months. If he loses we leave the woman here".

Eloise began to cry at this, and grabbed Banjo's arm, pleading for him not to leave her, and calling him a 'Selfish Pig'.

Banjo feigned to slap her, and she winced and cried even worse.

"Shut up, stupid slut!" he said, and pushed her back in her seat.

When his face was close enough to her face that they could smell each other, but no one else could see; he winked.

"Make it a hundred and fifty quid bet, and you've got yourself a ship".

The Captain paused, and pointed that fat finger at the two brothers, both of them, waggling it again, and then at each individually; then he continued as he turned squarely towards 'The Elephant', he laughed again and said through his laughter.

"You lose, and the woman can swim to fucking Australia", he turned back towards Eloise, and said again, "No offence love!"

He sat back down with a thump; Eloise carried on crying.

In a couple of moments Banjo had made the arrangements with one of the bet takers, and placed the bet; he had even tried to get four to one, saying that 'his man' could hardy see out of one of his eyes. But the bookies were adamant on three to one, so Banjo reluctantly took the odds.

After the bookies had marched 'The Elephant' around the cleared space a few times, and announced the match, taking bets as they went; a scrawny man in a red hunting jacket and a faded top hat scratched his way to the table-side.

"Have you got fucking fleas or something?"

Asked Captain Amberkan loudly, Eloise laughed a little, and then continued her bellakin.

"What does your man want to be called?" enquired 'The Scratcher'.

"Not my man", said Amberkan, he gestured towards Banjo, "This feller here is his brother I fancy, he can name him".

The Scratcher turned towards Banjo, his hand inside his coat clawing at his rib-cage.

"Call him 'The Big Ticket'", Eloise interrupted.

Banjo looked at her, a bemused grimace on his face. He could see she was about to start to cry again and so he spoke up, saying;

"That'll do for me, 'The Big Ticket' it is then".

The Scratcher acknowledged Eloise with a touch to his top hat, and then he said, in his flannelly Irish brogue.

"Two minutes to go then. I'll make the announcement so I will, get the punters off the seats you know, get my boys to walk the hats around one more time, then we're off. I'll do the reffing so there'll be no shenanigans or nothing like that".

'The Elephant' was now standing behind Captain Amberkan removing his jacket, his shirt and his vest, and handing them to his brother. As he did so, he said, as quietly as he could above the hubbub of the hall.

"Make sure you've got the coins, and find some bandages for later".

He turned and walked back towards the cleared area of floorboards. Banjo rummaged in his pocket and took out a small selection of coins. He pulled a half empty glass towards him on the table-top. He chose two coins and put them in his left hand, and clenched his fist; the other coins, he placed back in his pocket. He picked up one of the numerous bottles of whisky on the table and half filled the glass. Taking a box of matches from inside his jacket, he then struck one and passed each of the coins through the flame before plopping it into the whiskey.

299

Then, seated, he turned towards the cleared area, where 'The Scratcher' had waved the fight to commence. He found himself holding Eloise's hand so tightly that it made her yelp. He continued to squeeze it, but did not look at her.

Squasher Flannigan was a big lump, but his belly had begun to turn to lard, he was used to fighting drunks, and had a big right hand, trained to be hard and brutal. But he didn't have much else Banjo had figured. But then it wasn't Banjo standing across the square from him, it was his brother.

The big right came in first, like a monstrous windmill, The Elephant shielding his disfigured face with both forearms, taking the measure of this unknown opponent.

The Elephant took a dozen or so blows on his arms and body, and these had told him that Squasher's right hand was his main weapon, but even after just five or six swipes, the weight was leaving his opponent, he was too old, and too tired for this game.

'The Elephant' knew that his opponent was, (what Dykka used to call), 'A two minute thumper'. That is, a fighter who is unfit, and if he hasn't knocked you out in the first two minutes, then his legs won't take him the full distance.

After that he's easy meat.

'The Elephant' had decided that time was on his side, Squasher's blows were becoming lighter and less rapid, his two minutes were coming to an end. 'The Elephant' had even begun to think that he may avoid the usual fractured eye socket, and demolished cheek bone, the recurring injury, the pain, and the increasing deformity; all courtesy of his encounter with Crusher Hohner, that night at Scottsville Racetrack.

After another twenty or so blows from Squasher, received now with little actual damage, The Elephant decided that the time had come to despatch his opponent as gently as he could. As he lowered his guard, Squasher stumbled over the foot of 'The Scratcher', who could see the way this fight was going, and was hoping to call a draw before all his bets went south and he had to pay out. Squasher bundled forwards, and the top of his head smashed into 'The Elephants' cheek.

He felt his eye socket open and his eye twist inside his head. His cheek sank inwards and he was conscious of his entire face sinking and dropping on the one side. He felt the pain, the pain he had felt three times before, three times before today.

Rage enveloped him and he was once more 'The Bloody Elephant'.

Two straight lefts had squashed Squasher Flannigan's' nose flat to his face, exploding goblets of blood and mucus all over his cheeks, his chin his moustache, his leotard, and splatting over 'The Scratcher'.

Next, a thundering downwards driving right fist hit the nape of Squasher's neck. Like a pile driver hammer it tore through muscle and skin and split the collar bone like a dry twig, the one end of which dug its way out through the flesh and sinew to poke up at an ugly angle towards Squasher's face. It was hung with bits of fat and sagging snots of blood.

As Squasher crumpled, downwards and forwards, a final upper cutting left struck the point of his jaw, splitting the mandible clean in two at the chin, and dislocating both joints at the back of Squasher's mouth. As his top and bottom rows of teeth parted, and his lips opened wide, a torrent of blood spewed out and hit the floorboards a split second before Squasher's face smashed into the same spot.

He lay there; silent and unconscious.

"Three passengers then Captain; all the way to Brisbane?" asked Banjo, and put out his hand, ready to be shaken.

Captain Amberkan, said nothing for a moment, stunned by what he had just witnessed. Then, after a few seconds, he took Banjo's hand, and shaking it vigorously, said.

"Get the fucking money, grubs on me at the 'Lazy Arab', the food here's shit".

He looked around, and found the attention of his first mate;

"Cockleshell!" he shouted, "Get over to the 'Arab' and get Zuba to get a table ready to sit five, and make sure he's got his best steaks a sizzling on the griddle and a bucket of roasted sweet potatoes a piping hot and buttered".

He pointed at 'Cockleshell', then went on.

"And tell him I want a couple of bottles of good grog on the table, none of that fucking turpentine gut-rot he flogs to the niggers outside the dock gates, now on your way!"

He gestured to 'Cockleshell' and the door, making his instruction unmistakable. His First Mate made a semblance of a salute and headed for the exit.

Within fifteen minutes Squasher Flanagan could open one eye, move his left hand, and groan without assistance. 'The Scratcher' had coughed up (grudgingly) all of Banjo's winnings, and this with only the smallest suggestion of the threat of persuasion from 'The Elephant'.

After this, Banjo, with Captain Amberkan's help, had secured the use of a back room in 'The Frantic Chaplain Hotel', and had tended to 'The Elephants' wound, slicing his cheek again, forcing the smashed cheek bone back into position, and had slid the two whisky sterilised coins up inside to hold the bones steady while they knitted. He re-set his brothers eye socket, and bound it with a length of bandage which the good Captain had managed to procure for them.

By half past five according to the pissed clock on the Shipping Office, all of them, the brothers, The Captain, 'Cockleshell', and Eloise were sitting at the best table in the 'Lazy Arab' pub. Captain Amberkan's orders had been followed to the letter.

The meal was sumptuous, the grog was soothing, and the company was entertaining. Whilst the others tucked into large fat charred steaks running with warm blood juices, and buttered roasted sweet potatoes; The Elephant had to satisfy his hunger on a large bowl of mushroom soup, which Zuba had, 'made up special', because his injury would not allow him to chew quite yet.

Eloise gnawed at her steak with passion and lust, tearing at it with her knife and fork, and with her teeth. The greasy juice leaked over her lips and down her chin.

She devoured it.

In the same fashion, and at exactly the same time, as the rats on the Black Side of the Old Struet Dump in Pietermaritzburg, were beginning to devour and feast on the chopped up remains of Mambo, his sister Sinetta, and her friend Jonny Rickshaw.

South Africa to Australia.
Brisbane,

December 1928.

The journey across the gaping Indian Ocean had been blue and pure.

The trio had seen dolphins, storms, small islands, monstrous islands, and calms of polished mirrors that reflected the sky.

The 'West Honiker' had stopped for longer than planned in Madagascar and in Zanzibar. Captain Amberkan had no objection to waiting in the sunshine with fresh beer, hard liquor and easy women, until a lucrative cargo came along; and wait he did.

Itzak's face had healed and his feverous infections had ceased. The scars left from the bout with Squasher Flannigan had left ugly blueish raised tracks of lumpy flesh across his cheek, and the infection had devoured a section of his eye socket before abating. The whole effect was to distort one complete side of his face, as if an invisible hand were pinching the soft fattiness of the inside of his mouth, and yanking it permanently downwards. Strangely, the overall effect served to make Itzak appear less terrifying and more benevolent.

An effect not to be mistaken for reality.

Eloise had once more become a happy little girl, a new and fresh childhood had arrived, a late and welcome visitor.

She still never mentioned Dykka, Mambo or her Mother, or any other memory of Pietermaritzburg.

She swam with Itzak and Banjo, slept on beaches full of dreams and stars, and went naked to soothing sea whenever she needed.

Banjo watched her, and watched her, and watched her. Her nakedness was that of a small child, un-self-conscious and at peace.

Her body that of a woman.

For both Itzak and Banjo, the world had also developed an envious and enviable perspective. Experience had taught them that this time would end. This time and these places were not a destination, but a transience, a transition to somewhere new.

Australia, a promised land of beer and honey coloured women.

Itzak had learned to fish, and Banjo had learned about ships.

Eloise had learned how to forget.

Banjo still watched her with every spare eyeball moment, he could close those eyes and still see her in every milk coloured detail, every crease of her skin, every curve of her smile.

He would never tire of watching her.

He watched her all the way into Brisbane harbour.

The sinking of the SS Iron Knight.
And the transfer to the H.M.A.S. Waterhen.
March 1943.

It was another sweltering melting journey, chained up in the back of an Australian Army Marine Corps lorry; canvass backed, dusty, unbearably hot, and with a solitary water canteen which the squaddies' had pissed in.

The only difference this time was that he was the only prisoner, and there were five armed marines; which he had all to himself.

He was hungry, thirsty, dusty, too hot, and desperate for a fag.

They didn't give a fuck.

After the SS Iron Knight had been torpedoed, he had been in the water for over five hours, slicked in oil, and semi-conscious, before he had (literally), bumped into the only lifeboat the crew had managed to get away.

On that particular trip 'The Knight' had been transporting its usual two to three thousand tons of iron ore, and a mixture of drilling equipment and open cast spares; but it had also been retro fitted in Port Macquarrie with a rubberised hold liner, so that they could carry 25,000 gallons of 'Straight 70 Super Thick' heavy industrial oil to Freemantle in Western Australia.

Fully laden, she had been low in the water, probably the lowest ship in convoy OC 68 at that time, being full of high density cargo. The two torpedoes that hit her had been fired at one of the escort battle cruisers, the H.M.A.S. Townsville. But they

304

had *sortied* beneath her shallow draft hull and proceeded on to destroy the Iron Knight.

The first torpedo had struck her aft, just forward of the engine room and behind the number four hold. The second hit her almost square amid-ships, slightly forward of the bridge, almost in the dead centre of number three hold; plumb in the belly of the rubberised 'Thick Oil' container.

The explosion was colossal, and apparently visible for over thirty miles. The 'Knight' went down in under two minutes, bow up, and screaming as her metal bulkheads buckled, and her keel plates popped, sending shrapnel showers of rivets and steel shards whistling through the night air.

The remainder of convoy OC68 sailed on into the night. The escort ships, The H.M.A.S. Townsville and the H.M.A.S. Mildura, pursued the submarine. Primarily to chase it away, and discourage any other attacks, but always with the hope of finding it, and destroying it. Either below the waves with depth charges, or by forcing it to the surface, and bringing superior gun-power to bear.

In any event, the ships would radio the position of the sunken vessel, and notify appropriately. But stopping to collect survivors, if there were any, was definitely not on the agenda, in the dead of night, with a live 'Jap Sub' in the neighbourhood.

His head struck hard against the clinker planking of the lifeboat. It was Lifeboat Number One, slung from the bow davits of the SS Iron Knight; number one of three, the only one to be launched. He had drifted in and out of consciousness for some time, he could not hear, apart from a shrill squawking which would not stop.

His head felt like two gorillas were fighting inside it.

The bump woke him; and he became aware of the man, or body, he was holding across his chest. He made a noise, a grunt, though he did not hear it.

Suddenly several pairs of hands were reaching down, clawing at his tattered overalls, slipping over the soaked in oil, grabbing at him and the passenger he knew, or could remember, nothing of.

In the back of the transport lorry, the marines were smoking fags and telling dirty jokes.

"Fancy a fag chum?"

One of them had asked of their prisoner. He had replied that he could murder one. The marine had responded with;

"Well you'll just have to wait till we get to Port Keats chum. It shouldn't be more than another seven or eight hours".

The squaddies' had all laughed, and the truck continued on.

Seven more hours of drinking piss, and having the piss taken, he thought to himself.

Brisbane,
Queensland,
Australia.
The end of a 'Simple Life'
1931.

Australia had been good to them.

They had found lodgings in Carville Street, in the Wooloongabba district of the city, just south of the Dutton Park Railway Sidings. A rail yard where Itzak and Banjo had found work; loading the steam train coal tenders, and the coal carting wagons of the 'East Greta Coal Mining Company'.

It was long hard work, but it was what they were used to.

They were playing the banjo once more.

Aboard the West Honika they had been known as the Anderson brothers, at Dutton Park they had become the Andersons or the Andrews, dependant on who they were shovelling for.

Eloise had reverted to her Mothers maiden name of Hunter.

Together they were all happy.

Eloise kept house for them all, washed their clothes, cooked, and generally looked after them. On Mondays and Wednesdays she worked at a flower shop up on Highgate Hill, and on Saturday evenings she sang at the Gulliver Restaurant on Annerley Boulevard, while the 'Toffs' wined and dined.

Her singing voice was not great, but her presence and appearance made up for its shortcomings.

On Sundays, she and Banjo would go for a picnic in Goodwin Park, and walk along the green and shaded banks of the Brisbane River, watching the artists painting boat scenes or landscapes, and laughing at the jugglers, dancers and acrobats who busked there.

Occasionally there was an opera soprano who performed outside the Riverside Cafe for copper coins thrown into her straw hat. She had become a favourite of the pair, and they missed her greatly if she was not there of a Sunday.

Itzak rarely attended their Sunday sojourns, preferring, (if the work was available), to fill coal wagons at Dutton Park Sidings, as the rate was a quarter better for working on a Sunday. Afterwards he would go by tram to the bare knuckle fights over at Coorparoo. Though strictly as an observer these days, his knowledge of the game gave him a good insight, into each fighter's strengths and weaknesses, and he would often double his Sunday pay with shrewd bets on the bouts.

For Banjo, his time with Eloise was far more precious than 'a quarter on the rate', and even if the weather was poor they would still make for Goodwin Park, and if necessary spend all day in the Riverside Café, drinking thick milkshakes and eating Strawberry Rum Cake.

Eloise would talk as she ate, and Banjo would smoke and watch her, and they would both laugh incessantly.

The only people who did not know how far in love with each other they were, were Eloise and Banjo themselves, for they spent their lives in each others souls.

Eloise's desires still pulled her away from the brothers sometimes, but it had also been what had pulled them all together in the first place, and it was only desire. Her desires may have belonged to her own, and other people's bodies; but her heart was Banjo's and they all knew it.

That was all that mattered.

They had been settled for over three years by this time. The money they had brought from South Africa had lasted well, and they had not really suffered any hardships. It had been a blessed respite to all of them to have gained this period of 'invisibility' as Itzak had referred to it, in a rare moment of self awareness.

They had all earned wages, they could afford occasional luxuries, and they still had Dykka's diamond and the egg shaped emerald to fall back on if ever emergency beckoned; though they all knew the risks inherent in trying to dispose of such stones.

Most evenings they would listen to the radio set which Itzak had bought from his winnings on the bare knuckle bets. Their favourite show was 'The Shadow', which always started with the same line:

Who knows what evil lurks in the hearts of men? The Shadow knows!'

They would say the words aloud, and feign dastardly intent as they did so. They would drink wine now, and whisky only before bed-time.

This particular evening, they had drank two bottles of red Shiraz while listening to 'The Shadow', and after it, they had tuned in to some band music, and then some opera. They had drank another bottle and eaten a whole slab of soft cream cheese with blue streaks through it, which they ate with crusty bread and a bowl of red-currents.

Eloise and Banjo had danced together, slowly, to one of the opera arias, and Itzak had said:

"You two need to get married!"

He took another large slurp of his wine;

"I can't stand all this creeping around the apartment in the dead of night".

He took another glug of his wine.

"At least I could have a bedroom to myself then".

He belched, loudly, and they all laughed again, and agreed unanimously that it was a good idea.

Itzak's face distorted awkwardly as he laughed. The fractures to his cheek bones and eye socket had failed to heal well. A cruel infection had set in after the bout with Squasher Flannigan in the 'Frantic Chaplain Hotel' at the dockside in the Eastern Cape just before they had left South Africa. He had spent nearly three weeks in bed aboard the West Honiker, and twice Captain Amberkan had reprised the burial at sea verses from his Ships Bible in preparation for the worst.

"When shall we do it then?" asked Eloise still giggling, still dancing.

"Any Sunday, suits me now", answered Itzak, "They stopped all overtime at the Sidings yesterday, so me and Banjo are on bare money".

The mood declined, Eloise told them that she had seen something in the newspapers about The 'Government Savings Bank of New South Wales' closing its doors for good. Banjo said he had seen groups of men outside the rubber factory over at Greenslopes, and they were fighting amongst themselves over a days work.

"At least we've got work for the moment", said Eloise, "It's all so sad, I know; but it's not sad for us".

She pulled Banjo into her embrace and led him towards Itzak, she held both of their hands, and said:

"Whatever it takes, whatever we need to do, we will always be alright, we will always be together".

She kissed them both in turn on the cheek. Then she smiled, and when the brothers looked at her, looked at that smile, they knew she was right.

The wedding took place on a Sunday evening in August 1931 at The City Tabernacle Baptist church in Wickham Terrace, Brisbane.

There were few guests; some of the other labourers from Dutton Park Sidings came along with their wives, as did Dylan Gunn the yard manager for the 'East Greta Coal Mining Company'. He was a decent and fair man, a Welsh immigrant, who had started as a 'pick swinger' in the mines down south, but who had won promotion by night time study, and now managed the companies railway coal operations in Brisbane. He had brought his German wife with him, and their two baby daughters, Sabina and Bronwyn. Eloise had given them small bunches of carnations decked with pink wisteria to hold, and they had become flower girls and smiled all day. Itzak had danced with them at the reception, carrying one girl in each of his huge arms.

Eloise's Boss from the florists came and donated the bouquets, and the pianist from the band at Gulliver's Restaurant played the organ for the ceremony.

Religion had become something of an abstract concept for them all, and they had lied about their denomination with indifference. The Vicar had done a superb job on both sentiment and ceremony, and a small reception had been arranged at the

Riverside Café where Itzak had made a Best Man's speech which lasted less than thirty seconds.

Later, the newly married couple, Mr. and Mrs. Anderson, and the Best Man, had gone to the coast for three days. They had travelled by train, and had stayed in the Sunshine Guesthouse at Fraser Island. It had rained constantly, but they had a wonderful time. They had eaten well, drank plenty, been to a Music Hall show, and had even seen their first moving picture at one of the new Cinema's, an Odeon with red velvet seats and a golden ceiling.

Again they were happy.

They had returned to Carville Street on the Thursday morning in time for Banjo and Itzak to start their six a.m shift at the Railway Sidings.

They had bought some bread and Italian Salami outside the Railway Station in Frazer Island, and Eloise had made them both Salami sandwiches with piccalilli to take to work.

The next three weeks were delightful at home, every evening was a celebration, and if it were possible, Banjo and Eloise fell ever more in love.

Work however was becoming difficult.

The freight trains had nothing to carry; the coal stocks became an ever increasing pile of black despair and misery. Banjo worked a Monday Wednesday and a Friday, and Itzak Tuesday and Thusdays, with an occasional Saturday.

Even the bare knuckle bouts had been suspended due to lack of attendance.

By December 1931 the situation had worsened considerably. 'The East Greta Coal Mining Company' had gone into liquidation, and over three quarters of Dutton Park Railway yards lay idle. Bracken began to grow where once huge steam monsters had lined up to be fed.

Gulliver's Restaurant had been forced to shut down as their Bankers; 'The Primary Producers Bank of Australia' had foreclosed on their mortgage.

The only bright spot for the trio was that Eloise had managed to secure an extra day a week working at the florists. Apparently depressions are good for funerals, and funerals need wreaths, so florists are busy, she had explained.

The South African money had long since gone, and inflation had taken hold of the economy. The raw materials for the salami and piccalilli sandwiches Eloise used to make for her husband and brother-in-law now cost five times what it cost six months ago.

At least the stove in the apartment was always hot with both Banjo and Itzak being able to steal coal from the sidings, and they still had their radio set and 'The Shadow' to cheer them up of an evening.

It was a week before Christmas, and Eloise had gone off to the florists shop to make up the festive roundels of fake holly and mistletoe, for people, (at least those still with jobs), to hang on their front doors.

Itzak and Banjo were heading to the sidings to see if there was any casual work shovelling coal for the few locomotives that remained there, mostly passenger trains now, but any work was good, and they were managing to get one or two days a week. They were good workers, and were known to the train companies as such, and even on the days when they got no work they could still steal some coal for the apartment stove. Fish stew and potatoes with boiled onions were now the staple diet for them, and there was always a pot bubbling there. When they could get flour Eloise would bake bread, occasional eggs would sometimes result in a sponge cake, or scones.

Today there had been a morning's work loading a pair of tenders for a southbound passenger locomotive. The fireplate man, who they knew, had given them a dozen eggs from his own hen house. They had also stolen two sacks of coal.

So all in all not a bad day, as days went now.

On the way home, knowing that Eloise would not be back until early evening, the brothers decided to call on Dylan and Martina Gunn, and present them with a sack of coal and half a dozen of the eggs.

They called to Dylan's apartment regularly, where they were always assured of a warm welcome and a cup of tea, despite his lack of work and their clear and increasing impoverishment.

When they arrived at the apartment block in Lilly Street, near Langlands Park they were greeted by an almighty hullabaloo on the pavement outside the entrance steps to the shabby black-stone apartments.

There were police there with two black vans with bars on the windows, and a big white ambulance truck with a red cross painted over its back doors.

311

The doors were open and inside Banjo and Itzak could see the sheet covered forms of two small bodies, quite still, quite dead.

As they watched, two men in white trousers and shirts came out of the building and down the concrete steps towards the pavement and the ambulance. They were carrying a stretcher, covered as well with a crisp white sheet, again covering something quite dead.

As it passed by, a light gust of wind blew the sheet up a little, and dislodged it from the face of the corpse.

It was Martina.

Then, from the doorway came Dylan Gunn, he was being supported by two police constables, and a woman in a nurse's uniform. He was weeping and screaming uncontrollably. Itzak tried to attract his attention but was unable to get close enough through the swelling throng, and the police.

The ambulance and the police vans were loaded up, and within seconds had sped off along the sparse street.

A neighbour had told the brothers that Dylan had gone out to look for some work at the Rubber Factory. When he had returned he had found his wife hanging in the stairwell outside their apartment. She had smothered the two girls first as they slept in their bed.

The neighbour had explained that two days ago all the residents of the apartment block had received eviction notices from the 'Brisbane St. John's Bank'. She went on to tell them that the building had been owned by 'The East Greta Coal Mining Company', but since they had gone bust the bank had repossessed the building, and wanted everyone out by the end of the week. The neighbour said.

"It all got too much for poor little Martina; I guess she just couldn't take it any more; and those poor babies".

The woman began to sob.

Itzak and Banjo gave her two eggs, then walked away. As they did so, they asked a beat constable who was still standing by the steps, if he knew where Dylan would be taken in the van. The constable replied that he was going to St Catherine's Hospital, where he would have to formally identify the bodies for the district coroner.

The brothers decided that Dylan would need looking after for a while, and that he should come to stay with Eloise and them. They walked to the end of the road then took a tram to St. Catherine's.

It took over a week before Dylan Gunn could speak of the deaths of his wife and daughters. Banjo had plied him constantly with cheap whisky and strong tea, and Eloise had fed him hot fish stew.

Itzak had given up his bed to Dylan, and had slept on one of the comfy chairs in the living room. He and Banjo had taken it in turns to go out work hunting; not wishing to leave Dylan alone in the apartment, or even alone with only Eloise for company.

Last night he had listened to 'The Shadow' with them, for the first time since they had brought him there, and he had shown a glimmer of a smile.

"It will take time", Eloise had said as she gave him a mug of tea, and kissed him on his forehead, "It will take a long time, but it will pass, and in the meantime, you will have us".

She smiled at him, and although he had not been convinced, he found himself, (almost), at some sort of peace.

The I-21.
Two hundred and fifty miles north east of New Zealand.
May 12th 1943.

The giant Japanese Imperial Fleet submarine had been caught on the surface by the American Battleship U.S.S. Charleston. She had surfaced to drain a sea water contamination from her battery bay, a problem which could produce chlorine gas.

The Charleston had been re-stocked with ammunition only two days earlier by the Royal Australian Navy Vessel, H.M.A.S. Waterhen.

The American Naval Rating that loaded the first fired shell into the gun bay breach, had noticed that someone had scrawled on its side in white chalk the words.

313

'To the Japs. A present to you little yellow bastards, from Stoko, 1943.'

It was an observation error by Captain Kanji Matsumura, which had allowed the Charleston to come up astern of the I-21 and allow her to get close enough to fire two 110mm shells through the huge submarines deck planks.

Matsumura had ordered the crash dive instinctively, and without checking the extent of damage, merely wishing desperately to seek out the cover of the waves.

The submarines engine rooms, and rear sleeping quarters and gallies had all been holed. She took on water rapidly, and despite the closure of the bulkhead doors, she had sunk, rear end first like a wounded behemoth.

She now sat on the sea bed in eighteen hundred feet of water.

The maximum escape depth was one hundred and twenty feet.

The surviving one hundred and eight officers and men, including Captain Matsumura, had been trapped in the bridge and helm area for over fifty hours.

They would last another twenty hours or so, before all would be dead from suffocation.

Their bodies would never be recovered.

The Brisbane Bandolero's become famous
March 1932.

By the time the gang had hit their third bank, 'The Sunshine Farmers Bank Of Queensland', the press had dubbed them the Brisbane Bandolero's on account of their red bandanas, and that the first robbery had taken place in Brisbane.

They had managed not to kill anyone in the second raid, a heist which had netted them over thirty five thousand dollars from a branch of the 'New South Wales Expansionist Bank' just south of Frazer Island. It was a Friday, and more by luck than judgement a steel company had arranged for its payroll to be gathered there.

They were not so lucky at the third bank, at least in terms of casualties.

314

It was the north Sydney branch of the 'Landsman's Bank', the only bank in Australia that opened on a Saturday morning, and it was a Saturday morning which Eloise had chosen. She and 'The Elephant' had watched the bank for a few days before, and had found out that it had a large old safe, a staff of eight, made up of five cash windows with tellers, (three women and two men), an accountant, a deputy manager, and a manager.

Banjo and Dylan Gunn had discovered by idle chit-chat while changing a twenty dollar bill at one of the windows, that the security company did cash collection from the branch every other Monday, so every other Saturday would be the time when the branch had the maximum cash in store.

The first phase had gone to plan, with Banjo and Dylan Gunn handling the public in the banking hall, and getting them all on the floor in the usual fashion. 'The Elephant' had threatened his way into the back office area with little opposition.

Behind the cash windows and the teller's stools was a single large desk at which the accountant sat, half hidden behind a hillock of thick ledgers, some open some closed. To his left were two glass and timber screened offices, like a small pair of semi-detached gold fish bowls, each contained a desk, a phone, some filing cabinets made of green metal, and a man in a suit.

"Touch those phones and I'll blow your fucking heads off!"

Itzak had shouted as he drew the long barrelled Colt and pointed in through the windows.

On the door of the office on the right was painted the words, 'Mr. Dan Stucky, Deputy Manager'; and behind his desk stood the safe, big, black and fat with cash. The other office had, painted on its half glass door the words, 'Mr. Grenville Sullivan Machin, Branch Manager'; its letters were slightly larger than those indicating the office of Mr. Stucky, but in the same solid black lettering.

In the office of Mr. Machin there also sat, on the opposite side of his desk, a youngish couple, somewhere in their thirties, the woman had been crying, the man had made an effort to look smart in a shirt and tie, with a jacket; but had failed.

"Who are you?"

The Elephant had demanded of them curtly, waving his revolver at them as he spoke. He stood between the two doorways so that he could keep both offices covered as well as the tellers and the accountant's desk.

Dylan Gunn covered the customers that were lying on the floor, and Banjo leaned on the counter with his short nosed revolver poking through the bars at the tellers, who were now filling Itzak's hessian sacks with the cash from their till drawers. Dylan carried a crudely sawn off double barrelled shotgun, and said nothing, occasionally he would poke one of the people on the floor on the back of the head, or on their shoulders with it, just to remind them of their predicament.

"Ohn and Hega Beskiss", the woman had said with a slight accent, and pleaded not to be shot.

Itzak had persuaded the accountant, (with nothing more than a raising of his voice), to unlock the safe. He and the Deputy Manager now began to fill more hessian sacks distributed by Itzak.

"What are you doing here?" Itzak asked of the Beskisses'.

"Our farm is being re-possessed by the Bank", the woman replied, "Today was our last day, so we had to come in and sign some documents".

Mr. Machin's face needed no explanation, no translation, he was scared, he looked scared, he even smelt scared. Itzak told him to stand up; as he did so, 'The Elephant' surfaced once more:

"How much do you owe?" Itzak asked of Ohn Beskiss.

"Twelve hundred dollars and some change", he replied in blunt terms.

"Got any kids?" itzak enquired further.

"We had a little girl, she got took by the Diphtheria last winter", was the simple response.

'The Elephant' was out of its cage, the revolver barked twice and Mr. Machin was hurled backwards across his desk with two fist sized holes in his chest.

"You two", Itzak shouted into the other office, "hurry up with those sacks and get them out front, and collect the sacks from the tellers on your way, then back in here and on the floor with you".

Banjo shouted at the tellers through the cash window bars to get on the floor as well, once their sacks had been collected; and for them also to stay quiet, and be calm. The demonstration with Mr. Machin had put everyone ill at ease and nervous.

As he left the back area, Itzak again told everyone to stay on the ground face down, and not to move for half an hour, he jerked the phone lines from the wall. He gestured to Mr. And Mrs. Beskiss to go before him out towards the front area. As they passed him, and almost as if a fledgling thought had just hatched his head, he returned to the back area, and re-entered Mr. Machin's office. He collected up the documents they were signing from the desk. He looked around the expanse of the inlayed work surface, and found a fountain pen; he then walked across to where the accountant and Mr. Dan Stucky lay together. He crouched down next to them both, and, throwing the document on the floor in front of them, whispered:

"Sign these, both of you, date it, and time it an hour ago, and write across it, 'PAID IN FULL'".

He tossed the fountain pen onto the polished floorboards next to them. He added, as he pressed the Colt hard against the accountants' temple.

"And if I hear that you deny this document, I'll come back and pay you Mr. Machin's wages, got that?"

He broke the skin at the accountants' temple with the barrel of his revolver.

"Got it! Got it!"

Both men replied, as they scribbled in turn, then added without prompt.

"We promise!"

Itzak snatched up the duly notarised document, and cuffed Dan Stuckey hard across the back of his head as he rose, for no particular reason.

Once in the public area, Itzak rummaged in one of the hessian sacks, and counted out ten fifty dollar bills. He wrapped them in the document, and, somewhat overly surreptisciously, he pressed the bundle into the hand of Mr. Beskiss, then yelled at both of them to get on the floor, and stay there.

The gang then left the Bank, as calmly as they could, and jumped into the old green Austin Twenty which their new driver, one Tuffy Boyden had stolen from a petrol station outside Brisbane. He had been a onetime lodger of Dylan Gunn and his late wife, when he had been at collage with Dylan some years earlier.

He had lost his home when he had lost his job at the timber mills at Kooble Bar, in the southern Industrial area of Brisbane. Like many others, he had found himself suddenly, and irrevocably destitute. Tuffy Boyden was a poor individual, but a first class mechanic, and a reasonable driver, and displayed a strange and natural propensity for theft and dishonesty.

Itzak and Yuris had learned long ago that ordinary people can do devastatingly extraordinary things when their individual circumstances changed for the worse. There is nothing more dangerous in all the world than a man who thinks he has nothing more to lose.

The car was running, and the drive away was smooth, and along a well planned route. Eloise would meet them in an hour's time at an old deserted warehouse building she had found near Benning Island in Sydney Harbour.

She had purchased legitimately, (though in a false name), a brand new dove grey Riley, big enough to seat them all, and in some comfort.

After this third robbery, (and another death, another murder), they all knew that they would be even more brutally hunted by the police, and equally brutally dealt with if caught. They had already decided that Eloise must be kept away from the robberies themselves, more truthfully, Banjo had decided. He knew she must have no part in them. He knew that notoriety would make examples of them all, knew that the Government would want them as examples, knew there was no turning back. Knew how it all must end. Knew how much he would miss her when that ending came along.

The next five robberies came and went with two more murders, a close shave with the cops outside Adelaide, and many more sackfulls of dollars of various denominations.

As a diversion, (to their own enforced monotony), the gang had robbed occasional jewellers or watch makers, they had even stuck up a payroll train outside Fremantle. But it was the robberies of the Banks that kept them on the front pages of the newspapers, kept them, (at least in part), in the public's mind, in part with the public's sympathy. The Banks were bastards; there was almost open public support for the Bandolero's. The Government needed them caught, needed them to be made an example of.

This treadmill they were on could not be stopped, they could not decide one day to retire and buy a fishing boat, or start up a restaurant, or a trucking company. There were no turn offs on this road they had taken, Banjo, of all of them knew this best.

En-route around the Southern Ocean coast of Western Australia, Banjo had found a craftsman jeweller, who was a single shop owner, struggling to make a living, and to keep his business. He had given the craftsman Dykka's old tie pin diamond and asked him to make something special of it in the form of a ring. The man, an old Jew, Ashkenazi, by the name of Shimon, had fashioned a simple but perfect circle of seasoned Ironbark, grey wood, polished, and with the feel of mercury, and with a clasp of delicate platinum to secure the stone.

It was a thing of absolute beauty, and Banjo had paid the man two hundred dollars for his work, twice what he had asked. Eloise fell as deeply in love with the ring as she had with Banjo. She and it were the two most beautiful and unique objects in the universe, Banjo had told her when he had given it to her.

She swore she would never take it off.

The duality of the gang's morality was not lost on Banjo, though he suspected it may be on the others. Eloise had never considered their adventure a crusade, merely the latest stepping stone in their lives. Itzak and Dylan Gunn viewed themselves as 'The Shadow' avenging wrongs and amassing wealth as they went, they still thought that one day they could stop, go back to Brisbane and pick up their lives. Tuffy Boyden just wanted the money, and had said that after Christmas he would take his share and, "Fuck off", as he put it, "to America".

Eloise just went with the tide, Banjo held her heart in his hands, and had she known how precarious his grip was, then she would have surely lost her own grip on her tenuous reality.

She wanted today, that thing which she had always wanted that thing which Mambo, Bernard Van De Kyper, and a host of others before and since could never give her. Unconditional love and freedom, and unquestioned understanding, that thing that Banjo could give easily because he had known nothing else. He had been stolen from expectation, so had never required it, never missed it, never regretted its failures, as to him, it had none.

By the time they had all arrived at Payne's Find and hit the payroll at the Bank there, they had collected another pair of gang members, a young communist named Ambrose, and a thick set former miner named Sonny McClure.

The pair had befriended Eloise at a cinema one Friday evening, at the coastal town of Caernarvon. To the chagrin of Itzak and Dylan Gunn she had brought them back for drinks to a bungalow they had rented near the beach. Banjo knew that this was the nature of Eloise. She had opened her soul to the pair and had adopted them, as experienced parents adopt and take in lonely waifs.

Ambrose had left the gang a week before the Payne's Find robbery, as the life he had found himself on the cusp of was not truly for him.

He had fallen in love with Eloise, but not as much as he had loved his own life. His communist principles clearly did not extend that far towards the 'good of the many'. He would reject communism as he had rejected Eloise, as a proposition tasted, but a proposition discarded.

He had been orphaned some years earlier and been shuffled from Church homes to charitable care establishments right across the south coast. Someone had given him a book by Karl Marx, it was his only possession, and he had read it over and over. He had escaped from the last home as prisoners escape from gaols. He could have been no more than fifteen or sixteen, maybe even younger.

Banjo and Itzak had given Ambrose a thousand dollars and a good watch, and had wished him well. Eloise had kissed him on the cheek, and had given him a small blue flower.

The Western Australia Police were close on their tails by the time they had headed inland. By now they were a habit. It was the planning that would fuck them up, as Banjo had known. The net was closing behind them; the Northern Territories would be expecting them, if they got that far.

They made a pledge that they would not let themselves be taken alive, and that they would not allow the stolen loot to be captured by the Police.

They decided to bury it, all of it.

Banjo knew the pledge would not hold. He knew that Itzak would hold to it, and possibly Sonny, the new man. He had proven to be reliable, a quiet individual, but with a resolute edge to him. He had taken the young Ambrose under his wing when they had first found one another. But, as for the others, Banjo knew they could not be relied on. Tuffy Boyden was inherently weak, and Dylan Gunn, despite the loss of his wife and kids would fight to hold onto life's last seconds irrespective of what it may cost him. He would lie and turn them all in if he had to, not because he was disloyal, but because he was an ordinary man.

At his heart he was you and me.

As for Banjo, he was unsure of himself, if he had to die, then he had to die, but it was Eloise who distorted his view. He was not Itzak, not like his brother any more, Eloise was the difference. Eloise was his reason; live or die, eventually he knew he would lose her, he expected nothing more.

The capture and the hiding.
The Wylachi stockman's hut.
Daggar Hills, Western Australia.
July 28th and 29th 1933.

It was past noon when Malakye Jnr. Galloped through the wrought iron gateway of the Sandstone Farmstead. His mare and the new black stallion were both thick with slimy white sweat-scum, and he shouted a general instruction for someone to take them, as he pulled up and dismounted. He passed the reins to two aborigine farmhands who had responded to his shouts. He told them to get the beasts, cooled down, fed and watered and put in separate corals.

In the same fashion that he had instructed Toby 'J' and Linus the day before, Malakye Jnr. did not wait for a response.

Ever!

He ran up the stone steps and into the house, pushing open the two huge Ironbark entrance doors with little ceremony. Two doors which had been made and carved a few years earlier from the very thinnings of the tree which he had overlooked last night.

An aborigine housemaid scurried into the hallway, and Malakye asked her what time his father had left home that morning for The Sainted Tee. She confirmed that 'Old Man Mal', ('Big Mr. Wylachi' to her), had left the Farmstead in a truck with 'Mr Mordichae', before six a.m.

Malakye Jnr. already had the phone in his hands. It was a 'candlestick phone' made from dark brown bakelite with a thick platted flex. It stood in the hallway as a symbol of power for all who entered the Wylachi Farmstead to see. It said that this was not the household of some small 'Hairy Arsed Ozzy Bushman', but the headquarters of people who mattered in this area.

People who had contacts out there, in the big bad world.

People who needed a phone, when not many people had ever used one.

He told the operator at Coolinar Hill, to put him through to 'The Sainted Tee', and gave her a three digit number. There was no need for this extra information, the operator recognised Malakye Jnr.'s voice, and knew by heart the plug in connection for 'The Sainted Tee'.

The phone was answered by his father, and without pausing, or sparing a single word or detail, Malakye Jnr. relayed the events of the last sixteen hours.

'Old Man Mal' said that he knew what needed to be done, and that he would get hold of the New Norcia Police Station, making some rather uncomplimentary comments about 'Fat George' and 'Sergeant Monkey' over at Coolinar Hill 'Cop Shop', as he called it.

He told Malakye Jnr. to bring the small green pick up truck from the Farmstead, and meet him later in the afternoon at the 'Wylachi Horse and Livery' at the south end of 'Cutters Lane'. Old Man Mal also told him that Toby 'J' and Linus Sabak would probably still be there, as he had passed them, heading that way, early this morning with the collection of 'round-ups'.

He told Malakye Jnr., that he should tell them to 'stay-put, but keep '*stumm*', and make sure their rifles are cleaned and loaded up, just in case the cops from New Norcia need some guides'.

As an afterthought, 'Old Man Mal' had added that Malakye Jnr. should swing by Coolinar Hill on his way, and call to Ray Ballous' gunsmiths and collect his fathers old Spencer rifle which Ray had fitted a new stock to. A stock which 'Old

322

Man Mal' had spent about a month of evenings, sitting on the porch with a couple of gallons of good whisky, whittling away at from a seasoned hunk of old Ironbark. Ray had polished it so it 'shined like the face of the moon', or so he had said in the 'Night Time Bar' of the 'Shillington' three evenings ago.

Malakye Jnr. objected, as Coolinar was at the other end of Cutters Lane, and was a good bit more than a 'swing by'. But 'Old Man Mal' was insistent, and Junior knew that further argument was pointless. He reluctantly agreed, and said he would collect a couple of boxes of shells at the same time, just in case.

The reluctant detour would change his life.

Malakye Jnr. put the phone down and yelled towards the kitchen for someone to make him a sandwich and a big mug of coffee. He then dashed out onto the porch, clattering again though the Ironbark doors, and shouted across to the corals, (where the two aborigine farmhands were still unsaddling, and settling down his mare), for one of them to bring his rifle over to the house, and to 'make it snappy'.

He turned and went back inside.

Having eaten his sandwich, drunk his coffee, and cleaned and re-loaded his rifle, Malakye Jnr. collected the keys for the green pick-up from the desk drawer in his fathers study. He left the house, and began the forty five minute drive to Coolinar Hill, and then, afterwards, he would undertake the additional twenty or thirty minutes back to the 'Livery and Horse'.

It was a quarter past two p.m. as he drove out of the Sandstone Farmstead through the same wrought iron gate he entered only an hour earlier.

About fifteen minutes into the journey, Malakye Jnr. began to regret not changing his denims or his check shirt. He could smell himself in the cab of the truck, and he smelt of horses, sheep, manure, animal and human sweat, with a hint of chicken sandwich and coffee. He wound down the window, and decided to let the afternoon breeze blow some of the odours away.

By just past three o'clock he was leaning sloppily on the counter of Ray Ballous' gunsmith and hardware store, while Ray had gone out the back to collect 'Old Man Mals' gun. He was alone in the shop, slouching forward and tousling his hair, and surprising himself as to how much red dust and grit was still falling onto the glass topped counter.

He felt dirty, tired and uncomfortable. He could see in his reflection that he felt, exactly how he looked.

The brass bell above the half glazed door tinkled, and only half interested, Malakye Jnr. turned his head; silhouetted against the streaming late day sunlight which poured through the shop front windows and the glazed door, stood a woman.

The backlight of the shop windows made her thin turquoise dress transparent. Malakye Jnr. found himself standing up straight and turning full towards the woman. Her pale skin was flawless, and he felt his mouth hanging, half open.

She was possibly the most beautiful thing he had ever seen.

Even lovelier than his new black stallion.

Even lovelier than a thousand black stallions.

Ray Ballou came out of the back room, having heard the bell, without looking at the woman to his left; Ray put the Spencer Rifle on the counter.

"There you go, just like I told your old man, shiny as a new moon".

He stroked the silky Ironbark stock.

Ray was right; it was beautiful, grey and grained, polished and perfect.

As he looked up, he noticed his new customer.

Malakye Jnr. had not even glanced at the rifle, and now, as if rabbits caught in car headlights on a country track; the two men stood, motionless and silent.

They allowed her to wash over them, soak them and squeeze them, stun them and revive them.

She smiled, not coyly, but a big wide all consuming smile, then, putting her left hand to her mouth, she coughed, a demure cough, a cough requiring an answer. On her finger, the sunlight caught and danced upon a diamond ring, the diamond the size of the woman's little finger nail.

Ray deserted Malakye Jnr. in a micro-second, and stood in front of the woman, adjusting his tie, sweeping his hair back, and brushing down the buff coloured apron which he always wore.

"What can I get for you Miss?" he asked, and smiled.

His dozen or so remaining teeth doing their best to look welcoming.

Matter of factly she replied:

324

"Four box's of 303 shells, a box of 38 smoothes, and a box of twelve bore heavy buckshot cartridges please".

Ray replied, with something about it being good to see a woman who new her 'artillery', and then he apologised, (as he rummaged through the shelves behind him), for not having any '38 smooth'.

"Oh", the woman responded, "38 regular will do just fine then; thank you".

Malkye Jnr. was bathing in her voice, it washed over him, sucked him in. It had a strange accent, but the words were a piece of impressionism, a suggestion of, but far enhanced reality. His mouth had still not fully closed.

While Ray returned to the shelves, hunting out the '38 Regular'; the woman turned to Malakye.

"Oh my", she said, almost whispered. "You look like you could do with a stiff drink, a sleep, and a hot bath young man".

All other thoughts had left him, and he cursed himself for not looking more respectable.

Ray bagged up the woman's purchases, and rang them into the ornate bronze and silver till on the counter. It was one of those tills, where the price clangs up on little white scalloped cards behind a glass window at the top, and all the keys have inlaid ivory discs, with prices on, in black or red lettering.

The woman commented that the till was indeed one of the most wonderful things she had ever seen, and she rubbed a painted fingernail across its little glass window.

Ray replied by commenting on the ring she wore on her wedding finger, saying that it was unusual. The woman held it forward, and explained that the stone was an old family heirloom, and came from South Africa. But that the surround was made of a native Hardwood, and had been purpose made for her, at her husband's request, by a jeweller in Esperance on the shores of the Southern Ocean of Western Australia.

"Damn it" said Ray, exclaiming loudly, "If that woods not old Ironbark then I'm not the finest craftsman in this here shop."

He reached for Old Man Mals Spencer, and, turning it, pointed the stock towards the woman. He smiled broadly, and stroking his workmanship, offered her up the stock for inspection.

The woman smiled again, with the same affect; again, she turned to both men and said;

"Yes, I do believe you're right, it is, it's exactly the same, polished and grey: and, as shiny as the moon".

She looked up at Ray, as her hand fell gently on the stock, then smiled once more, and repeated:

"As you said, shiny like a new moon".

The shop fell silent.

She handed Ray a twenty dollar bill, and told him to keep the change, picked up her bag of purchases, turned and walked out against the creeping sun beams. The two men watched her from floorboards to rafters as she left.

Watching every sway, and every twitch in every muscle.

Malakye Jnr. snatched up his father's rifle, and forgot all about the extra shells.

"Send us the bill Ray", he shouted as he headed for the door.

In the street, the woman was about thirty yards ahead of him on the pavement, she stopped next to small group of parked cars, hers was concealed by the vehicles behind and in front, but was facing him. As she unlocked it, and swung open the driver's side door, the metal skin faced him. He recognised the grey Riley.

Malakye Jnr.'s smile died on the pavement.

The woman placed her shopping in the passenger seat, stretching across the front of the car with one foot on the pavement and one knee on the driver's seat. A perverse wind sighed between the door and the pavement as she stepped back, and eased open, for a second, the turquoise dress, and revealed the briefest instant of stocking top and alabaster thigh.

Malakye Jnr. found himself shouting for the woman to:

"Hold on a minute!"

As she turned and stared at him along the pavement, she smiled. She knew the boy would be hers.

Malakye found himself wishing she could be his.

<u>**Naval Dockyard Gatehouse.**</u>

<u>**Port Keats,**</u>

<u>**Northern Territories,**</u>

<u>**Australia.**</u>

<u>**The last day of February 1943.**</u>

It was raining.

A blessed rain, noisy as the hot days were hot, and the tarmac roads were black. It beat like a blacksmiths hammer on the tin roof of the security hut. Inside, Officer Arthur Du-Pont, of the 'Northern Territories Police Force', looked through the rain streaked window at the blurred world beyond.

Half turning, and half not, he said over his shoulder to the shorter, other officer that shared the eight till six shift with him; and who stood diagonally behind Du-Pont, pouring coffee from a thermos flask.

"There's a woman standing in the rain over there, across the road, by the 'Bus Stop' sign. She got off the nine thirty from Darwin; it was on time, I put it in the log".

Officer Arthur Du-Pont looked at his wristwatch. Then spoke again.

"She's been there for twelve minutes, she's got her umbrella up, but she's getting soaking, it's fucking lashing down out there".

The shorter policeman stepped forward, and, still holding his flask in one hand, and his cup in the other, pressed his face close to the glass, he mused, only half caring.

"She'll catch her death out there, this weathers' in till midday they reckon. Then a blisterer this afternoon".

The short officer, then handed Du-Pont the coffee he had poured, and began pouring one for himself, having picked up a tin mug from the little table with the phone on it.

They debated the womans intentions while they sipped their coffees. Then, Du-Pont put his cup, (only half drunk), down on one of the little tables in the hut. He took down from a large nail, (which had been banged into the timber wall), a much too small black umbrella.

"Fuck this, I can't leave her standing out there in the rain, she'll have bloody pneumonia before long".

He stepped out onto the small concrete and tarmac island, between the, 'ins and outs' barriers, on either side of the security hut. He shouted across the road.

"Miss; hey, Miss, can I help you with anything? There's not another bus along here for another hour or so".

For a moment she didn't answer, but looked across the road, she must have heard him; Du-Pont thought to himself. He was just about to shout again as the woman, without saying a word, stepped off the pavement and began to cross the road towards him.

As she walked, nearing him, Arthur Du-pont, could see that the woman was probably in her late thirties, attractive, and absolutely drenched. Her thin summer dress clung to her thighs and breasts, and swayed heavily, but slowly, as she moved. Despite the umbrella, her bare shoulders were glistening with the warm rain. As she approached him, and even through the lashing torrents of water, Arthur could see that her eyes were sad; sad, as a winter night is dark; and her lips quivered in the expectation of words that would not come. She held her umbrella in the wrong direction to have any hope of stopping the rain; and as she reached him, Arthur took it from her and pulled it down.

He ushered her gently into the dryness, but noisiness of the hut.

In her left hand, and at her side, she held a canvass shopping bag. There was something not too heavy, but quite large in it, probably about a foot square. He took it from her soaking wet hand with no resistance, and no comment.

"Come on in love, and sit down a while in the dry".

He turned to the short officer, and said;

"Pour the lady a nice hot coffee, please, and pop this bag over in the corner".

He handed the bag to his associate, then turned back to the woman, who still remained absolutely silent. She appeared as a strangely attractive mixture of bemused, frightened, brave and just plain wet.

Du-Pont said, in his best kindly voice.

"We'll have to take a squint in the bag Miss, if you don't mind, after all this is a Naval Base, and there is a war on".

He smiled, his best re-assuring smile, and pulled a face at his short associate to quickly check the bag.

From it, the short officer withdrew a square, metal, orange, Jacobs Biscuits tin. Removing its lid, and rummaging inside for a brief moment; he turned back towards Du-Pont and said:

"Just some photo's, letters and some newspaper clippings, just 'bits and bobs', nothing to write home about Arthur".

He closed the lid.

"Good enough", replied Arthur.

Then, crouching down towards the woman, and in his best 'putting at ease manner', and with his best smiley face on; he continued, half speaking to the woman, and half to his side-kick.

"Now, let's put the tin back in the bag, and get this lady a nice hot cup of coffee; then she can tell us exactly what we can do to help".

The shorter officer made a quizzical sideways glance at Arthur Du-Pont; and mentally concluded that the rain must have got inside his head through his 'lugg-holes'.

What had happened to the big, brash, gruff, 'tough as old boots' cop he knew and loved? He had suddenly, and without warning, turned into a really nice feller. The short cop, (mockingly), smelt his coffee before taking his next sip, just in case some invisible Devil had slipped a dollop of some 'make you suddenly lovable' potion into it.

He then looked at the woman, sitting there, dripping: her dark hair pasted to her shining white cheeks and forehead with the sticky clinging rain. Her shoes squelching on the huts' planked floor, her stockings wrinkling around her ankles, sodden with the sagging down-pour.

329

He found himself smiling.

As he handed her the cup of coffee, she returned his look, and smiled as well, only a suggestion of a smile, a hint of what a smile could be.

The short cops mouth went dry, and he found himself saying:

"Just like Arthur said Miss, drink your coffee while it's hot, and then we'll see what we can do to help".

The capture and the hiding.
The Wylachi 'Livery and Horse'.
Off the south end of Cutters Lane,
East of Sandstone,
Western Australia.
July 28th and 29th 1933.

By five o'clock, he had arrived at the 'Livery and Horse'. His father, his Uncle Mordichae, and his crippled Uncle Stan who had a withered left leg, were waiting for him on the brick-built mounting platform, just in front of the main coral.

Linus Sabak and Toby 'J' sat on piles of timber fencing, across the yard, a little way back towards the timber cabin everyone called 'the Office'. They were smoking roll-ups with some other Aborigine farmhands and stockmen, and drinking sweet tea from Billy Cans, which they passed around between them. All the time they were laughing amongst themselves.

Their jokes and their laughter were beyond the language of the white men.

The white men who occupied the high ground of the mounting platform.

The white men who had the last laugh.

Next to the Aborigines stood two other white men, not laughing; stock hands, Roustabouters', freelance drifters looking for casual work wherever, whenever and whatever could be found.

The depression of this decade had bitten hard into the Outback and the Bush, as well as leaving deep scars in the Cities and Towns of Western Australia. The antipathy between these white men and the Aborigines, was self evident, they did not speak, nor share the tea or tobacco, the white 'casuals' worked for food and lodge and a dollar a day.

They were separated in the yard by three piles of wrapped barbed wire, and 'Old Man Mal's' black 'Morris Ten'. He kept the car at the 'Livery and Horse' offices for Linus Sabak, (or one of the other hands who could drive), to collect his brother Stan from his house every morning for work, and to take him home each night.

The distance between the two groups of men standing, and sitting to either side of the 'Morris Ten', was probably less than a dozen yards; but none-the-less it was an age. An age crammed with mis-shapen superiority, and in-bread disadvantage, each now blamed the other. Each convinced they were right.

Malakye Jnr. avoided the questions of;

"Where the fuck have you been?"

And the sarcasm of the remarks like;

"We were just about to send out a search party!" by volunteering the information; (the lie): that he had suffered a puncture in one of the tyres on the green pick-up truck.

He saw his Uncle Stan thumping his way around the trucks tyres with the crutch he always carried. A crutch which Old Man Mal had made for him twenty something years earlier.

It had a rich, dark brown leather armpit crook, as soft as a 'Virgins Quim', Stan used to say, made from the stretched belly skin of one of the first heifers he and Mal had ever butchered. Its shaft, which split to a 'V' as neat as any line on printed paper, was made from a single piece of Ironbark, cut from the old tree up at the far end of Cutters Lane on The Sainted Tee boundary. Across its middle, separating the two forks of Ironbark was a piece of polished horn that was the hand grasp, as white as an Aborigines eyeball.

Uncle Stan had once told Malkye Jnr. that it was hewn from the forearm bones of a poaching 'Abo'. An 'Abo' that his Great Great Grandfather had caught stealing sheep. Uncle Stan had told the (then) youngster that Great Great Granddad, had lopped off the man's arm with a scythe, as a warning to other Aborigine's not to steal from Wylachi land.

Malakye Jnr. was grateful to see the three Police Cars turn off Cutters Lane and head up the track towards the 'Livery and Horse', it meant he could escape the imminent interrogation of his Uncle Stan, who was still beating the living daylights of every tyre on the green pick-up truck.

The New Norcia Police Cars were dark green and white, the doors, the boots, and the bonnets were white, and everything else was dark olive green. Each had a big polished klaxon on the roof, and an equally shiny spotlight fixed incongruously with ugly rusty iron bolts on each of the passenger doors.

The Cars were British 'Railton Invicta's', four litre straight eights. Superb machines with sweeping front wings and running boards, lovely vehicles, and the worst possible choice for this part of the world. Every one of them would probably need complete sets of new springs after a nudge out to the Old Stockman's Hut at the foot of Daggar Hills.

The cops had even brought a couple of motorcycles with them, dark green 'Rex-Acme 750cc Sturmey Archer' machines, with armed patrolmen sitting uncomfortably astride them in peaked black caps, goggles, knee boots, and jodhpurs with wide white stripes down the outside.

They may as well have brought some water skis and snow shoes.

"Fucking idiots".

'Old man Mal' had remarked to his brother Mordichae. Both men had laughed.

When the convoy had pulled into the Livery yard and parked up in front of the mounting platform, next to Malakye Jnr.'s green pickup, and his Uncle Mordichae's stock transporter, the lead car disgorged its passengers.

From the passenger seat of the leading car squeezed out a fat elderly officer with big epaulettes with lots of shiny metal on them, silver buttons, and First World War ribbons across his chest. He had an uncomfortable moustache, a shock of grey hair and an ugly scar across his lip, which his moustache tried but failed to hide.

Across his black uniform was a gleaming leather diagonal belt attached to the wider belt which circumnavigated his ample middle. He introduced himself, and saluted.

Funny and incongruous; all the Aborigines laughed. He paid them no attention.

He spoke with a slightly 'affected', 'English Country Gent' type clip.

"Gilbert Van Der Faisey, Police Chief Van Der Faisey", he said, and smiled.

He seemed a daft old stick, but nice enough, and probably as brave as only daft people can be.

He introduced his second in command, calling the man over from the middle car; they all had swish black uniforms and caps, and all looked the part.

"This is Sergeant Killing; he'll be in charge of the arrest party in cars two and three, whilst I, Constables Armsby, Tremayne, and Matrik in car one, will provide any back up and support action which may be required".

He gestured behind him at the two motorcycle patrol cops, and continued;

"Patrolmen Summersby and Dolenz, will act as rapid response; to cut off any attempts at escape, and to be communication runners if needs must, in the event".

Unsure of the meaning of anything that had just been said, but certain that there was some sort of strategy in there somewhere; even if they did have all the wrong vehicles, 'Old Man Mal' asked:

"What do you want from us then Chief?"

The Chief told them that he wanted guides to lead them to the south of the Stockman's Hut, and that they wanted to be two or three miles away from the hut by just before dark. He said that they would then proceed on foot, 'for silences sake, and for expedition', to within fifty or so yards of the hut, placing officers, 'surreptitiously all around, and at points of pertinencey'.

The Chief was concise, but in a convoluted kind of way.

He then went on to explain that Sergeant Killing, 'by use of megaphone amplification', would announce the presence of the New Norcia Police Force, and request that the, 'miscreant's present themselves in the fashion of an orderly surrender'.

"Well: good luck to you fellers", said 'Old Man Mal' matter of factly, and followed up with:

"We'd best fuck off then, it's a good two hours to the bottom of Daggar Hills, even in those jalopies".

He pointed, (somewhat disparagingly), to the Police convoy of vehicles, and then, as if to re-enforce the tightness of the timescale, he added;

"And it'll take another hour or more's walk to the Old Hut after that, probably a good bit more with you lot done up like Pox Doctors' clerks".

He asked Van Der Faisey, before they left, if the 'cops', had 'water and grub'.

The Police Chief assured him that, "His men were adequately provisioned for the *sortie*".

"Good enough", replied Mal.

He turned towards the Aborigines and shouted that Toby 'J', and Linus should jump in the green pick-up, and, 'top the tank up, and chuck a spare wheel in the back'. He told them there were a couple of wheels in the 'kit shed' next to the office.

He also reminded them to bring their rifles, and some spare ammunition.

He asked Malakye Jnr. where his refurbished Spencer Rifle was from Ray Ballou, and Mal Jnr, retrieved it from the green pick up and passed it to his Father. 'Old Man Mal' looked at the new stock, and polished it with his sleeve.

"Will you look at that?" he said, and showed it to Mordichae and Stan, "A thing of bloody beauty that; a thing of bloody beauty", he turned to Mal Jnr., and asked rhetorically, "Did you ever see anything so bloody beautiful?"

Malakye Junior most definitely had, but said nothing.

'Old Man Mal' then told Mordichae to jump in the Stock Truck with him, and shouted across for the two white 'casuals' to jump in the back, and collect a shotgun each from Toby 'J' on the way. 'Old Man Mal' had promised each of the men, including Linus and Toby 'J', 'Ten Bucks a piece for the nights work'.

Gilbert Van Der Faisey, raised a hand in gentle protest as 'Old Man Mal' barked instructions across the yard. The Police Chief explained that this was a New Norcia Police operation, and that he was not happy with the Sandstone Farmsteads' men being fully armed.

'Old Man Mal' explained to him in words of one syllable, hyphenated with the odd 'fuck'; that it was his land, his Stockman's Hut, his trucks, and his men, and that the Chief would take three days to find the Old Hut on his own; and if 'Old Man Mal' and his men were guiding, then they would be armed.

The police Chief, 'acquiesced', as he put it, and made some noises about possibly deputising them all, 'pro-tem', he had said, 'upon their arrival at the point of designation'.

"Good enough!" said Mal again, and headed for the truck after his brother Mordichae.

"What about me?" piped in Malekye Jnr.

Without turning around, 'Old Man Mal' said;

"You take the Morris, and drop Uncle Stan home; I'll see you back at the Farm House sometime tomorrow morning".

The expected objection from Malakye Jnr. was cut short by his father.

"And don't leave the shearing logs in the boot of the car; the bloody termites could eat them to shreds if they get in there this time of year. Make sure you take them in the house, and put them safe in the study".

A look of momentary puzzlement drifted over Malakye Jnr.'s face. His father continued, and then left, regardless.

"You'll find the keys on the dashboard, don't forget your Uncle Stan; and for fuck sake don't crash it, and try not to get another puncture".

His Father pulled himself up into the passenger side of the Stock Truck next to his brother Mordichae.

As he did so he gave Mal Jnr. a look that fell somewhere between, 'just do as you're told', and, 'I know you've been up to something', with a possible touch of, 'now's a time when you should know to keep your mouth shut' mixed in for good measure.

The two white 'casuals' were already in the back of the truck, they were standing in the cattle bed, holding onto the roof rail.

As he closed his door 'Old Man Mal' waved lazily towards his son, and gave him the look again as Mordichae started the trucks engine and began to pull away from the mounting platform. The entire convoy circled around the yard, about Malakye Jnr. and his Uncle Stan, like planets spinning around a star; then headed off down the dirt track towards Cutters Lane.

"Come on Young 'un", said Stan. "You can treat me to a beer in the 'Shillington' on the way, Dunder's got his new radio machine up and running, and there's a 'rugger' game on, or so your Uncle Mordichae reckons".

He laughed out loud, as he did a kind of hobbling twirl on his crutch, turning awkwardly towards the car. The laugh was more of a chuckle really, more demented somehow, not really a chuckle even, a kind of cackle. He hawked noisily, and spat on the dust floor of the yard. Then finished with;

"Poor cunt, he'll miss it now", he said, presumably referring to Mordichae.

Malakye Jnr. watched him from behind, still a little puzzled as his Uncle Stan waddled towards the 'Morris Ten'. He turned again and looked down the dirt track, he watched the vehicles tail lights grow dim in the distance.

"Come on Young 'un, don't want to miss the kick off do we!"

"I think we already have!" said Malakye Jnr. under his breath, and began a slow trot towards the car.

The sinking of the SS Iron Knight.
The time adrift;
The time locked up in Newcastle, New South Wales.
And the road to Port Keats;
March 1943.

In the lifeboat, he had laid in the hull-well; prone, between two timber cross seats, someone had crouched over him, and given him a drink of brandy. They told him not to swallow it.

"Swish it round then spit it out Stoko".

He did as he was told.

"Have another pull, and do the same again".

Before he could reply, the bottle was back at his lips; again he did as he was told.

Next, a metal cup, a good pint, full of fresh water was placed in his right hand; he began to focus on the sailor standing over him, even in the darkness he recognised him as a 'Jib Operator' from the ship.

"Now, get that water down you, and try for a kip. Bloody good job on the Captain Stoko; bloody good, saved his bloody life, no two ways about it, bloody good job. You get yourself together, we'll get him sorted".

The man rose, and in an instant was gone; stepping over things and people towards the stern of the lifeboat.

Prisoner number 89855812, looked around, he had not really heard what the 'Jib Operator' had said to him over the shrieking in his ears, but he knew well enough to drink the water, as he had known well enough not to swallow the brandy mixed with a gob-full of oil.

He now guzzled the water greedily, and drained the whole pint. Pushing himself up on one elbow, he could see that there were about a dozen or so other men in the lifeboat, some injured, some not so injured, others badly injured; none, save for the 'Jib Operator', absolutely un-injured.

The lifeboat, and the night stars, began to spin and swirl, completely beyond his control the cup dropped from his hand, his eyes began to roll, and the blackness sucked him in. He passed out completely, utterly, peacefully, and most of all; thankfully.

The lorry ride from the New South Wales port of Newcastle had been a pile of shit from start to finish. When they had been brought ashore, he had been separated from the other men who had been in the lifeboat with him, and scuttled off the local police station.

He had spent two nights in a cell there.

The coppers had been decent enough to him, and had let him know, (by way of paper notes; his hearing still having not returned); that an army lorry would be picking him up to take him to his next ship.

He could not recall being asked if he wanted another ship, and he thought to himself that no-one out there in the vastness of all the 'Australian Regional Prison Services' really gave a flying fuck, as to whether or not he ever wanted to see a fucking wave ever, ever, ever, again.

He had however, as Captain Tynsdale had reminded him only twenty eight days earlier, on the deck of 'The Iron Knight'; 'Put his hand up for this'. And he recalled the words, 'For the Duration', being screamed at him somewhere along the line.

He presumed that, 'For the Duration', meant having ship after ship blown from under him, until he eventually went down with one of them.

He realised, still, that he was a prisoner, and choices were for others, not for him.

When he came too, the 'Jib Operator' explained to him, (by a mixture of sign language and exaggerated word forming and lip reading), that he had been out for two days, but that he had drunk some water, and was looking a bit better now. He found the latter bit hard to believe, as he still felt like shit, and his head felt like there was a bell ringing contest going on in there.

The 'Jib Operator' also told him that the Captain was hanging on, but had not come around yet.

He pulled himself up, and looked around the boat, he needed a piss, but could not yet stand properly, so he knelt on one of the cross seats, and pissed over the side. As he buttoned up the fly of his filthy, oily, and still damp overalls; he recognised Midshipman Greener Hawks, sitting cross legged on the triangular timber seat in the prow of the boat. Greener was looking out over the empty vast sea with a pair of, (much too small), ships binoculars.

Somebody, a deckhand he had seen on board, a man they called Joey, handed him a mug of water, and two thick biscuits with a slice of corned beef between them.

"Get these down you Stoko, and if you're up to it; you can give us a hand to get the sail rigged later, if the wind picks up a bit".

The man licked his finger, and held it in the air. Prisoner number 89855812 did not understand why, neither, probably did Joey the deck-hand.

He had fallen asleep in the back of the lorry, and was now being shouted at to: "Get out, and stand fast".

His welcome at Port Keats was only marginally more affable than his previous one at Albany.

Port Keats was in the Australian Northern Territories, to the east of Darwin. It was the major port entry to the Timor Sea, and as well as a shipping hub, it also contained the northward facing bulk, (if that is the right word), of the Royal Australian Air Force. Mostly based at Fairbirn Arfield in Canberra, Archenfield in Brisbane, and Tabbyfield, two miles in-land from Port Keats.

As Prisoner number 89855812, stood at the rear of the dropped down lorry gate, and raising his hands against the noon sun, he saw some planes, flying overhead, and heading out to sea, only a few hundred feet above. He didn't know it but they were a squadron of 'Hawker Demons', escorting a dozen or so 'B25 Mitchell Bombers'.

They were, in reality, left overs from the 'Netherlands East India Air Force', which had fled to mainland Australia ahead of the Japanese. Most of the Dutch pilots had been shipped back to Europe, but some had stayed to train up Ozzys' to fly the planes they were leaving behind.

The 'Hawker Demons' were almost relics, and no match for a Japanese 'Mitsubishi A6M Zero' in a bad mood. The 'Mitchel's' however, were a different kettle of fish. They were reliable, long range bombers with a good payload. They had earned their reputation in the famous 'Doolittle Raids' on Tokyo on April 18th 1942, launched from the U.S.S. Hornet in the Western Pacific.

This particular day they were on a short range coastal defence training mission. There had been substantial bad press recently when a B25 had crashed at Port Keats on the 31st January 1943, killing and injuring eight civilians.

So the R.A.A.F., were trying hard to regain public confidence.

"Come on chummy", said one of the sqauddies, and gave Prisoner number 89855812, a gentle prod with his rifle butt; "Just head towards the sea, and stop when I tell you".

They were walking towards a small bright yellow, wooden security lodge, on a little concrete and tarmac island. To either side spanned heavy looking red and white striped barriers, blocking the roads in and out of the docks. There were two police officers standing in the double, front facing doorway.

They wore dark blue uniforms, with shorts and white socks, a white bush hat with a silver badge on the front, and a white side arm holster hung from a webbing belt, also in white, their shoes were white plimsolls.

The next two days passed in a mixture of lucidity, boredom, sea-sickness, sleep and the desire for semi consciousness. Stoko, (as he was now, apparently, called), had helped Joey and two other rescued crewmen, raise the lifeboats single sail, bail out any sea water, and collect, in tin mugs and bailing pots, any rainwater that came their way; which had been plentiful.

The last twelve hours had been full of horrendous swells, and driving torrential rain, stinging cold rain that bit your cheeks like little darts, and kept your eyes squinted. Twice they had nearly lost the boat, and Joey, who had been tasked by Greener Hawks with trimming the sail as the weather rose, went over the side once, but his tether, held to a rowlock, had saved him, the rest of the men had managed to heave him back aboard.

There were exactly fourteen occupants of the lifeboat.

Today, as the sun rose, was day four in the lifeboat.

Midshipman Greener Hawks, by use of the stars, his pair of inadequate binoculars, the sun, and the Captains waterproof watch, had somehow managed to keep them in the convoy lanes, and, (he hoped), within a dozen or so miles of where the 'Iron Knight' had gone down.

The morning had passed with the usual attempts at good humour, little conversations about wives, girlfriends and kids, some profanity about Japs and Krauts with attached colourful banter about Hitler and a generic 'Tojo'.

At one point Stoko had been asked by the 'Jib Operator', what he had done to, 'wind up in clink for such a stretch'. Any answer he may have given was cut short by the Captain, who had shouted from the stern for all hands to, 'check the boats caulking leaks and springage'.

The subject of Stoko's crimes was never raised again on the lifeboat.

Captain Tynsdale still lay in the stern with an injured calf and a badly bruised and swollen knee; but he had now recovered all his mental capacities. He made it clear to everyone that he had full confidence in Greener, and that he was certain that rescue would come in due course.

Amidst the disjointed conversations that occupied the lifeboat, and at irregular intervals, someone would often start up a song, or a quiz to break the monotony.

The sea was by now glass calm.

It was day five.

The sun had just passed overhead, and Captain Tynsdale had just asked:

"Who shot Abraham Lincoln?"

Greener Hawks had said quickly, 'John Mudd'; one of the other men, Stoko thought he was a Ships Steward, interrupted, and said, that John Mudd was the doctor who treated the assassin, and that it was a 'bloke called John Wilkes Booth what did the shooting'. Another man, a Second Engineer interrupted with;

"Don't be daft, he invented the Salvation Army".

Then he called the steward a 'dozey prick'.

Captain Tynsdale laughed out load, and said that it was moments like this when he most regretted not saving his pipe and tobacco. The mood on board was good, and the Captain and Greener Hawks, made sure they kept it up.

"Smoke; smoke!" shouted Joey, who had jumped up, and now stood on the centre board slot, balancing himself against the sails solitary mast.

Every man heaved to starboard, nearly capsizing the lifeboat in their enthusiasm.

"There's another one!"

This time Joey screamed the words.

Every arm was now raised aloft, every hand waiving, every mouth shouting, screaming, yelling.

"Hey, hey".

Or

"Ahoy".

Or

"Over here",

Or anything else that could not possibly have been heard at such a distance.

The ships had now transcended the horizon, and were about ten miles away. For the next twenty minutes, every man shouted himself hoarse, and waived his arms till his biceps screamed for rest. Eventually, at about six miles distant, the lead ships Morse Lamp burst into life…. It signalled…..

'Sit tight, we've seen you, have got
the bacon and eggs on ready'.

It kept repeating.

Not all the crew could read Morse, so Greener Hawks and Captain Tynsdale translated, almost in unison.

The lifeboat erupted in whoops and cheers, which did not subside until the two huge grey battleships were towering above them and, small tenders had been launched to usher them in.

As the marines approached the security hut, one of them took a familiar looking slip of pink flimsy paper from his breast pocket, and handed it the shortest of the two policemen.

'I've seen one of them bits of pink paper before', thought Prisoner number 89855812 to himself.

"G'day", the marine said, as he passed over the document.

"We've got to deliver this feller", he pointed a thumb backwards at the prisoner; "To that ship", he pointed a forefinger at the pink flimsy.

The marine reached into his other breast pocket and pulled out a brown leather I.D. wallet, and handed it to the taller of the policemen.

"This is me", he said and laughed.

He was the only one that laughed.

"Wait here", said the shorter policeman, and went in to the hut.

They could all see him as he talked on the phone, put it down, checked a list on the wall, then dialled someone else, then checked a thick book on one of the little tables that littered the wooden hut, then dialled someone else.

After about five minutes he came back out, still holding the pink flimsy.

"Right; you're expected", the Police Officer fired a withering glance at the marine as he handed the flimsy back to him; then remarked with an edge of vinegar in his voice.

"You were expected three hours ago", he paused for effect, but not long enough to allow the marine private time to formulate an excuse.

"Wharf three; pier five", he then stepped off his concrete island and directed them.

"Down here to the end, about five hundred yards, then turn right. You'll see 'Wharf One' on your left, go past all the 'Wharf One' piers; they're all signposted in red, and all the 'Wharf Two' piers; they're all signposted in blue; that's about a thousand yards each. Then you'll see the 'Wharf Three' signs in white. Pier five will be on your left, about another five hundred yards".

The Officer made no pauses, and no further explanations, and stepped back onto his concrete island; re-securing the upper ground.

"Thanks", said the marine private, and turned to waive the lorry over.

He was interrupted by the tall policeman, who had taken a bit of a dislike to them all; and him in particular.

"Got a pass for that wagon?" he asked casually.

"What"; replied the marine private.

The short Policeman now interjected.

"Looks like you lot are walking then".

He leant forwards slightly from his concrete island, then continued,

"Officer Du-Pont here, will escort you", he turned a quarter turn, and shooed the lorry away with a condescending flick of his risk.

"You can wait across the road", he shouted to the driver.

Then, turning to his colleague, simply said, "take them over Arthur", and he went back into the security hut and started making more phone calls.

Officer Arthur Du-Pont then took out from behind the hut, a black and white push bike that was a little too small for him. It was clearly of a size that he, and the shorter officer could both use, but which was ideal for neither.

As he hopped across the saddle, and stood with one foot on the ground, and the other leg hanging nonchalantly over the cross bar, he told the marine private to collect the rifles and side arms from his team, and leave them in the security hut until they got back, and to leave the handcuffs on the prisoner.

He patted his own side arm, and said,

343

"Don't worry. I'll be watching him all the way".

The weapons were collected without question and stowed inside the door of the security hut. Officer Du-Pont, asked the marine private, for a quick further glance at the pink flimsy, he re-read it and handed it back;

"Right then; 'The Waterhen', it is", and he set off, shouting as he went, "Keep up then laddies".

He cycled off at a measured pace, just quick enough to keep the squaddies and Prisoner number 89855812 jogging at slightly more than a gentle trot. Within a few minutes, the required sweat rings were appearing on all the marine fatigues and the prisoners overalls. Officer Du-Pont smiled, and whistled as he pedalled.

The H.M.A.S. Waterhen was a lend-lease, Town Class Battle Destroyer, ('V' and 'W' class pre-fixed).

It was part of the American/British trade off deal, of ships for Great Britain in return for permission for U.S. military bases to be set up in places such as New Foundland and Diego Garcia.

The Americans loaned the British their old ships on wartime leases, and the British loaned the Americans offshore land for American military bases on almost eternal leases. The Yanks had driven a hard bargain, and the old adage 'Needs must when the Devil drives' most definitely applied to the British at the time; (and the Yanks knew it), well done Mr. Roosevelt.

Also seconded to the Royal Australian Navy from this deal, were the other Town Class Destroyers, Vampire, Vendetta, and Voyager. The Class was generally known as '4 Stack Flush Deckers'; they were poorly armed with only four 4 inch guns and six 21 inch torpedo tubes; and at only 1100 tons and 312 feet long, were small to shoulder the name Destroyers.

'The Waterhen', had been laid down in Palmers British Shipyards at Hepburn-On-Tyne in July 1917, and launched a year later. The design had a reputation for instability, and, being so light, this was exacerbated, when half full oil tanks sloshed around in even moderate seas.

The risk of capsize was very real.

The now, newly re-fitted, (and re-commissioned; for the third time), H.M.A.S. Waterhen was at Port Keats, having completed her sea trials out of the re-fit yards at Darwin, further up the Northern Territories coast.

In 1940 and 41, she had seen action in the Mediterranean, having assisted in the Allied evacuation of Crete, and the earlier, so called 'Spud-Run' supply convoys into Tobruk, and North Africa generally.

She had been holed during a German Luftwaffe dive bomber attack off Sollum near Alexandria. Though badly damaged she had been taken in tow by H.M.A.S. Defender, and pulled into Valletta harbour at Malta, for emergency repairs. From there, via several convoy attachments, and several, 'wet dock' port repairs, she had been limped back to Darwin for the well overdue re-fit.

She now sat, at Wharf Three, Pier Five, at Port Keats harbour, in shining new grey and black livery, with orders to sail with the midnight tide, and to rendezvous with convoy AOC188 at various designated points off Indonesia, South of Ceylon; Mauritious, French Reunion Island, and Madagascar. Thereafter to make all speed to the straits of Gibralter, and link up with the British and American Mediterranean Fleets.

The rescue ships tenders pulled smartly alongside the lifeboat.

"Drop the mast and take the rope on the bowsprit, sharply now we don't want to hang around here too long". Came the command from the tender.

The Royal Australian Navy Midshipman threw the rope to Joey, who did not need a second instruction. The rope was lashed in a clove hitch, in a dry spit, and the motorised tenders put about, back towards the bigger of the two Battleships. It was clear from the tender crew's hat bands that the big grey ship was the H.M.A.S. La Triomphant.

Within a few moments the tenders were back aside the battleship, at a drop down ladder staircase point, and the passengers from the lifeboat were being ushered onto the semi-deck, and up the steps. Joey and Stoko helped the Captain; Greener and the 'Jib Operator' helped one of the other men who had injured his ribs, and the Steward and all the others were fit enough to climb the steps unaided.

The lifeboat was kicked away by the Midshipman from the tender.

The pair of tenders were rapidly hitched to their davits, and winching started immediately. The drop down ladder staircase was hauled up, and the lifeboat was left to drift aimlessly away.

Once all the men were securely on deck, the Midshipman, turned, leant backwards slightly, and, cupping his hands around his mouth shouted up to the level one gallery above them.

"Now Gunney!"

A Bren Gun burst into life, and discharged a hundred or so ungrateful rounds into the drifting lifeboat. She sank within seconds, a small wound of detritus littering the sea where she had sat a wink of time earlier.

All fourteen men watched in silence.

All felt the sadness of the lifeboats cruel fate.

They felt the screws engage through the vibration in the deck plates, a wake formed, and the big ship sliced through the sea once again. The relief sagged like treacle in the air. The moments of stillness had seemed an eternity; dollops of sweat had plunged from every forehead on board. Once more in line astern the two warships turned 30 degrees to port. They were heading towards the Australian mainland, and the port of Newcastle, a short distance down the south coast from Sydney.

"Right"; said the Midshipman, calmer now, and wiping his brow with the back of his hand, "Let's get you all to sick bay, and then those bacon and eggs we promised you".

He, and two other ranks, then led them all below.

As the squaddies bundled Prisoner number 89855812 up yet another gangplank; a strange and familiar smell assaulted his nostrils, he, and his guards were panting from their trot around Port Keats Dockyard; and as he sucked in air through his nostrils he recognised the unmistakable whiff, of self rubbed, Navy Rough Shag tobacco.

As he looked up at the gangway gate, he felt himself smile, a reflex smile he could not stop, nor that he would wish to.

There in front of him stood Commander Iestyn Tynsdale, of the Royal Australian Navy. After the loss of the SS Iron Knight, and the fantastic feat of seamanship in the lifeboat, by maintaining position to aid the search; (they had in fact been picked up, less than five miles from the sinking). Tynsdale had been re-called to Active Service, and promoted to Commander. In his mouth he clutched in a grinning corner a brand new Meerschaum pipe, a homecoming gift from his wife and girls, and in his right hand he now carried a walking stick, carved from seasoned Ironbark.

Next to him on the deck, stood First Lieutenant Greener Hawks, seconded at Tynsdales request, and also duly promoted. On each of their uniform shirt breasts they had an additional medal ribbon. The ochre coloured flash with two inset narrow pink stripes at either side, of the Sea Gallantry Medal. As the Iron Knight had been a British built and registered vessel, its crew were eligible for such civil awards for bravery. And the British Government had seen fit to award these decorations on this occasion to two Australian Merchant Seamen, with some degree of publicity.

Commander Iestyn Tynsdale, and his brand new First Lieutenant Greener Hawks greeted Stoko with self evident enthusiasm. As before, Tynsdale took the key and the pink flimsy from the marine private, without even acknowledging his salute. He signed the paper and returned it, used the key to unlock the handcuffs, and then, without a further word, took both key, and cuffs, and threw them both over the side, and into the deep blue waters of the Timor Sea. The three men shook hands warmly, and walked, chatting and laughing, with arms around shoulders, like infant schoolboys, across the deck.

At the foot of the gangplank, the squaddies fell in, once again behind officer Du-Pont and his bicycle, and began the long sweaty run, back to the security hut. Du-Pont whistled brightly as he pedalled.

He promised himself that he would shave a good minute or so off his outward journey to H.M.A.S. Waterhen, on his homeward journey back to his gatehouse hut. Turning his head backwards over his left shoulder he shouted at the marines to:

"Keep up back there!"

<u>Mrs Amethysts Living Room.</u>
<u>'The Four Terraces'</u>

Senghenydd,

South Wales.

Sunday evening April 12th 1972

Maldwyn lounged languidly on Mrs Amethyst's floral chintz settee. He held in his hand, a monster green china mug, (which Mrs A. kept specifically for him), of Nescafe with nine sugars in it. At regular intervals, he would slurp it noisily, and, (when Mrs. A. was out in the back kitchen), he would lean to one side and break wind as silently as possible.

He announced to both Dilwyn and Ellis, (who were seated at the big oak table), that horrendous flatulence was a symptom of severe haemorrhoids.

"I want to send over to Murray and Wilf a list of things we could do with from down under, but I had the thought that Harry 'H', could phone Murray in Perth, and just give him the list over the phone. Save a bit of time and money see".

Dilwyn and Ellis, demonstrably deliberated.

With some theatricality; they debated, (for Maldwyn's benefit); the merits and difficulties of using 'untrained' researchers; (this discussion contrived for the prime purpose of not wishing to belittle Maldwyn's idea, with the suggestion, that they had already arrived at such a conclusion some days earlier).

They then, (again with a degree of drama, to re-enforce the illusion that it was Maldwyn's sole concept), agreed that this was a sensible suggestion, as long as Murray was up for it, and could spare the time do it.

"We'll have to keep the list simple, make sure it's stuff they can find without too much stress", said Ellis.

Dilwyn then added,

"We'll also have to pay Harry 'H' for the phone call; that'll be a couple of quid; but Maldwyn's right, it will save us time, therefore I agree".

Ellis confirmed that the 'Historical Societies' coffers contained thirty two pounds and eighteen pence, however Maldwyn was owed three pound and sixty eight pence for train and bus fares, and another Five pounds and twenty eight pence for annual library memberships which were coming up due. He also reminded everyone

348

that, Dilwyn was owed ninety three pence for photocopies, and he himself was owed one pound and twelve pence for a large box of Cadbury's Milk Tray, which he'd sent to 'Tin-Tin', for all her help.

This last item caused some debate, as Dilwyn reckoned that Ellis was getting a material gain from it, in the form of Tin-Tin. Or; as Maldwyn put it: 'A benefit in kind, in the form of a good shagging when he next went up to London'.

They all eventually settled on a fifty percent re-imbursement of this item, and a photo of Tin-Tin, for the file.

After the usual banter between them all, they settled down to discuss the possibility of formulating the list for Harry 'H' to relay to Murray, and the format the list should take, so as not to prove too daunting for the 'Down Under Connection', who was, after all, not as familiar with research as the members of 'The Historical Society'.

But firstly the Amethyst brothers congratulated Maldwyn on his efforts in Cardiff, concerning the maritime details, and the casualty lists etc. Dilwyn also made a point of saying:

"I think we should speak with The Reverend Pugsley as well, at some point".

Both Maldwyn and Ellis nodded and mumbled in agreement, Maldwyn said;

"You'd never think it to look at The Rev would you, 'Military Cross' and all".

Ellis interrupted;

"What we still lack is definitive proof that our 'Stalin', was one hundred percent guaranteed, actually, 'Yuris Pavel Androskewowiczs' at some time in the dim and distant".

The others both contended that the evidence so far was conclusive, or at least highly indicative. Maldwyn, suddenly became animated, (though not animated enough to get up off the settee).

"Yer!" he said, reaching into his overcoat inside pocket, "I forgot to give you this".

He held up a small coloured photograph. He then waited until Dilwyn rose from his chair, and walked across the room to collect it, as he took the photo; Maldwyn smiled at him, half apologetically, and said the single word, 'Piles', as an excuse for his apparent indolence.

Back to the table, and Dilwyn studied the photograph, and then handed it to Ellis. They both enquired as to its origins and content.

Maldwyn explained that he had got it from Bethany Harrington last Saturday night, down at 'Caerphilly Social Club'. Evidently she had been seated on the same table as Maldwyn during the performance of, 'Mr Mephisto and his beautiful young assistant'. Who; Maldwyn assured the 'twins', and contrary to their amusing previous comments, had been extremely entertaining.

Indeed, at one point, 'Mr Mephisto' had promised to, 'turn Maldwyn into a Prince': (the suggestion in this comment, that Maldwyn was actually being likened to a 'Frog', seemed to pass him by completely). The boys chose not to illuminate him, and went back to examining the photograph.

"So what is it then?" asked Ellis, holding it up to the light.

"Well it's Beth and 'Stalin', on the 'Social Club Outing', it's about ten years old I reckon, maybe less. But look at 'Stalin', it's the only time I've ever seen him without his glasses on. Fuck me! He was even buried wearing the bloody things, like jam jar bottoms with thick black frames. 'N.H.S. Specials' they were".

"So?"

Said the Amethyst boys in unison.

"Dew, dew, I'll tell you what; you pair, with more degrees than a fucking thermometer between you……"

"Language Maldwyn!"

A shout exhumed from the depths of the back kitchen, then added, after a rebuking hesitation;

"Fancy another coffee, and a current bun?"

Mrs. A. poked her head around the scullery door.

"Oh, yes please Mrs. Amethyst; and sorry about the 'Fucks'. Nine sugars for me, please".

Mrs Amethyst acknowledged, and walked across and collected Maldwyn's mug from the coffee table. As she walked out she 'tutted' at her two boys, and gave them that look that only Mothers can give.

"So?"

Repeated the twins.

Maldwyn told Ellis, (who was still holding the photograph), to grab the big magnifying glass, that was always on the table; and to dig out the photo of the horse racing party, that had been in the tin box.

Now that all the box's contents had been copied, annotated, cross referenced, and filed in as near chronological order as possible; it was not a difficult task. And within less than a minute, the two photographs were side by side in front of Ellis.

"What am I looking for Mal?" he asked.

Maldwyn, silently adjusted himself on the settee, leaned back, and said simply;

"Spots".

The two brothers looked at him incredulously.

"Spots?"

They repeated; Dilwyn walked around the table and stood behind Ellis looking over his shoulder, and both of them sharing the magnifying glass. In front of them were two photographs, one, the coloured one, about five inches by three inches, showing a close up of a man and a woman, with Blackpool Tower in the background. It had nothing written on the back, but was easily recognisable as 'Stalin', and Bethany Harrington, and both were clearly a decade or so younger, and 'Stalin' was alive and not dead.

The second photograph was black and white and smaller about three inches square. On the back, in pencil, tight to the top margin, and in very small neat writing, and barely discernable it said; 'Railwayman's Cup Day, Scottsville Park, 1924'.

Maldwyn reminded the boys that they had already made the horse racing connection, and that the Dykka Van Hoost and Vienna Sunday Hunter wedding certificate issued in London, (that Tin-Tin had found for them), filled in some of the chronology of events.

Both Dilwyn and Ellis, nodded that they were aware of all this. They also retorted with the fact that they knew that Dykka Van Hoost had come to a sticky end, and referred to the newspaper article that Maldwyn had come across.

Maldwyn then went on to tell them, that Bethany, when she had showed Maldwyn the photograph at the 'Social' last Saturday; she had recalled that 'Stalin' had smashed his glasses that day. Apparently they had been thrown off when

351

Bethany had been squeezed against him in a 'Spinning Waltzer' ride at Blackpool Fun Fair. So, Maldwyn explained; this was the only photo she had of him without glasses.

"Blind as a door post without them", she had said.

Evidently either confused about sensory simile's, or a bit pissed at the time.

Neither Maldwyn, nor the Amethyst twins, had ever seen 'Stalin' without glasses. Maldwyn began to titter, then said, with some satisfaction.

"Look under 'Stalin's' left eye in Bethany's photo".

He paused while Ellis crouched over the magnifying glass.

"See it? See it?" Maldwyn enquired further, literally wriggling now with excitement.

Ellis looked up; beaming, smiling, grinning, sucking in the evidence, this is why Maldwyn can charge the amounts of chocolate and sandwiches he does, Ellis thought to himself.

"I see it", he said, slowly, and in a drawn out kind of way, then handed the magnifying glass to Dilwyn, tapping the small black and white photograph with his index finger as he did so.

There was a moment of study, then.

"Me too", said Dilwyn, again slowly and drawn out; "It's on both photos!"

Maldwyn almost stood up.

"Those photos are forty years apart; that's either the worst 'blackhead' you've ever seen, or it's something more permanent".

Maldwyn then went on to tell them, that Bethany had confirmed to him, (while 'Mr Mephisto' was sawing the head off his beautiful young assistant), that 'Stalin' had a birth mark under his eye, and that his thick black glasses frame hid it. Maldwyn said that he had recalled also seeing the same position 'spot', on one of the young men in the little black and white photograph.

Ellis rose quickly, and rushed to the scullery, returning in an instant with a small bottle of purple 'meths', some rags, a toothbrush, and a broken razor blade. He turned the small photograph over again so it was face down on the table. He set about it with a determined delicacy.

Mrs. A. returned from the kitchen with a tin tray, with 'Mackeson' written on it. It contained Maldwyn's mug, two cups, (each with saucers) for her sons, and a volcano sized pile of toasted current buns, lashed with flowing rivulets of molten butter. She distributed the drinks, and placed the plate of buns on the coffee table in front of Maldwyn. Rubbing her hands on her 'pinny', (which was always on), she walked into the passage and shouted;

"I'm off across the road to Dot's to borrow a cup of sugar; I won't be two ticks".

The boys, and Maldwyn, knew she would be at least an hour, 'Songs of Praise' was due to start, and she couldn't watch it properly with the 'Historical Society' in the house. Mind you she probably did need sugar, what with Maldwyn guzzling it at nine spoonfuls per cup. It's amazing he had a tooth left in his head.

"Look at this!"

Exclaimed Ellis, he held his magnifying glass to the back of the small photograph, and, turning briefly to Dilwyn said:

"Write this down in case it disappears as the 'meths' dry out".

Dilwyn grabbed a pen and notepad, and indicated to Ellis that he was ready. Ellis continued, as Maldwyn struggled to his feet, desperate to hear the discovery.

'Railwayman's Cup, Scottsville Park 1924, Me, my Mother, Dykka, Gonda, Banjo Androskowowicsz, his brother The Elephant, Mambo our chauffeur, and Kerasons'.

The small neat pencil written script was signed simply; as Ellis relayed: *'E.H.V.H'.*

The entire 'Historical Society', screeched to a man, and almost in unison:

"Eloise Hunter Van Hoost!"

Ellis flipped the photograph back over, so it was face up. He pointed at the extremely attractive young girl resting against the bonnet ornament of the car. She was holding a parasol and wearing a long, well tailored dress.

"This is her then! It was too small to see before, and her face is half hidden behind this big bloke, he must be the one called '*The Elephant*'".

Dilwyn interrupted;

353

"It is her! It's the same *bird* in the photograph from Brisbane, her hair is lighter in this one, and she's not looking straight at the camera; but that smile is the same, it's definitely her".

Maldwyn leaned over his shoulder, and placed a fat finger on the photograph.

"And this is him", he said, "Stalin!"

He paused briefly, and then with succinctness only Maldwyn Somerset could muster, he added:

"Fuck me! He's changed".

Dilwyn, choosing not to expand on Maldwyn's observations; said that this photo gave them faces to match names, and that it also linked to the other document provided by Tin-Tin, and tied the South Africa documents into the Australian documents.

When he referred to the Tin-Tin documents, he made it clear to Maldwyn and Ellis what he meant. Not the marriage certificate of, 'Dykka and Vienna', (he now evidently felt comfortable enough to call them by their first names). No, the document Dilwyn was referring to, was the other marriage certificate.

The Australian one.

The one between Eloise Hunter and Banjo Anderson.

The one they had agreed never to mention to Bethany Harrington.

Dilwyn turned to Maldwyn, and asked simply, (just to confirm for his own peace of mind); that this part of their discoveries had not reached the sensitive ears of 'Stalin's' former landlady. Particularly given that Maldwyn had indulged in a few pints at the 'Social', whilst in the close company of the, (sort of), 'adulterous party'; the question posed itself in Dilwyn's head concerning the sanctity of this elements current secret status. The delights of Mr. Mephisto and his beautiful assistant, coupled with the narcotic and heady effect of several 'Newcastle Brown's' and mixed roll-ups, could, after all loosen lips: and loose lips sink ships.

Dilwyn did not relish the thought of bumping into a demented Bethany while collecting his Mothers fruit and veg. order from Aber Square shops on a Sunday morning.

"I trust you didn't mention our suspicions on that front to Bethany?"

"You trust damn right I didn't", replied a very definite Maldwyn.

354

"I didn't fancy sitting in the concert hall of 'Caerphilly Social', with a pint of 'Mann's Top' chucked all over me by a screaming drunken mad woman from 'Sneggy'"

As he listened to Maldwyn's re-assurances, Dilwyn reached across to the end of the table, and picking up the now empty 'Jacobs Biscuit Tin', he removed the orange and black metal top. He then turned it upside down, to expose the bronzed and faded inside face of the square tin lid.

He wiped it over with his sleeve, and tilted it so that the living room light bulbs played on its surface. There, scratched very faintly on the inside, with some coin, or a key, long ago, and in letters no more than a quarter inch high, raggedy and uneven, was the piece of information, that the Amethyst boys, and Maldwyn, had shared, (as yet), with no one except Tin-Tin.

It said:

'To Banjo A from Mrs A All my love now and always. Forgive me E.H.V.H.<u>A</u>.'

Dilwyn raised his head, quite solemnly, to look at the others, who were both standing, and were both silent. He said simply, as he drew his hand across the scruffy inscription, with its last 'A' being underlined with three little scratches, and slightly larger than the other letters.

"'Eloise Hunter Van Hoost Anderson'. Look at the 'J' in 'Banjo', I know it's scratched on some tin, but the tail on that 'J' is unmistakeable. It's the same 'J' as on the back of the little photograph. She wrote them both; maybe twenty years apart, but she wrote them both".

He then made a long pause, unnecessarily long, then, putting the lid gently on the table, this time face down, he continued. Addressing Maldwyn primarily.

"I'm happy that 'Stalin' was Banjo Anderson when he married Eloise in Australia, I think we all are. And that he was Yuris Androskewowicsz, when he was aboard the *Cok Guzel Denizala Baligi*. The casualty list Maldwyn dug up proves that. And the photo at the races proves the same, for later in South Africa. But what we need from you now Maldwyn is...."

He paused again, and his voice was more serious. "What we need is an answer to when, and why Yuris Androskewowicsz became Banjo Anderson? And also why,

355

on the ships compliment list from the H.M.A.S. Waterhen in 1943, he's back to Androskewowicsz, and with a number after his name, that ties up to a Prison inmate?"

Maldwyn took a large noisy slurp of his coffee, and replied:

"Ah; yes, well this is why I need Harry 'H' to phone Murray and Wilf down under. There's stuff I need now that only Ozzy archives and the like, can give us. If we can crack out the list with some well placed questions, and some search proposals for them; keeping it simple like; I'm pretty confident that, given what we've got already, we can fill in a lot of the gaps".

Dilwyn and Ellis, looked at each other, and then back to Maldwyn; they all agreed to the efficacy of the proposal, and Ellis said, as he took a seat at the oak table;

"Right, let's get this list together then!" and he picked up a pen, and notepad.

Maldwyn took another bellowing slurp, pulled out a chair, broke wind, (only slightly quieter than he had slurped at his coffee), and parked himself at the end of the table, apologising as he did so.

The H.M.A.S. Waterhen.
Across the great Indian Ocean.
For his second time.
Then off to War in Europe.
June 1943.

The journey had been different to the last time. Eloise had still intervened, still been with him, albeit locked away in an old tin box that once held Jacobs Cream Crackers.

He had wept when he had exhumed its contents in Captain Tynsdale's office, he had squeezed the Ironbark ring, (now devoid of its stone, devoid of its heart), so hard, that despite its smoothness, it had broken the skin on his palm.

It was a wound he knew may never heal.

He had returned the rest of the box's contents to its tin coffin, but had tied the Ironbark ring around his neck on a piece of string which he withdrew from his overall pocket.

Over the next year the Waterhen saw action off North Africa, and patrolled routinely the waters around Sicily and Sardinia. She carried supplies and munitions to Malta and Cyprus, and came under attack more than once.

Banjo had seen men die, had seen boys turn into men, and sometimes had, in turn, seen those men die too. He was not given to reflection, and just did his job. He had stayed alive, and had tried where possible to keep those close to him alive.

Sometimes he had succeeded, sometimes he had failed. This, he had concluded, was the nature of life.

Maldwyn Somerset's List.
April 18th 1972.

'Things to get Harry 'H' to ask Murray in Oz to find out about'.

The note on the top of the paper said, in Maldwyn's scribbly green biro. He then enumerated each item:

1.) *Where is Captain Alec Hawks?*
2.) *Ditto Iestyn Tynsdale?*
3.) *Anything Murray can dig up on 'The Brisbane Bandolero's'?*
4.) *Anything Wilf can find on a Banjo Anderson, or Andrews or*
       Androskewowicsz or Akpaganathos?
5.) *Anything on places called Sandstone, Coolinar Hill, Payne's Find, New*
       Norcia, and Daggar Hills?
6.) *Any connections between these places and the 'Brisbane Bandolero's'?*
7.) *Any court records for the 'Brisbane Bandolero's'?*
8.) *Anything else that might spin off from the above?*

9.) Any W.W.II Naval casualty lists relating to the H.M.A.S. Waterhen.

Maldwyn would give the list to Harry 'H' and await any results.

The Old Stockman's Hut.
North of Cutters Lane, below Daggar Hills.
Western Australia.
July 28th and 29th 1933.

By nine p.m. the small convoy of Police Cars, motorcycles, and pick-up trucks, had turned off Cutters Lane, about three miles before the Payne's Find junction, and were ricketing over the unmarked scrubway that led to the Old Stockman's Hut. They had suffered a good ten miles of this painful crawl, and probably had the same, if not more still to endure. It would be at least another two hours before they would be set up, and in position.

Malakye Jnr. and his Uncle Stan were on their fifth beer in the Shillington. Aside from themselves, in the Night Time Bar, there was just Old Nillica, the street sweeper and local 'Abo' drunk, who Dunder made use of from time to time to give the place a general clean up. Today had been one of those times; and now Nillica was drinking his wages.

The Rugby match had finished, and no-one remembered, or cared about the score. The radio now rattled and crackled some 'Orchestra' music, which was apparently 'Live from Fremantle', and by some German dead feller.

By the time Malakye Jnr. had arrived at the 'Livery and Horse' earlier that afternoon; the grey Riley, dust caked, and dull in the fading light; had driven west through Payne's Find Junction and was heading towards Meekathara.

By eight thirty, this small town of Meekathara was dwindling in the Riley's rear view mirror. It would spend the night at a nameless truckman's stopover between there and Gascoyne, where the woman would drink away her first night of absolute loneliness.

She would mix her way through bars and bedrooms, and Scotch and strangers, all the way to Carnarvon at the coast near Shark Bay.

Over the next five days and nights, she and her Riley would hug the sea roads through the blind date towns of Onslow, Dampier, Purdoo Roadhouse, Port Smith and Cape Leveque. She wept her way across mile after desolate mile of tarmac, seeking comfort where she could, and collecting blurred, hazy memories along the way; shedding others.

Eventually she arrived at Point Blaze:

"Just a kick in the arse away from Darwin", as some mongrel ugly Road Layer had told her, in some flea infested bar, over some bottle of 'Possum Piss' whisky.

He told her this, told her how absolutely gorgeous she was, told her how he had waited for a woman like her all his life, told her shit, dribbled on her, bundled her into the stinking filthy toilets, and fucked her with five of his puke smelling friends; then punched her unconscious as an encore.

His name was……..she couldn't remember.

Fifteen hours later she checked into the 'Duchess Mag Hotel'; opposite the Railway Station in Darwin; she bathed, she ate, she put fresh make up on her bruises, cleaned her teeth, and lipsticked her lips. She painted her nails, creamed her skin, and curled her hair. She threw her turquoise dress, shoes, bag, gloves, stockings and underwear into the rubbish chute on the landing outside her room; and then slept for two whole days.

Malakye Jnr. delivered Uncle Stan to his Auntie May, and apologised for his Uncle's condition. She commented that there was not much to choose between them, and forced Mal Jnr. to stay for a coffee, and to help her get Uncle Stan up the stairs. He drank the coffee, as quickly as he could without scalding the roof of his mouth, but needed to get back to the Sandstone Farmstead. The time was falling off midnight now, and the Grandfather clock in Auntie May's parlour, was beating out the quarter hour; he needed to be home, needed to be near a phone, just in case.

By half past midnight, Malakye Jnr. had made his excuses, pecked his Auntie May on the cheek, and was heading across Cutters lane by the old Ironbark, and swinging off left behind Sandstone, and out towards the Farmstead.

As he made the left hand turn behind the Ironbark tree, the headlights of the 'Morris Ten' swept the small irregular area of scrub away to his right. He saw the small depression about twenty or thirty yards away, saw the faint remains of tyre tracks. He saw the night-time winds from the Daggar Hills falling softly across the scrubland, and tilting the fine dry dust, stealing it from here and there, smuggling it up and around, and dumping it into everything, and everywhere else.

Tilting and sifting it into tyre tracks, and into small depressions.

By morning the suggestions of deeds done would be gobbled up and eroded.

An hour later, he was sitting at his Father's desk, in the study, with the double doors which lead to the entrance hallway, very firmly locked.

On the floor, he had scattered, in hasty unwrapping, like a Christmas morning in a house where small children live; the hessian sacks, and small boxes of the 'Shearing Logs'.

The 'Shearing Logs' which 'Old Man Mal', and his Uncles had placed in the boot of the 'Morris Ten'. The 'Shearing Logs' which were nothing to do with shearing, not 'Logs' at all.

Malakye Jnr. had never heard of 'Shearing Logs'; but already; HE LOVED THEM.

He had In front of him, on the oversized boast of the desktop; sat, squared and ordered in neat piles, counted and calibrated, sorted and denominated, just a morsel over three hundred and eighty eight thousand scruffy, stolen, crinkled and lovely, lovely, lovely Australian Dollars.

Scattered around the pillars of notes were dozens of pocket watches, wrist watches, gold cigarette cases, women's brooches, necklaces of all descriptions, rings, bracelets and all-sorts.

Malakye Jnr., found himself sitting, lounged back in his father's big red leather, rocking and swivel desk chair, with his feet up and crossed on the edge of the desk, with a large Scotch, in one hand, and a hand rolled cigarette smouldering in the other. He could not help the canyon like grin that sliced his face, nor the glints he knew must be flashing in the backs of his eyeballs, they were rich now, and rich forever.

He didn't forget his promise.

He took from the bottom drawer of the desk, a short, but fat, roll of thick brown wrapping paper, which he knew his father kept there for when he needed to send the ledgers to the accountants in Perth. There was also a wide roll of sticky tape and a small ball of twine.

Malakye Jnr. counted out twenty thousand dollars in the largest denomination bills, (to keep the package as small as possible), and placed them in front of him next to the wrapping paper. He also selected what he considered to be a very elegant, and very valuable, diamond and gold bracelet. He took a swig of his whisky, and, with his roll-up hanging from his mouth, he thought for a moment in the new silence of his world.

He concluded that twenty thousand was too much, and he reduced the pile by half to ten thousand dollars, plus the necklace. In any event, as long as his father, Uncle Mordichae and the New Norcia cops were doing their end properly up at the Old Stockman's Hut, there should be another ten thousand bucks coming their way in reward money. So; he concluded, no great loss; give her the ten grand, and she'd sit still forever.

Once he'd finished his wrapping, double papered, and using half the roll of sticky tape, he then tightly twined the package for extra safety. He withdrew from the centre drawer of his fathers desk, a long white envelope made of heavy gauge paper; expensive quality.

He wrote on the front of the envelope, with a thick soft pencil which sat in slot-tray, next to the empty cut glass inkwell on the desk; and in his best print:

Eloise Anderson;
Care of: The Duchess Mag's Hotel,
Station Forum,
Darwin,
Northern Territories,
Australia.

He left the envelope unsealed, but tucked it underneath the twine of his parcel, ready to receive the locker key.

Malakye Jnr. knew that 'Old Man Mal' and his Uncle's couldn't have had any chance to count up their haul, because they simply hadn't had the time, and, in any event, when Malakye Jnr. had unloaded the boot of the 'Morris Ten', all the sacks and boxes were still tied and had some dust on them.

He would tell them of his arrangement with Eloise, once he had sent the parcel, and it was too late for them to talk him out of it.

Or he may never tell them; he hadn't quite made up his mind.

In the stack of jewellery and watches, there was one package Malakye had yet to open.

He had left it until last.

It was a small brown coloured, suede, silk lined pouch with a matching silk chord. It was, he considered most likely, the last item he had seen Eloise place in the burial hole, as he had watched through binoculars from his vantage point, on the small escarpment in Daggar Hills.

It was the item she took from her bag, and placed on top of the pile of bags and boxes.

He thought how short a time ago that was, and yet how great a distance he had travelled since then.

He pulled apart the pinched top of the pouch, and loosened the silk chord. Turning it upside down, he emptied the single item from within into the palm of his hand. A single, perfectly cut and faceted, large egg-shaped Emerald fell from its nesting place and rested across his life-line.

He had never seen such a thing before. It was perfect; symmetrical, flawless, beautiful.

It reminded him of her.

He finished his Scotch, stood up, turned and began loading the bundled piles of cash into the bottom of the family safe, which stood behind his Father's chair. Only 'Old Man Mal' and his son knew the combination, no one else; not even Stan and Mordichae.

The safe was a '1930 George Bloch Protectall Special'. It stood five feet tall, and was three feet wide and the same measurement deep. It had taken ten men to move it into the house, where it now rested on a chunk of concrete, at least a yard deep, cast beneath the floorboards. It also had thick iron cleats on each corner, which were bolted into the concrete with one foot long steel bolts. It was fire proof, thief proof, water proof, but not deceit proof.

By one a.m. Police Chief Gilbert Van Der Faisey, and his men, along with 'Old Man Mal' Wylachi, his brother, the two Aborigines and the two white 'casuals', were sheltered in a low drainage rill about a hundred yards south of the Stockman's Hut.

Though well out of sight in the darkness, and out of earshot beneath the light breeze which swept down from the Daggar Hills; the men still crouched, and kept their voices low. The Chief had despatched Sergeant Killing, and Officers Summersby, Dolenz and Armsby to reconnoitre the area around the hut and report back in two hours time with positions of cover and the like.

He had told the other Officers to get some rest, eat and drink. He issued the same instruction to 'Old Man Mal' and his men, and forbade them all to smoke, for fear of the match strike, or burning cigarette, being spotted from the hut.

From their vantage point they could see a thin column of smoke rising from the huts solitary chimney pot, and the shimmering glow of paraffin lamps wobbled within, and leaked out through its small mis-matched windows.

The shadows moving against the lights suggested that there were a number of people in the hut. 'Old Man Mal' had told the police that there were at least five or six, during his phone call of the previous day. Outside was parked the large stock truck.

Van Der Faisey checked his notes in his pocket book, and said to Mal, in a whisper, and in his usual, but natural manner.

"I have a notation here, summarised from your initial telephonic report, that there are possibly in excess of half a dozen miscreants, with two vehicles".

He paused, and looked back to 'Old Man Mal', awaiting a response.

Malakye Snr., had been deliberately vague in his original phone call, and responded with;

"That's what I thought my son said, but I could have been wrong, it was all a bit rush and tear, know what I mean Chief".

He poked his head up over the rill, and then, crouching back down, continued with:

"Well, at least they're still here, I reckon you've got the buggers cornered this time!"

The Police Chief stated, 'with categorical certainty', as he put it, that the truck they could see parked outside the hut, illuminated by the half light easing from the windows, fitted the description of the one used in the robbery at Walebing, and that it was definitely the one stolen from the Railway Yard at Payne's Find. That; after the Railway Companies, 'Wages purloynment, and wholly unscrupulous, and unfortunate wounding of one of their employees that had been occasioned there ', as Van Der Faisey dressed it up.

It was also, (the Chief had continued); 'according to the detailed notations of the participating Officers; still in the possession of the gang at the close call at Bindi Bindi'.

Van Der Faisey tangentially mused for a moment that he was concerned that not all of the gang may be in the hut. He concluded however that this was an issue for a future bulletin pending the successful outcome of today's operation.

'Old Man Mal' said that he reckoned that the whole gang was in the hut, but in any case he wanted the full reward money, paid in full for getting them this far.

The Police Chief agreed that he would ensure that the reward payment would be made. He then went on to tell 'Old Man Mal' about how close they had come to capturing the gang at the Bindi Bindi filling station.

"During, and after the execution of that felony, the gang had very nearly been justly captured. When they were leaving, and, having just 'stuck up' to use the vernacular, a petrol station there, they were observed by one of our Police vehicles. Apparently they had 'Pistol Whipped' the cashier, and two of them urinated on him whilst their accomplices emptied his till and rifled his store, 'Foul Swine', an altogether bad lot if you ask me Mr. Wylachi ".

He looked at Mal Snr. squarely again before carrying on with his tale.

"Shots, apparently were exchanged with the Police Officers on that occasion, with a clear intent by the miscreants towards injuring, if not murdering duly accredited Officers of the Commonwealth of Western Australia".

"Fucking Bastards!" replied 'Old Man Mal' with contrasting, but equally accurate brevity.

"Quite so", responded Police Chief Van Der Faisey.

In the passenger side glove compartment of the grey Riley, was a Mauser C96 pistol and around five hundred and fifty dollars, in crumpled, and stuffed in bills.

The gun rested on the paper sweet packet, with the map of the hole drawn on it.

No writing, a stylised tree indicating the big old Ironbark, a rough bearing point on the far left peak of Daggar Hills, a thick wiggly line marking the track of Cutters Lane. There was a second bearing point picking up a distant water tower next to the rail tracks, a mere spec in the far off touch between land and sky. The third and last reference point was marked with a sketched crucifix, eyeing over towards the spire of the Non-Conformist Chapel, which stood across the road from the Shillington Arms, in Sandstone. A spire which could just barely be seen from the Ironbark on a clear night, thanks only to its artificial illumination.

That eerie incandescence was provided by a small, and hopelessly inadequate electric light bulb nestling at its apex, and upwardly illuminating the carved Crucifix above. A carved wooden Cross; six foot tall complete with our Saviour, nailed, crowned and chastised stood atop its pinnacle. '*Iesus Nazarene Rex Iudeorum*' nailed skew-iff across its top for the pigeons to perch on.

Our Lord gazing mournfully down upon the dwindling customers of the Shillington Arms, and incanting:

"Forgive them, for they know exactly what they do, but they do it anyway".

The crucifix, rough and expressive; had been carved by 'Old Man Mal's' Father, from whom he had inherited his love of whittling hunks of rock hard Ironbark into things of beauty.

For the balance of the map, only small 'x''s marked out paces, and a big 'X' marked the hole.

The paper bag stayed in the glove compartment.

'Old Man Mal' leaned comfortably against the warm earth of the drainage rill, and felt the sweat beginning on his back. Mordichae and the others rested all about him. He found himself caressing the new Ironbark rifle butt, and whispering to his brother how the shimmer of the moonlight picked out the different shades of grey grain in the deeply polished stock.

He said he would get a brass plate made with today's date on it and get Roy Ballou to inset it in the end of the stock as a commemoration of this adventure. Mordichae told him to 'Fuck off', and that he should just concentrate on 'Staying alive'.

'Old Man Mal' laughed, as quietly as he could, and patted his brother on the shoulder.

It was after three a.m. when Sergeant Killing returned along the drainage rill, Officer Dolenz was with him, but Summersby and Armsby were not.

He explained that he had found a position of perfect concealment behind a small rocky outcrop not more than half a dozen yards beyond the parked up truck. Having got that close without being discovered, he had decided to leave the other two Officers, complete with rifles and side arms in position there rather than risk moving up to that spot later with other officers, and the incumbent danger of being discovered at that stage.

The Police Chief agreed wholeheartedly, and designated one of his other officers to replace Armsby as a reserve.

He then told Officer Dolenz to find out if any of the other constables could ride a motorcycle, and to appoint one of them as a 'runner' in lieu of Patrolman Summersby. Mal Snr. And Mordichae were quite impressed by the general efficiency and manor of both Killing and Van Der Faisey.

'Old Man Mal' made a mental note not to say too much to either of them, they were too cool, and too sharp for his liking.

Sergeant Killing then ran verbally through a series of encircling positions and proposals with his Police Chief; and the two men made a collection of notes and sketches in their pocket books.

Once they had reviewed them, altered them, discussed them, and finalised them, Gilbert Van Der Faisey tore out individual leafs of paper from the note books, and distributed each to individual officers.

He went along the rill speaking with each man, making sure that everyone knew his place and his responsibilities in this plan. For a man in his sixties, and with a 'beer-belly' to die for, the Old Chief moved along the rill with the practiced experience of someone who had spent long dark, cold, wet and terrifying months in the trenches of Paschaendale.

He glanced at his watch as he issued his orders, it was approaching four thirty, and the morning sun would be creeping up in an hour or so.

It was time to move out.

As the policemen crept out of, or along the rill, depending upon their orders and dispositions; Van Der Faisey, and his reserve constables returned to 'Old Man Mal' and his crew. Sergeant Killing was at his shoulder and the Police Chief said, with rare economy, and with no discussion.

"I am authorised to temporarily deputise all men here; and I now officially do so".

He turned to his Sergeant and requested that:

"He entered a confirmatory note of this deputisation in his pocket book, along with the names of all those present".

Killing acknowledged, and immediately began taking everyone's details down, in hushed tones. Once he had completed, he informed the Chief that he would now go and occupy his position, he took with him a constable who had sat silently for the last two hours about twenty feet further along the rill, the constable had been nursing his 'Springfield M1903' rifle and a battered old megaphone.

Sergeant Killing carried a 'Thompson M1' sub-machine gun of 1928 vintage.

'Old Man Mal' had noticed that two or three of the other cops carried 'Thompson's', but that Sergeant Killing looked like he really knew how to use his.

For the most part, the rest of the cops carried old 'Enfield 303's', and every one of them, including Van Der Faisey, had a holster with a 'Colt Police Positive' six shot 38 revolver in it.

The next hour crept like a sick slug.

"Sit tight gentlemen", the Police Chief said as he drew his revolver and checked its action.

He glanced at his watch.

The sun was washing the scrub towards the hut with a blood red hue, turning to orange as it rose, second by second.

The megaphone battered the still of the yawning dawn.

Then, it began.

"This is Sergeant Atticus Killing of the New Norcia Police Constabulary, Commonwealth of Western Australia. You are surrounded come out with your hands on your heads, and leave your weapons inside the hut".

Killings voice boomed across the emptiness.

He boomed it another three times, repeating his demand word for word, it seemed to get a little louder each time he said it, or a little more forceful, or a little more desperate.

The old carved Ironbark door of the hut, was pulled open, inwards, and a man, young, twenty one or twenty two maybe, fair haired and fresh faced, bare breasted and stripped to the half ran outside. His hands were held high in the air, and plumes of dust danced around his trouser bottoms up to his knees, as he galloped back and forth in front of the hut, agitated, frightened.

The dust he kicked up hid his boots, and he looked like a ghost floating about, a couple of inches off the ground. He drew to a halt, six or eight yards in front of the hut door.

"Don't shoot, don't shoot, I give up, it's me Tuffy Boyding, I give up!"

Another man, also shirtless appeared in the doorway. This man was bigger, broader, dark hair with an ugly scar on his left cheek, and a distorted shape to the one side of his face. He held a sawn off double barrelled shot in one hand, and some sort of large calibre revolver in the other, it was in fact an 'extra long barrel American Colt 45 Peacemaker', in black gunmetal, with a pearl handle.

Unlike the first man, who was clearly Australian, this man spoke, or rather screamed with a strange suggestion of an accent?

"You fucking coward Boyding!"

Gilbert Van Der Faisey turned to 'Old Man Mal' as they both peeped above the top of the rill, The Police Chief had a puzzled look on his face, and whispered;

"South African? I served with some in the Great War. That sounds South African to me!"

Before he could continue further, the man in the doorway unleashed both barrels of the sawn off. The first shot hit Boyding from behind in the small of his

368

back, and blew his guts out of his belly in a misty haze of red, and a shower of dissected bits of intestine that landed about three yards in front of him.

The single high pitched yell was deafening.

'Old Man Mal' didn't realise a man could make such a noise, it was like a thousand pigs squealing and slipping on a slaughterhouse floor as they saw their compatriots being sliced, and knew their time was coming. Mal had heard that noise hundreds of times, from screaming pigs, lambs and cattle.

He hated it, but accepted it.

He accepted this.

That was who the Wylachi's were.

The scream did not even last a second before the shot from the other barrel smashed into the back of Boydings skull. His face exploded into another puff of blood red dust that would have filled the Daytime Bar of the Shillington Arms.

All the wrath of hell broke loose in an instant, and the rat tat tat of Sergeant Killings machine gun spewed shells into the doorway of the hut. The big South African jerked backwards, as if connected to some huge elastic band, as round after round thumped into, and through him. Abstract lumps of flesh and bone flew off him in all directions. For a brief fibre of time he seemed to float, horizontal above the floor of the hut, the soles of his boots facing outwards, and in mid air. Then, time caught up, and what was left of him, dead now, thudded back to the ground.

Rifle and pistol shots spat from the windows of the hut and from around the riddled door jambs. The gunfire from the cops was pouring into the hut, like pigswill into troughs; onto the hut, through the hut. Its retirement years of gentle decline and decay being shattered by the horror of this sunrise. Huge fist sized holes being punched in its wooden walls, fractured shingles and shrapnel's of corrugated tin spun off its roof, hurled upwards by the never ending gunfire.

Occasional screams and curses hid beneath the noise of battle. The rate of fire coming from the hut declined as each villain fell. It seemed now that only two, or maybe three men remained firing from inside.

'Old Man Mal' glanced across to his left, and forwards, he saw the long morning shadows of Sergeant Killing, and the Constable with the 'Springfield M1903' rifle, flitting behind odd outcrops, and dodging on the open ground between

369

them. The young Constable was hit, a single shot took his kneecap clean off, and he fell like a sack of 'spuds', crumpling and yelping. Sergeant Killing stopped briefly in that instant, checked his run and turned towards the young officer. In that infinitesimal flick of a half tick of a good watch, a rifle shot struck him in the groin.

Gilbert Van Der Faisey immediately instructed his reserve officers over the lip of the rill, and towards, Killing and the young Constable:

"Get those men out of there now!" he ordered, waving and pointing to his left.

In the momentary distraction, two men darted from the hut, both with a revolver in each hand. The taller was dragging his right leg; it had a tourniquet of an old belt, strapped around his thigh. His light beige trousers shimmered with the sticky thickness of his blood, with which they were saturated.

He wore no shirt, like the others. The younger man was dressed in dark trousers and a dark shirt, unbuttoned and flapping wildly as he ran toward the stock truck. As he reached the drivers door Constable Frederick Armsby rose from behind the cover of his small rocky outcrop, and fired his 'Enfield 303', somehow, and from close range, the shot missed and shattered the windscreen of the truck. The man with the tourniquet, pointed both his revolvers in Armsby's direction and fired each in turn, the first shot struck the policeman in his right hand, sending the rifle twirling into the air. The second shot hit Fred Armsby plumb in his Adams Apple; two or three pints of blood drenched his uniform tunic in as many seconds. He fell gurgling, and spluttering to the floor, in just as few seconds later, he was dead; his wife was a widow, and his children orphans.

Patrolman Summersby remained behind the rocks, crouching, shivering with fear. He had not fired a single shot in the entire engagement.

The man in the dark shirt had clamboured into the driver's seat of the truck, and had started the engine. He was already turning the stock-truck around as the second man; the wounded man, dragged himself in through the passenger door.

He was still firing with both pistols as the truck swung round towards the rill.

The vehicles wheels spun insanely on the sandy scrub, and threw up huge clouds of thick dust. This obscured the views of everyone, created confusion, and distraction. Within a dozen yards of the rill, the truck threw sharp right, and accelerated over small humps and troughs of the open scrub towards Cutters Lane.

The bumps and jives of the truck smashed its exhaust off and the engine roared, as if in pain, panels and rails bounced, broke and fell from the back gates, crashing into the scrubland as they fell.

Police Chief Van Der Faisey, was standing in the well of the drainage rill, and firing with his revolver at the rising, fleeing cloud of dust.

'Old Man Mal' clanged the bolt of his Spencer rifle, and wedged the new Ironbark stock hard into his shoulder, he loosed off one round; his only shot of the day.

He could see no target, and it was a random shell into an ever widening vagueness of dry dusty air.

The bullet crashed through the rear window of the stock trucks cab, and hit the back of the driver's right hand as he fought with the huge steering wheel. It drilled a neat one inch hole through the thin bony flesh, and blew a hole twice that size in the young man's palm as it exited. It also removed a six inch section of the steering wheel as it continued on, outwards through the smashed windscreen.

His agony was deafening.

The two men, against all the odds, had escaped. Somehow, they were still alive, and heading away from Hell.

Patrolman Fuzzy Dolenz was the first man to reach Fred Armsby. As he knelt over the corpse, and as the buzz and dust of the battle, and the stirred scrub of the stock trucks escaping tyres began to settle around him; he heard the feint sobbing, of what he thought to be child.

As he rose to his feet, listening harder, and walking towards the sound, rifle in hand; he came across the weeping, and terrified, Patrolman Frank Summersby.

Dolenz bent over him and leaned his rifle against the rocks; he shook him violently, and began to drag Summersby to his feet. Then he stopped, and looked around, there was not another Officer within thirty yards. He leant forwards, to within two inches of Summersby's face, and through clenched teeth, said to the quivering Patrolman:

"I'm about to save you're reputation Frank, just make sure you remember it, and when you come to, say you were clubbed by the feller who got away".

371

Dolenz scanned the scrub about where Frank was cowering. His eye fell upon a thick piece of old Ironbark, as thick as his forearm, knarled and twisted and about eighteen inches long. He snatched it up quickly and struck Frank, hard across the forehead, leaving a deep gash above his eyebrow. As the unconscious Summersby slumped to an untidy pile behind his rock; and as much in fury as anything, Patrolman Dolenz drove his heavy motorcycle boot hard into Frank Summersby's face, breaking a couple of teeth and splitting wide his bottom lip. He then slackened Franks tie, and undid his top shirt button for effect. Dolenz then stood up straight, tugged at his own shirt collar below his uniform tunic, and shouted loudly:

"Over here, quick, over here, two of our blokes are down!"

Murray and Wilf,
Payne's Find, and the old Ironbark,
July 4th and 5th 1972.

The morning had been crammed with cornflakes, toast, bacon as stripy as a Yankee flag, black pudding speckled with fat, splitting red sausages and runny eggs a small man could swim in.

There had been a sea of steaming tea, and on the side table, threatening an avalanche, teetered a mountain of thick fried bread so sumptuous that dwarves would fight for the right to sleep on one of the mattress slices.

Coffee was available for the less cultured, and in the corner of the dining room a young couple with jeans, a head scarf and a beard embarrassed a *croissant*. They had clearly watched a programme about *Province*.

My Uncles demolished their breakfasts with the lust demanded of ex-pats from a dingy mining valley, so far away and yet now almost in their pockets, almost in their dreams.

"Fantastic!" said Wilf, as he leaned back in his chair and smoothed his belly, as if easing the 'Full English' along its intestinal voyage.

"Can't fault that", exclaimed Murray, wiping his lips with the giant thick cotton napkin.

Serviette is a word the bearded *croissant* eaters would have used.

The two men poured another cup of tea each, and over their consumption, along with two more slices of toast and a dollop of marmalade the size of Seville, they planned their moves for the day.

They would drive to the local library, (the old landlady, who they now knew to be Ernestine Bug, had given them directions over the cornflakes), and pick up whatever material they could find, concerning the shootout at the Wylachi Stockman's Station nearly forty years ago.

Then, they would make their way back to Coolinar Hill, and see if they could get any information regarding the arrest of Banjo Anderson.

Once they had completed these tasks, (as set by Maldwyn Somerset), they would either camp out for the night, or find another B & B over towards, or indeed in, Coolinar Hill itself.

They had already driven through the fading idea of a town that had once been Coolinar Hill, earlier in their journey. It had seemed to them a place with no hope, a town that the good roads no longer went through, and where the people sought escape from, even just a short distance, a spit in the dust filled wind to a land where hope still flourished. Like young Toraya, waitressing her way out as far as Sandstone, and maybe with Payne's Find in her sights.

Then, tomorrow morning, as early as a bed cock could rise, and before a real cock could crow, they would un-muddle the map.

Seek by torchlight the cryptic symbols, and, like a couple of masons without the funny handshakes and ten to two feet, they would pace out the pacings and see if 'X' really did mark the spot.

They collected their kit from their simple but comfy room, paid their bill at the reception table, and made their goodbyes to the elderly Mrs. Bug. She parted reluctantly with their change, took back her keys, smiled a horrible grin, and almost kissed them farewell. Their respite at the Captain Cooke Bed and Breakfast had come to its end.

The Payne's Find Municipal Library had proven to be surprisingly efficient. It was a modern building of little aesthetic merit, made largely of concrete, and a mish mash of unsuitable multi coloured bricks, with metal windows and wooden doors. It was so ghastly that it must have won dozens, if not hundreds of awards for its architect, who doubtless tormented himself for days over the depth of the dull grey fascias, or whether to make the brick paviours' in the entrance foyer vomit coloured, or to give them the delicate changing hues of pig manure, which he had eventually settled on.

Internally however, the structure was utilitarian and well sign posted. The 'Newspaper Archive' section was where Murray and Wilf found themselves by ten o'clock in the morning.

Within an hour a very helpful young lady by the name of Glynnis, had collected for them, (and set them out on a large table in the first floor reading gallery), nine large volumes of aged newspapers, each one leather bound in grey, and a good three inches thick, and each the size of the Financial Times. The volumes contained copies of every local newspaper from Mount Magnet to New Norcia, which had been published between July 1933, and March 1934.

They found some detailed accounts of the shootout, including some first hand accounts from a few of the Policemen who were actually there. There was one from Motorcycle Patrolman called Fuzzy Dolenz, who said that he had witnessed one of his fellow officers; a Patrolman Frank Summersby single handedly try to stop two of the 'Brisbane Bandolero's' escaping in a stock truck after they had shot and killed Officer Fred Armsby.

'Bravest darn thing I ever saw'.

Patrolman Dolenz was quoted as saying, he had concluded with,

'Frank Summersby deserves a medal the size of a frying pan!'

Several editions later, there was a small column which stated that Patrolman Summersby was indeed to be awarded a Police Gallantry Medal.

374

Murray and Wilf trawled through the back editions of the newspapers until just before two o'clock in the afternoon. Glynnis had brought them other volumes containing more distant publications as they had requested them, and took away the volumes which they had finished with.

At two p.m. she had came over to their table and asked if there was anything else she could assist them with, as she was finishing early today, and her fiancé was picking her up.

She explained that they were going shopping to pick a wedding ring. She was eager, as are all impending nuptualists to share her good news; even with total strangers.

She pointed across the reading gallery at a good looking and smartly dressed young man in his mid twenties; she said that his name was Hugo.

Murray told her that they only had another one or two months worth newspapers to plough through, and that they should be finished in an hour or so. Glynnis smiled happily, and as she left the two men, amidst the large grey leather volumes, and their own scatterings of notepapers strewn across the table top, she said.

"Just leave everything where it is when you've finished, one of the other girls will collect it all up at the end of the day and put it back in its proper place".

She smiled again; even broader than before if that was possible, and said 'Cheerio'. Then she was gone, heading towards her new life with Hugo.

Murray and Wilf had winkled out tons of new stuff about the Brisbane Bandolero's, and Wilf had made notes as copious as a brothels laundry list about their exploits.

"Wait till Mad Maldwyn and the Amethyst weirdo's get copies of all this".

They knew of the 'Historical Society' and its members long before their emigration.

They recalled them all.

Unfortunately.

He waved the sheets of papers in the air at shoulder height; he looked like Neville Chamberlain, only more suntanned.

"Stalin is like the Ronnie Biggs of the 1930's", he paused, and looked left and right, then lowered his voice, and leaned forward towards Murray, who was sat at the opposite end of the large table.

"Eighteen bank jobs they did. Eighteen!"

He repeated the total for emphasis.

Murray, equally furtively, slid across the table towards Wilf, a single sheet of paper he had been scribbling on. He folded it in half first, with the writing inside so that no one else could see it.

Then he also whispered, all of this was absolutely unnecessary as they were the only two people in the reading gallery. Murray started to speak, a hushed, quite hoarse speech, less than a whisper really.

"Half a million dollars!"

His eyes opened wide, and a huge smile sliced his face, he pointed at the piece of paper.

"That's what that lot adds up to, there's the figures, there from each of the Bank robberies in all these newspapers".

He waved both arms gracefully above the grey leather volumes, as if casting spells on them to make them levitate. He continued, still furtive.

"Wilf; that's half a million bucks in 1930's money, that's, that's......"

He hesitated.

"I don't know how much that would be today, but it's a fucking shit load!"

Both men could resist no longer and erupted into fits of laughter and whoops of expectation. They both stood and did what can only be described as a little dance around the table. Like two small boys inadvertently locked in a sweet shop by its absent minded owner, they were as happy as the Sun was big and far away.

An hour and a half later, they were driving into Coolinar Hill. Wilf had wanted to take the route via Sandstone again, as he wanted to look at the old Church steeple, and the carving of Christ at its top.

He had told Murray that when he had seen it the previous day, just as they were leaving 'The Shillington Arms', there was something about it that caught his eye, but he couldn't make any connection as to why it felt such an important observation. Now after having seen it for a second time, and coming at it from the other direction, the direction of Payne's Find; he knew what that connection was.

It was one of the reckoning points on the old map. He checked the photocopy in the 'East Light' lever arch file, as Murray drove.

"I'm bloody sure it's this".

He pointed to a cross marked on the map.

"And this, this kind of zig-zaggy thing"

He drew his finger along a sketch of what looked like some roughly pencilled sharks teeth. Then waved the same finger towards the mountain peaks in the distance.

"This, I'm fairly sure is that, but not quite from this road".

He gestured again at the range of mountains which filled the cars windscreen.

"Those must be Daggar Hills, they stretch all the way behind Sandstone from Payne's Find, and out to the west beyond Coolinar Hill".

Wilf paused a long moment, looking backwards and forwards, as Murray drove, occasionally leaning across his brother to peer out of the drivers side windows. Then he said:

"If we were further west of here…." he stopped mid sentence, and then rummaged in the cars door pocket for the road atlas. Having found the correct page, he leaned across Murray again to get a better view westward. He then consulted the hand drawn map in the lever arch file, returned again to the road atlas, and then looked all around several more times.

"If we were over there", he said, pointing towards the sinking Sun, "and looking this way", he pointed through the windscreen, then continued with, "and then if we looked back there", he now pointed out of the rear passenger window in the approximate direction of Sandstone. "Then", pausing again, said, "then; I think we'd have two of the reckoning points on the old map, and I think they'd line up".

He then returned his attention to the road atlas, saying, almost excitedly, almost pensive, but with still a kind of considering, calculating, meter to his voice.

"There's a railway line over there".

He pointed again, this time pressing his finger hard against the passenger seat window of the Taunus.

"It loops around from Mount Magnet away to the west, swinging by Sandstone, and edging along The Daggar Hills, off towards Payne's Find, it doesn't go through Coolinar at all".

Wilf looked up from the atlas, and twisted around in his seat so that he could look out of the rear window.

"According to the road atlas there's another road, about two miles over there, it say's here", he gestured to the atlas's open page, "that it's a private track, marked as 'Cutters Lane'".

He put his head down towards the ring bound atlas, struggling to read the small print on the map at that location.

He spoke as he studied.

"It seems to lead no-where except from this square thing, I think it say's 'Abattoir and Stockyards', and goes from there straight to the western and eastern intersection of the main highway, that intersection is called 'Payne's Find Junction', or so it says here".

Wilf looked across at Murray with the same look that some unemployed labourer in Dublin would have had on his face the day he won the Irish Sweeps Stakes.

"That's the place", he said, astounded at his own powers of navigation, "two of the three reckoning points on The Amethyst boys map tally with it, from over there," (he pointed against his window), "it all works out. If there's a bloody big tree of some description along that 'Cutters Lane'", he pointed yet again, westwards out of the car windows, this time through the rear passenger window behind him, and hopefully for the last time, (Murray had thought to himself); then he said, and with something of an air of finality:

"If that tree is there, and if you can see the crucifix on the steeple at Sandstone from it, and if the shape of the Daggar Hills in front of you look like the sharks teeth zig-zags on the photocopy, then all you need to do from there is pace it out and break out the shovels".

"And the Champers!" Murray added.

The two men turned into small boys once again, and whooped and hollered as they passed the signpost indicating that they were entering Coolinar Hill.

Murray suggested that as it was nearly four o'clock, they should find a chip shop or something and get a bite to eat; after all they had not eaten since the giant's breakfast at the B & B. Maybe even get a beer or two, before snooping around to see what they could dig up about the capture of Banjo Anderson.

They already had partial transcripts of the trial, (obtained from the Perth Criminal Records Office), in the 'East Light' file. They had found these for Dilwyn and Ellis after the phone call from Harry 'H' and had sent them back to the Amethyst boys by air mail. They had also collected some newspaper cuttings about it from the Perth Archive, and sent these back as well.

In fact, with the photocopied translation of Sister Lubia's note pad in there, the grey 'East Light' lever arch file had become a fairly thick and very complete document. In fairness to Dilwyn and Ellis, they had done a first class job on pulling all the pieces of information together into one composite document. By the time they had forwarded the completed thing to Wilf and Murray it was in a condition that even the average monkey could follow.

Murray relied on Wilf.

The initial quest for sustenance in Coolinar Hill did not take long; they found a very nice 'sit down' fish and chip parlour almost in the centre of the town's main drag. They parked next door to it; outside a timber and glass shop-fronted store, with a sign on the fascia above the large windows that said, 'Ray Ballous & Son, Gunsmith'.

The fish and chip parlour was replete with fully tiled walls, big stainless steel fryers oozing the thick vapours of bubbling lard, and the subliminal spitting of crisping batter, and moisture being terrified from fresh cut spuds.

It was not yet five p.m. but already the parlour was busy, with most of its plastic topped tables sagging under the weight of greedy guzzlers.

"G'day gents what can I do you for?" shouted a fat man from behind the fryer.

He was as wide as he was tall, and evidently a lover of his own produce.

"Battered Plaice and chips twice please", replied Murray, reading from the chalk board menu on the wall behind the fryers.

The entire menu consisted of either the chosen Plaice and chips, or Cod and chips, or sausage in batter and chips. The Plaice looked the best option, less bones than Cod, and less fatty than the sausages, a display of which sat crinkling, 'like old men's knobs', (Wilf had remarked quietly), behind the glass fronted top shelf of the fryers.

Murray added, after not much deliberation;

"And bread and butter for two and two mugs of tea please, I don't suppose you do beer?"

The fat fryer laughed loudly;

"You suppose right Sport, tea, tea, and more tea, that's all you get in here, along with the best fish and chips in Coolinar Hill of course".

He laughed again.

"The only fish and chips in Coolinar Hill"; piped in one of the two old ladies in blue plastic aprons who were clearly his assistants.

The fat man, whom they supposed to be the owner, told my two Uncles to take a seat, and he would give them a shout when it was ready. They duly sat down, and examined the table for the essentials of fish and chip parlour enjoyment. They were all there, a jug with pairs of cutlery wrapped in paper napkins, a huge white plastic translucent salt cellar about eight inches tall, a small cardboard and plastic pepper pot with all the holes blocked up, (Murray set about freeing these with the tip of his fork), a monster bottle of malt vinegar, and a plastic squeezy tomato shaped thing with a green nozzle containing ketchup. There was a bottle of H.P. Brown Sauce on an adjacent table, which Wilf leaned across and re-located.

"Not from around here then, judging by the accent?"

Enquired an ageing voice from the table behind, both men adjusted themselves to see the speaker.

"No, we're from Perth", replied Murray, but from Wales originally.

"Not Poms' then?" said the old man, and laughed.

"No; Taffs really" retorted Murray, and laughed too.

The old man, who must have been in his eighties, introduced himself as Ray Ballou, from the Gunsmith shop next door.

"I think we met your daughter yesterday", interjected Wilf, "Lovely girl, we met her over at a restaurant in Sandstone, Toraya wasn't it?"

"That's her all right, except she's not my daughter, she's my granddaughter; my son Ray Juniors' girl, he runs the shop with me. Toraya's a smashing kid, too good for round here, sharp as a tack, and twice as pretty she is".

My two uncles nodded in agreement. Ray was tucking into a piece of Place, battered and drenched in vinegar. As far as they could see, he had only one tooth in his mouth, just left of centre and in the bottom.

"So what brings a couple of Taffs' like you to these parts then?"

Ray spoke a sort of idle conversation that only the twighlight years of ones life can engender. A sort of forensic discussion interlaced with incisive insights, pertinent truths and remembrances delicately mixed with absolute bollocks.

Wilf had gone up to the counter and collected the meals and drinks on a large blue plastic tray, which he unloaded onto the table then returned it to the 'Fat Fryer'. Murray continued talking to Old Ray, but was trying not to give too much away, he said, as Wilf returned to take his seat at the table, that he and his brother were writing a book on Australian Crime in the Great Depression, and that they were researching the so-called, 'Brisbane Bandalero's'.

Ray slapped his fork on the table, and smiled, his solitary tooth sparkling against the half eaten, and now fully exposed content of his mouth. He tapped his chest and said with some pride.

"You are looking at the man who made the gun who shot the last of them!"

Suddenly, Murray and Wilf were more interested in 'Old Ray' than in battered their Plaice.

They bought him two more mugs of tea, and over a half hour period he told them everything he knew. All about the shoot out at the Wylachi Stockman Station, all about the dead and wounded cops, all about Stan Wylachi and Dunder McFall, and the capture on Cutters Lane. He told them that the only survivor of the Bandolero's, 'a young feller by the name of Banjo something or another', as he put it, had been taken to New Norcia Police Station, and from there after a local 'quack' had fixed him up, they shipped him off south for a trial.

Ray also said that the police reckoned there were a few others who escaped, and that they kept the search up for a good while after, but no one else was ever found. He told them that 'the cops' had come across other car tracks over at the Wylachi Stockman's hut, and so they thought there could be others that got away.

He took a good large noisy slurp on his tea, then said.

"There was no one else I reckon; I spoke with Stan Wylachi, and he told me there was no room in that old stock truck him and Dunder came across on Cutters Lane, for anyone other than the two fellers in there, and they were shot all to hell and back".

Old Ray paused, and gazed for a moment out of the Fish Parlours window; he scratched his chin, then carried on.

"It was 'Old Man Mal' Wylachi who fired the shot, the one that hit the driver, I saw what it did to the steering wheel after the bullet had gone through the young feller's hand, and that must have been from a good few hundred yards. Only a good Spencer Rifle like the one I worked on could have done that".

Without wanting to give too much away, Murray and Wilf tried to nudge him further, particularly on the ill-gotten gains side of the storey.

"Did the Police ever recover any of the money the Bandolero's stole?"

Asked Murray, attempting to be indifferent.

Failing.

"No way!" said Ray; "That's one of the reasons the cops wanted there to be more of the gang that got away, gave them an excuse for making such a balls up of the shoot out in the first place. They liked everyone to think there was a bloody army out there at the Stockman's Hut, couldn't have got more than a half a dozen blokes in there anyway, bloody place was only the size of good double bed."

He looked into his empty tea mug; Wilf translated the silence and called to the 'Fat Fryer' for three more teas.

Ray continued.

"The money was long gone I reckon before they ever got to Payne's Find. If it was me I'd have split it up all the way across the country, shoved it in odd Banks here and there, bought some houses, some land, left some with mates, that kind of thing".

The new tea's arrived, via my Uncle Wilf; and Ray took a fresh glug.

"No, that loots long gone, forty years gone now, scattered all across the country".

He paused again, and looked out of the window once more.

"That young feller got life at hard labour you know, poor bugger's probably long gone by now, I don't reckon they last long smashing them rocks all day every day. And it was my work on that gun that caused it really".

Murray and Wilf would speak later of how the old man seemed to regret the work he had done on the gun, how he appeared to almost felt guilty about it. It was all my Uncle Murray could do not to blurt out that the 'young feller' as Ray referred to him, had lived as happy as a sand boy in Senghenydd in Old South Wales for the last twenty seven years.

But he bit his tongue, it was nearly seven p.m. now, and the Fish and Chip Parlour had emptied once and was beginning to re-fill. The 'Fat Fryer' was making it clear by body language, that he wanted Ray's and my Uncle's tables vacated; and soon.

Wilf paid for the meals, and also settled up Ray's tab, feeling it was the least that he could do.

As the three of them left the Fish Parlour, Ray stopped, just outside the doorway, he said, grabbing Murray's arm as he did so.

"It was the very day before you know, only one day before the shootout, that I gave that gun back to young Mal Wylachi Junior".

He shook his head and pursed his lips.

"He's 'Old Man Mal's' son alright, ruined this town with that highway of his, all the way up Cutters Lane to Payne's Find Junction. There's only one thing that interests him, and his two boys Hugo and Robbo".

Ray rubbed his ageing thumb against his index and forefinger, in the universal sign language for 'money'. He winked then said;

"Course I can't say too much, his young lad Robbo's got a bit of a sweet spot for our Toraya, but I reckon they're all little shits. Their father Mal. Jnr. drove his missus into an early grave with all his womanising; even today, always searching for something, never seen a man with so much, who's so dissatisfied. He owns half the

383

bloody territory; you can't have a bacon sandwich these days that the Wylachi's are not taking a slice out of".

My Uncles walked with Ray a little way, until they stood on the pavement near their car. Ray said to them, as they both shook his frail but still dexterous hand.

"It was the day she came into my shop. The same day Mal. Jnr. collected his old man's gun, in fact, the same time as I recall".

Ray smiled, a huge smile, a joyful smile crammed with vivid sensuous images that he would never allow to escape from inside his head.

"My God she was gorgeous, pretty as a bunch of spring flowers she was, somewhere in the land between girl and woman I'd have said, somewhere between dreamed perfect and real perfect. She stood there".

He pointed in through the front windows of his shop, paused briefly then carried on remembering.

"She wore a turquoise dress, and the sunlight streaming through the window made her almost naked".

He jarred back to the present with a jolt, for a moment there he was tumbling back forty years.

"Anyway, after that, she was gone, she had a curios ring on her wedding finger, beautiful it was, made of Ironbark, same as 'Old Man Mal's' rifle stock. It had a huge diamond in it, the size of her little finger nail. Don't know who she was, or where she went."

"Did she buy anything when she came into your shop?" asked Wilf, being casual.

"Some shells, that's what most folks buy when they come to my shop, that's it".

My Uncles thanked Ray for all his help and reminiscences, and Ray asked if he'd get a mention in Wilf's book.

He was assured that he would, and if possible it would be on the front page.

Before parting company with him, Murray asked Ray if he could recommend a guest house locally, as time was now getting on, and they would probably now like to stay overnight at Coolinar.

Ray directed them to Old Mrs Armsby's place out towards the old railway tracks. He had said that the food was good, the sheets were clean, and the rates were cheap.

As Murray and Wilf turned to walk away, Ray shouted after them:

"If you get as far as the railway tracks, you've gone too far, but you won't miss it I'm sure; good luck fellers".

He also then turned away, and was gone.

As Murray and Wilf got in the Taunus, and before driving off, they once more, and for a brief and fleeting moment became small boys again.

"It was her!" said Wilf quietly.

"You bet it was!" whispered Murray.

"What a woman!"

The Ironbark strikes again.
Banjo's last taste of freedom.
July 29th 1933.

Sonny McClure winced and cursed at every bump and pothole that the stock truck hit. He had lost all feeling his leg, and every time he loosened the tourniquet a small fountain of blood drenched his trousers and the floor of the drivers cab.

Banjo was fairing no better at the wheel, his right hand was useless and he had tucked it inside his dark shirt. He had had no opportunity yet, to stop and bind it. The shoot out at the Stockman Station was now over an hour old, and the truck was just turning northwards onto Cutters Lane.

They would have to stop, only for a moment, but they would have to stop.

It was now early morning, and the sun was shining a bright searchlight down onto the dusty snaking dryness of Cutters Lane.

There was no longer any darkness to hunt out for cover.

Banjo pulled the truck over in a cloud of the dust. He left the engine running, and it roared like a traction loco now that the exhaust pipe had been knocked off during their escape.

Sonny was fading fast; he had lost a lot of blood, and was slumped against the passenger door. Banjo had parked the truck over to the roadside, (if that was the right word for Cutters Lane back then), at a slight incline and roughly against a scrub embankment. He rummaged through the glove compartment for something to wrap his smashed hand with. He found nothing, so quickly took off his shirt and used it in the form of a bandage and a sling.

He tried to slacken the belt on Sonny's leg to get some blood flow back into the limb for a moment. He jerked the strap away from the buckle, and Sonny groaned as the blood moved downwards again; into, and out of the gunshot thigh.

Using his left hand only, Banjo could no longer re-tighten the belt-strap tourniquet and struggled to stop the blood from spurting around the cab and across his face, into his eyes.

Above the scream of the engine, (which now roared louder and louder as Banjo's foot hit and slipped around the accelerator peddle as he wriggled in his seat, pulling and jerking at the tourniquet belt), Banjo was momentarily oblivious to the world outside the drivers cab of the parked stock truck.

He could not stem the bleeding from Sonny's leg, and the warm red liquid was now swilling over the floor, across the seat, squirting over the dashboard, and still finding its way into Banjo's eyes and mouth.

It is unlikely that he knew anything about or even saw, the heavy Ironbark crutch which swung like a sledge hammer through the open smashed windscreen of the stock truck. It hit Banjo full in the face with an almighty collision, shattering his nose and removing several teeth on its passage.

The crutch had been wielded by Stan Wylachi.

He had cadged a lift to work that morning from Dunder McFall, owner of the Shillington Arms. He had made the arrangements the previous evening while listening to the Rugby with young Mal. Jnr. in Dunders' Bar. The Shillington's owner had mentioned that he was taking an early trip up to Coolinar Hill to collect some kegs of beer, and Stan had asked if Dunder could run him over to The Sainted Tee, as he didn't know what time 'Old Mal', Linus and Toby 'J' would be back.

This arrangement also suited Mal Jnr., as he wanted to wait at the Farmstead in case his Father made contact by phone.

The two men had pulled up behind the battered stock truck in Dunders' not quite as battered pick-up. It had not taken them long to realise what they had stumbled upon.

Banjo had not heard them over the sound of his own engine, and the struggle with the tourniquet had distracted him long enough for Stan, even with his gammy leg, to creep along the driver's side of the truck, clambour up onto the running board, and swing his crutch like a cricket bat into the cab. Banjo crumpled over, and then behind the steering wheel, he was spark unconscious even before his forehead crashed into the side window, ricocheting with the force of Stan's blow.

Dunder had simultaneously crept up the other side of the truck, carrying a half full bottle of lemonade which he kept under his seat in the pick-up. Without even surveying the scene inside the cab, he threw open the passenger side door. The already unconscious body of Sonny McClure cascaded out, slumping headfirst towards the ground. Dunder struck him hard across the forehead with his lemonade bottle. It didn't break, but Dunder felt the skull beneath it fracture under the vicious whack of the impact. He pulled Sonny all the way out, and allowed him to fall, hard to the scrub floor. Dunder dropped the bottle, and reached into the cab, he snatched up the two pistols that were on the seat, and stuffed them into the waistband of his old trousers.

Sonny McClure would bleed to death where he lay, at the side of the stock truck, unconscious on the scrubby ground.

Dunder and Stan dragged Banjo out of the cab and tied him up to the heavy tow ball at the back of the pick-up, using some old ropes which Dunder kept there to lash beer kegs on with.

Every ten or fifteen minutes, or between fags, Stan would give Banjo a stiff, sharp poke in the ribs with the end of his Ironbark crutch, just to make sure he was still alive. Banjo would yelp and groan, then pass out again.

The two old friends would wait until someone else came along Cutters Lane, they would drink what was left of Dunder's lemonade, and smoke roll-ups until that 'someone else' arrived.

The 'someone else' turned out to be the small convoy of Police Cars, motorcycles, and 'Old Man Mal's' trucks; all of which arrived about three hours later.

The end of Murray and Wilf's 'Fishing Trip'.
1972.

The Ford Taunus had pulled onto the north end of Cutters Lane about half an hour earlier; it was not yet nine a.m. They had passed a plethora of roadside signs proclaiming that this was a 'Private Road', and that a maximum speed limit of thirty miles per hour was in force, there were other signs proclaiming that 'Trespassers would be prosecuted', and that there were, '24 Hour Security Patrols'.

The pristine gleaming black tarmac shimmered in the morning temperature gradient; its single white central line scored it like a rapier, dividing south bound and northbound traffic.

The Taunus was travelling behind a gargantuan eighteen wheel stock truck with high slatted metal sides, and containing hundreds of sheep. On its rear end drop down gate was emblazoned the dark blue and sky blue logo that Murray and Wilf had seen so many times this morning, a stylised 'M' and 'W', mirroring together, one letter above the other, set against a white background; below this logo was written, (in dark blue italics), the single phrase:

'Another delivery from Wylachi Herds of Australia. Serving the needs of the Nation.'

Murray and Wilf both recognised the logo, they had seen it in every freezer aisle of every supermarket their wives had ever dragged them around, but they had never paid it any attention. It had just been an abstract label on a leg of lamb, or a rump steak, or a pack of smoked streaky.

Today, it was on every lorry on the road; crammed stock trucks, like warped Noah's Arks heading south towards the abattoir, with squealing pigs, sheep and cattle squeezing their steaming noses through the side gratings, gulping, and snorting in those last precious sniffs of warm air.

On the opposite lane empty trucks headed north for re-loading at Wylachi farms, they were interspersed with articulated refrigerator units, again with the blue logo, this time on their sides, as well as their tails. Presumably these carried the frozen carcasses of the dispatched animals, on their way to Wylachi packing plants or Wylachi canneries for onwards processing and distribution.

As they drove, the two brothers recalled seeing the logo on the bodies of Milk Transport Tankers, Murray had even remembered it on the sides of tins of cat food which my Auntie Flo kept stacked in the utility room at their home in Perth.

"This lot's got its fingers in everything", remarked Wilf as he glanced around them while the vehicle continued south along 'Cutters Lane'.

"You got that right Wilfy boy," replied my Uncle Murray, "I think I've even opened packs of sausages with that badge on them at barbies' before now", he gestured at the logo on the lorry in front of them, and the ones that passed them on the opposite side of the road.

Occasionally, they would see another car, or a motorcycle, even an odd push-bike. They concluded that these must be employees, driving in or out of the abattoir, commencing or ending shifts. They had gleaned from discussions in Sandstone, Payne's Find, and at Coolinar Hill, that the abattoir operation was a twenty four hour a day business, and running non-stop three hundred and sixty five days a year.

Their discussions with Ray Ballou at the Fish and Chip Parlour, and others in the 'Toady Bar and Grill' in Coolinar, (where they had both enjoyed a late night 'T' Bone), had also made it clear that the 'Cutters Lane Abattoir' was not their biggest plant. Apparently the abattoir at Mount Magnet was over five times the size, and that there were at least three more throughout Western Australia, with others in the Northern Territories up towards Darwin, with yet more in Queensland and New South Wales. Ray had also said that he had heard talk that the Wylachi Group were trying to buy a Tuna Fisheries and Canning Company up towards Cairns.

"Look at that!" exclaimed Wilf loudly, and he pressed his index finger smudgeley against the windscreen. Murray leaned across to get a better view, and pulled a face at the fingerprint on the glass.

"What am I looking at?" he asked.

"There!" said Wilf, and stabbed the windscreen again, leaving another smudge.

"Up ahead, about a mile or so!"

Murray squinted and forced himself forward over the steering wheel.

"The bloody tree, up there in the distance!" Wilf continued excitedly, and a little frustrated, "It's got to be the one on the sketched map, the photocopy from Dilwyn and Ellis".

He paused, and slapped Murray on the shoulder, he was smiling broadly now.

"Remember I said that there should be a big tree somewhere on this road?"

He made another smudge on the windscreen, my Uncle Murray tutted, Wilf spoke again.

"Well there it is, that's got to be the starting point, and look at the direction", Wilf was now animated.

"I'll bet you can see that steeple in Sandstone from there".

He waved an arm across Murray's line of sight:

"And those Dagger Hills, they must be right, you can almost see the zig-zag sharks tooth shapes from here".

He slapped Murray's shoulder again, this time laughing loudly; he was a schoolboy once more.

"It's here, I'm telling you, this is the place, it ties up, it's only bloody real, it's only a bloody treasure map".

Murray joined him back in their infancy, and if the car had been bigger they would have surely danced.

The smudges on the windscreen were forgotten.

It took about twenty minutes to arrive at the place where the tree stood. The traffic was slowing, and to their dismay, they could now see that the big, grey, knarled old tree occupied the entirety of a constructed roundabout, with red and white paviours' marking a two metre demarcation line around its circumference.

390

As they approached there was a large square road sign with a stylised roundabout on it with four black lines painted into it, in the form of a Celtic crucifix. The stem of the sign was clearly the road which they were on, then directly over the roundabout it said 'W.H.C. Abattoir Number One', the spurs to the left and right said, respectively, 'Wylachi Livery Stud Farm', to the left, and the one opposite, pointing to the right said, 'The Sainted Tee Sheep lands and Wool Production'.

The Ford Taunus circumnavigated the roundabout at least three times, and the two brothers viewed the tree from every possible perspective. Wilf indicated that Murray should take the road towards the 'Stud Farm'. He did so, and after a hundred yards or so, another roadside sign proclaimed, 'Wylachi Livery and Stud Farm, eight and a half miles'. After ten more minutes of driving, Wilf suggested to Murray that they should pull in.

The road was reasonably quiet with just the occasional pickup truck towing a horse box passing by them. The horse boxes all had the now familiar dark and light blue logos' on them, contrasting against their galvanised shininess. One had pulled up next to them, and a young man had shouted from his cab;

"You fellers o.k.; broken down or something?

Murray had said that they were just letting the engine cool down, as the radiator had an air lock, but that they would be fine in a half hour or so.

"Quick thinking Batman!" Wilf had said, as the horse box tower waved and drove off.

He rummaged on the back seat and recovered the 'East Light' old grey lever arch folder, and turned up the photocopy of the map. He got out of the car, and standing at the roadside, took some rough bearings. He could see the shark tooth hills, and they were dead ringers from this position for the sketched peaks on the map. To his right, and at a considerable distance, he could just make out the tip of the steeple on the Church at Sandstone, which must have been at least twelve or fifteen miles distant.

They could certainly see the tree, which was less than a quarter mile behind them.

Murray had also now got out of the car, and the two men studied the map in the open folder, which they rested on the roof of the Taunus. Wilf did some mental calculations and traced the dotted lines on the map with his index finger.

"If you work on one pace being about three foot long", said Wilf, almost in a thinking out loud kind of way, then if 'X' does mark the spot, then as near as I can figure it, 'X' is about thirty yards the other side of the tree."

He looked up, some despondency crept across his usually, and naturally happy features, as he said, gloomily:

"That puts 'X' smack in the middle of that junction".

He pointed back towards the tree.

"Smack in the middle of that tarmac road that leads to that Wool Factory thing".

He looked directly at Murray; the two small boys had now grown up again.

"We're fucked!" he said, "these roads are non-stop; anything over there is buried forever, lost forever, incarcerated under thousands of tons of stone and tarmac when they laid these fucking, fucking, fucking, fucking, fucking, roads".

My Uncle Wilf's despondency was becoming apparent.

"Shit!" said my Uncle Murray, with (it must be said), remarkable composure, given the circumstances.

"So bloody close too".

Murray concluded with.

Before the brothers could commiserate further with one another, they were disturbed by three shiny new security trucks, with blue lights flashing, pulling up near to them, one behind, one in front and one adjacent.

Each vehicle was white as fresh cleaned teeth, and had the, (by now), ubiquitous two tone blue Wylachi logo on its doors, with the words 'W.H.C. Security' written underneath in non-conformist bright red lettering.

Three burley men emerged from each vehicle, they wore two tone blue uniforms to match the logo, dark blue trousers and sky blue shirts with the logo also embroidered above the breast pocket, the shirts had dark blue epaulettes, and the trousers had a sky blue stripe down the outside of each leg. Gleaming heavy black

392

boots poked out from the trouser ends, and a long black truncheon hung from each thick belt.

There was an old Aborigine, (over sixty year's old and nudging retirement Murray guessed mentally), standing next to the driver's door of the adjacent truck, and was speaking into a hand held walkie-talkie thing with a curly black lead.

"We'll bring them right over Sir".

Wilf heard him say.

The man walked over to my Uncles, and told Wilf to get in the truck at the rear of the Taunus, and Murray to get in the one parked at the front.

Murray noticed his name badge, black plastic with white inset lettering, it said, 'Senior Security Supervisor Linus Sabak'.

Within moments, and brooking no argument, the Security men had placed my Uncles in the trucks, with two guards and a driver to accompany each of them, and were turning left at the roundabout by the old tree, and heading south on Cutters Lane towards the main gates of the abattoir.

One of the other officers from Sabak's truck, had sat in the driver's seat of the Taunus, turned it around and followed behind. It took another fifteen or twenty minutes before they were in front of the abattoir, and at the end of 'Cutters Lane'.

At the gates of the abattoir, Linus Sabak, waved at the guards in the security lodge, and the red and white banded barriers rose gracefully.

The complex was immense, office blocks to left and right, huge car parks containing queue's of animal filled lorries, other queues of refrigerated lorries pulling off or parking up, with security guards ticking off paperwork and checking the vehicles in and out, then mulling back and forth to the security lodge and filing out yet more paperwork, and stamping passes, and buzzing between the vehicles, getting each one in and out as quickly and efficiently as possible. Sticking different coloured numbered labels on each vehicles windscreen's, each sticker overlaying many previous stickers, from innumerable previous visits.

The security trucks passed a petrol station area where the lorries were tanked up, more security guards processed the re-fuelling stickers, and then tore off the confirmation slips as the attendants dealt with each vehicles fuel allocation. Re-fuelling tankers parked at the end of the filling area, waiting to unload their cargos into the underground tanks, waiting for a security guard to put a tick and their initials in the right box on their delivery tickets.

After the fuelling station, the Security trucks swung right around a large hanger like building with 'Freezer Compound Number 2' written on a sign above its sliding metal doors.

They then passed several buildings with men in white hats and overalls and aprons walking between them. The men's aprons and white wellingtons were blood splattered, and from their waist belts hung monstrous looking knives and sharpening irons, each man wore what looked like a chain mail gauntlet.

They must have driven by at least eight such buildings, each of which had a large sign on its gable end, saying 'Slaughter House', every description followed by a number.

Outside number '5', the trucks, (followed by the Ford Taunus), drew to a halt. Between this, and the adjacent building, 'Slaughter House 6', there nestled a low level collection of small portacabin type offices, all linked up by adjoining doors and corridors, a real hotchpotch.

There was a metallic pale blue Rolls-Royce parked in a white lined space outside the offices main entrance, a gold and black Jaguar snuggled next to it, with a pair of bright red MGB GT's, in spaces at the far end.

Other cars filled spaces opposite and around the corner.

Murray and Wilf were ushered through the entrance doors, into a small reception area, where a woman, (they later found to be Mrs. Hulme), offered them tea or coffee, Wilf declined but Murray asked for a coffee, white with two sugars. The woman smiled affably, and said she would bring it to the meeting room.

The brothers were guided by Linus Sabak, and three of the Security guards, down an adjacent corridor, and into a utilitarian room at the far end.

The room contained cheap plastic chairs and some old Formica topped tables, all pushed together to form one big table. All of the tables were topped in slightly different coloured laminates, and all clearly of different ages, and different manufacture, which made the whole room look somewhat makeshift.

Linus directed them inside, and told his security guards to wait outside in the corridor, he told my uncles to take a seat each, and make themselves comfortable.

394

Then to make this request absolutely impossible, he then took a seat directly opposite them, and glared at them with some menace and contempt.

Mrs. Hulme arrived with Murray's coffee, and a plate of chocolate digestives.

Almost simultaneously two men, well dressed, and both in their fifties came in, one in his late fifties, the other in his early fifties.

The elder of the men told Linus Sabak to leave, and he did so without discussion; Mrs. Hulme placed a cork coaster from a side table under Murray's coffee mug, then she too left the room.

The two men sat at the far end of the table. The younger man had the grey lever arch file open on the table in front of him, and was reading it, making occasional notes in it with an expensive looking fountain pen, and thumbing quickly through the pages. Occasionally he would lean towards the older man, and whisper in his ear, cupping his hand as he did so. The older man remained impassive.

Wilf looked hot, and was sweating; Murray drank his coffee, and finished off all of the chocolate digestives.

After about twenty minutes, or possibly more, the younger man asked:

"Which one of you pair is Murray and which is Wilf?"

The brothers introduced themselves.

The other two men did not.

"Can you both read?"

The younger man asked further of them.

Murray and Wilf both confirmed their literacy.

Then the younger inquisitor asked why then, had they ignored the signs which clearly said, 'Private Road', and the like.

There was silence.

The younger man went on:

"Do you know what the penalty is in this State for trespass? We have already contacted the Police at New Norcia, who will be here within the hour".

Wilf protested their innocence, but was silenced by an authoritative wave of the younger man's hand.

"Your car will be impounded and crushed"

Then, almost as an afterthought, he asked, looking up inquisitorially:

"You're not animal rights protesters are you?"

As if on cue, Linus Sabak knocked the door and poked his head around, and asked for the younger man to step outside for a moment. He did so; the older man remained insitu, and said nothing, nor moved, nor blinked for several long seconds.

The younger man returned.

"Apparently you've been asking questions locally about this establishment; there a several people who will provide statements".

He looked hard at each of the brothers in turn, and then said.

"The penalty for criminal damage and attempted murder are extremely harsh gentlemen. You animal rights protesters are after all exactly that. Criminals, I mean".

The man sat down; as he did so he said:

"Mr. Sabak; our Head of Security, informs me that he has found two five gallon jerry cans of petrol in the back of your car."

The man paused, probably for effect, then continued with:

"Do you have any idea how much damage, and the potential loss of life or injury that the explosion of ten gallons of petrol could cause in an establishment such as this?"

Murray had by now begun to sweat as much as Wilf, and both of them tried to explain it was just spare fuel for their fishing trip.

There was no reply.

The younger man spent the next half an hour berating the brothers and giving them an unsolicited dissertation on the moral imperfection of the Animal Rights Movement.

Eventually Linus Sabak returned to the office door, and said that the New Norcia Police had arrived.

The officers spoke with the younger man for several long minutes in the corridor. There were three of them, one with Sergeants stripes on the sleeve of his brown and cream uniform. They all carried guns, and looked like they had each suffered a humour and compassion by-pass.

The two brothers were about to suffer and spend the worst forty eight hours of their lives.

They were escorted out of the room and along the corridor.

The 'East Light' lever arch folder stayed on the table in the meeting room.

At New Norcia Police Station they were separated, and each was interrogated as Animal Rights Agitators. They were threatened with charges of 'Planning Mayhem and Destruction', 'Criminal Damage', and, as the younger man said earlier, even 'Attempted Murder'.

During the two days and nights, the two brothers received no food, no sleep, and only occasional cups of tea, which tasted of piss.

They were told after about forty five hours, that they were to be charged with 'Trespass', 'Planning Mayhem', and 'Attempted Murder', and that they were to be transferred to Adelaide Prison the following day to be 'Remanded in Custody'.

Three hours later, they were each conveyed from their respective cells, (in handcuffs), into the charge room, (for that was what it said on the door). They now met each other again for the first time in two days.

They both looked like shit.

The Police Sergeant told them to take a seat, and an armed Constable stood behind each of them. He then proceeded, (with some officialdom), to read the charges. The two brothers, my Uncles, were wide eyed, red eyed, unshaven, dirty, sweaty, still handcuffed, and justifiably terrified.

The Police Sergeant said that he would now phone for a duty solicitor to come and speak with them before they were transported to Adelaide. The Sergeant explained that the 'Paddy-Wagon' as he called it was, 'parked up out back'.

At that moment the ominous and solitary black phone on the Sergeants desk began to ring. He picked it up, and with not many words, other than 'Yes', 'No' and 'If you're certain?' he replaced the receiver.

He breathed out a huge sigh, and threw his pen angrily on the desk top.

"That was Mr. Suda-Iwo, the solicitor for the Wylachi Herds Group of Companies".

He paused, clearly annoyed, then leaned forward and said through gritted teeth, and in a horrible grunting sort of voice.

"They want to drop all charges. You're free to go".

He turned to one of the Constables.

"Get their car around, and get them out of here".

Then he turned back to Murray and Wilf, who still sat there in their handcuffs. He said:

"If I ever see either of you pair up here again, I won't pay any attention to Mr. Suda-Iwo or whatever his fucking name is next time. You've got my word I'll have you in Adelaide nick before you can tell me to go and fuck myself, I've got a cabinet full of unsolved shit filled crime files, and I can put your names on any of them I choose!"

He turned to the remaining Constable and said, almost screaming now with rage.

"Get these pair of cunts out of here, and keep them company with a squad car as far as the Northern Highway, and make sure they get on it, and point them towards Perth".

As they left the 'Charge Room', Sergeant Waldo Summersby picked up the black phone, and kicked the door shut with his boot as he did so.

Somewhere in the English Channel,
H.M.A.S. Waterhen,
February 1945.

The Australian sailor lay on the small bed in sick bay with a huge puddle of blood on the floor beneath him. The medical orderly, (for they had no doctor on board), had sent word to Captain Greener Hawks that the man would die.

The Captain entered the sick bay with his cap under his arm.

The orderly explained, (as quietly as he could), that the piece of shrapnel had cut a gaping swathe across the ratings stomach and had removed three quarters of his liver in the process.

"There's nothing we can do Sir", said the orderly.

The medical orderly, who was really a seaman with two stripes known affectionately on board as 'Doc', (with not much invention), told the acting Captain that the injured sailor was in extreme pain, and that he had been dosed up with just enough morphine to allow him to remain barely conscious.

Doc continued whispering as quietly as he could, explaining that the man was insistent on speaking with the Captain.

Captain Hawks had known the wounded man since the days aboard the old Iron Knight, he had been a 'jib-operator' on the deck crane, and had spent time with him in the lifeboat.

His name was Yarris Joseph, and had become 'Able Seaman Akpaganathos' when he had been seconded at Captain Tyndale's request into the Royal Australian Navy, and had secured a posting aboard the H.M.A.S. Waterhen.

Today, as for the last six months, The Waterhen had been on duty assigned to 'Operation Gooseberry', the sinking of old freighter ships, (vessels which were long past their serviceable condition), in locations along the Normandy coast to form breakwaters and temporary jetty's. The ships were being sunk, one on top of the other, where Royal Engineers filled them with stone or concrete.

They were turned into safe harbours.

Captain Greener Hawks had collected the rusted old steamer 'West Honiker' from Lisbon, as ordered, (and as he had collected many old hulks from various ports over the last months). He had taken her in tow to the Normandy coast, where she had been anchored in the designated position, and shelled by H.M.S. Belfast, and the U.S.S. Charleston until sunk.

The rating in the sick bay cot was in clear and substantial pain. His mid section was wrapped tight in a thick swaddling of bandage, through which the blood still soaked, and dripped to the deck plates.

"I've given him all the morphine I can Sir; he's getting saline, but it's a losing battle; he keeps saying he just needs to see you, wouldn't take no for an answer", the orderley whispered again, somewhat apologetically.

"No problem Doc", replied Greener Hawks, then, even quieter he asked in return, "Does he know how badly injured he is?"

The orderly replied that he must do, and that, "The wound very near chopped him in two, the piece of shrapnel was as big as a dustbin".

"Thanks Doc", Greener whispered, and touched Doc on the arm before asking;

"How long has he got?"

Doc considered the question, but not for long, and then replied:

"Left to his own devices maybe an hour, an hour in bloody agony, sweating and screaming".

'Doc' looked deep into Greener's eyes, then added.

"Left to MY devices, about two minutes, both of those minutes in peace and quiet with the help of five or six ampoules of morphine".

Captain Greener Hawks returned the medical orderly's gaze.

"Understood!"

He said, and moved towards the cot.

As Greener Hawks stood next to the bed, the orderly at his shoulder, his feet slipping on the blood-soaked deck plates, he took the ratings hand, and said simply.

"You wanted to see me Jo: what can I do for you?"

Seaman Akpaganathos gripped his Captains hand, his eyes wide, his teeth gritted and his face thick with dirty sweat.

Without raising his head, the rating said, almost at a level which was inaudible; something. Greener Hawks leaned towards him, placing his ear next to the man's quivering lips.

"Say again Jo, I'm sorry but I can't hear you".

The rating tried again.

"I've got no relatives, my parents are both dead, I've never married, got no kids, no one to tell".

His hand again squeezed at Greener's.

"You must promise me you'll do as I ask now!"

Greener replied that he would do his best, but that he couldn't promise until he knew what Jo Akpaganathos wanted.

"Promise! No conditions, you must promise me now!"

Greener raised his head and looked the dyeing man in the eyes. He could not, nor would not refuse.

"I promise Jo, whatever it is, I promise".

He returned his ear to Jo's lips, and listened intently, for at least five minutes.

Captain Hawks rose up, still holding Jo's hand, and said.

"I understand Jo, you can consider it done, and for what it's worth, it'll be my honour".

He turned to Doc, and said, more in the fashion of an order than discussion.

"This man needs morphine Doc; and he needs it now".

Captain Greener Hawks, replaced his cap on his head, and left the sick-bay. As he did so, he stopped a rating in the companionway outside, and told him to find Stoko, and bring him to the Captains quarters. On his own journey back to his quarters, Greener Hawks swung by the bunk area of the lower ranks, and found the locker of Able Seaman Yarris Joseph Akpaganathos. He removed its entire contents, along with his own hat from his head, and placed the former within the latter, and carried it back to his cabin.

In the ships log, (as requested by Jo Akpaganathos), he recorded the unfortunate incident of the explosion under shelling of the 'West Honiker', and the sad death of Ships Mechanic and Boilerman, Prisoner number 89855812 on secondment from the Western Australian Prison Service. Every other detail, except the name of the dead man was entered with religious accuracy, and Military scrupulousness.

There was a knock at the door.

"Enter", the Captain shouted.

Stoko stepped inside, and saluted. He wore his usual blue oily boiler suit, and heavy boots. As ever his hands and face were dirty.

Captain Hawks offered him a seat, and a Scotch, both of which he accepted.

"Jo Akpaganathos is dead", he said as he poured the drinks, he kept all emotion out of his voice, and handed Stoko his drink.

Both men took a huge gulp, and Greener topped up their glasses before taking his seat behind his desk.

"Jo had no next of kin, no one to write to, no one to miss him".

He took another large swig of his Scotch, and looked across the desk to the man opposite him. Stoko looked to be in his mid forties, and was lean and fit, but he could have been ten years older. Jo Akpaganathos had been thirty eight. As Greener

401

studied his guest, he concluded that the age was acceptable and close enough. He said simply:

"It's you lying on the bed down in sick-bay, you, Prisoner number 89855812, you are dead. From today you are Jo Akpaganathos".

Greener rummaged about his desk and collected up some papers which he waved towards Stoko, who still sat silently, sipping at his Scotch.

"These orders send us to the port of Cardiff to collect an old clunker called 'The Marquis Of Bute', we're to tow her to Le Havre where she will be sunk as part of Operation Gooseberry; after that, we're instructed to make all speed back to Port Keats, and home to Oz for decommissioning".

Captain Hawks rose from his seat and walked around his cabin and collected up the bottle of Scotch, he re-filled both their glasses once more. Then, sitting down again; he added:

"If I were you, I'd get off at Cardiff; I'll take you ashore with me when I collect the paperwork for the 'Marquis of Bute'. We'll be there for a day or so, getting re-fuelled and re-provisioned. It'll be a good two months or so before we dock back at Port Keats. When we get there I'll complete the paperwork for Jo Akpaganathos to say he was discharged there. No body will be any the wiser. I'll let your mates on board in on some of the tale, and they can cover things. There's plenty of new men on board which will add to the confusion, and you keep yourself to yourself anyway. So no real problem".

Greener took another huge mouthful of Scotch. He was a first class officer, and this was against the rules, and he was a rules kind of man. But he had given his word, and he knew that if Captain Tynsdale had still been aboard, then he too would have acceded to Able Seaman Akpaganathos' last wish.

"We're burying you in the morning Stoko, over the side as YOU requested. We'll be in Cardiff in three days time, get your kit ready, and you'll need these".

The Captain handed Stoko the bundle of documents he had collected earlier from the ratings locker.

"This is you now Jo", he said, "Make your namesake proud of you, no slipping back, it would be very embarrassing for all of us if anyone ever found out you were still alive; understand?".

Jo nodded, rose, and finished his Scotch, at the door of the cabin he stopped, and turned. He said:

"Thank you Captain Hawks, it's been a privilege to serve with you and Captain Tynsdale. I promise you will never hear of me again".

Greener Hawks rose to his feet as well, and also drained his glass, he walked over to Jo and held out his hand, which Jo took appreciatively.

"It's been a pleasure and an honour for me too Jo, and I'm sure I speak for Captain Tynsdale as well; make a quiet life for yourself".

Greener squeezed Jo's arm and smiled broadly. Jo left the quarters, truly a new man.

"And don't forget that old biscuit tin when you leave", said Greener as he closed the door, "I won't be able to post it on to you".

The funeral at sea, (at the dead man's request), was a solemn, but brief occasion, with Captain Hawks reading the lesson. Stoko's body was slid into the English Channel from beneath an Australian flag. The sea was calm, and the splash was gentle. The crew sang 'Waltzing Matilda', and then went back about their duties.

As Captain Hawks had said, the port of Cardiff came along in a few days, and The H.M.A.S. Waterhen left with one more rusting hulk in tow astern, and one less mechanic in her engine room.

The former inhabitants of the lifeboat from the old Iron Knight, (those who had found themselves aboard the Waterhen), had organised a secret a whip-round, and raised over a hundred quid, in a mixture of Ozzy Dollars, British Pounds, and a mish mash of Canadian and Yank currency. 'Doc' had supervised it, after the real Jo Akpaganathos had repeated his last desires to him, and had made him promise too; just to make sure the Captain honoured his word. 'Doc', (thankfully), had not needed to enforce his own promise, and had donated a good woollen jacket, a packet of Players cigarettes and a crisp ten dollar bill to Jo's 'escape fund' as he had termed it.

As the man in the thick coat walked out of the dock gates into the rain soaked darkness of Cardiff's West Bute Street, he saw the railway station opposite.

At one of its platforms was a small green steam locomotive puffing and whistling in exultation, behind it sat three carriages in the cream and brown livery of the 'Great Western Railway Company'. The sign above the stations entrance gates said, again in cream and brown, 'Butetown'.

"Where does this train go?" asked Jo of the windswept Station Master.

"Up the Rhymney Valley", the man said, his lantern swinging in his hand, "Stopping at Cardiff Central, Queen Street, Heath Park, Cefn Onn, Llanishen, Caerphilly, Aber Junction, and Abertridwr".

The man smiled, a wide welcoming smile, then added.

"If you need to go any further, you'll have to catch a bus from Abertridwr up to Senghenydd, apart from the road to Lady Windsor Colliery, that's where the world ends. Senghenydd I mean".

The man laughed loudly.

"Sounds perfect!" said Jo and laughed as well.

He bought a single ticket.

Sydney,
New South Wales, Australia.
January 15th to 18th 2013.

The Virgin Australia Airlines 747 Jumbo, touched down at 8.48 a.m. local time at Sydney's Kinsford Smith Airport. Aboard, comfortable in their business class seats, and well rested after their long journey from London Heathrow, was my Father, my Uncle Bryn, and Johnny Spinks, (Spinksy).

The three men were all in their late seventies or had even just touched eighty. The journey was always destined to be arduous for three such senior citizens, but their unexpected benefactor had provided for their comforts as best as could be expected. Their flight had been luxurious, and there had even been a British Doctor and a Nurse provided for them, for the journey from London to Sydney.

Doctor Lau and Nurse Traynor had met the three men at the V.I.P. Lounge at Heathrow, where they had been introduced by Neville Cartajhena, the solicitor from Mundle Specter-Wilde & Company, the man who had made the original approaches.

Neville had also travelled with them to Sydney, and, (so he had informed them), was responsible for, 'all the arrangements', as he put it.

After landing and disembarkation, the small group were ushered through passport control, by four well dressed, and sunglass clad thick set, very tall men, who had met them at the terminus. The most senior of the men introduced himself as Dean Amberkan, of the New South Wales Personal Security Company, (a subsidiary of W.H.S. Group). He provided Neville with some identification papers, which Neville then checked against some documents he had in his briefcase.

Neville Cartajhena was a smart young man, no more than thirty five, who looked like he had been born in a three piece suit and black rimmed glasses. He was about as boring as they came, but affable enough, and extremely efficient. My Father, My Uncle Bryn and Spinksy looked exactly how elderly blokes in foreign countries are supposed to look, light coloured 'slacks' as my Father calls them, stripy polo shirts, thin zip up lightweight bomber jackets, (windcheaters, either light blue or buff, generally), and sandals with socks.

Neville had all their passports, flight tickets, hotel reservations and the like, snuggled in his brown soft leather briefcase, which never left his side. The only thing the three senior citizens were apparently responsible for, was a long thin white envelope each, (of very thick and expensive paper), which Neville had handed out once they were settled down on the aeroplane before take off from Heathrow. All of them had placed their individual envelope in the respective inside pockets of their 'windcheaters', (another one of my Fathers expressions).

The envelopes had each contained ten thousand Australian Dollars; all of it in cash.

Outside the main exit doors of the airport concourse, there were three large black Bentley limousines, each parked against the kerb, and each with a uniformed female Chauffeuse standing by, and holding open the rear doors.

Doctor Lau and Nurse Traynor were escorted to the rear-most car by one of the big smart security men, while Dean Amberkan gestured to the three old gents that they should get into the centre car, along with Neville. He then instructed that one security man should ride in the front passenger seat of Doctor Lau's car, and that two of his men should ride in the rear of the front car, and that he would sit 'up front' in the middle car.

The journey to the Sydney Park Hyatt was as smooth as silk, and the route had evidently been chosen to show off the city to its absolute best. The five star service continued all the way to the men's suite, which had three individual bedrooms and bathrooms, and a spectacular view from 'The Rocks' across the bay to the Opera House.

Doctor Lau and Nurse Traynor occupied the suite to the left, and Neville must have drawn the short straw as he had a single room to the right.

It was about 10.30 a.m. by the time Neville had checked everyone in, and had organised hotel staff to get everything packed away.

Dean Amberkan informed them that he and one of his men were staying at the room directly across the hallway. He gave each of the men, Doctor Lau, and Neville, an 'I-phone', and told them that the phones had been voice programmed, and if they just said, 'Dean Amberkan' into the microphone, each 'I-phone' would automatically dial him.

He further explained that two of the limousines and their Chauffeuses would be on permanent station at the Hotels forecourt. And, that if anyone wanted to go anywhere they need only pick up the room phone, (he gestured to it, as if no one had ever seen a phone before), and inform reception, who would then have one of the cars brought up to front the doors.

Room service then turned up with a ridiculous amount of food, which two waiters set about distributing on the huge dining table in the old men's suite. They unanimously agreed, that, as days went, today was a 'good un'.

Two hours later My Uncle Murray, and his brother Wilf landed at the same airport, on an internal Quantas flight from Perth, Western Australia. They too had unexpected envelopes in their pockets.

Their version of Neville Cartajhena was an Australian solicitor from Fremantle called Suzie Cabot-Fitzgerald, she was a female Neville. They also had medical staff, supplied in the form of Doctor Zubic, an obese Eastern European, and his anorexic Nursing assistant, Nurse Spotkins.

When they were checked in, they too were given equally opulent suites and rooms further down the corridor, and 'I-phones' from Dean Amberkan.

My Father noted later, that their limousines were maroon, as opposed to the black ones provided to my Dad's party.

Today was Thursday, and Dean Amberkan had explained that everyone could do as they wished, but that a full tour of the city had been arranged for Friday if they wanted to partake. This would include a guided private viewing of the Opera House, and luncheon on a boat trip around the harbour.

As for today they could just, 'chill out' as he said, and let the jet lag settle down.

Finally, Dean Amberkan explained that a 10.00.a.m. meeting had been arranged for them all for Saturday morning, at the offices of 'Mimex, Fuller, Mimex Law' at the Chifley Tower in the city centre. He said that the limousines would collect them all at 9.30 a.m. from the hotel reception lounge.

The gentleman they were to meet with was Mr Ambrose Suda-Iwo, the Senior Partner in the firm.

As he left the suite, he turned, as if just remembering something, and said;

"And don't forget, whatever you need, drinks, more room service", he waved a casual finger at the waiters still decorating the dining table, "just charge it to the suite, the W.H.S. Group of Companies are picking up all your expenses", he waved both hands slowly in front of him, as if he were patting the air to demonstrate this limitless bounty.

He then turned to the others in the suite, and continued, "that goes for you too Mr. Cartajhena, and you Doctor Lau and of course you Nurse Traynor". Dean Amberkan smiled at them all with glistening white teeth and a time perfected tan. His accent was not heavy, and for such a large, and obviously powerful man his voice was somehow most soothing.

Nurse Traynor had already fallen in love with Mr Amberkan, and in reality, who could blame her.

The rest of the day, and all of the next flashed by in a mixture of heady excess with the seemingly un-ending consumption of ice cold lager, rich red wine, and broiled and fried shellfish of various colours and description; each portion being the size of the average family dog.

They had all taken the pre-arranged tours and the boat trip, and had enjoyed every hurtling second. My Father, Spinksy and my Uncle Bryn reminisced at every opportunity with Murray and Wilf, and crammed the half century since they had last seen each other, into less than fifty hours.

Saturday morning arrived all too quickly.

The limousines, with their usual efficiency, delivered the five men at 9.55 a.m. to the huge glass revolving entrance doors of the Chifley Tower. Dean Amberkan and his men escorted them, and their two solicitor accompanists, inside to the deliberately imposing marble and bronze atrium. The respective medical teams had been asked to wait in the limousines, but to ensure they had their I-phones turned on.

Above the central reception island, (where three black men in green blazers and white shirts, each with a crisp teal coloured tie, busied themselves); there loomed a ridiculously large plasma display screen. It was the sort of screen one sees at departure halls in airports, or railway stations. On it were displayed the illustrious business residents of this prestigious address.

The screen told everyone who traversed the travertine floor, (from the electronic revolving entrance doors, to the bronzed and gleaming reception island), it told them that floors eighteen to twenty were occupied by 'Mimex, Fuller, Mimex Law'.

After every floor entry for the firm, (displayed on the screen), there followed an impressive list of solicitors names, each with long abbreviations of accreditations after their initials and surnames. There were smaller font bracketed descriptions next to each name, indicating their specialisms.

On the display for the twentieth floor, the first name indicated, and placed strategically, next to the firm title, was Mr Ambrose Suda-Iwo. In turn, and in brackets after his name, and after a long list of impressive letters; the screen said, (in red italics):

'Senior Partner, and Head of Corporate'.

Neville Cartajhena noted that Mr. Suda-Iwo was the only person on the 'Mimex, Fuller, Mimex Law' section of the screen, whose Christian name was displayed, everyone else just had an initial. This re-enforced the impression he had formed during the initial meeting with Dean Amberkan, concerning the elevated status of Mr. Ambrose Suda-Iwo.

As he glanced across at his Australian counterpart Suzie Cabot-Fitzgerald, Neville observed from her body language, (and her own speed read of the display screen, which he noted as she glanced upwards), that she too shared his impression of Mr. Suda-Iwo.

He also, incidentally, noted that Miss Cabot-Fitzgerald, (with no engagement or wedding ring, and in her mid-thirties), looked extremely attractive this morning, in her rather fetching, and figure hugging peach coloured two piece business suit, with pencil skirt and matching stilettos.

Neville found himself, (for a brief instant), musing as to which perfume she wore, the odour from which he had captured a brief waft of, as they came through the revolving door. He wondered whether her long shoulder length auburn hair was a natural colour, or applied. Her glasses were black framed, rectangular and neat, similar to his own he mentally observed.

Her briefcase was soft pig-skin, and as full as his.

Dean Amberkan instructed his three men to remain in the entrance atrium foyer, and to await their return. He gestured to the numerous small clusters of brown leather and bronze chairs which proliferated in the foyer, each cluster surrounding a small pale grey, circular polished wood, (coffee type) table of thinly slatted Ironbark.

As the burnished bronze doors of the lift car swished open on the twentieth floor, they were greeted by a smart, black clad woman in her early fifties. She knew by name each of the five men, and Neville Cartajhena and Suzie Cabot-Fitzgerald.

She greeted each of them personally.

The woman had clearly been well briefed, and had done her homework. She ushered everyone out of the lift, but raised a polite hand in front of Dean Amberkan, which she allowed to come to rest on his granite bicep.

"If you could possibly wait here Mr. Amberkan", the woman gestured to a pearlite cream leather settee, which was placed in the corridor, in front of the lift doors; "I'll have some coffee and juice sent out for you".

Dean Amberkan nodded, and took his seat with no further discussion.

As the group walked along the wide corridor, turning right every twenty or thirty yards or so; the woman pointed, almost randomly at small portraits hung on the expensively papered walls, introducing each, as 'Partners' or 'Associates'. She had introduced herself as Nicola Haye Sant, 'Associate Partner in Corporate'. She had made the introduction as she walked passed her own small portrait.

Her accent told Neville that she was French, but had lived in Australia for some considerable time.

At the eventual end of the corridor, they came to a pair of double doors, very dark, very smooth, and very modern. She pushed them open without knocking.

Inside was a monstrously large, long and narrow boardroom table, which matched the doors in its minimalist simplicity. Around it, were parked at least two dozen rich red leather chairs with high backs and dark wooden arms, again matching the doors and table top.

The one wall, opposite the entrance doors, was glass, and bronze tinted; in keeping with the buildings architecture and affording a panoramic view across, and down upon, the cityscape stretching out twenty storeys below them.

At the head of the table and to their right, sat a man in a three piece, blue pin striped suit, with a white shirt with a horrible orange tie. As they entered he stood up, the laboured rising of a man in his eighties, he removed his half moon spectacles as he rose, placing them on the table in front of him, on top of a small collection of blue files, and an aging 'East Light' grey, A4 lever arch folder.

Nicola Haye Sant introduced the elderly man as Ambrose Suda-Iwo, Senior Partner. As if on cue, and from a small side door, two young ladies in green jackets, (similar to the ones worn by the black men on the foyer reception island), came into the room and placed trays of fresh orange juice, tea and coffee, cups, saucers, small jugs of cream, and pastries on the table. They smiled politely as they did so. As they left, Nicola asked them to take some coffee and orange juice out to Mr Amberkan who had remained seated near the lifts.

Ambrose Suda-Iwo shook each mans hand personally, and kissed the back of Suzie Cabot-Fitzgerald's. A gesture she seemed not wholly happy with. Neville noted the wry smile from Nicola Haye Sant, and realised it was Mr Suda-Iwo's way of putting people off-guard or on the wrong foot. 'He's a clever old duffer', Neville thought to himself.

"Shall I be Mother?" asked Nicola, as she poured the teas and coffees, asking each person for their preferences as she went.

"Please, make yourselves comfortable", said Mr. Suda-Iwo, in a very broad 'Ozzy' twang.

Cultivated 'mateyness' thought Neville; 'definitely a clever old duffer'.

Everyone took a seat, my Father, Uncle Bryn, Spinksy, Murray and Wilf, on one side of the table facing the glass wall, and Nicola, Neville and Suzie on the other, with Mr Suda-Iwo resuming his position at the head of the table.

He stood in front of his chair.

Suda-Iwo was smart, his grey hair was thick, and combed back exposing a tanned but creased forehead. His features were wrinkled, and he made some attempt to hide them with a well trimmed and tailored beard and moustache. There was a sniff of vanity about him. His suit was not 'off the peg', and the watch which squinted from his shirt cuff was a gleaming, wafer thin, very expensive 'Raymond Weil'. The fountain pen which lay on the table in front of him was a 'Mont Blanc', cut from translucent blue crystal.

His after shave only hinted at the air in the room.

'Gautier', Neville thought.

"I suppose you're all wondering why you're here?" Mr. Suda-Iwo asked initially.

No one spoke.

He turned to Murray and Wilf, and said, picking up the old grey 'East Light' folder as he looked at them:

"The last time you gentlemen saw this file was July the fourth 1972, at the Cutters Lane Abattoir Buildings of the 'Wylachi Herds Meat Packaging Corporation', as it was then, I believe you were planning a fishing trip up towards Mount Magnet?"

He smiled, lightly.

He put the file back on the table and slid it towards my Uncle Murray. He pointed at it, and said as he did so;

"That file has been in my safe, and has moved with me to every office I've ever occupied from that day to this."

Murray and Wilf opened the file.

Their faces indicated the recognition, and they both looked towards my Father, my Uncle Bryn, and Spinksy.

Murray said simply:

"Stalin!"

The memories cascaded back to each of the old men, their eyes widened, some scratched their heads, some opened their mouths as if to speak, but none of them did.

Ambrose Suda-Iwo smiled, resumed his seat, and leaned back in the chair.

He carried on:

"I'm pleased you remember gentlemen, it saves me considerable time".

He tapped a finger on the other files on the table, the pile of blue cardboard files.

"These!"

He tapped again.

"These, are your lives; I've got a file here for you Harry", he nodded at my Dad, "One for you Mr. Spinx, and one for you Bryn".

He nodded at each in turn.

"And not forgetting you Murray, and you Wilf".

Mr. Suda-Iwo then began moving the blue files around the table top, reading aloud the small white label with each man's name on as he went, sliding them across to each of the men, distributing them.

He then began reading off the names on the other blue files which sat in front of him. Shuffling and moving them around like a deck of cards.

"Maldwyn Somerset; Dilwyn Amethyst, Ellis Amethyst, Bethany Harrington, Eloise Van Hoost, Gustav Amberkan, Gilbert Van Der Faisey, Frank Summersby, Fuzzy Dolenz, Iestyn Tynsdale, Alex 'Greener' Hawk, Arthur Du-Pont, Iolo

Pugsley, The Van Der Kyper brothers, Captain Karem Tortruk, Major Switch-Rillington, Sister Lubia…. blah, blah, blah, the list goes on".

He let the last blue file he had picked up flop onto the table top.

"You gentlemen; and your associates back there in 'The Old South Wales'".

He pulled a bit of a face, and waved a thumb over his shoulder, to suggest distance.

"Have cost my client hundreds of thousands of dollars over the years".

He leaned back again in his chair, and paused. After a short while, he erupted into deep exploding laughter.

He said loudly, and with good humour:

"Mind you, most of those hundreds of thousands of dollars came to me, so I can't really grizzle too much".

The old men, and the two solicitors remained silent. Mr. Suda-Iwo took a large swig of his coffee, cleared his throat and continued.

"The thickest blue file on this matter is that one", he pointed a crinkly old finger towards the opposite end of the table.

There, alone at the far end, sat a scruffy dog-eared cardboard file of faded pale blue. The old men, Neville and Suzie turned their heads and stared at it.

Mr. Suda-Iwo spoke again.

"The names on the front of that file say 'Banjo Anderson, Itzak Anderson, Itzak Androskewowicsz, Yuris Pavel Androskewowicsz, Yarris Joseph Akpaganathos, and 'Stalin': a lot of names for two brothers from Odessa don't you think?"

Everyone still remained silent, while Mr. Suda-Iwo reprised the investigations he had instigated over the past forty years, and the lengths he had gone to, for his client, to ensure that 'this matter', (as he had now started to refer to it), 'Never again saw the light of day'.

He stated that:

"When you leave this room today, and by the time your lift reaches the foyer of this building; these files, will be shredded."

He paused again, this time he became pensive, more serious, almost supplicant in his manner.

"When you leave today, some wrongs may have been righted, some guilt assuaged. An old man, Malakye Wylachi Jnr., who I have known, and sometimes loathed, but sometimes loved, for over half a century, may well sleep a little more comfortably in his grave".

He reached inside his jacket pocket, and took out a single sheet of paper, folded three times. He opened it out, and handed it to Neville Cartajhena, he said that he and Suzie should read it, and advise the old men.

He said that each of their respective firms had received instructions by fax and e-mail within the last two hours, along with appropriate fees by telex transfer; confirming that both Neville and Suzie, are released, (at 10.30 a.m. Sydney time), from their obligations to the W.H.S. and W.H.C. Group of Companies. Thereafter they are free to represent the old men.

Ambrose Suda-Iwo asked them both to turn on their mobile phones. They both did so, and both confirmed receipts of e-mails and text messages from the heads of their respective practices, confirming that arrangement which Mr. Suda-Iwo had just stated.

"Now please advise your clients as to the content of the contract I have just handed you".

Neville and Suzie read, then re-read the document Mr. Suda-Iwo had given them. The two solicitors, read aloud sections of the document to the old men, and explained what little 'legalese' there was contained in it. The document was short, concise, and deliberately simple.

Neville and Suzie explained that it was basically a confidentiality agreement, and that no one was ever to speak of or divulge anything they knew about anything or anyone in the 'blue files', ever. They said that each of the five old men were to sign it, and that Neville and Suzie were to witness it.

Neville leaned forward resting his elbows on the table top, and removed his glasses, in monotone he said:

"The document also states that each of you will receive into your bank accounts, by five p.m. today, the sum of one million Australian dollars".

Neville had never seen five signatures applied to a document with such rapidity. The two solicitors duly witnessed the item, and returned it to Mr. Suda-Iwo, who re-folded it, and placed it back in his jacket pocket.

He breathed a long sigh, a kind of sigh of relief that had waited forty years to be exhaled. He looked comfortable. Turning to Nicola Haye Sant, and pointing to the blue files, he said:

"Get rid of these Nicola please, and have the shreddings bagged up, and placed in the boot of my car".

He waved across the table top at all the files:

"And don't forget that one", he pointed again to the far end of the table.

"And this one too", he pointed at the grey 'East Light' lever arch folder in front of Murray.

"I never want to set eyes on any of them again".

He picked up and drained the remains of his coffee cup, which by now must have been cold.

No one had touched the pastries.

"There are a couple of last things before we break up the meeting", continued Mr. Suda-Iwo; "I understand that the Reverend Pugsley, both the Amethyst brothers, Miss Harrington, and Mr Somerset, have all sadly passed away. With this in mind, the late Mr. Malakye Wylachi Junior, O.B.E. has bequeathed to the…..um..um….."

He hesitated, as someone who has forgotten a difficult name or event hesitates. Nicola, helped out, and intervened:

"The Senghenydd Community Council", she said.

"Ah yes", Mr. Sudo-Iwo picked up the conversation, now suitably reminded.

"He, Mr. Wylachi, has bequeathed, anonymously, to the Senghenydd Community Council, the sum of five million Australian dollars. This with the specific instruction that it is to go toward the construction of a leisure centre for the use of local residents."

He turned again to the old men from The Old South Wales.

"Tell the Community Council, that the local authority has also received a similar anonymous donation for this purpose, and that they have already agreed to provide the site for the development free of charge."

He gave a little chuckle at this point, and concluded the item with:

"I handled that bit of the negotiation myself, put the squeeze on them a treat if I may say so. Haven't lost the old touch, eh Nicola?"

He reached into his suit again, this time into the outside breast pocket. He handed my father a cheque, a bankers draft made out to 'Senghenydd Community Council' in the sum of five million dollars, and said:

"I presume you will know who to give this too?"

My father acknowledged that he did.

Then, Mr. Suda-Iwo returned to Neville and Suzie. He now reached into the side pocket of his jacket, and took out a small white envelope, and said as he did so:

"It was a hard job picking you two, took me three weeks before I settled on you pair".

He scratched his ear as he spoke.

"I'll want a confidentiality agreement from you as well before you leave", he gestured at Nicola Haye Sant, "Nic's got it already drafted", Ambrose nodded at her, and she seamlessly adopted the conversation;

"It's next door in my office, I can witness it", she smiled affably.

"There's also a certified cheque for each of you, for your services", she paused briefly, and then added; "I mean that's for you personally, not the firms you work for; they're getting their fee's anyway".

Ambrose now regained the discourse.

"You can call it expenses if you like; hell, I don't care what you call it, just make sure you keep it," he paused again. "Anyway the cheques are for fifty thousand dollars each".

He handed the white envelope to Neville, and told him to open it.

Inside were two railway tickets to Darwin, they were overnight sleeper train tickets, for two private compartments. There were also, nestling in the envelope, two reservations, each for double rooms at 'The Duchess Mag's Hotel', for seven days and seven nights.

The last item in the envelope was a key.

Ambrose Suda-Iwo explained that the key was for a left luggage locker; locker number 888 at the Railway terminus building opposite the hotel. He also explained that the locker enclave of the terminus building was conservation listed, and really was a thing of beauty. He said that the preserved lockers were stainless steel, with rich polished Ironbark doors.

He told Neville and Suzie that inside locker 888 they would find an old brown suede purse with a silk string draw chord. He concluded by saying:

"If this all pan's out, as I think it will; the thing you'll find in the suede purse, you will pass on to your children".

He waved a silencing arm before any response from the pair could be formulated.

Ambrose, creaked up from his seat, and made his goodbyes as the meeting broke up. The other participants also stood up one by one, and made mutterings of polite meaningless chit-chat. He shook hands again as he moved slowly around the table, nodded and patted shoulders as one does.

As he came to Suzie Cabot-Fitzgrald; he once more leaned forward, and kissed the back of her hand. As he did so, she noticed, peeking over the top of his waistcoat, and fixed to his ghastly bright orange tie, an ornate gold tie pin; it had, set in it's clasp a beautifully cut diamond, as big as the little finger nail of a woman's hand.

Eglwys Ilan Chapel,
South Wales
January 28th 2013.

At the graveside, Kaddish had been delivered in stunning purity and simplicity, almost, but not quite sung by the Rabbi Jacob Weiss-Blumen of the Cardiff United Synagogue.

His breath had condensed against the chill morning as he spoke, and wistful puffs of white air had left his words as they settled.

The snow was thick on the ground, and the Landrover's had only just managed to fight their way to the Chapel's lich-gate: up the climbing narrow lanes

417

from Abertridwr on the one side and Pontypridd on the other. It had begun to snow once more and yesterdays tracks were already collecting new smoothed edges from the fresh falls.

The whiteness hung from the trees bare branches and shivered in the new morning.

Present, in addition to the Rabbi, had been the well wrapped Reverend Lionel Imperious of The Church In Wales, the mitten clad Johnny Spinks, my woollen scarf spun Uncles Bryn, Murray and Wilf, my long coated Father, (all accompanied by bobble hats or trilby's well pulled down, gloves and pairs of sensible well soled boots); the incongruously tanned Dean Amberkan with several unknown men in dark suits and pointless umbrellas:

And me.

I had watched the early morning proceedings from the top of Senghenydd Mountain, squinting against the worsening snowstorm through a pair of illicit binoculars. Shivering and snivelling through the open window of my Nissan 4 X 4, and puffing on a thin roll-up to keep warm, my heater did not work, and I was rolled in turn in woolly sweaters and a coat which thickened my arms, a 'Thinsulate' snow cap with a hole in it, and two odd gloves which completed my ensemble.

Inside my 'wellies' nested three pairs of poor socks.

A black Landrover had collected the Rabbi at seven in the morning, from the slippery steps of his Synagogue at Llanedeyrn in Cardiff, South Wales.

At the same time, another black Landrover had collected my Uncles Murray and Wilf from the Cardiff Hilton Hotel, a third had collected my Father, my Uncle Bryn and Johnny Spinks from their homes in Caerphilly and Abertridwr, just north of Cardiff; and yet a fourth had been driving along the white and frozen M4 motorway from central London.

It contained Ambrose Suda-Iwo and his guest.

It had been a difficult arrangement to bring to fruition, and Ambrose had made a personal donation of thirty five thousand pounds towards the external re-pointing of the stonework of Eglwys Ilan Chapel, in order to start these particular wheels turning.

418

The Reverend Lionel Imperious had proven a very difficult protagonist to win over. Particularly given the necessity to avoid the wholesale exposure of the full details of the storey; and yet Ambrose had made this promise to himself and to God.

He had no intention of letting either down.

The Rabbi Weiss-Blumen had demonstrated a similar reluctance, until Mr. Suda-Iwo had persuaded a certain very senior member of the Israeli Government to make a personal intercention with the Rabbi on his behalf.

After that conversation, (apparently by long distance telephone, not e-mail), the Rabbi had relented.

Life-long favours had been called in, and silent debts that only lawyers can recall had been wiped off ageing slates. It had cost Ambrose Suda-Iwo time, money and influence.

They had been items well spent.

At the end of these 'negotiations', Ambrose had achieved that which would normally have proven un-achievable.

By judicious argument with all parties, he had arranged that Kaddish would be said by a Jewish Rabbi over the grave of a Russian man buried as a protestant, in a churchyard overlooking a small Welsh mining community over forty years ago.

Today's service, which had lasted less than twenty minutes, had taken nearly a century to arrive.

Yit-ga-dal v'yit-ka-dash sh'mei ra-ba,
b'al-ma di-v'ra chi-ru-tei, v'yam-lich mal-chu-tei
b'chai-yei-chon uv'yo-mei-chon
uv'chai-yei d'chol-beit Yis-ra-eil,
ba-a-ga-la u-viz-man ka-riv,
v'im'ru: A-mein.

Y'hei sh'mei ra-ba m'va-rach
l'a-lam ul'al-mei al-ma-ya.

Yit-ba-rach v'yish-ta-bach,

v'yit-pa-ar v'yit-ro-mam v'yit-na-sei,
v'yit-ha-dar v'yit-a-leh v'yit-ha-lal, sh'mei d'ku-d'sha, b'rich hu,
l'ei-la min kol bir-cha-ta v'shi-ra-ta,
tush-b'cha-ta v'ne-che-ma-ta, da-a-mi-ran b'al-ma,
v'im'ru: A-mein.

Y'hei sh'la-ma ra-ba min sh'ma-ya,
v'cha-yim, a-lei-nu v'al kol-Yis-ra-eil,
v'im'ru: A-mein.

O-seh sha-lom bim-ro-mav,
hu ya-a-seh sha-lom a-lei-nu v'al kol-Yis-ra-eil,
v'im'ru: A-mein.

Glorified and sanctified be God's great name throughout the world
which He has created according to His will.
May He establish His kingdom in your lifetime and during your days,
and within the life of the entire House of Israel, speedily and soon;
and say, Amen.

May His great name be blessed forever and to all eternity.

Blessed and praised, glorified and exalted, extolled and honoured,
adored and lauded be the name of the Holy One, blessed be He,
beyond all the blessings and hymns, praises and consolations that
are ever spoken in the world; and say, Amen.

May there be abundant peace from heaven, and life, for us
and for all Israel; and say, Amen.

He who creates peace in His celestial heights,

may He create peace for us and for all Israel;
and say, Amen.

Ambrose Suda-Iwo and his guest didn't leave their Landrover, they sat in the back seats with the darkened windows wound down no more that three inches, and smoke from Ambrose's Cuban cigar billowed occasionally from the opened window.

Before the Landrover's left, Dean Amberkan took from the back of the one in which Ambrose was seated, a carved marble 'Star of David', no more than a foot across. He handed it to one of his ill-suited associates who took it into the Churchyard and slotted it into a pre-prepared stainless steel clamp which had been mounted at the top of 'Stalin's' old headstone. The suited man placed it position, and snapped off the locking pins.

It said simply, etched across its centre in small Cyrillic script:

'Yuris Pavel Androskewowiczs. Once, you were loved.'

Epilogues

The Reverend Iolo Pugsley.

It was a Saturday afternoon, a fortnight before Christmas 1972.

Dilwyn and Ellis arranged to meet The Reverend Iolo Pugsley in the Lounge Bar of the Piccadilly Inn, at Caerphilly. They sat, with a pint of Trophy Bitter in front of each of them, and a half eaten, communal bag of 'pork scratchins' crouched next to the ash tray on their small, but private table. They awaited the arrival of three portions of 'Chicken in a Basket', which they had ordered earlier.

Maldwyn was due to be there, but a last minute call from the Bus Depot Manager, to say that Walter Bracken had phoned in sick, had persuaded Maldwyn do

421

Walters' Pontypridd and Taffs-Well run for the day. After all Saturdays was time and a half, and Christmas was coming.

The two brothers had spent the last two hours explaining to the Reverend Pugsley, all that they had discovered about Yuris 'Stalin' Androskewowicsz.

There had been some tears; the boys had shown 'The Rev' the citation. They had not 'gilded the lily' they had shown 'Stalin', 'warts and all', so to speak.

The young waitress delivered the food.

They then consumed their 'Chicken in a Basket' whilst answering any other questions 'The Rev' raised.

It is clearly something of a sobering thought, to realise that you have officiated at the funeral of the man who saved your life almost thirty years earlier. A thought which must arrive with certain, shall we say, "Baggage", as to ones own validity.

The waitress returned half way through the 'Chicken in a Basket', as waitresses do, to ask if everything was alright with the meal, and to ask if any more drinks were required. The meal was indeed very nice, and the 'twins', and 'The Rev' said so in glowing terms. Had Maldwyn been able to attend, he would have undoubtedly asked for more chips, and some bread and butter, the Friday night, self inflicted sickness of Walter Bracken, was indeed a blessing all round.

Dilwyn and Ellis ordered two more pints of Trophy for themselves, and 'The Rev' requested a bottle of 'Orange Juice, Topped up with Lemonade'. The waitress nearly had a 'clutcher' on the spot; and, stuttering in disbelief, asked 'The Rev' to repeat his order; which he did without batting an eyelid.

Over the next three days, 'The Rev' moved out of the Piccadilly Inn, and in, (as a proper lodger), with Bethany Harrington, still a spinster of HIS parish.

That Christmas, he organised 'Carol Services', a collection of tinned foods from local supermarkets for distribution to 'The Needy'. He spent Christmas Morning outside Cardiff General Railway Station distributing soup and bread to the 'Tramps' that lived under the arches there. He arranged a Christmas Dinner for the afternoon, for the Old Age Pensioners, (as a joint venture with other Vicars and Priests in the vicinity), at the Wesleyan Chapel on Crescent Road in Caerphilly. He even roped Bethany Harrington in, to cook the Yorkshire Puddings, which, by general consensus; were absolutely disgusting.

There was also a rumour flying around that on Christmas Eve morning, he went to Caerphilly Miners Hospital, dressed as Santa, and dished out sweets, chocolates and toys to the kids in the Children's Ward.

Over the next few years the pews of Eglwys Ilan Chapell became increasingly full, with every passing Sunday. And there were not many days when The Right Reverend Iolo Pugsley M.C., would not be seen knocking the doors of the terraced houses of Senghenydd; HIS parish, ministering to the sick, and gauging the needs of his flock, Church-goers or otherwise.

He performed the Christenings of over six hundred babies, and the funerals of over three hundred parishioners. He tended the graves that were untended, painted gates in the graveyard, fixed doors and pews in the Chapel, and made sure that every wedding he officiated at was a very special day for all concerned.

When he died in 1987, over two thousand people lined the route from Bethany Harrington's House, to Eglwys Ilan. The Chapel itself was full to bursting, and the Bishop of Llandaff Cathedral came up from Cardiff to deliver the eulogy.

The 'Rose and Crown', (The Eglwys), put on a dozen free kegs of beer, and nearly everyone in the villages of Senghenydd and Abertridwr provided Sandwiches and Sausage Rolls. Two minute silences, followed by a toast; were held in the Piccadilly Inn, Caerphilly Social Club, The Wheatsheaf, The Bowls Inn, The Kings, The Pontygwindy, The Goodrich, The Aber Hotel, The Royal, and every pub within a three mile radius of Eglwys Ilan.

His gravestone, provided by donations from his flock, and in accordance with his last wishes; said, quite simply:

The Right Reverend Iolo Pugsley, M.C.,
1923-1987.
Vicar of this parish.
It has been a privilege.

Lucien 'Banger' Smutz.

'Banger' Smutz was hanged at Port Elizabeth on January 14th 1929.

After 'The Elephant' versus Crusher Hohner fight at Scottsville Park, in 1924. 'Banger' had found himself wealthier than he had ever been, with a little over three hundred pounds in his pocket.

He had returned to Durban, and bought a small house with his 'winnings', on the outskirts of the city. The neighbourhood was largely Indian, so the price was reasonable, and there was a tolerance of his unusual (for that time), mixed race relationship.

He had continued to work for Dykka's old outfit at the 'Baccy Thinners', in the yard near Durban Docks, and his wife had continued in her cleaning in her job. Except now they worked directly for Silvo Vischer, who had taken over the operation after Dykka's demise.

By the middle of 1925, 'Banger' had developed something of an over-fondness for Dykka's whisky and iodine, which had evolved to a necessity for neat Gin by the end of that year. By June 1928, he was drinking at least two bottles a day. It had taken its toll on his health, and his personality, what there was of it. Already with a propensity towards violence, his moods had become extreme, and he had already begun beating his younger black wife.

One Friday evening in November 1928 he had travelled by train to Ladysmith, about a hundred miles north, to watch some fights, and hopefully win some money. He had arranged to stay with some old 'thumpers' up there, and would travel back the next day, or maybe even Sunday if his winnings were good enough.

However, he had heard at the railway station in Ladysmith upon his arrival, that the fights had been cancelled, because of an outbreak of cholera in the town. He had used his return ticket, and jumped straight back on his train; not wishing to stay a moment longer than necessary in the vicinity of the disease.

The return journey had passed slowly, and he had disposed of, (by self consumption), the bottle of Gin he had brought with him 'for his old mates'. He had returned to Durban Station at just after ten o'clock, and flagged a taxi outside to take him the three or four miles to his little house on the outskirts.

The taxi dropped him off at the end of the road, he paid the driver, and he walked with his small overnight bag the sixty or so yards to his front door.

Inside, he found his young wife with Silvo Vischer, and two other white men, all were naked, his wife on all fours, astride one man, with Silvo kneeling behind her with his hands on her hips, and a third man in front of her, holding her by the hair.

Within three minutes, all four of them were dead. 'Banger' had beaten the men senseless in a blur of rage that lasted no more than thirty seconds, all three were semi-conscious and scattered about the floor like so many crumpled rugs. He had then grabbed a serrated bread knife from the kitchen, and, with no further consideration, plunged it deep into his wife's chest, he yanked it out, and repeated the action twice more. The spurting blood left stripes about the plastered walls as she whirled and twirled and screamed before collapsing, quivering, on the single settee.

Turning to the men, some of whom were coming round, and with the same knife, and with no further thought than he had given his wife; he sliced each of their penises off. He then returned finally to Silvo, and cut his throat for good measure.

He sat in his kitchen drinking more gin, until the police arrived an hour or so later.

All except one of the men died, as did 'Banger's' wife. The survivor gave evidence at the trial, which was held in Queenstown in front of a District Judge, and a Crown appointed prosecutor, due to the brutality of the crime. It took the all white, all male jury, eight minutes to find 'Banger' guilty. His charge, 'the murder of two white men'. His wife had not even appeared on the charge sheet.

He was hanged at Port Elizabeth Prison at the last stroke of the midnight chimes from the prison clock tower, on 14th January 1929. It took 'Banger' eighteen minutes to die.

When cut down, his corpse was buried in an unmarked grave in the unconsecrated grounds of Port Elizabeth Prison. He received no sermon, no flowers, and no headstone.

He rests there still.

425

Arthur Du-Pont.

Arthur Du-Pont, exempted from wartime service as a reserved profession, rose through the ranks of the Northern Territories Police Authorities to the office of Deputy Commissioner.

He never married, but there were rumours of a once torrid affair with a woman from Queensland, who, it was said, broke Arthur's heart.

He died in 1988 at the age of eighty nine.

He left all his worldly goods, according to his Last Will and Testament, to the 'Australian Society For Penal Reform'.

Fuzzy Dolenz.

Sergeant Fuzzy Dolenz was dishonourably discharged from the Western Australian Prison Service in 1960, after a complaint against him by the wife of an inmate. He had been innocent of the charge, but the complaint had been supported by Warden Frank Summersby of the Perth Correctional Facility.

Mr. Dolenz, and his wife, to whom he was devoted, emigrated to New Zealand in 1962.

Both died within weeks of one another in the summer of 1970.

They had one son, a Policeman in Christchurch.

He returned to Western Australia after his parent's death, to take up a position with the New Norcia Police Constabulary.

Warden Frank Summersby.

Committed suicide in the late summer of 1970.

He and his wife had three children, all of whom joined various departments of the Western Australia Police Force.

His eldest son, Waldo, is today the Custody Sergeant at The New Norcia Police Headquarters, and is due to retire in 2015.

Frank Summersby's wife, who was considerably younger than him, re-married and moved to Hobart.

She lives there today.

The Van Der Kyper Brothers.

Both lived to be centenarians, eventually passing away in the new millennium; Louis in 2001, and Bernard in 2003.

They had funded Ian Smith's campaign for the Rhodesian Unilateral Declaration of Independence from Great Britain in the 1960's, and had profited hugely from its success.

They had seen the 'Writing On The Wall' as Louis had phrased it, when Rhodesia became Zimbabwe, and had moved all their business interests and their money to Botswana.

They both died peacefully in their sleep. Each in one of the two largest houses in Gaborone, the Botswana capital. Each a wealthy and lonely old men.

Their immense wealth reverted, (upon their deaths), to the Government of Botswana, and now funds the construction and management of Hospitals, Schools, Railways and Roads, in one of the most successful states in the continent of Africa.

Mordichae and Stan Wylachi,
Old Man Mal, and the 'Wylachi Herds'.

Both were retired by their brother 'Old Man Mal' in 1940, with substantial financial settlements in return for all their shares in all the Wylachi Businesses.

Watertight 'Confidentiality Agreements' were drawn up by Ambrose Suda-Iwo, a young solicitor at the Fremantle office, of the Sydney law firm of Mimex Fuller.

Mordichae nor Stanforth ever spoke with their brother again. The agreement was finalised, (it is said), with some acrimony. Both brothers succumbed to heart attacks and died in the early 1960's.

'Old Man Mal'., nor Malakye Jnr. attended their funerals.

As for Old Man Mal himself, he passed away, (again from a heart attack), in 1968. He had retired from the family business in 1953, and handed full control to his son Malakye Jnr.

Mal. Jnr., had expanded the businesses beyond all expectations, by the early 1970's they were a National series of large corporations, with interests in farming, dairy and stock, as well as fisheries and food processing.

He had married and divorced twice, and had two sons, Hugo and Robbo one by each wife. Both sons had discovered little interest in the family business, but a joint and shared love of fast cars and fast boats. They had both married, and in turn had produced one son each, two grandsons for Malakye Jnr. their names were Hugo Jnr. and Stanforth Wylachi.

Hugo, (although under ten years old at the time), dropped the 'Junior' when his father and uncle were both killed in a motorboat racing accident in 1973.

The two cousins had run the Wylachi business empire with their grandfather, Malakye Jnr., (who had never rejected his suffix 'Junior'), since 1985.

They had taken the businesses to ever greater heights; by the new millennium they had interests in Canada, The Philippines, South America, and Europe.

They would miss their grandfather.

Gilbert Van Der Faisey.

Became the first 'Head of Security' at 'Wylachi Herds' as it was known in 1938.

He volunteered at the outbreak of the Second World War, and used his connections, (despite his age), to secure a posting attached to the Royal Dutch Air force in The Philippines.

He was killed in a Japanese air raid in June 1941.

He left a wife and nine children.

Toby 'J' and Linus Sabak.

Toby J died in mysterious circumstances, having fallen from a horse at the Wylachi Livery Stables in early 1935. His neck had been broken, and his skull crushed.

The investigating officers, Sergeant Dolenz, and Inspector Summersby, both of the New Norcia Police had found the death to be accidental. 'Old Man Mal', in recognition of their strenuous efforts and investigations, had presented each, (very privately), with a blank cheque for five hundred dollars, 'to be made out to their favourite charities', he had said.

Those charities were, (predictably), Fuzzy Dolenz, and Frank Summersby, he had found this out via a local Bank Manager, one Daniel Stucky who had provided him with photographs of the completed cheques. 'Old Man Mal' had kept them in his personal safe, until 1973, when he had burnt them in his desk ashtray.

Linus Sabak married Toby J's widow in 1936. He took over the position vacated by Gilbert Van Der Faisey, as Head of Security in 1940.

He was a loyal retainer to the Wylachi Family until he retired in 1980.

He died ten years later, peacefully, and in his sleep.

Captain Gustav Amberkan.

By 1945 Gustav had turned his back on the sea, sold the 'West Honiker' to a freelancer running sherry from Portugal to the newly liberated, and greedy, ports of Europe.

He had settled in Port MacQuarrie, New South Wales, having developed a taste for Australia in the 1920's and 30's.

He married late, and he and his wife had one son, Friedrich in 1958.

Friedrich had married in 1978, to Joanna, and in turn, in 1980, had produced a son, who they had named Dean, for no apparent reason, other than that it was quite modern.

Friedrich and Joanna had been killed in a house fire in 1990, and Dean had become a Ward of the State. He had in due course been awarded a scholarship at 'Sydney University' funded by the Wylachi Foundation.

He now works as 'Head of Mainland Security' for a subsidiary of the W.H.C. Group of Companies.

Iestyn Tynsdale and 'Greener' Hawks.

Captain Tynsdale, as he was always known, worked tirelessly as a fundraiser for charities catering specifically for 'The Blind'. He raised over one million dollars up until his death from a stroke in 1988.

'Greener' married the Captains youngest daughter in March 1947.

At the wedding, 'Greener', for the first time, shared with his old Captain, and his new Father-in-Law, the truth about their mutual friend 'Stoko'.

Captain Tynsdale had smiled all day long.

In turn, he had shared with 'Greener' the secret of his W.W.1 gallantry award. He had told him how he and three others had sunk a huge Russian destroyer with 'Limpet Mines' in October 1916 to prevent her being captured by the Germans prior to the Russian Revolution. The Russians had of course been allies up to this point, and so the operation, even to this day, had remained secret. The Russians had said that the explosion was the result of electrical fires in the ships magazine.

The stricken ship had been *The Imperatritsa Mariya*, and the action had taken place at Varna.

In early 1972, 'Greener' had received a curious telephone call from a person who had introducd himself as Wilf Swayzee.

The man had told 'Greener' that he was calling from Perth. He had given 'Greener' some details over the phone concerning certain enquiries he was making concerning a former mutual acquaintance. 'Greener' had said that he had no idea what the caller was talking about, and had put the phone down.

That same day Captain Tynsdale received a similar call from someone introducing himself as Murray Swayzee. He provided a similar response, and again put the phone down.

'Greener' Hawks, and his wife Angharrad, still live in New South Wales.

Eloise Hunter Van Hoost Anderson-Androskewowicsz.

Thus far, I have been unable to find out anything further regarding Eloise after her journey to Darwin in 1933, save for her fleeting visit to Port Keats a decade later.

If anything more comes to light; I will let you know.

Lightning Source UK Ltd.
Milton Keynes UK
UKOW032015231112

202692UK00002B/6/P